the Murmur of Masks

The Murmur of Masks

CATHERINE KULLMANN

Ardua Publishing

Argus House, Malpas Street, Dublin 8

Ireland

© Catherine Kullmann 2016

ISBN 978-1-912732-75-3

Cover image: Portrait of Lady Morgan (Sydney Owenson) (1776-1859), Writer, c.1818 by René Théodore Berthon, Collection: National Gallery of Ireland Photo © National Gallery of Ireland and reproduced with their permission.

For my parents, John and Kitty,
for whom time spent reading was never wasted.
With love, to mark their hundredth birthdays.

Book One

Chapter One

Portsmouth, England, 1803

"When I write to you now, Papa, I shall picture you here in your cabin reading my letter or imagine you on the quarter-deck with your telescope."

Captain Frobisher laughed. "And I shall no longer think of you as a schoolgirl with her hair down her back but as a beautiful and accomplished young lady. Please God we'll soon defeat the French and the next time I come home it will be to stay. Your mother should start thinking about where she would like to live. We'll buy a neat estate not too far from the sea. I must have the whiff of salt! Come, it's time to go."

Up on deck, he hugged her to him and kissed her fondly. "Goodbye, my darling Olivia. May God protect you until we meet again."

She blinked the tears from her eyes. "And you, Papa. May you always have fair winds in your sails and the enemy at a disadvantage." She settled herself somewhat nervously in the boatswain's chair.

"Stop fidgeting," her father muttered as he looped a ribbon around her skirts close to her ankles to prevent any immodest fluttering while she was lowered to the boat that would take them back to shore.

"You're a real sailor's daughter now," he teased. "Hold tight, my darling."

3

The boatswain's pipe trilled and Olivia held her breath as she was swung over the side of the ship and gently lowered to the captain's gig waiting below. It rocked as she stepped in to it and she had to clutch the hand of the young officer to steady herself before she could take her place beside her mother.

As the gig pulled away from the *Hector*, the women twisted in their seats to wave a final farewell. Above them Captain Frobisher stood motionless, his telescope fixed on his wife and daughter and they knew he would remain there until, safely ashore, they disappeared from view.

Early the next morning, it was the women who watched from the ramparts until the ship vanished over the horizon. "First Robert, then Papa," Olivia said sadly. "We'll miss them."

"Yes," her mother answered, adding briskly, "now we must get used to being without them again. If we find Weymouth agreeable, perhaps we should take a house there for six months from Michaelmas. Your father may have his estate, but I should like to be near a town with good shops. Thanks to his Majesty's interest, Weymouth should be better in that regard than other coastal towns and the society will be more refined."

Olivia completed a neat pirouette out of sheer excitement before continuing more sedately along the landing to her mother's room. A sunny day and a new costume! There could be nothing more elevating to the spirits. She smoothed the skirts of her gown, enjoying the feel of the cool cotton against her palms. The pattern of autumn leaves on cream was most becoming and later the deep gold redingote would bring out matching tints in her eyes and hair. Weymouth had indeed proved agreeable and Mrs Frobisher had found a charming house there at a reasonable rent. There was so much to do in these last days in Portsmouth.

She and Mamma must first visit the shops in the High Street and then they could stroll on the ramparts.

No doubt there would be many others taking advantage of the first fine day in a week. If Mamma is agreeable, I'll send at once to the *Blue Anchor* to order a carriage, Olivia thought. Smiling to herself, she tapped lightly on the bedroom door and slipped into the room. The curtains were still drawn and soft autumnal sun filtered through to deepen the sheen on the satin counterpane.

"Mamma?" Olivia said quietly and then, more cheerfully, "Good morning, sleepyhead!" There was a smile in her voice as she repeated the morning greeting from her childhood. That was how Mamma had woken her each morning. As she moved closer to the bed, she was struck by an unusual silence. Mamma did not precisely snore, but it could not be denied that she was inclined to breathe more heavily while sleeping.

"Mamma!" she said more insistently. "Mamma!"

There was no reply. She darted to the window and tore open the curtains, then hurried back to the bed. All was quiet; she could hear only her own quick footsteps and the sound of her agitated voice as she called again. There was still no reply. Frightened, she drew back the bed curtain, deliberately letting the rings rattle, but her mother did not stir. Olivia's hand covered her mouth, as if to repress a silent scream.

"Mamma. Mamma!" She leaned forward to touch first a still hand and then a waxen cheek. There was no reaction from the sleeper, no breath stirred her breast and she felt cold, too cold. Olivia seized her shoulders and shook her. "Mamma!" She gasped to see her mother's head sway eerily back and forth, the eyes slightly open and the features fixed and unmoving.

"Mamma," she whispered as she gently laid her back on her pillows. The hand that had rested on the counterpane slipped to one side in an unnatural movement like that of a rag doll.

Olivia's knees buckled, collapsing her to the floor where she remained for long minutes clutching her mother's cold hand. There was no sign of life but she could not, would not accept the evidence of her senses.

"Miss Olivia! Whatever is the matter?"

The shocked exclamation of the maid who entered with the breakfast tray brought Olivia back to herself. Slowly she lifted her head from the soft eiderdown. "Oh, Betty, 'tis Mamma— she's—she's gone. She has left us."

Mr Samuel Harte, whose black arm-band bore mute witness to his recent loss, stripped off his sodden greatcoat and handed it to the footman before going to hold his hands to the blazing fire.

"Where is my niece?" he enquired over his shoulder.

"Miss Frobisher is in the morning-room, sir."

"Tell her I'll be with her as soon as I've changed my clothes. I feel as if the cold of the churchyard has seeped into my bones."

"Yes, sir." The man hesitated. He did not know his late employer's brother very well. "Might I send up something hot, sir? Coffee or punch, perhaps?"

"A glass of punch would be just the ticket."

Thirty minutes later, dry and warm if not reconciled to his lot, Mr Harte reluctantly acknowledged that he could tarry no longer and left the sanctuary of his room to seek out his niece. He stood for a moment in the door of the morning-room, observing her still figure. She sat turned away from him, the white of the handkerchief clutched in one hand a stark contrast to the dull black of her mourning gown. Her head drooped as if her neck could no longer support the mass of hair that was piled up loosely in a way that would have elicited a reproof from her now-dead mother and her shoulders slumped as if unable to bear a heavy burden. He cleared his throat softly.

"Olivia?"

At the sound of his voice she squared her shoulders and raised her head, turning to face him with the barest hint of a smile that owed more to the habit of courtesy than to any emotion.

"Uncle Samuel! Come and sit by the fire. What a terrible day for a burial—it's as if the very heavens weep to see her gone. I've been sitting in her chair—I thought I might feel the memory of her dear embrace. But no. All is cold and empty."

Instead of taking the chair across the hearth from her, Mr Harte picked up another and set it beside that of his niece. He gently laid his hand over hers. "My poor girl. I should have arranged for someone to sit with you."

"Mrs Carr offered to come," she said listlessly, "but I said I wanted to be alone. Were there many at the church?"

"A couple of dozen, I suppose; some old tars who had sailed with your father and brother and the husbands of some of your mother's friends."

"At least Mamma and Papa could spend some time together this past year," Olivia said with a sigh. "And Robert was home as well. I don't know when we were last together as a family. Although I think Robert was pleased when the peace failed and he was recalled. He has a better chance of getting his step now."

Mr Harte was pleased to see that this last remark was accompanied by the ghost of a rueful twinkle. "Have you breakfasted?" he asked abruptly.

"Oh, here I am delaying you and you must be famished," Olivia said remorsefully. "I told them to wait until you had returned, but it must be ready now."

"You will join me, I hope?" He stood and offered her his arm, sighing inwardly. With his brother-in-law and nephew both now recalled to the navy until Boney was defeated, he supposed he was now responsible for his niece. There was no-one else available, as far as he knew. The mere thought caused him to break into a cold sweat. He was an established pillar of gentlemanly society, moving in bachelor contentment between his clubs and those *haut ton* entertainments that appealed to him; that is the ones that provided him with a good hand of cards, a tolerable supper and intelligent conversation. What did he know of fatherhood? His wife and only child had died on the same day so long ago. He had been a father for only a few despairing hours and indeed most of his acquaintances were unaware that he had ever been married.

Glancing at Olivia's white face, he summoned a smile. She had eaten very little since he had arrived post-haste in response to the tear-stained note advising him of his sister's unexpected passing. "Come, my dear, here is a pretty dish of eggs and here some tarts to tempt your appetite. Pray try a little of each. And I think a small glass of sherry will not go amiss. We are very late today, it is almost noon."

"There is a gentleman to see you, Miss Frobisher. He said it was important."

"Theobald Edmondsen, solicitor," Olivia read on the ornately engraved ivory card. "What does he want, I wonder? I must see him, I suppose. Show him into the drawing-room and request my uncle to join me there."

As the footman left the room, a sleek gentleman of middle years slipped past him and bowed. "My dear Miss Frobisher, may I express my heartfelt condolences on your sad loss? I felt it incumbent on me to call, for your dear, departed mother entrusted to me her last will and testament, so I feel a responsibility for you." He smiled, all teeth, as he seized her hand and patted it.

"Indeed, sir." Olivia pulled her hand away, resisting the impulse to wipe it on her skirt. She heard rapid footsteps outside and her uncle stormed into the room.

"Kindly explain this intrusion, sir! You may apologise to my niece and take yourself off."

"Theobald Edmondsen, solicitor of the late Mrs Frobisher," the visitor declared hastily.

"Hmmph!"

"He says he has Mamma's will," Olivia informed her uncle.

Mr Harte was unimpressed. "Indeed? I was not aware she had made one."

"While, as a married woman or '*feme covert*' as the law has it, Mrs Frobisher was not permitted to hold property or sign legal documents," the solicitor instructed his unwilling listeners, "she did however have the right to dispose of her 'paraphernalia' as we men of law say." He gave a little tittering laugh. "That is to say her clothing and personal ornaments. Your late mother availed herself of this right, leaving everything to you, Miss Frobisher," he made a little bow, "with the exception of some jewellery that belonged to her maternal grandfather. This she leaves to her son Robert, along with any gifts her said son made her in the past, with the hope that one day he will pass these on to his own children."

Olivia was bewildered. "But if Mamma may not own property, what about the contents of this house? And the bank account?"

"They remain Captain Frobisher's, as heretofore."

"But Heaven knows when he'll be home. Mamma managed everything. He used to laugh and say he was happy for her to rule on land."

"Indeed?" The solicitor tutted disapprovingly. "Be that as it may, as far as I am informed, the captain has regrettably made no provision for anyone to—eh—take over the administration of his affairs in your late parent's stead, should she predecease him. I regret no arrangements have been made for an independent appanage for Miss Frobisher. I took it upon myself to enquire at the captain's bank today, seeking to spare you, my dear Miss Frobisher."

"Damned encroaching of you," Mr Harte snapped.

Loftily disregarding this remark, the solicitor continued, "I was informed that only Mrs Frobisher was entitled to draw on his account."

"But what am I to do? How could Papa treat me so!" Olivia was horrified.

Mr Harte took her hand and said gently, "Olivia, you wound me grievously by implying that I would ever see you want for anything."

Her fingers clutched his. "I'm sorry, Uncle," she apologised on a sob. "It was such a shock."

"I understand, my dear," he soothed her before addressing the solicitor. "That will do, Edmondsen. You may hand me my sister's testament and take your leave."

"But it must be probated," the man protested.

"The will, if you please." Mr Harte held out a commanding hand. "We will not detain you further. You are not to approach my niece again or involve yourself in any way in family matters. You have overstepped the bounds, sir! Now, this way, if you please. John will see you out."

He closed in on the solicitor and possessed himself of the will before urging him to the door. Having delivered their unbidden guest to the footman, Mr Harte lingered at the top of the stairs to satisfy himself that he departed without delay.

Mr Harte returned to the parlour where he found Olivia pacing up and down, her handkerchief crumpled between her fingers. Whenever she passed the portrait of her father that hung over the mantelpiece, she paused briefly to cast it a reproachful look before continuing her nervous motion.

"Olivia! This will not do. Come and sit down, my dear."

She burst into tears. "I feel a wretch for thinking about such a thing as money when Mamma is barely in her grave. I should be mourning the far greater loss. But what am I to do? I know you will look after me, Uncle Samuel," she continued hastily, before he could repeat his previous reproof, "but supposing something happened to you? It's not as if Mamma had been ill; she just—just didn't wake up that morning. I still can't believe she's gone."

"Have you no idea where your father is?"

"They sailed first to Bantry Bay. The last we heard was that he was to join Lord Nelson in the Mediterranean. That is all I know. I've written to him and Robert care of the Admiralty, such sad letters too." She choked back a sob.

"I shall write again," Mr Harte decided. "In the meantime, I think we should look through any papers your mother might have left. And tomorrow we shall make plans. But, Olivia, no matter what arrangements Frobisher might have made, you are too young to be setting up your own establishment. And Portsmouth, even Kingston, is no place for a young lady on her own."

He thought wistfully of his comfortable house in London. It was managed capably by a married couple who greatly appreciated the independence afforded by the lack of a mistress and were assiduous in ensuring their master's well-being. How could he introduce a niece with concomitant duenna and maid into such an abode, frequented by gentlemen of all types at all hours?

"We were to remove to Weymouth at the end of the month," she said dully, "but it's all the same. I had not thought that my whole life must change."

He smiled sadly at her. "In the midst of life, we are in death, my dear. But you will be brave, I know."

A search of Mrs Frobisher's writing table yielded no further information although the locked cabinet in her bedroom contained a strongbox containing about one hundred guineas as well as a handsome collection of jewellery.

"She rarely wore it," Olivia said, "generally just Papa's ring and the locket with his and Robert's hair. That reminds me, Uncle," she continued awkwardly, "Mrs Carr cut some locks of Mamma's hair for me and I thought to have a mourning ring or fob made for you."

"That is very thoughtful of you, my dear." Mr Harte was not sure if he wished to avail himself of this melancholy offer, but did not see how he could refuse. Well, he need not wear the thing, he supposed. "I should prefer the fob. Now, I think I should consult my own man of law. Perhaps in the circumstances I may be appointed your temporary guardian." He hesitated. "Do you think Mrs Carr would be agreeable to your staying with her for some weeks until we can get this sorted out? My house is a bachelor establishment and not suited to a girl like you."

"We could ask her, I suppose. I like her well enough and I know she is lonely since Miss Edith Carr married, for her husband is also at sea. But could I be a sort of boarder, Uncle? I should not like to throw myself on her charity."

"There can be no question of that," Mr Harte answered, appalled. "And you must tell me what you need."

"The most important thing now is mourning," she said wanly. "I shall see if I can have some of Mamma's gowns made over. She had a black cloak made when my grandmother died three years ago and there will be other things as well that I may use."

"Very well, very well," he said impatiently. "You are not to stint yourself, Olivia, but go on just as you always have. You're a sensible girl and will not overdo things, I know. Margaret brought you up too well for that."

"Yes, with Papa away so much, she was used to fending for herself—and me."

Chapter Two

Derbyshire, England, September 1803
"Enough! It was just the shock."

Mrs Adams pushed the hand that held the smelling salts away from under her nose and struggled from her husband's embrace. She sat up and fixed an imploring gaze on her younger son. "Say I didn't hear you correctly, Luke."

I might have known it, Luke Fitzmaurice thought resignedly. A pretty woman who had captured the devoted hearts of two husbands, his mother adroitly wielded an air of feminine fragility to ensure that her sensitive feelings must be of primary concern to all within her ambit. But at almost twenty, he was too old to fall for such tricks.

"I'm afraid you did, ma'am," he replied calmly. "I am sorry to distress you, but I hope I know my duty when England is threatened with invasion. I intend to defer my return to the Varsity and buy a pair of colours."

"Absolutely not! I forbid it."

"Forbid it? You cannot."

"I can and I will," she asserted. "You can't ask that of me, Luke, or expect me to bear the constant suspense and worry, never knowing if you are safe."

"If every English mother thought that, we might as well spread carpets at our ports to welcome the First Consul to our shores," he retorted, "that is if he were still interested in invading a nation of cowards."

"Mind how you speak to your mother," his stepfather snapped.

"I beg your pardon, ma'am," Luke said, returning immediately to the fray, albeit in more moderate tones. "I have always intended to join the military. In fact if it were not for my illness, I should have done so sooner, but I felt it prudent to work on my sword drill and my riding until I was sure I had regained my strength. And with the peace last year, I thought I might as well take my degree first. But now all has changed."

His mother looked dumbly at him, tears trembling on her eyelashes.

"What did you think I would do when I came down from Cambridge?" he asked more gently. "Sit and twirl my thumbs or saunter from one fashionable lounge to the other, idling the day away? It's not as though I'll inherit a father's estate like my brothers. I must make my place in the world. What is open to me in the line of gentlemanly occupation? I'm not cut out to be a parson and got deuced queasy the only time I was aboard ship. No. It's the cavalry for me."

"There's the law," his stepfather suggested, "or politics."

"If I wish to go down that road, there will be time enough once Boney is defeated."

"You can't access your capital without the approval of the trustees until you're twenty-one," his mother said suddenly.

"Oh? Who are they?" he asked casually. "That's just a year away, so I'm sure it won't be a problem. Any true Englishman will understand."

"They are bound to respect my wishes and I'll forbid it," Mrs Adams declared, stretching her hand towards him. "How can you do this to me, Luke? Think of my nerves. It's barely a year since we lost dearest Cecily and it is not so very many years since you yourself were so grievously ill." She brightened suddenly. "In any case, the doctor won't permit it. He said that he had known acute rheumatism, such as you had, to cause a subsequent weakness of the heart and that you must always be careful not to over-exert yourself."

Luke looked at her in amazement. "He never said anything of the sort to me!"

"I suppose it never arose, dearest. But there can be no doubt about it. You're not fit to be a soldier."

"And that pleases you, ma'am?" he asked cuttingly, shaken by the almost triumphant note to her voice."

"That is quite enough, Fitzmaurice!" Mr Adams barked. "You are not too old for a thrashing."

This was beyond everything! Luke rose to his full height and stared down at his stepfather, gratified to see the older man take a step back. "I beg you will not try it, sir," he said softly, "for I should not submit meekly, I assure you and would be loath to be forced to defend myself against a man of your years."

"Luke! How can you threaten your father with violence?" His mother's voice faltered.

"My stepfather, ma'am," he corrected her coldly, "and he it was who threatened me. I am no longer a schoolboy to be chastised at will."

At this Mrs Adams subsided again into her cushions, her sobs growing louder and louder.

"Now see what you have done," Mr Adams accused.

Luke turned on his heel and stormed into the hall. He clapped his hat on his head and left the house as if the hounds of hell were at his heels.

He followed the path through the gardens down to the lake automatically, wanting only to get away. He felt weary, his bones aching as if he had indeed been thrashed and his heart aching at the sense of cruel betrayal. Neither his mother nor his stepfather had even tried to see his side of it. She had never mentioned any lingering weakness before, so why suddenly raise it now? It sounded damned smoky to him. He had a good mind to find the nearest crimping sergeant and take the shilling! His steps led him around the lake to the small summer house and he sat on the steps looking up at the milky river of stars that flowed across the dark sky.

My mother can't stop me volunteering, he realised after a while. That doesn't cost anything. And I must find out about the trustees. She never explained anything about my father's will. I could ask Jer. As our father's heir, he must know about it as well. And in a year I'll be of age and may do as I like.

Comforted by these plans, he made his way back to the house. To his relief it was in darkness. A sleepy footman lit a candle for him at the one burning on the hall table and as Luke slowly climbed the stairs he could hear the man locking the front door.

Good morning, Mother, good morning, Father."

"Good morning, my boy," Mr Adams said heartily. Mrs Adams looked up from her correspondence but neither smiled nor returned his greeting.

Luke sighed inwardly. He had every intention of apologising, but the fact that she would not speak to him until he had done so made him want to ignore her as comprehensively as she did him. But that would be unfair to his stepfather, who was always willing to accept an olive branch.

"Mother, Father, I wish to apologise for my intemperate words yesterday evening." He spoke formally; while he regretted his tone, he could not deny his sentiments.

His mother looked reproachful. "I have to say I was very disappointed in you, Luke. You may no longer be a child, but you are a gentleman."

"Yes, Mother."

"Just promise me you will put this notion of a military career out of your head and we'll forget all about it, won't we, my dear?" She glanced over to where her husband perused yesterday's *Times*.

"I'm sorry, but I can't do that, ma'am," Luke replied firmly. "We are all called to serve. Even Jer is raising a volunteer corps for home defence."

"Will you at least speak to Dr Wilton first?" Mr Adams interrupted.

"Mr Adams!"

"My dear, I have considered the matter overnight. Luke has the right of it. If he is well enough to serve, we should not prevent him from doing his duty. Wilton treated him during his illness and should be able to advise him now."

"Thank you, sir," Luke said gratefully. "I'll ride down to the village this morning."

"I am sorry, sir but I remain convinced that prolonged exertion might put an undue strain on your heart. I cannot in good conscience recommend a military career."

Luke felt ill. He had been so sure the doctor would support him. "And if I were to join a volunteer corps at home?" he suggested hopefully.

"Not even that. Be grateful you're as well as you are, sir. There were times we despaired of your life and you will recall how long it took you to build up your strength."

"I see," Luke said dully.

Unable to face anyone, he did not turn for home but headed towards the hills, picking up the pace as soon as he was free of the village confines. For some time he was aware only of the rhythmical surge of the big gelding between his thighs, the answering movement of his own body, the wind in his face. Leaning forward, he urged the horse into a gallop. 'Don't think, don't think', pounded through his head in time with the hoof-beats and then, 'Useless, useless'. The ground grew steeper and he slowed his mount, patting its neck. "You shouldn't suffer for my failings," he said apologetically.

He continued more slowly, letting the horse pick its way up an uneven path to a rocky outcrop that looked out over the surrounding countryside. A rough shelter had been built from grey stone to protect any wanderer or shepherd caught in a storm. Luke dismounted and loosely looped the reins around the branch of a bent and twisted tree. A little spring burbled nearby and he went to scoop up the fresh water in his hands, first drinking and then splashing more onto his hot face. He took a deep breath, drawing in the sun-warmed air, scented with grass and gorse. A skylark rose overhead, singing its heart out. He looked up at the tiny bird, a black dot against the blue sky. He had felt like that, ready to soar and be free. What now? He shook his head. A rough-hewn plank had been balanced between two piles of stones and he went to sit on the make-shift bench. Ignoring the wild beauty of the surrounding scene, he hung his head, frowning at the clasped hands that dangled between his spread knees.

He felt—*un-made*—was the only way he could describe it. To be told he was more or less an invalid, infirm, not even an old crock, but a young one! And yet he didn't feel unwell—he could ride all day and stand a bout as well as the next man. He was tired at the end of a day in the saddle and if his heart beat faster and he was out of breath after swordplay, well that was usual, wasn't it? Everyone got out of breath when they ran a race or engaged in sports. It was part of the fun, to push oneself to the limit. But his limit was to be less than that of other men? He had never noticed it.

What was he to do? He felt aimless, purposeless, worse than when he had finally been permitted to leave his sickroom three years previously. Months of intermittent fever combined with aching joints had left him a gawky, gangling youth with pudding rather than muscles who had grown several inches during his forced bed-rest. It was Mr Adams' head groom, a former cavalry sergeant, who had stepped in then to help him. Observing the boy's struggles to regain his strength and revive his riding skills, he had suggested that a little sword drill might be of benefit. Fired by dreams of a commission in a cavalry regiment and gratified by the prospect of not appearing a complete Johnny Raw when this should come to pass, Luke had put himself in the hands of his instructor who, on occasion, had gone so far as to pronounce his prowess 'not bad'. But it had all been to no avail.

Tomorrow he must travel to Dorsetshire for his sister's betrothal party. Was that to be his future, to go from one engagement to the next as a society fribble, for ever looking on while others acted?

Chapter Three

"Frankly, Rembleton, while I have no issue at all with pro-
viding for my niece financially, the thought of assuming
social responsibility for a young lady who must be launched on
the marriage market has thrown me into an abject funk."

Mr John Rembleton, generally known as Rambling Jack,
waved to the footman to bring another decanter. Of an enquiring turn of mind and endowed at a young age with a handsome
fortune courtesy of his godfather, he had roamed the world for
more than twenty years, sending back natural specimens to be
stored for him as well as furnishing the Royal Society with regular reports. On his return to England the previous year, he had
purchased a ramshackle farm on the outskirts of London where
he and his collaborator Bartholomew Wilkins processed the
fruits of their travels. It was their intention to publish a revised
natural encyclopaedia in the style of Buffon, reflecting their own
more recent discoveries and conclusions.

From time to time Jack met Mr Harte over a glass of port at
the Society of Eccentrics, but he had never before encountered
the other man in such a state of distress. Having listened sympathetically to Mr Harte's confession, he sat back, ran his hand
over his short dark hair and remarked, "Familial duty is the very
devil! I know it all too well." He was silent for a moment and
then enquired, "What sort of a girl is she?"

"Very sensible, not at all missish, "Mr Harte replied. "That will make it easier. It's not that she's empty-headed or foolish. A little shy, perhaps. They lead an odd sort of life, these naval wives and daughters. On the one hand they must manage their lives and their households without the masculine support and protection that is their due, on the other they seem to move in almost exclusively feminine circles except when a husband has liberty, as they put it. The sons frequently join the navy at a very young age, so the daughters are generally more sheltered than our society young ladies. But they are also more self-reliant. Olivia has been well-educated—she attended a good academy in Bath, or so I'm told, but doesn't give herself any airs and has very pretty manners. For all that, at eighteen she can't be permitted to set up house on her own."

"I see that." Mr Rembleton drank deeply before saying, "Do you know, Harte, I think we may be able to help one another."

Jack stripped off his clothes and climbed into the steaming bath. With a sigh of relief, he rested his head against the towel-draped back of the metal tub and began to sort through the day's events in his mind. The door behind him opened and a slim, long-fingered hand reached over his shoulder to present him with a tumbler of cool rum and lemon punch. He seized it gratefully.

"You're much too tense—lean forward so I can attend to your back."

Smiling, he obeyed, letting his head dangle as the strong fingers kneaded and caressed, easing the tightness in his neck and shoulders, but creating another tension lower down. He sighed again.

"How did you fare in London?"

"Not too badly—apart from being accosted by Rembleton, that is. I saw him too late to evade him."

"What brings his exaltedness to town? Parliament isn't sitting, is it?"

"No. But surely you don't think that the country can manage without his advice, especially in these perilous times? He's hovering around the politicos, revelling in his own importance."

"God help the country if we must depend on him."

"More to the point, I think I may have solved one of my problems, although you may not like the solution."

The fingers dug in tight and then eased. "Oh?"

"I ran into Samuel Harte at the Eccentrics. He was in the dumps because his sister has just died, leaving him with an eighteen-year-old niece on his hands. Her father and brother are God knows where with the navy, so there's no recourse to them."

"So brave Harte quails, does he?"

Jack groaned acknowledgement of the pun. "He doesn't want to disrupt his bachelor life and Rembleton's pressure on me to sire the heir he has failed to provide increases all the time."

"And of course you always do what brother wants." Knowing hands ran down Jack's spine and cupped his buttocks. Jack shifted obligingly to allow more access.

"His insinuations become excessive," he said flatly, "and I've no wish to be hanged for sodomy or even pilloried for the attempt. Have you?" The hands stilled and Jack twisted round to face the only person he loved.

Bart Wilkins shuddered. The mob rarely showed any mercy towards those pilloried. Men accused of attempted buggery were subjected to its worst excesses and it was not unknown for them to be carted off unconscious to their dank prison cell at the end of the prescribed sentence. He pictured Jack and himself, locked in position for hours, unable to move or defend themselves as they were pelted with filth and all sorts of missiles, cut and bruised by stones and shards, plastered with rotten vegetables, mud and dung.

"Would he do it?"

"Not deliberately, I think. After all, it must reflect on him, mustn't it? But you know Rembleton—he's incapable of thinking before he acts and his temper is easily triggered. 'Cursed sodomite' was the worst insult he could think of to hurl at me, but if he gets into the habit of doing so, then tongues may start to wag. If I marry Harte's chit, we would be safe, she would be properly established in her own home and Rembleton would have his heir."

"If she's only eighteen, is it fair to her?" Bart asked

Jack shrugged. "I think such a marriage would work. And don't forget that my brother is eighteen years older than I. He's over sixty. She would one day be Lady Rembleton."

"That would be a sufficient inducement?"

"Perhaps." Jack shivered suddenly and climbed out of the bath. "Damn water's got cold," he said, towelling himself vigorously before donning a soft woollen dressing gown. "Oh to be back in the tropics!"

"No hope of that for the moment," Bart said wistfully. "But to return to our muttons—."

"Don't you see?" Jack said urgently. "These naval wives and daughters are used to doing without their men. If I purchase her an estate within an easy distance of here, we may generally retain our way of life. I can point out a dozen couples and more in every ton ballroom, where the husband has not altered his habits after marriage. I need not spend more time with her than it takes to get a child or two on her."

"Can you?"

"Sire an heir? That I don't know. But perform with a woman? After I left Harte I went round to Madame Sybilla's—told her I wanted an experienced woman who could play the virgin."

Bart shook his head, laughing. "I might have known you would take the empirical approach."

"It's not as though we were never with a female before," Jack retorted. "Remember Immodest Meg?" They both grinned at the memory of the barmaid who had made it her business to initiate the boys of Rembleton into more adult pleasures.

"She took us together and never guessed that it was watching the other that excited us, not her attentions. She was too young to be your brother's first. Maybe if you ask him who filled her place in his day, it might deflect his suspicions."

"You cunning dog," Jack said admiringly.

"But what was it like today?"

"Once I told her to stop her theatrics—'Ooh, sir pray do not hurt me'," he piped in a falsetto voice, cowering back as he did so, "and lie still, it was about as satisfying as boxing the Jesuit; a release, no more."

"You'd be kind to your bride, I hope?"

"Of course," Jack answered indignantly. "I wouldn't hurt her, not more than is necessary to take her maidenhead. And should she be ignorant of what happens between a man and a woman, I'd explain it to her first. The whore said it's surprising how many girls don't know what will happen and that many men like that."

"You had quite a chat with the wench."

"I told her I was getting married and had never had a virgin before. She said a real virgin would be much tighter than she was and gave me a little phial of oil to ease my way." Jack picked up a jug of water that had been set beside the fire to keep warm. "I must shave."

"Don't," Bart said. "That is unless your previous exertions have left you too—weak for more."

Jack untied his belt and shrugged the dressing-gown from his shoulders. "You'll have to come and find out," he said as he went towards the bed.

Chapter Four

*L*uke's blade slithered against that of his opponent. This was the first time he had picked up his sabre since his military ambitions had been thwarted. Even today he had not sought the bout, but could not ignore his mentor's challenging, "I suppose you've got soft at that university, Mr Fitz!" He turned his wrist so as to lock the sergeant's sword with his own and grinned broadly.

"What do you propose to do now, sir?" the sergeant asked drily. "It all comes down to which of us can disengage and thrust first, don't it? Very pretty in a duel or fencing salon, perhaps, but on the battlefield? There they fight dirtier." He brought up his left arm, slashing out with the edge of his hand towards Luke's throat. "Or I could give you a punch in the bread-basket or a knee in the cods if you brought me in close enough."

"I'm never going to be near a battlefield," Luke snarled. The sergeant relaxed his hold for a moment and Luke knocked his sword out of his hand.

"That's better sir," the man said approvingly. "'Ave you changed your mind about the military, then? Especially now, with the peace broke, I'd 'ave thought—."

"So did I," Luke flung at him. "But my mother forbids it and that damned quack says my heart may have been damaged during my illness and he can't recommend it." He wiped his brow with the back of his wrist and stooped to pick up the other's sword, handing it to him hilt first.

"Billy," the sergeant called to a passing stable lad. "Run and fetch two pots of ale. Quickly now."

He put his sword on the narrow table at the side of the practice room, straddled the bench beside it and took up a cloth to wipe the blade. Luke silently followed suit.

"Now, Mr Fitz," the sergeant demanded once they had sampled their ale. "What's that you said about not being fit for service?"

Relieved to have an unbiased if well-disposed listener, Luke unburdened himself haltingly, feeling as if he were stripping himself bare. "I feel such a sham," he finished. "Look at me! Almost six foot tall, as healthy a specimen as you might meet. I can ride, swim and fence, but am not considered fit to be a soldier when any looby might enlist at will."

"What exactly did this doctor say?"

"Pure speculation," Luke said angrily, "all coulds and mights and perhaps. He put his ear to my chest and took my pulse and said there might be an irregularity—he couldn't be sure there wasn't. And how it had been reported that men who had had acute rheumatism had suddenly dropped dead years later. But that doesn't say anything, does it? The one may have nothing to do with the other. People drop dead all the time. But he has my mother convinced and she won't listen to me and Mr Adams says I should heed what the quack said."

The sergeant frowned. "I don't know what to say to you, sir. A soldier's life is an 'ard one—"

"I know that," Luke interrupted hotly. "I'm not an idiot with a head full of dreams of glory."

"'ard in ways you mebbe can't imagine," the sergeant continued unperturbed. "You're abroad in all weathers, much of the time in wet duds, for you've 'ad no chance to dry 'em after a soaking, sometimes short on rations and mebbe on sleep too, and then the order comes for a forced march—through the night if your luck's really run out." He put a hand on the younger man's arm. "Mr Fitz, there's no denying you was grievously ill with the rheumatics and they left you very weak. I reckon there's none knows better than me 'ow 'ard you worked and 'ow long it took you to recover. But what if it did leave a weakness? What if it was to 'appen again? I've seen too many men collapsed at the side of the road, too weak to march on."

Luke's shoulders slumped. "So there's no hope for me?" he asked, dejected.

"Not as long as you're determined to be sorry for yourself," the sergeant said tartly. "By my way of thinking, it's not the cards 'e's dealt that make a man, but 'ow 'e plays 'em. I'd never 'ave thought you'd be one to want pluck."

"I don't," Luke protested indignantly. "But I feel all at sixes and sevens."

"I'm not surprised. But you still 'ave your brains and your ballocks, 'aven't you? Why did you want a pair of colours? For the glory? To fight? To seek adventure? To serve your country? To escape petticoat government?"

"All of those, I suppose," Luke acknowledged with a reluctant smile.

"You're not trying to outrun the constable or 'ave got a mort in the family way, 'ave you?"

"No, no," Luke said, laughing, "nothing like that."

"You'd be surprised at the reasons why some men enlist. And there's always the ones who need the pay. There's no shame in that."

"No," Luke agreed. "It's more honourable than running away from your responsibilities." He got up and went to the door. "Billy! Fetch two more pots of ale or, better still, bring a jug."

"Yessir!"

"Then you're going to 'ave to make the best of it, ain't you, Mr Fitz?" the sergeant demanded. "You 'ave time, you'll be at Cambridge for another couple of years."

"But what am I to say to people?" Luke asked despairingly. "I may not even join a militia. People will wonder. The whole world is sporting a uniform these days. Even the Prime Minister came down to the House in some version of regimentals."

Sergeant Quant drank deeply. "That's the advantage of being a nob! If you're stiff-necked enough, few will dare ask you and you can out-stare them as do. There's no need to wear your 'eart on your sleeve, is there?"

"True."

"As I see it, you've come to a cross-roads in your life, Mr Fitz, earlier perhaps than some, but it 'appens to us all. Don't go off at 'alf-cock either, but consider what direction you want to take. We don't always 'ave to follow the crowd. There's a lot of work to be done at 'ome to keep an army marching. And there's plenty 'olding office as won't see it. There are other places and ways to serve, if that's your wish."

" 'They also serve who only stand and wait'," Luke murmured.

"That's it, sir. As long as your 'eart is willing, you'll find your way."

Luke drained his tankard and stood. He held his hand out, almost bashfully. "Thank you, Sergeant."

The sergeant clasped his hand, putting his free hand over their joined ones. "You'll do, lad," he said gruffly.

"And you may have this little parlour for your own if you wish." Mrs Carr opened the door of the return room between the first and second floors. "My girls were used to regard it as their own sitting-room and indeed it gave us all some privacy, for they did not always wish to sit with my callers."

"Edith and I had many a comfortable coze here," Olivia said with a warm smile. "You are very good, ma'am."

"Nonsense! I am only grateful that your uncle had the sense to propose your coming to me."

Mrs Carr was a lively woman of about fifty, who took a greater interest in matters of fashion and style than Olivia's mother ever had and was more than happy to advise on a suitable mourning wardrobe.

"You will not wish to invest too much in full mourning, my dear Olivia, for you will wear it for only three months after all, and will not be going out much in that time. If we put a deep border on your mother's cloak, it will be more than adequate, but you must have a new bonnet and several pairs of gloves. A pretty bonnet may be retrimmed with lighter ribbons and you will continue to wear black gloves while you are in half-mourning."

"Do you know of a good glover, ma'am? I confess I should like to have them made for me if it is not too expensive. It is my little finger, you see." She held out her left hand, showing that this digit was much shorter than usual.

"I never noticed it," Mrs Carr said, amazed.

"We were used to put some wadding in the tip of the glove, but I have wondered if a skilled glover could not do better. Fortunately one does not in general offer one's left hand but at times, when joining hands when dancing, for example, I wonder if the wadding might not be noticed."

"There is a very good man, an émigré, in town. We shall see what he can do for you," Mrs Carr said sympathetically. "Now, I think two morning dresses and two dinner gowns should be enough, don't you? Your white muslins will be perfect for half-mourning, perhaps with a black net shawl. I think you should have one evening gown for half-mourning too—it is best to be prepared."

It was a melancholy task looking through her mother's belongings, but Mrs Carr's practical approach helped shake Olivia out of the lethargy into which she had fallen. Her kind hostess encouraged her to recount little anecdotes of happier days as they sorted through her mother's 'paraphernalia', as Olivia remarked with a muffled laugh, describing Mr Edmondsen's intrusion.

"A dreadful man," Mrs Carr agreed. She gracefully accepted the gift of a selection of pretty caps, "for you are far too young for them, my dear and I shall remember Margaret fondly when I wear them," and suggested that the female servants would be pleased with gifts of some of the simpler garments. "They will do them very well for church on Sunday and your maid Betty will dispose of whatever you do not wish to keep. We may refashion the black silk for you now, the other gowns can be packed away carefully for the moment."

By the time this was done and Olivia had consulted with a jeweller regarding the creation of mourning rings for her father and brother, the fob for her uncle and brooches for herself and Mrs Carr, she had somehow come to accept that her mother was gone although the gap she left could never be filled.

"Uncle Samuel!" Olivia went into her uncle's outstretched arms. "I thought you had quite forgotten me."

Mr Harte kissed her cheek, satisfied that she no longer looked as forlorn as she had on the day he departed for London. She still presented a pallid appearance in her mourning, but her features were alive again. She seemed older, more mature.

"Come. Mrs Carr has kindly given me my own sitting-room so we may be undisturbed while you tell me how you got on. Would you like some tea?"

"Or a glass of port, sir," the housekeeper suggested.

He gave her a grateful nod and followed his niece up the stairs.

His niece managed to restrain herself until he was installed by the fire, a glass in his hand. "Well?" she asked imperiously.

He laughed at her cocked eyebrow. "You're the image of my mother. I feel as if I'm expected to account for myself and my misdemeanours."

"Uncle, pray don't tease. What have you discovered?"

"Quite a lot," he replied meekly. "Firstly, I spoke to your father's solicitor and discovered that he holds a document appointing me to act *in loco parentis* to his children should anything happen to your mother." He smiled ruefully at her. "This was signed more than thirty years ago, before your brother was born, so you must forgive me for not recalling it although I have to say I was very surprised at Edmondsen's revelations and did not like his categorical denial of any provision your father might have made. In fact, his solicitor feels sure it will be possible for us to come to some arrangement with your father's bank that permits you to draw funds for your daily subsistence—although I would be very happy to frank you until we hear from him, Olivia. You know that."

"I do, Uncle," she said softly with a speaking glance.

"What that encroaching quill-driver Edmondsen did not know was the details of your mother's marriage settlement. I did not wish to raise your hopes unduly, my dear, and said nothing until I had spoken to my own solicitor whose firm has acted for the Hartes these many years.

"In brief, Margaret had a marriage portion of ten thousand pounds, handsome enough in those days. It was settled on her, giving her a life interest and on her death it was to pass to her children. As I recall, your father was very insistent that he would not touch his wife's money, although he did benefit indirectly because she was able to some extent to support herself." Mr Harte smiled at Olivia. "So you have five thousand pounds from your mother, as a marriage portion; a very respectable amount if not a fortune. You will receive the interest—a couple of hundred pounds per annum—until you are wed."

"Oh. She never mentioned it."

"I suppose she never felt the need to do so," he replied shortly. "There was nothing to suggest she was in poor health, was there?"

"No. That's why it was such a shock. She was looking forward to Weymouth. We had found a pretty little house to rent and if she liked it there, she hoped to find somewhere we could make a permanent home. I am so relieved to know my parents didn't abandon me, Uncle. Mr Edmondsen made me feel as if I would be cast out onto the street at any moment. And I didn't like the way he looked at me," she disclosed. "I was glad you were there."

Girls are very vulnerable, Mr Harte thought, shocked. Had the solicitor been aware of the settlement and thought to gain the heiress while she still suffered under the shock of her mother's death? Who knew what may have happened, especially if she had thought she had no-one else to turn to and Edmondsen had offered succour?

"You need have nothing more to do with him. I shall have my own solicitor deal with your mother's will."

"Thank you, Uncle."

"But, my dear, this does not solve our most pressing problem, which is the question of your home. Where are you to live? You will need a more permanent abode. Could you remain with Mrs Carr?"

"I would be reluctant to impose upon her for too long. She has three married daughters and is in the habit of going to one or the other for long visits. I would not wish her to feel obliged to include me. We can hardly expect her to offer me a permanent home."

Mr Harte squared his shoulders. "Then you must come to me," he said resolutely. "We shall need to arrange for a respectable lady to live with us as your chaperon and also introduce you to society once you are out of mourning."

"Introduce me to society," Olivia repeated faintly, not knowing which prospect, the duenna or the ton, was more daunting.

"You are my niece after all," Mr Harte said rather haughtily. "It was your mother's choice to live so retired." He thought for a moment. "Do you have any admirers here? Is there anyone you favour in particular?"

She smiled and shook her head. "Most of the eligible men I have met are naval officers and, to be frank, sir, I have no desire to marry a sailor. It's a hard life for the wives left behind. Robert feels the same and does not intend to marry while he is on active service."

"But you are not opposed to marriage?"

"It is a woman's lot, is it not? I have been wondering how I might earn my bread if it came to that. Now, don't be angry, Uncle Samuel. It was purely idle speculation. I suppose recent events have made me more aware of my circumstances. All that occurred to me was to be either a lady's companion or a governess, dependant on the whim of my employer. Marriage to a good man would be better than that."

Heartened by this pragmatic response, Mr Harte announced. "There is an alternative which I would like to put to you as it was put to me. May I do so?"

"If you please, sir."

"I happened to discuss your situation with a fellow member of the Society of Eccentrics. I know him as well from the Royal Society—he is a fellow and his papers are very highly regarded. I beg you will not consider this a breach of confidence but he noticed that I was in a brown study and I sometimes find it useful to tease things out in conversation. He's a younger man than I, about forty, I'd say, the younger brother of Lord Rembleton. He returned to England last year, having travelled far and wide for over twenty years in a spirit of scientific exploration and finds himself under pressure to marry as the viscount has no sons. Both his lordship and his wife are considerably older than Mr Rembleton so it is very likely that he will succeed his brother in the fullness of time. He has suggested that if the two of you could come to an agreement, a marriage between you would benefit both of you."

Olivia's mouth fell open at the astonishing suggestion that she marry a complete stranger. "He must be a very odd sort of man to propose such a thing," she said faintly.

"Not odd exactly, but—I suppose it is the habit of an enquiring mind to recognise a problem and attempt to find a solution. He was very clear that it would be a made match, as they say, one based on mutual respect and esteem. His only reason to marry is the need for heirs to the title. He would be generous; he is well-to-do and has no knowledge of your fortune. He would set you up in your own establishment while continuing to spend a considerable amount of time at his property north of London, near Primrose Hill, where he pursues his scientific interests."

"What kind of man is he? Do you like him, Uncle Samuel?"

"If I did not, I should not have mentioned this to you. He is at times a little awkward and can be very direct, as with this proposal, but I judge him to be an honourable man. He is not a ladies' man either; you need have no fear on that score." He saw that his niece looked stunned. "It would be an advantageous match in the eyes of the world and I thought I should mention it."

"I suppose I should think about it," Olivia said. "Should you object if I discuss it with Mrs Carr?"

"Not at all, my dear. Do exactly as you like. Now, I must pay my respects to her before I see Edmondsen."

"Edmondsen holds no other papers on your mother's behalf," Mr Harte announced on his return to Mrs Carr's pleasant home.

"I remember Mrs Frobisher saying she had passed his office on High Street and stepped in on a whim," Mrs Carr said. "The previous day she had called on another lady who mentioned that it was possible for married women to bequeath their personal effects and she wished you to have hers, my dear." She looked a little conscious. "We women can take strange notions and dear Margaret did not like the idea of her jewellery and so forth going to a subsequent wife if she were to die and the captain to marry again."

Olivia froze for a moment at this comment but then replied, "She was always so thoughtful, so caring."

"What do you think, ma'am?" Olivia finished describing Mr Rembleton's unexpected proposal as relayed by her uncle and looked across to Mrs Carr. "It is a preposterous idea, is it not?"

"But not one that I would dismiss out of hand," that lady said once she had recovered from her surprise. "A viscount's brother, especially when he is also the heir, is not to be sneezed at, as they say."

"But I've never even seen him, let alone spoken to him," Olivia protested.

"I understand that his offer is contingent on the two of you coming to an agreement," Mrs Carr pointed out. "I do not see why you should not consider it sensibly and prudently. What would your circumstances be if you were to accept this offer? You must compare them to your other opportunities. I am not saying you should decide rashly, although there are many women who would leap at such a chance. But if you clarify your thoughts in general, then you will know whether you wish to proceed with the particular.

"Allow me to give you one piece of advice. Although I know many couples who were almost strangers when they married, I consider there must be a fundamental understanding between a man and a woman if a marriage is to be satisfactory. I am not talking about love, you understand, for that may grow afterwards, but more the sort of common sympathy that has us enjoy one person's company at dinner while we find another irritating and intolerable. After all, if you could not bear a man's company for two to three hours, how would you stand being married to him?"

Olivia had to smile at this down-to-earth view of things. "So you are saying, ma'am, I should consider whether I could contemplate such a marriage and, only if I think I might, should I ask Uncle Samuel to arrange a meeting with Mr Rembleton, to see how we get on together."

"Exactly, my dear."

Chapter Five

*C*larify her thoughts? It was easier said than done. It had never occurred to Olivia to wonder about her life, ponder what she wanted from it. It had all seemed so clear-cut. But now the very foundation of that life had crumbled under her feet. She wrapped her shawl more closely around her and drew up her feet to huddle into the armchair beside her bedroom fire. Some days she felt she would never be warm again.

Mamma's loss cut deeply. They had been so close, the two of them, probably because Papa and Robert were at sea. Mamma had even removed to Bath so that Olivia need not board at her school but could return home each afternoon. How many happy hours had they spent together, taking turns to read as they sewed or planning little outings? This last year, they had enjoyed the whole round of entertainments indulged in by a relieved nation, weary after over ten years of war and longing for merriment. They had looked forward to removing to Weymouth and to finding a permanent home. Where was Olivia to live now? And what would it be like without Mamma?

She felt uneasy about imposing herself on her uncle. He had said he was 'happy to frank her' but only 'you must come to me' when he spoke of her living with him. His house was a 'bachelor establishment' and he would employ a chaperon for her. Would that be like having a governess? Supposing Olivia didn't like her?

How would it suit Mr Harte to have not one but two females taking up residence with him? And what if he were to suffer a sudden death just like his sister? Who would then claim responsibility for Olivia? The questions tumbled through her mind.

Mamma had been so concerned that Papa might marry again that she had made that will. Her father might well consider that to be the best solution. Olivia should then live with her stepmother, he would say. How could she bear to see another woman in Mamma's place? Come to think of it, Papa would not require a second wife to make such arrangements for her—he could send her to live with some lady of his acquaintance, perhaps a naval widow. And what if he lost his life? A sailor's life was perilous at the best of times and England was fighting a cruel opponent.

The more she brooded, the worse her situation appeared. None of these options seemed to offer real security and stability. Mamma had been her anchor, she realised—it hadn't mattered how often they had moved to suit Papa's postings, she had always been there. Without her, Olivia felt adrift.

She needed to find a safe harbour. Mr Rembleton seemed amenable to considering her point of view—he had spoken of their coming to an agreement, not of dictating his terms. He would be generous, set her up in her own establishment. It was somewhat surprising that he proposed spending much of his time elsewhere, but neither her uncle nor Mrs Carr had remarked on this as being particularly unusual. What did gentlemen do all day? Now that she thought about it, they probably pursued interests outside the home, which was traditionally the wife's domain. Certainly, when she had paid calls with Mamma they had only encountered the ladies of the family.

There was a tap on her door. "Are you still up, my dear?" Mrs Carr enquired.

"I've been thinking about Mr Rembleton's suggestion, ma'am. At the moment I feel like a cork spinning in rough seas—I could be tossed anywhere. I have never had a real home the way other girls at school had. Mamma was my home, it seems."

"You would like to put down roots." Mrs Carr nodded understandingly. "There can be no doubt that the situation of a married lady is in general much more favourable than that of a single woman, especially a young one. While Miss Frobisher may not have her own home, Mrs Rembleton could."

"And if Mr Rembleton were to die? What would be the position of his widow?"

"It would depend on the settlements and whether there were children. If you were still young, it might be necessary for you to engage a companion. But you would certainly be able to retain your own household. Once you are married, you are deemed to be of age so that while you might have trustees, you would not be subject to the authority of a guardian or even a parent or elder brother. But you need not come to a decision tonight."

"So I am to tell Rembleton that if he chooses to present himself, he may court you?" her uncle asked some days later.

Olivia took a moment to answer. "Not court me," she said finally. "I would not expect him to profess an affection that cannot yet exist between us. He does not offer a love match, but more a practical way to meet our two needs, his for an heir and mine to feel secure in my own home. We should spend some time in one another's company, see how we get on together, make sure that neither is possessed of an habitual peculiarity that the other finds insupportable. Like Mr Edmondsen's little titter," she explained in answer to her uncle's look of amazement, "or the way the curate sniffs perpetually. But I don't know how that might be managed while I am still in mourning."

"Wait until the first month is over," Mrs Carr recommended. "If you are still of the same mind, your uncle may return here with Mr Rembleton. I should be happy to invite you both to dine," she said to Mr Harte, "and we might go for another walk. Olivia can then decide if she wishes to take matters further."

Olivia felt very fine in her black silk dress and comforted by the new mourning brooch which she had pinned where the neckline of her dress dipped at her bosom. She carefully smoothed her black kid gloves. M. Renard had cunningly lengthened and stiffened the little finger of the left hand just enough so that one really would not notice the slight deformity.

Well, I've donned my best armour, she thought as she studied her reflection. I wonder what he'll be like. Her cheeks were faintly flushed with nervous excitement and her heart thumped suddenly to echo a knock at the hall door. She hastily turned away from the mirror over the fireplace and, with a quick smile for Mrs Carr, went to sit decorously on the settee. Men's voices were heard in the hall, her uncle's deep one and a lighter one answering him, then there were quick, firm footsteps nearing the door.

"Mrs Carr, may I present my friend Mr Rembleton," Uncle Samuel said. Olivia studied their visitor as he made his bow to his hostess. He was of medium height, with a trim figure displayed to advantage in fawn knee-breeches and a dark blue coat. His black hair was cropped unfashionably short all round—here were no curls combed forward 'a la victime'—and she was struck by the unusual shade of his complexion, a strange, faded brown that reminded her of her father when he returned from the tropics.

"My niece, Miss Frobisher," her uncle was saying and she curtsied.

Mr Rembleton smiled, displaying deep crow's feet at the corners of dark brown eyes. "Miss Frobisher, I am honoured to make your acquaintance."

"The honour is mine, sir," she replied politely and was relieved when Mrs Carr stepped in to enquire about the gentlemen's journey and if they were comfortable at the *George*.

Mr Rembleton was an amiable dinner companion, punctiliously seeing to her comfort. As they were only four, the conversation was general. He was curious about the effect of the vast naval presence on the town.

"It is not the most salubrious place in the country," Mrs Carr answered, "and one is much more aware of the war here than in other towns. At the end of May, for example, within two weeks seventeen French prizes were brought in but another time it could be our own ships limping into port carrying many wounded. A ship in full sail is a truly magnificent sight but to see such a splendid vessel brought low, her sails and rigging torn, her masts splintered, her sides holed, is dreadful. And then one remembers the thousands of sailors who have no grave; for whom at best the service for burial at sea was read before they were consigned to the ever-rolling ocean."

Olivia broke the moment's respectful silence. "I understand you have undertaken many voyages yourself, sir," she said to Mr Rembleton.

"Yes. My imagination was fired by Anson's voyage and those of Cook. I remember my excitement on being presented with a copy of Cook's journals of his first voyage on my thirteenth birthday. From then on, I was determined to explore the world and discover its wonders."

"My father sailed on the Discovery, Captain Cook's companion ship on his third voyage."

Mr Rembleton looked at her respectfully. "My goodness, Miss Frobisher, it is indeed an honour to be in your company."

"I may take no credit for it, sir," she replied drolly. "It was before I was born."

Mr Rembleton's eyes gleamed. "Do you happen to have any mementos or souvenirs from the voyage?"

"I have Papa's letters of course—Mamma kept them all from when they first met when she was nineteen. That was in

1769—they did not marry until 1772. And there are small items, curios such as shells and beads that he brought her. They are all in that big sandalwood box we looked at only the other day," she reminded Mrs Carr.

"Could I see them?" Mr Rembleton was almost stammering in his excitement.

Olivia hesitated. "I don't feel I should show you Papa's letters, sir," she said at last. "Parts of them are very personal. When Mamma read them to me, she always skipped some paragraphs."

"No, no, of course not," he replied at once. "I just thought if there were passages describing natural occurrences or landscapes, foreign ports, that sort of thing; to read it at first hand would be capital and we naturalists always like to see corroborative reports."

"There are many such descriptions, in my brother's letters too, for sailors tend to write their letters like a journal, day by day, so as to be ready to send one off whenever the opportunity arises. It can be quite monotonous when they are at sea so anything that is different will be mentioned."

"My husband does exactly the same," Mrs Carr put in. "Miss Frobisher, would you be willing to review your father's letters and copy out any interesting passages for Mr Rembleton? It would be a pleasant task for the winter months. Indeed, Mr Rembleton, if you would find Captain Carr's narratives of any interest, I should be happy to do the same."

"Ladies, I should be forever in your debt," Mr Rembleton vowed.

"Yes, I think I would like to," Olivia agreed. "It would bring me closer to him."

"If you are interested in first-hand accounts, Mr Rembleton," Mrs Carr said, "there is a very old man here in Kingston, one George Gregory, who sailed with Lord Anson on his voyage of discovery."

"He must be over a hundred," Mr Harte exclaimed.

"One hundred and eight, they say," Olivia confirmed.

"We must try and see him tomorrow, eh Rembleton? Who knows how long he'll last."

"By all means," Mr Rembleton replied. "And perhaps the ladies would join us for a walk on the famous ramparts in the afternoon."

When Mr Rembleton arrived at the appointed hour the next day, he carried a large parcel.

"As you have agreed to undertake a task on my behalf that I acknowledge may be tedious, I hope you will allow me, ma'am," he bowed briefly to Mrs Carr, "and, with your uncle's permission, Miss Frobisher, to provide you with the tools for your labours." He opened the parcel to display two handsome mahogany writing boxes which contained every implement a writer's heart might desire, a score of notebooks beautifully bound in leather and the crowning glory of a silver quill-cutter, "Which I hope will spare you much of the work in mending your pens."

Olivia looked at her hostess. It was a kind thought, but was it beyond the permissible? Yet, the donor's honest eyes and appealing gaze banished any thought of declining his gift. Taking a breath, she said, "You are too kind, sir."

"Indeed," Mrs Carr chimed in. "Thank you, Mr Rembleton."

"These will now become scientific documents and provenance is most important, so I have inscribed the first page of each set." He opened a notebook to display the inscription:

Observations of Captain Robert Frobisher R.N., transcribed from his letters by his daughter in the Year of our Lord Eighteen Hundred and Three Volume the First 17 to

"I have made a similar inscription for you, ma'am, and you must both adopt this title, amended as appropriate, for succeeding volumes. And, Miss Frobisher, if you are kind enough to peruse your brother's letters as well, pray take a separate notebook and do not include his observations with those of your father. Pray note the place and date of any extract, the time as well if it is given."

"Well! Such clipped tones, my dear. He might have been giving instructions to his secretary" Mrs Carr remarked later, not a little miffed at the notion.

"I liked it," Olivia replied. "He was not treating us as silly females, but explaining the way he wanted things done and assuming we were intelligent enough to understand. It was the same with the passage headings. He trusts us to do it properly, rather than assuming it is beyond the limited capacity of our little minds."

"That is true," Mrs Carr conceded.

Ensconced beside the fire in the *Quebec Tavern*, Jack lit his pipe and gratefully drew in the aromatic smoke. He had been in Portsmouth for three weeks. Despite the need to spend some hours with Miss Frobisher, earlier that day he had been able to inspect the immense dockyards and in particular Brunel's truly innovative assembly system for making the wooden blocks so essential to ships. He brooded over what he had seen. An array of steam-driven machines made it possible for ten men to do the work of one hundred, with the additional advantage that the blocks thus manufactured were all to a common standard. He looked up from his jottings. Was this the start of a new future? Where would it lead?

"Another pint, sir?"

He nodded to the tavern wench who put down a brimming tankard, leaning over the table to give him a good view of her ripe breasts.

She smiled invitingly. "Will there be anything else, sir?"

"No."

Tomorrow was Sunday. He and Harte were to return to London the following day. He must make up his mind about Miss Frobisher. She was a sensible girl. She didn't giggle or flirt, nor had she seemed to expect any lover-like attentions from him. They had met every day, mostly for walks although once or twice her uncle had had his horses put to so they could drive out. He must come back again to inspect the area more closely. Bere was still a royal forest, but by all accounts badly neglected, so it was very likely that old habitats had not been destroyed in the modern passion for enclosures and improved agricultural yields. It would be interesting to go over to the Isle of Wight, too. With a sigh, Jack dragged his thoughts back to his prospective bride.

She was intelligent, interested in his descriptions of his travels and could follow his train of thought when he explained his conclusions. He could talk to her the way he talked to his assistants. He liked her, he realised. He did not feel uncomfortable with her, as he so frequently did with females, as if they were inhabitants of another world. And it might actually be quite pleasant to have a son, someone who could continue his work after him. They were to accompany the ladies to church tomorrow. He would ask to talk to her privately afterwards.

"I should like to speak freely, Miss Frobisher."

"Pray do, sir,"

"We are two intelligent people. I think we would deal well together, but I should like to be sure that there is a clear understanding between us. May I proceed, or do you feel you could not support the idea of a match between us?"

"I should like to hear what you have to say," Olivia answered. Having encouraged him for some weeks, she could hardly do less. And she had enjoyed his company. He passed Mrs Carr's dinner companion test, she thought with an inward smile.

Despite this encouragement, silence grew between them until Mr Rembleton suddenly exploded into speech.

"Hang it, Miss Frobisher, I'm no good at this sort of thing! I'm not a man who makes pretty speeches or indeed one who goes much into society although I realise that that must change if I marry. My work is my life. We—that is Bartholomew Wilkins, who accompanied me on all my travels—he is the son of the steward at Rembleton and I've known him all my life, well Bart and I are deeply engaged in evaluating, cataloguing and reporting on the specimens we collected on our travels and that have been waiting for us at our home near Primrose Hill. It is an old farm that we have restored and adapted to our purposes, a combination of library, museum, laboratories—what you will. We also have an experimental garden as well as glass houses and even a few animals that we brought with us—not many, a couple of lemurs and some monkeys, though their numbers are increasing. They inhabit an island in our little lake. It is not a place to which one would bring one's wife and children," he concluded. "I should however be happy to establish you properly in a place of your choosing, and visit you regularly."

"I should not like to be regarded as a deserted wife, sir, nor my children to have an absentee father," Olivia said firmly. "I know how much the presence of such a parent is missed."

"I accept that, but the greater part of my life would not be spent at your home. However, that would not be unusual for men of our class, whose various responsibilities and interests frequently take them away from their country estates."

"Hmm."

"If we found somewhere within half a day's journey of Primrose Hill, I would endeavour to come every week," he offered. "If I appear at church once or twice a month and we are seen together in society, perhaps invite our neighbours a couple of times a year, that should still any wagging tongues, especially if we are observed to be on cordial terms with one another."

It was a lot more than her parents had had. "You are aware that I have not been much in society?" Olivia asked him. This was something she had not thought of.

"I'm sure my sister-in-law would support you," he offered. "My brother is pressing me to marry after all. When is your mourning up?"

"At the end of March," she answered shortly.

"In time for the Season then."

"For one who does not go much into society, you are well-versed in its niceties, sir," Olivia could not help observing.

"One must know the enemy in order to be able to take defensive action," he replied with a grin. "What would you think of taking a house in town until the summer? It would give us more time to find a suitable place for you. Have you given any thought to where you would like to live?"

"I had not thought so far ahead, sir." Her heart beat faster and she smoothed her damp palms over her black skirts. He seemed to assume it was settled between them.

As if he had divined her thoughts, he said, "What of you, Miss Frobisher? Have you any requirements or stipulations?"

Apparently he was willing to consider her wishes, treat her as an equal.

"Although it may seem mercenary, Mr Rembleton, my reason for considering a marriage between us is to secure my own future. I have recently become aware of my own—vulnerability, I suppose I could describe it, as a young, unmarried woman who is to all intents and purposes orphaned. I may receive word any day that my father is no more. My uncle will, I know, do all in his power to assist me, but what if something were to happen to him? You offer me the opportunity to establish myself permanently in a way I cannot as a single girl and I judge you to be a fair-minded and rational man, who would not seek to take advantage of my situation. The mere fact that we are having this conversation demonstrates that."

Mr Rembleton looked very serious. "I give you my word, Miss Frobisher, that I will do everything in my power to guarantee your independence and security."

She took a deep breath. "As a married woman I would have a recognised position in society that is denied to me now. But I must be assured that my home is not only mine, but would remain mine in the event of your own untimely demise. I hope you will forgive my plain speaking, but you are considerably older than I."

"You are quite right," Mr Rembleton said, apparently unoffended by this frank assessment.

She thought for a moment. Better to say it all now, while she had the chance. Over the previous weeks she had sought Mrs Carr's views regarding marriage settlements. As that lady had not only approved those of her daughters but also regularly read the journals as well as the law reports, she had not laughed off Olivia's request but had encouraged her to consider matters realistically. "It's better to prepare for the worst, even while hoping for the best," she had said one evening.

"I must also know that my financial security and that of all my children is assured, not only that of the son who would eventually inherit your brother's estate." Olivia informed her suitor. "In addition, I must be named as the guardian of all our children in your will. I have never met your brother, so it is not personal animosity when I say that I would not wish him or anyone else to be entitled to remove my children from my care." She stopped and looked him in the eye. "And I want your word of honour that should I die, leaving my child or children motherless, you will do everything in your power to be a good father to them, even if it is at the cost of your own work."

"You have it," he said simply. "May I say how much I value your clear-sightedness and frankness? I had not thought beyond our marriage, but you are right to point out that we must be prepared for all eventualities. Have I your permission to speak to your uncle, to tell him we have agreed terms?"

"You have, sir," Olivia held out her hand to him. "I should like to express my appreciation of the confidence you have placed in me. God willing, I shall be a good mother to our children." A little worm of excitement wriggled deep inside her at the thought of being a mother. Her family may have been torn from her, but she could make a new one.

He did not bow over her hand but took it in a firm grip. "I am sure of it," he said.

Chapter Six

A bride did not wear mourning.

She looked like a ghost. The gown and redingote of cream figured silk seemed strange after over four months of black bombazine and the matching brimmed cap that covered her hair and shaded her eyes, made her cheeks even paler. Hadn't Mamma had a coral necklace? The three strands were made to sit close around the throat and she had always said Olivia should have it when she grew up as it was better suited to her long, slender neck. She smiled sadly as she looked through her mother's ebony and ivory jewel box, remembering the many times Mamma had explained to her where the different pieces had come from. We never thought she would be taken from me so suddenly. What would she say if she saw me now? Would she approve of this marriage?

Olivia found the necklace and held it up to her neck. Papa brought the beads back from that voyage with Captain Cook. He had loved Mamma so—his letters positively radiate his affection. Will Mr Rembleton and I come to love one another? Mrs Carr said love could grow after the wedding. I trust him, and that's a good beginning.

There was a tap on the door and Mrs Carr came in. "Are you ready, my dear?"

Olivia held the necklace out to her. "Please help me with this, ma'am. I present an altogether too washed-out appearance. I need a little colour."

"This soft pink is perfect," Mrs Carr said as she fastened the clasp. "Now, if you move your hat back just a little so that some of your curls show and your eyes are not in the shadow," she gently tilted the cap as she spoke, "and pinch your cheeks and bite your lips, it will give a more rosy hue to your complexion. That's much better. Here are your gloves and reticule—you may hand me your gloves in the church, for you must remove them while you make your vows." She reached up to embrace Olivia. "I wish you every happiness, my dear Olivia, and please know that you may turn to me at any time."

"Thank you for all your kindness, ma'am. I don't know what I would have done without you these past months."

"I am so glad I was here to help you," Mrs Carr said simply. "You have been very brave—your parents would be proud of you, I assure you."

"Thank you." Olivia sighed. "I wish we might have heard from Papa before today. I should have liked to have had a parent's blessing."

"I know, my dear. Do not forget that you also have an eternal father, who will be with you today, I am sure."

Jack waited calmly at the altar of the little Norman church. He felt no guilt nor did he consider what he was about to do hypocritical or even mendacious. His intimate friendship with Bart was something set apart, a private life developed and nurtured over decades that did not, could not exist in the outer world. In public he would be Olivia's husband; it was only in secret that he could be Bart's lover. This separation of worlds had become so ingrained in him that it was almost as if he were two distinct individuals and, although it was his nature to dissect and analyse everything, he had never questioned this anomaly but simply accepted it as it was.

He repeated his vows steadily, his bride's hand resting in his. What a cruel world it was, that he could not make them to the one he loved. He repressed the fleeting thought and slid the ring onto her finger. Odd that her little finger is so short, he thought, I wonder what caused it. Now they knelt together for the prayer and he felt the priest take his right hand and join it to hers.

"Those whom God hath joined together, let no man put asunder."

It was done, Olivia thought, as she felt Mr Rembleton's firm clasp. She was married, *'for better, for worse'*. The remainder of the short service passed over her head. She signed the register and repaired with her new husband, Mrs Carr and her uncle to the *Crown Inn*, where Mr Harte had ordered a breakfast to be served in a private parlour. She found she had very little appetite and crumbled rather than ate a slice of toast. Mrs Carr had explained what her wifely duties would be, but it was strange to think that the man sitting beside her now had such intimate rights to her person. He too was quiet, but he smiled fleetingly when he caught her eye.

"It is odd, is it not, almost a transformation?"

"From two to one?" She nodded agreement. "I will take the final words to heart and endeavour not to be afraid."

"Or amazed?" he asked. "I wonder what is meant by that. I think it would be a poorer world if we lost our capacity for amazement."

"I dislike standing on ceremony," her new husband said as the carriage pulled away from the *Crown*. "May I use your name, Olivia?"

"Pray do, sir."

"And you must call me Jack."

"Very well, Jack." It seemed astonishingly personal to use a gentleman's Christian name, but perhaps it would assist them to grow closer. "Where do we go today?"

"Directly to London—we should be there by evening. I hope you like the house. I have taken it until the end of June and by then we should have acquired your home."

While more spacious than any Olivia had lived in to date, the house in Bolton Street was not so large as to be intimidating. She was welcomed respectfully by the butler, who introduced her to the rest of the staff.

"May I show you around the house, ma'am?

Olivia smiled at the housekeeper. "Tomorrow, if you please. For now, pray take me to my bedchamber and send up hot water, also to Mr Rembleton."

"Very good, ma'am. When do you wish to dine?"

"In an hour," Olivia decided, thinking she would need at least that amount of time to recover from the journey. Seventy-two miles, even in the new barouche-landau which, to her surprise, was to be for her sole use, had been exhausting. Jack had been pleased they could average nine miles an hour, including the short stop to take a hasty nuncheon at the *King's Arms* in Godalming. He had been able to read, but reading in a carriage made her ill. After exchanging a few desultory remarks, she had closed her eyes and tried to doze, but her thoughts raced too much for this to be restful. In the end, she had idly watched the passing scene.

"Oh, and send one of the maids to assist me," she added, recalling that, on Mrs Carr's advice, she had let Betty go. 'She does well enough here,' she had said, 'but does not have the à la modality you will need in your new life.'

'Better wait to have most of your bride-clothes made in town too,' Mr Harte had agreed. 'You will not wish to be stigmatised as a provincial dowdy.'

This stricture had so flustered Olivia that Mr Harte had had to promise to take her to see the London shops at the earliest possible opportunity.

The clock on the mantelpiece struck ten silvery chimes. The tocsin, Olivia thought whimsically and then scolded herself for reading too many horrid novels.

"I think I'll retire."

Her husband looked up from his notebook. "Very well, my dear. I shall join you in half an hour."

"As you wish."

He didn't stand when she did. He must have noticed her surprise and said bluntly, "It is not a lack of respect if I fail to stand when you do; it is a custom I find singularly senseless and do not propose to observe when we are on our own."

"You must do as you wish in your own home, sir," Olivia replied coolly and left the room. Now that she thought about it, it was rather foolish to expect gentlemen to act the jack-in-the-box, popping up out of their seats according to a lady's movements. It was becoming apparent that Jack was disinclined to observe the usual politenesses. Her father and Robert had always stood when she and Mamma had, but it seemed a natural reflex on their part, just as Mamma would frequently say, 'don't get up' if she was just stepping out of the room for a moment. It did seem odd that Mr Rembleton would not rise to wish her a good night. But then, it wasn't 'good night,' she reflected.

The maid helped her undress and handed her a fine lawn nightgown, a gift from Mrs Carr. It was so sheer that she could see the outline of the tips of her breasts in the dressing-table mirror. The fabric felt cool and smooth against her skin. The maid unpinned her hair. Olivia sighed with relief when the tension at her scalp eased and shook her head vigorously to encourage the heavy locks to fall.

"Shall I brush it out, ma'am?"

Another change. She was no longer 'miss'.

"Yes."

"Do you wish me to braid it, ma'am?"

"No, leave it loose," she replied, remembering Mrs Carr's suggestion that she wear her hair down on her wedding night. "Thank you. That will be all."

"Good night, ma'am."

She wondered what she should do next. Mrs Carr had said, 'your husband will come to your bed', so presumably she should get into bed. Was she to blow out the candles or leave them burning? The sound of a door closing in the room next to hers put an end to this nervous musing and sent her scrambling towards the bed, anxious not to be discovered standing in front of the fire in what she had been shocked to discover was a translucent garment. She gained the safety of her pillows, noticed that the candles were still lit and shrugged. It was too late now to snuff them.

Mrs Carr had said not to be missish. 'Mr Rembleton strikes me as a considerate gentleman and, although it will seem strange to you initially, you will soon get accustomed to it. I will not deny that the first time may hurt a little—it is the way women are made; why I have never understood—but I hope that later you will find pleasure in your husband's company. Remember, a man and a woman coming together is the most natural thing in the world and there is nothing to be afraid of.'

I wonder will I be amazed, though, Olivia asked herself just as the door connecting her room with that of her husband opened. Mr Rembleton—no, Jack—came in. He was wrapped in a dark blue banyan and carried two gently steaming glasses.

"I thought we might have some punch," he said cheerfully. "It will help ease any trepidation you may be feeling." He handed her a glass and sat facing her on the edge of the bed. "There is no point in my telling you not to be alarmed, for the unknown tends to scare us, doesn't it? But let me see if we can alleviate your fears." He raised his glass to her. She followed suit, the heady, spicy aroma encouraging her to taste the contents. The warm, sweet liquid slipped down easily and soothed her a little.

"It's very good," she told him, taking another sip.

He smiled encouragingly. "Olivia, do you understand what I, what we are going to do tonight?"

She nodded. "Mrs Carr explained it to me."

"What did she say?"

Olivia gazed at him, appalled. Surely he didn't expect her to repeat it out loud? But then she thought sensibly, if I can't even say it, how am I going to do it? Blushing fire, she took a fortifying gulp of punch. "You will put your member into my— between my legs and when you spill your seed there, it might start a baby growing inside me," she finished on a whisper.

"Good girl," he complimented her.

"It may hurt the first time."

"I will do my best to prevent that. If you finish your punch, you will be less tense and that will help."

She drained the glass obediently.

"Finished?"

She nodded and he took it from her hand. She felt drowsy and a little lightheaded. The room had got very warm and it was almost a relief when he pulled back the covers.

"May I?" he asked, and without waiting for an answer lifted her nightgown to above the join of her thighs. She didn't resist, but lay against her pillows, her eyes fixed on his face. He took a little phial of oil from his pocket and showed it to her.

"If we put a little of this on you, it will be easier for you. May I?"

She whispered her consent.

He slipped his hand between her legs and smoothed the oil over her feminine folds, working gently but briskly, like a nurse applying a salve. It felt strange but not unpleasant and she liked the exotic, aromatic scent.

"Open your legs further apart and bend your knees so that you can set your feet on the mattress," he instructed.

Olivia complied. She saw him touch himself below his nightshirt but did not look too closely. He came to lie between her spread legs, nudging them further apart and then she felt something bigger and firmer than his fingers prodding at her entrance.

"Open for me," he murmured.

She gasped as he pushed in and went deeper, stretching her uncomfortably. How far did he have to go?

"There's a good girl, just a little more, easy now," he muttered.

It's as if he's trying to soothe a nervous mare, Olivia thought, suppressing a little giggle. It wasn't too bad. He felt thick and hard and as he continued to thrust it burned a little and she stiffened against him.

"Easy now," Jack said again. He pressed harder, something within her gave way and she felt him surge within her. Despite her resolve to bear everything stoically, she gave a little whimper.

"It's almost over now," he said encouragingly, moving faster.

She lay quietly beneath her husband. It had stung quite badly for a moment or two, but now there was just that strange fullness rocking her from within. Jack groaned, jerking abruptly and then stilled. He was gasping for breath. After a short while he removed himself from her and lay beside her. He reached over to touch her cheek in a fleeting caress, the first she had received from him.

"Thank you. I hope it didn't hurt too badly."

"No," she answered.

"Good girl," he said again.

But I'm not a girl any more, she thought.

After a few minutes, he said "You'll want to sleep." He got out of bed and shrugged into his banyan. "Good night, Olivia. Shall I blow out the candles?"

"No, don't. Good night, Jack."

She waited until the door closed behind him before climbing gingerly out of bed and going over to the washstand behind the screen. The water was still warm. She dampened a linen towel and wiped between her legs. It came away reddened and she washed again until the towel was clear and she no longer felt sticky. Taking another towel and a candelabrum, she went back to the bed. There was no more blood than might come at the beginning of her courses, but there was a strange, musky odour. She blotted the sheet as best she could. It would do until morning. She went to the dressing-table and quickly braided her hair into a loose plait.

The worst was over, she supposed, as she blew out the candle beside her bed. It was strange how something so intimate could be so impersonal. According to Mrs Carr, it would get better once she and Jack grew more accustomed to one another. And he had been considerate. The girls at school had whispered of brides being torn open, ravished on their wedding night by a brutish husband. Olivia wondered how they had been able to reconcile this with their dreams of adoring lovers. One was as unreal as the other, she supposed, as she drifted into sleep.

"Good morning, Jack."

Mr Rembleton looked up briefly from the *Times*. He had almost finished his breakfast—a plate stained with egg and toast crumbs was pushed away to accommodate the newspaper and a half-empty coffee-cup was at his right hand.

"'Morning, Olivia."

Olivia sat, striving to maintain her composure. She had anticipated some embarrassment when they met in daylight after the previous night's activities, but this grunted greeting, as to an acquaintance passed on the street, was more upsetting. Had it, had she, meant nothing to him? She stared at the back of his newspaper. Perhaps she should take breakfast in her room in future. But today she was determined that her husband would at least acknowledge her.

"Mr Rembleton? Jack!" she said more sharply when her first attempt was ignored.

He laid the *Times* to one side. "Yes, Olivia?"

His tone lacked rancour and she felt encouraged to continue. "While I accept that you wish to disregard 'singularly senseless' social customs, I did not take this to mean that you would ignore me completely, or is it just that you despise conversation at the breakfast table?"

He blinked at the tart remark and then grinned boyishly. "I beg your pardon. You are quite right to take me to task. I have become too accustomed to my bachelor ways. I should have waited for you as well, shouldn't I?"

"As to that, we must discover what suits us both. I should be happy to breakfast in my room, but now that I am here—,"

They were interrupted by the butler bringing Olivia's breakfast. When he had set it before her, he handed Jack a folded sheet of paper. "This has just arrived, sir. The lad said it was urgent."

After a quick look at the note, Jack leapt to his feet. "Have my horse saddled immediately! Please excuse me, Olivia; I must go to Haye Farm at once. There is an emergency."

"Is there anything I can do?"

"No. Thank you," he added as an afterthought as he reached the door.

"When will you be back?"

"I don't know. Tomorrow, I hope." He hurried out, his mind clearly elsewhere.

Olivia stared after him. However she might have imagined the first morning of her marriage, it was not like this. Dazed, she poured herself a cup of chocolate and broke a roll to dip it into the thick, dark liquid. If this were a Minerva Press novel, she thought, savouring the rich sweetness, my newly-wedded lord would be thrown from his horse and succumb to his injuries, leaving me a widow while barely a bride, but of course in expectation of a happy event. Naturally, I would bear a son who would soon be abducted by his evil uncle, the wicked baron.

As she continued her meal, she amused herself with additional convolutions to this plot. Perhaps her husband would not die, but lose his memory from a blow to his head. He would wander the world until fate brought him to her door, a ragged beggar. The sight of his wife would immediately restore him to his senses. Reunited, they would foil the machinations of his brother, who had substituted his own bastard for the rightful heir—easily identified by a distinctive birthmark. The baron would die, either of remorse or fury at being thwarted and her husband would take his place to the joy of the peasantry at the installation of the good baron.

She smiled and shook her head to dispel her fancies. She poured herself another cup of chocolate and reached across the table for the *Times*. Perhaps there would be some news of the Mediterranean fleet.

Jack sprang from his horse, tossed the reins to the groom who had come running at the staccato hoof-beats and hurried into the house to take the stairs two at a time. He forced himself to slow down before he quietly turned the door-knob and eased open the bedroom door. His housekeeper rose from a chair beside the bed.

"He's sleeping, sir," she murmured. "It's that dreadful ague again. The fever has eased for now. I've never known it go so high. He was burning up. The doctor was fearful it wouldn't break in time."

"Did you give him the cinchona?"

"Yes, sir. Huxham's tincture in a little port. We got it into him eventually. The fever must have come on in the previous night, so by the time we realised yesterday morning, it was almost too late."

"I'll sit with him now."

"Yes, sir. Shall I send up some ale?"

"Please."

The woman left the room and Jack took her place. How many hours had he spent watching here? They had hoped the return to England would improve Bart's health, but he still suffered from these recurrent fevers. He leaned over and gently smoothed the fair hair away from the pale face. The skin felt cool, almost clammy.

"Did you change the sheets?" he asked abruptly when the housekeeper came into the room.

"Yes sir, and got him into a fresh night-shirt, too. His was soaked with sweat, poor man."

"Good," Jack said and waved her away. He took a deep draught of ale and leaned back, trying not to think.

"What the devil?" A disgruntled voice croaked from the bed. "Don't tell me the idiots sent for you."

"You had them worried. How do you feel?"

"As if I fell into the copper on wash day and have been put through the mangle. Is there anything to drink?"

"Here." Jack poured a glass of small beer and helped Bart sit up to drink. When he was finished, Jack went to a table and mixed another dose of the tincture.

"Foul stuff," Bart complained but downed it obediently.

"Can you eat anything?"

"I'm not hungry, but I'll try some broth if there is any."

Jack went to the top of the stairs and shouted down instructions.

"You shouldn't have come," Bart grumbled when he returned. "What did you say to—her?"

"Just that I had to come here. The message was announced as urgent and I didn't offer any explanation. She didn't protest or complain."

"She's very accommodating."

"Yes." Jack went to the window and pulled back the curtains. Looking out, his back to the other, he said, "I can't talk to her about you, can I?" He turned and added painfully, "And I won't talk to you about her." He looked pleadingly at Bart. "I owe her that much loyalty at least."

Bart moved his head restlessly on the pillow. "Maybe it would have been better to let the fever take me."

"Don't say that!" Jack sat on the bed and took the other man's hand, stifling an unbidden memory of sitting opposite his wife in just the same way last night. "She could never be to me what you are; never doubt that."

Bart's hand turned and gripped his. "It's not our fault that we are as we are, or that society looks upon us as moral lepers."

"Or that I am saddled with such a brother. But I must keep my two lives separate. It's the only way I can do it."

"All's right. I understand. I won't mention her again."

Jack stroked Bart's bristly cheek. "I'll shave you when you've had your broth."

Bart turned his face into the caressing hand. "Thank you for coming. I would have forbidden them to send for you, and I will for the future, but—I'm glad you came."

"I'll always come if you need me," Jack promised him.

Chapter Seven

As promised, Mr Harte called at Bolton Street the day after the wedding. His niece was alone. She seemed content enough, he thought and the house was certainly adequate. He accepted her offer of refreshments and then wondered what he could say without appearing too personal in his enquiries.

"How did you find the new carriage?" he asked at last. "A handsome equipage, I must say."

"Yes, it was very generous of Mr Rembleton. Should you like to drive out in it?"

"Why not? There won't be much doing in the park this early in the year, but we could do the round, I suppose."

"And you promised to show me the shops. Could we go tomorrow? I think you will have a better idea of lady's fashion than Mr Rembleton," she added flatteringly.

"I suppose I will," Mr Harte said. "Town is still quite empty, so you will be able to gather your first impressions and place your orders while the modistes are still glad of the commissions.

"This is a very fashionable lounge and in the Season will be quite thronged with people, but now one may saunter very pleasantly," Olivia's uncle remarked the following day as they strolled along Pall Mall.

To her provincial eyes, the street was busy enough and many of the ladies were so stylishly turned out that she felt quite a drab hen among these swans. Just look at the younger of the two ladies approaching then. Everything about her was just so, as if she had stepped out of one of the modish prints and so well suited to her delicate form that she would have resembled nothing more than a Meissen figurine were it not for the liveliness of her expression as she talked to her companion, an older woman—her mother perhaps? Olivia was transfixed with envy of the elegant silver satin jockey cap, decorated with ruching and twisted braid, with a cunningly-wrought tassel mingling with the dark curls at the back of the wearer's head.

As the two ladies drew level with Olivia and Mr Harte, the elder inclined her head in recognition. He stopped immediately, raised his hat and bowed in acknowledgement.

"Your Grace, Your Grace."

"Why, Mr Harte, I had not expected to see you in town at this time of the year," the older lady exclaimed. "Have you lost your taste for sport?" Her eyes lingered curiously on the young woman on his arm.

"Not at all, ma'am, but I have more pleasant duties at present. May I present my niece, Mrs John Rembleton? Mrs Rembleton, the Duchess of Gracechurch and the Dowager Duchess of Gracechurch."

Not a little alarmed by this introduction, Olivia curtsied to the two ladies.

"Mrs John Rembleton?" the younger duchess exclaimed. "Never say that you are married to Rambling Jack! Now, pray don't poker up," she implored. "I am sure I wish you both happy; it is just that I am so surprised. I had thought he was a confirmed bachelor."

"I saw the notice in the *Morning Chronicle*," the dowager remarked coolly. "My felicitations, Mrs Rembleton. It was more than time he faced up to his duty," she added severely.

Olivia was horrified by these frank comments—were they a sample of what she might expect from the ton? A polite smile pasted to her lips, she glanced at her uncle but said nothing.

Mr Harte considered his niece. She held her head high and had raised her left eyebrow infinitesimally, suggesting a faintly surprised amusement that her private affairs should arouse so much interest. She certainly has a look of my mother, he thought, entertained by the way she almost seemed to look down her nose at the petite duchess. However, it will not do for her to offend either lady.

"May I express my condolences on Your Graces' bereavement?" he said. "The late duke will be a sad loss to the nation, particularly now when the country is in such a perilous state." He spoke sincerely and the dowager nodded in acknowledgment.

"Thank you, Mr Harte."

"Do come to dinner tomorrow evening," the younger duchess invited impulsively. "And Mr and Mrs Rembleton, of course," she added smiling at Olivia. "It will be a small gathering, as we are not really entertaining yet."

"We should be honoured," Mr Harte bowed.

"Then we shall take our leave of you until then."

Mr Harte watched for a moment as the ladies continued down the street. He sighed as he and his niece walked on. "She and my wife were second cousins," he said unexpectedly. "They were of an age and came out together. Lady Ottilia, as she was then, was always destined for a great marriage. My Kate used to say she didn't envy her."

"That's the first time I heard you speak of your wife," Olivia said.

"It's so long ago—as if it happened to another man. They were very like. It makes me wonder what my wife would look like now. And my son. He would be thirty. I might be a grandfather." He sighed again.

Olivia patted his arm. "I hope you will be a grandfather to my children, if I am so blessed. You are the only relative I have in England. Papa is the surviving child of only children."

He put his free hand over hers. "Your marriage is opening all sorts of doors, my dear. It does me no harm to be jolted out of my set ways, I suppose."

"Thank goodness I have my wedding dress. That will be suitable for tomorrow, will it not? Mrs Carr thought of just such an eventuality and we had it made so that it can be easily adapted for evening wear."

"I'm sure you will look most charming."

It was after five o'clock when Jack appeared in the door of his wife's parlour. She wrinkled her nose when he came nearer. He must reek of the stables.

She made no comment but simply enquired, "Is all well?"

"Yes, thank you." He didn't elaborate and she didn't ask more.

"We dine at seven. You'll want to bathe beforehand," she informed him. "I'll have them bring up hot water."

She makes her expectations very clear, he thought, amused. But then, you didn't want a clinging vine, did you? Fair is fair. He saluted. "Aye, aye, ma'am."

"To your duties, sir," responded the daughter of the navy and waved him off with a smile.

"I must engage a lady's maid, Jack, but what about you? Do you have a valet?"

"No. I'm perfectly capable of shaving and dressing myself. My housekeeper looks after my clothes—I leave it all to her."

"But you'll be leaving things here as well, won't you?"

"You're right. I'll need more dress clothes too, I suppose. I must see my tailor tomorrow."

"Mrs Mullins suggested we employ another footman—apparently most families who take the house bring some of their own servants; she was quite surprised we didn't, apart from the coachman and groom. I'll need one to sit on the box when I am paying calls, she says, or escort me when I go out. Perhaps we could find one who would also act as valet when you are here."

"Do whatever you think is necessary, Olivia," Jack replied impatiently. "The domestic is your sphere—I shan't interfere."

And don't want to be involved, Olivia translated silently. She changed the subject. "My uncle and I met the Duchesses of Gracechurch in Bond Street this afternoon. The duchess invited us to dinner tomorrow evening."

"I'll dine at my club, then."

"But you are included in the invitation." Olivia was surprised that he would think she had been invited without him. London society was clearly very different to that in the provinces.

"Are you sure?"

"Yes. She specifically mentioned you."

"Very well," Jack said, yawning. "I'm for bed. Good night, Olivia. I won't disturb you later."

"What exquisite pearls," the younger duchess said to Olivia the next evening. "The lustre is quite exceptional."

"They were my mother's. My father brought them back from one of his voyages."

"And she gave them to you as a wedding gift?"

Olivia nodded. "In a way. She died quite unexpectedly in September. My father and brother had not long been recalled to active service."

"And you were left alone?"

"Apart from my uncle."

"So that is why," the duchess said slowly. "Forgive me, Mrs Rembleton, I do not mean to pry, but it strikes me that you might be in need of a friend. We are more or less of an age, are we not?"

"I am nineteen."

"I am twenty-three."

"Is that all?" Olivia had blurted the question before she could stop herself. "But your son is almost five."

When they arrived, the lively child had been carefully lining up pairs of animals so that they could enter Noah's Ark. To her astonishment, Jack had got down on his knees and entered into a serious discussion with the boy as to the advisability of separating predators from their prey before helping him re-sort his stock so that all might hope to reach Mount Ararat safely.

"I was not yet seventeen when I married," the duchess said simply, "so you see I know what it is to have one's life suddenly turned topsy-turvy. How long do you remain in town?"

"We have taken a house in Bolton Street for the Season, but once I have seen to my wardrobe—I decided to wait with the purchase of my bride-clothes until I came to London—we must visit Rembleton Place."

The duchess made a face. "I suppose you must. You are right to wait—it is better to have all your armour in place when dealing with Lady Rembleton. But you will not have much to do with her, will you?"

Olivia recalled the stiff note in which her ladyship had congratulated her new sister-in-law on her marriage and looked forward to receiving her at Rembleton. "Mr Rembleton thought she might introduce me to society, but I don't know if she is agreeable to the proposal,"

"Pooh! I can do that. After all, your late aunt and my mother-in-law were cousins, were they not? We need only say there is a family connection if anyone should ask—which they won't."

"Your Grace is very kind," Olivia stammered.

"Then that is settled. Now, your wardrobe. Madame St. Jean's style should suit you to perfection. She prefers tall willowy females. I do better with Madame Lemartin, but St. Jean will jump to serve you, especially if I introduce you. Some of these modistes give themselves airs and like to pick and choose their customers, but no one denies a duchess." This was said in so disarming a fashion that Olivia could not possibly take offence, especially as the duchess continued, "If one has to endure the tedium that comes with such a rank, one might as well enjoy the advantages as well. Do you have a good dresser? That is vital if you are to be properly turned out."

"Not yet," Olivia confessed. "My uncle was most insistent that Mamma's Betty would not do."

"I can imagine. Come with me." She swept Olivia across the room to interrupt Mr Harte's conversation with the dowager and skilfully deflected him to talk to the duke and Mr Rembleton about the welfare of climbing boys, a subject, she had learnt earlier, that was of great concern to him.

"Mamma, did you not mention something about Madame de Figeac's dresser?" she demanded, once the three ladies were alone.

"Eloise Martin? Yes she came to see Harper this morning. After dear Marguerite died, she accepted a position with Mrs Norris, not reckoning with Norris *père et fils*, for the one is totally degenerate and the other, although still at school, bids fair to follow in his father's footsteps. Martin found herself obliged to flee the premises and yesterday sought assistance here, for she had frequently come here in attendance on Marguerite. On learning I was in town, she spoke to Harper, hoping that she might know of a suitable situation for her." The dowager looked self-conscious. "I suppose I should have sought your consent, my dear, for this is no longer my house,"

"Nonsense, Mamma!"

"I told Harper she might stay here while we considered whether we knew of anything. But it is very early in the year. Why do you ask?" Her gaze was suddenly fixed on Olivia. "Is Mrs Rembleton in want of a lady's maid?"

"She is, and Eloise Martin would be ideal, for Madame was always perfectly attired. And Martin is not so old—about thirty I would think—that she will not adjust to a young mistress. Indeed I think she would revel in the thought of bringing her into the first style of fashion."

What a pleasant evening, Olivia thought, as the maid took the pins from her hair. She would not have thought she could be so at ease with two duchesses. The duke was more reserved, but perfectly polite. As a bride, she had sat on his right. He had been interested in hearing about Papa and Robert. And her husband's company manners had been impeccable.

When he came to her room, she felt no pain, but the act itself was as impersonal as it had been on her wedding night.

Jack surprised his wife the following evening by presenting her with a rectangular ebony box that was intricately inlaid with ivory. "I picked up some trifles on my travels. I heard you talking to the duchess about your mother's pearls and remembered these. They are yours now. Have them set however you wish."

"Thank you," Olivia said and opened the box. It contained several little packets of tissue paper. She unwrapped the first one to reveal a dozen or so exquisite rubies. The next one contained sapphires. "Jack! How beautiful!" Another one held a magnificent square emerald while others sparkled with diamond fire.

"You must keep those packets separate," Jack warned her as she stared in awe at the gems. "The colour is matched within each one, but they are each slightly different from the other."

"You cannot mean to give these to me," she protested. "They must be worth a fortune."

He shrugged. "Why not? What good are they doing in the bank? And you have a shapely neck and shoulders—you will display them to perfection."

"Thank you, Jack." She rose and went over to kiss his cheek. It felt cool beneath her lips, with just a hint of stubble. He accepted the caress but did not seek more or attempt to hold her when she went back to her chair. Her father would have put his arm around her waist and hugged her to him, Olivia thought, puzzled by her husband's coolness.

"Oh and I've heard from my brother," Jack announced. "They are coming to town and we may call on them at the town house. It'll save us going to the Place for the moment. It's so dreary there. Rembleton House too, but at least we won't have to stay there."

Chapter Eight

"A person to see you, sir."

The college servant stood aside to permit a stocky footman clad in the burgundy Needham livery enter Luke's room. Alarmed, he jumped to his feet. He was very fond of the Countess of Needham who was his mother's godmother, but why would she send one of her servants like this?

"What has happened?" he demanded sharply.

"Nothing, sir, that I am aware of." The man proffered a letter. "Her ladyship sends this. It will explain all, she said."

Needham, March 1804

My dear Luke,

Needham's secretary has contrived to break both right wrist and ankle and so will be unable to accompany us to town next week. We should be most grateful if you would be so obliging as to come with us and provide Needham with whatever assistance you can. You will appreciate that it would be difficult to find a reliable, confidential secretary at such short notice and for so brief a time. We expect Carruthers to be recovered within six weeks and I am sure the president will accede to my request that you be permitted to extend your vacation accordingly. I enclose a letter for you to give him in this regard.

Luke shook his head, grinning. He supposed he should be grateful she did not require him to seek out the vice-chancellor.

I have instructed the servants to remain with the carriage in Cambridge overnight and it is at your disposal for your journey here tomorrow. Pray do not disappoint me, Luke. It promises to be a difficult session and I should be easier about Needham, who is beginning to feel his years, if I know that you are at his side. You may also be intrigued by the insight you will gain into the machinations of the country's politicians and their hangers-on.

Your affectionate
E Needham

Luke folded the letter. "Where are you putting up?" he asked the footman.

"The *Black Bull*, sir,"

"Can you be ready to leave at eight in the morning?"

"Yes, sir."

"Very well. Talk to the gyp about my trunks."

"Very good, sir." The footman reached into his pocket and produced a purse. "Her ladyship's compliments and she sends you this in case you need to make any arrangements before you leave."

"Pay my debts, you mean?" Luke grinned as he took the heavy purse.

"I'm sure I couldn't say, sir."

"That's all for the moment, then."

Luke pulled on his gown and looked for his cap. He must take Lady Needham's letter to the president's lodge at once. I'd better have a word with my tutor as well, he thought. He looked distastefully at the desk piled high with books and notes. I'll be glad to be away from this frowsty backwater.

"That's excellent, Luke, concise yet pregnant." Lord Needham laid down the summary of the day's discussions. He came wincing to his feet and stretched gingerly. "My old bones are getting very stiff. I need some exercise. Do you fancy coming to Angelo's in the morning?"

Stiff Needham might be, but he displayed a refined technique with the foil. Invited to a bout, Luke acquitted himself creditably enough, although it was quite a different style to his drill with the sergeant. Here elegance and deportment were just as important as scoring a hit.

"You lack finesse sir," Angelo commented, "but you have very good control of your blade."

"You'll soon put a little polish on him, won't you Angelo?" his lordship asked jovially.

"Yes indeed, my lord."

It's really a sham fight, Luke thought disparagingly, but found he could not object when Needham insisted he take a daily lesson with the fencing-master.

"Excellent, Luke," Lady Needham said to him on learning of this. "I'll make sure he goes with you. It's just what he needs. I'm grateful for anything that takes him away from those interminable papers."

"What do you make of us?" Needham asked one night as he and Luke returned from a select male dinner; the type of occasion where, as he put it, 'the real governing of the country happens'.

"It's fascinating, like being behind the scenes of a theatre," Luke answered slowly, "but I confess to being surprised at the way so many have an eye to the main chance. I didn't realise it at first, but as much huckstering goes on as at a country fair. Does no one act disinterestedly, for the common good?"

"Very few," Needham said wearily, "and if you try, you are suspect. To get, you must be prepared to give."

"But what about your principles?" Luke asked hotly. "You heard Creevey. *'As a private of a party, there is nothing so fatal to public principle or one's own private respect and consequence as acting for oneself on great questions.'* He will follow his leader, even where he is of a different opinion. And whatever about compromising on lesser issues, surely one must remain true to oneself on the great questions?"

"I do not think he was speaking generally," Lord Needham temporised, "but out of respect for Fox, whom he greatly reveres."

"To the extent that he is prepared to ignore the voice of his own conscience," Luke said scornfully.

"You are still young and idealistic. As you gain more experience of life, you will come to see that there are many shades between black and white."

In the shadows of the carriage, Luke raised his eyes to heaven at yet another circumlocution of the older generation's favourite pronouncement: 'we are older and wiser, we know best'. Is there any age, he wondered, where you are neither ignorantly young nor patronisingly old, but simply adult? Is there an age where you genuinely regard all others with equal respect or do you slip without noticing from one extreme to the other?

Martin stood on a stool and skilfully dropped Olivia's ball-gown over her head. She jumped down and assisted her mistress to slip her arms into the short puffed sleeves before lacing the back closed. She twitched the white skirts to rights, ensuring that the over-layer, which was some six inches shorter than the silk under-robe, hung correctly.

"*Très bon,*" she approved.

"I have never looked so elegant," Olivia exclaimed. Bouquets of white embroidered flowers embellished the bodice and hem of the gauze overdress, the only colour coming from the coral ribbons that encircled the high waist and the cuffs and echoed her mother's beads around her neck. Martin had dressed her mistress's locks high on her head, in a seemingly artless pile that looked as if it might tumble down but in fact was securely anchored with tortoiseshell combs that, on the duchesses' advice, had been set with the smallest of Jack's diamonds so that they sparkled intriguingly in the depths of her hair. A few curls had been loosened to frame her face becomingly.

"Now the shawl," the maid said. Carefully spreading open the wide expanse of the finest black silk net, so delicate that, before the long fringe had been knotted at each end, it might have been drawn through a wedding-ring, she draped it over Olivia's elbows, so that it fell gracefully over her lower back. The ends of the shawl were embroidered with floral sprays similar to those of the gown, but in shades of coral, green and gold and these panels gleamed and shimmered against her front skirts.

"I'm terrified I shall catch it on something."

Martin shrugged. "You may be as careful as you like, *Madame*; it is the others who are more dangerous."

"That's true, I suppose."

Olivia picked up her reticule and fan and went downstairs to the hall where her husband waited for her. He was correctly dressed in a dark coat with cream satin knee-breeches and waistcoat, but was clearly not a man who lived to dress. The only sign of vanity was the dark sapphire pin in his cravat that matched the ring he always wore. He was freshly shaven, his skin smooth and inviting.

"Madam!" He made an elegant leg and offered her his arm.

So it's company manners tonight, Olivia thought, as she placed her fingers on his arm. She felt a faint tingle of excitement. He smelled different, she noticed, enjoying the subtle spicy odour that suggested some oriental unguent. She smiled as they took their seats in the barouche-landau.

"Your sister-in-law disapproves of this carriage," she remarked, "she calls it 'an over-stylish extravagance'."

"She's your sister-in-law as well," Jack pointed out, grinning. "You may not deny the relationship."

Olivia grimaced. She had been presented to Lord and Lady Rembleton some days previously when she and Jack had called in form at Rembleton House. Their hosts had been coolly gracious, but no more and Olivia could not but compare this aloof civility with the duchess's warm friendliness. Even the duke and the dowager duchess had been less stiff-rumped, she thought.

"Lady Rembleton returned our call today while you were out. Mrs Frome was with her. She is the eldest daughter, isn't she?"

"I think so," he answered carelessly. "What had they to say for themselves?"

"Very little. They didn't stay long, as they must prepare for the Gracechurch ball this evening. Apparently there has not been one since the present duke and duchess were married and they were at pains to impress upon me what a triumph it was to have been invited. It was amusing to listen to their allusions to the dear duchess, for I have never heard her mention them in such favourable terms."

"It is very likely they owe the invitation to you," Jack said astutely.

Just as Jack handed his wife down from the carriage, Lord and Lady Rembleton, accompanied by their unmarried youngest daughter, reached the top of the steps of Gracechurch House. Her ladyship glanced back and her look of outraged surprise made Jack chuckle.

"Didn't you mention we were also invited?" he murmured in Olivia's ear.

She shivered at the tickle of his warm breath and shook her head. "It was impossible to slide a word in edgewise."

Once inside the house, they joined the long line of guests moving up the grand staircase to greet their host and hostess. A warm smile and a quick word and they went into the magnificent ball-room. Newly decorated in the Classical style, it gleamed in gold and white, with touches of a soft duck-egg blue. Countless mirrors conspired with sparkling glass chandeliers to create a landscape of glittering light. A hum of conversation rose and fell as guests swirled and eddied in constantly changing groups. Olivia gulped and her fingers tightened on Jack's sleeve. The only other people she knew were his family who had made no attempt to wait for them but progressed steadily down the long room as if determined to avoid any unnecessary contact.

He glanced down at her. "Chin up, my dear," he whispered encouragingly, looking round to see who was near them. "Ah!" He steered her towards an elderly gentleman who reminded her somehow of her father.

"Admiral MacNamara," he said with a bow.

"Mr Rembleton," the man exclaimed. "You are the last person I would have expected to see here." He turned to the lady at his side. "My dear, may I present Mr Rembleton; he and I have voyaged together in the past. My wife, Lady MacNamara, Mr Rembleton."

"Mr Rembleton," the lady nodded graciously.

"Lady MacNamara," Jack bowed again. "May I present my wife, Mrs Rembleton? Admiral Sir Charles MacNamara and Lady MacNamara, my dear."

"Admiral, Lady MacNamara," Olivia curtsied.

"This is doubly surprising." The admiral shot Jack a look from beneath a furrowed brow.

"You may know Mrs Rembleton's father, Captain Frobisher," Jack continued smoothly.

"Not Robert Frobisher?"

"Yes," Olivia confirmed.

"I know him well. He served under me on the *Alexander.* How is he?"

"Well, I hope. He is at present with Lord Nelson in the Mediterranean."

"Are you newly-wed, Mrs Rembleton?" Lady MacNamara asked kindly.

"Since the end of January, ma'am."

"Why, you are still a bride! This must be your first appearance—it is so early in the Season."

"I suppose it is," Olivia said, startled, "on such an occasion at any rate."

Another couple came up to join them and after a few minutes Jack and Olivia strolled on. Musicians had by now taken their place in the gallery and the Gracechurches walked onto the floor with the Duke and Duchess of Rutland and two other couples to dance the opening cotillion.

"May I have the pleasure of dancing with you, Olivia?"

"Of course," she answered. She had always loved dancing and was pleased to learn that her husband apparently did too.

He led her to the set that was forming. The musicians struck up again, the long row of gentlemen bowed, the ladies curtsied, the two sides moved towards and away from each other and the top couples commenced the figure. Olivia was thankful that they were far enough down the set that there was ample time for her to note the figures they selected. When their turn came to lead, she discovered Jack to be a vigorous and proficient dancer, clearly delighting in the movement and their eyes met with perfect amity when they returned to their places.

Afterwards they continued their stroll, pausing to exchange pleasantries with Mrs Frome. "I had not thought you so good a dancer, Uncle," she commented.

"In all my travels I never encountered a society that does not dance. It is an excellent way of breaking down barriers if you are willing to join in or demonstrate your own steps. I've danced many a reel or jig to the sound of a tin whistle. Frequently though, the men and women dance separately, not together as we do." He looked around. "Things have changed since I left England; then such a ball would have opened with the minuet."

"It is still danced at court balls," the Duke of Gracechurch, who had come up to them, remarked. "And very tedious it is too."

"But so elegant," declared Mrs Frome.

The duke turned to Olivia. "Mrs Rembleton, the next dance is about to begin. I should be honoured if you would stand up with me. Mr Rembleton, you permit?"

"By all means," Jack nodded.

Olivia hid her surprise at this rather frightening honour—she had not met the duke since that first evening at Gracechurch house—and let him lead her to the top of the set.

"As a bride, you have pride of place," he commented. "You must call the dance."

Chapter Nine

Luke couldn't take his eyes off the alluring girl dancing with his host. Taller than average, she held her head high, displaying an elegant neck and shoulders. Her skirts fluttered over coral slippers as she moved, revealing shapely ankles clad in white stockings embroidered with coral rosebud clocks that trailed seductively up her legs. He was struck by her poise. She was neither unduly flustered by standing up with a duke, nor stiff or unyielding but moved gracefully yet with dignity. A soft smile lit her eyes and curved her lips while her lithe movements suggested an innate pleasure in the dance.

Now she and her partner danced down the set, each weaving in and out of the opposing row, she briefly joining hands with the gentlemen and he with the ladies. She came to Luke and their hands clasped for an instant. He had an impression of a mass of brown curls shot with gold that matched the eyes sparkling with enjoyment. She danced on and he waited impatiently for his turn to dance the figure, when they would again repeat their encounter. *'And palm to palm is holy palmers' kiss'*. As he approached her, their glances met. She did not lower her eyes and her smile deepened as if to acknowledge a mutual pleasure.

"Who was that dancing with Gracechurch?" Luke asked Lady Mary Hope as they promenaded after the dance.

"A Miss Rembleton, somebody said. Earlier she was with Mrs Frome who is Rembleton's daughter. She and the duke are talking to the dowager duchess now."

"Let's see if we can drift that way."

"Interested, Luke?" Lady Mary slanted her eyes towards him with a little smile.

"Who drifted towards Sir Harry Kimberley with you last night?" he countered.

She laughed. "I'm very grateful to you. I'm dancing the supper dance with him later."

They skilfully wove in and out of the throng, stopping to exchange a few words here and there until they reached their destination. For such a large gathering, the sound of the conversation was muted, Luke thought, just a murmur of carefully articulated speech in carefully modulated tones. Quite unnatural, really, with no raised voices or genuine laughter. Feminine satin slippers and masculine leather pumps slid soundlessly on the gleaming floor. Pale muslin draperies, punctuated by more richly coloured silks billowed and swayed as ladies walked or curtsied. There—in that corner—there must be a personage of high rank, one of the Rutlands, perhaps, judging by the deeper curtsies of the approaching ladies.

Most of the faces displayed the same polite mask so that the rare individual who revealed anything of his or her feelings stood out. That was what had attracted him to Miss Rembleton, he realised. She seemed to be enjoying herself in a more natural fashion that reminded him of village dances at home. He imagined she had not been long in town. The room was warm, heated by the hundreds of candles whose honeyed smell hung heavily in the air and the press of bodies that added an intricate layer of scents and perfumes.

"Do you like it, the Season, I mean?" he asked Lady Mary.

"Generally yes. It's a bridge between leaving the schoolroom and taking on the responsibilities of marriage and your own home. You see a bit more of the world, meet new people. I love the theatre and opera. It's at its best now, when town is not so full and everything is fresh. Later, when you have the real crushes, it can be quite unpleasant. I like to ride early in the morning, when the day is new, but frequently there is nobody to go with me."

"You may come with me if you like, as long as I'm in town," he offered.

"That would be famous. But, Luke, I wouldn't wish people to get the wrong idea about us."

"The wrong idea?" he asked blankly.

"That you're courting me," she replied and then burst out laughing. "If you could only see your face! I think it best if I speak to Mamma. She'll be able to put it about that we are like brother and sister."

Understanding dawned. "You don't want me to queer your chances with Kimberley."

"Or anyone else," she agreed serenely. "But you may assist them if you are willing to act as a brotherly escort while you stay with us."

"I'm at your ladyship's service," Luke proclaimed grandiloquently. "Or at least as far as my duties to your father permit."

Lady Mary curtsied to the dowager duchess and kissed her cheek

"You look delightful, child."

"Thank you, ma'am. May I present Mr Fitzmaurice?"

Luke made his bow and suffered through a long-winded round of introductions within the group surrounding the dowager. He casually eased his way around the circle until he was standing next to Miss Rembleton. Close to, she was even lovelier, her oval face marked by finely arched dark brows. Her Roman nose was perhaps stronger than conventionally acceptable for so young a woman, but it added distinction, he decided. Hers was no doll-like prettiness, but a sterner beauty that was softened by her charming smile. She listened with interest to the discussion of Grassini's London performances but did not join in.

"I haven't had the opportunity to see her myself," Luke said quietly to her. "They wouldn't approve at Cambridge if I were to take a jaunt to town to go to the opera. They're very strait-laced there."

"But you managed to escape them, sir," she observed, a twinkle in her eyes.

"Just for the vacation," he sighed dramatically.

The musicians began their preparatory sounds and he seized his chance. "May I have the pleasure of this dance, Miss Rembleton?"

Her amusement dimmed as if a cloud had veiled the sun. Her smile faded, her lips firmed and she raised her head, squaring her shoulders as she did. Luke was puzzled. She had all the signs of a lady about to deliver a set-down. Surely he couldn't have offended her with his request? Should he have approached her chaperon? Mrs Frome, perhaps?

"I am *Mrs* Rembleton, Mr Fitzmaurice." She glanced across the circle to an older man who was engaged in an animated discussion of Lamarck's theory that the environment gave rise to changes in animals.

"Consider the mole, ma'am" he was saying. "Is he blind because he lives in the earth or does he live in the earth because he is blind?"

Luke froze in a sort of sick mortification, made up of embarrassment at his *faux pas*, disappointment that she was not a single lady and horror that she was apparently married to a man who might be her father. He was angry with himself for having mistaken her status and annoyed at her quiet correction, although what else should she have done? To let his error stand could only lead to further, deeper embarrassment.

"I beg your pardon, ma'am." he said, adding weakly "I must have misheard when we were introduced."

"That can happen in such a crush," Mrs Rembleton agreed graciously.

Mr Fitzmaurice's eager look had faded and all at once Olivia understood that by accepting Jack's offer she had cut herself off from the world of youth. For her there could be no flirtations and courtships, no subtle wooings, no falling in and out of love. She had renounced that without having experienced it. The ice that had encased her emotions since her mother's death shattered and she was a girl again, with all of a girl's sensibility; one who now recognised that she had joined the ranks of the matrons without first having enjoyed her girlhood.

A small silence fell between them until he said steadily, "May I have the pleasure of dancing with you, Mrs Rembleton?"

Her heart aching, Olivia was inclined to refuse, but to do so would be a cutting rebuke to the young man who had bravely stood his ground and courteously repeated his request. "Thank you, sir," she said and permitted him to lead her onto the dance floor. She acquitted herself well enough, but the joy of the evening had flown. They did not converse much and she declined his offer of refreshments afterwards. A few steps brought them to Mr Harte's side. She presented her escort to her uncle and after a few moments of polite chit-chat, he departed.

"Are you enjoying yourself, my dear?" Mr Harte asked.

"Yes. It is a splendid evening, isn't it," she replied as if by rote.

How would it have been if I had refused Jack? Would my uncle have brought me into this society? She looked wistfully at the little groups of smiling girls and their attentive young men. Might I have been like them, able to flirt and pick and choose among my admirers?

"Well, Mrs Rembleton," the duchess stood before her. "Are you enjoying your come-out?"

Olivia blinked. She hadn't thought of it like that. "Oh yes," she smiled. "It was very kind of the duke to stand up with me."

"Pooh!" The duchess waved this away. "Come, walk with me," she commanded. "You will excuse us, Mr Harte, I know."

"Of course, ma'am."

The duchess took Olivia's arm and steered her across the landing to a small parlour. "It's too early for anyone to be in here," she commented, closing the door. "Tell me what is wrong. Has someone upset you?"

"It's foolish," Olivia said. "I should have been better prepared."

"For what?"

"Someone asked me to dance with him. He called me Miss Rembleton." Olivia stopped abruptly, her lips trembling.

The duchess reached over and took her hand. "It brought your circumstances home to you," she suggested gently.

Olivia nodded dumbly.

"I understand. I didn't have to contend with it in that particular way, for I was Lady Stanton from the day I was married." She shrugged, smiling wryly at Olivia. "Mine was a made match." Going to the tray of decanters, she poured a small glass of madeira. "This will help you feel more the thing. I shouldn't worry—people are already asking who you are and by the end of the evening no one will be in doubt of your situation. Now, let me introduce you to some other young wives. You will find you are not alone."

On their return to the ballroom, they were immediately accosted by gentlemen begging the duchess for an introduction to her companion. She frowned as she assessed them. "I will present you, sirs, but then you must excuse us, for my mother-in-law is looking for Mrs Rembleton. You may seek her out there if you wish her to favour you with a dance."

"I should have thought of this," she muttered in Olivia's ear as they moved as quickly as permissible across the floor to the alcove where the dowager sat with Mr Harte.

"Mamma, Mrs Rembleton needs a duenna," the duchess said gaily, "one who will help her separate the rakehells from the rascals. I know I may depend on you to help her, you were such a support to me in my first Season."

"I should be delighted, my dear Mrs Rembleton," the dowager said. "While most gentlemen may be relied upon not to go beyond the bounds of propriety, it is a sad truth that there are some reprobates who prey on young wives. They will know not to seek you out if you are with me and I shall ensure you have acceptable partners. Dear me, this will give an additional little fillip to the Season."

"You are very kind, ma'am," Olivia said faintly. Did the dowager mean to take her under her wing for more than just tonight?

"Nonsense. Was not your aunt my dearest cousin? I am happy to take her place, if you will have me."

"I am honoured, ma'am," Olivia said, while her uncle took the dowager's hand and raised it to his lips.

"Your Grace is all kindness."

"Mr Harte," the dowager said firmly, "if you 'Your Grace' me once more, I shall rap your knuckles."

"I'll behave, Duchess" he said meekly. "I have not forgotten how in dread we all were of your fan."

The two older people laughed. Olivia smiled with them and the first of her would-be partners approached.

"Luke," Lady Mary whispered urgently, "I'm very sorry but I misled you about Mrs Rembleton."

"So I discovered," he answered wryly.

"Oh!" She looked at him sympathetically. "Was she very offended?"

"No. In fact she was most civil and even consented to stand up with me after I had apologised. She agreed it was easy to mishear in such a crush."

"That was nicely done of her," Lady Mary commented. "But to be married to such an old man! Now, let me present you to Miss Jeffrey. Poor thing, she is just seventeen and really too shy to have been brought out this Season. But there are three sisters behind her, and I suppose her Mamma wants to fire her off as quickly as possible. You are such a good brother, you will have no problem in putting her at her ease. If you invite her to stand up with you for the supper dance, you may join Sir Harry and me and the others afterwards. It will give her a little confidence—that is all she needs."

Jack had escaped to the card room for a couple of hands, but now stood scanning the ballroom for Olivia.

"I want a word with you, Jack," his sister-in-law said haughtily.

"Indeed? First I must look to my wife."

Lady Rembleton sniffed disparagingly. "She has hardly stopped dancing since the duke led her out. She is quite the belle of the ball, I'm sure I don't know why."

The duchess came up to them. "Are you looking for your wife, Mr Rembleton? She is in the supper room. You need not be concerned about her. My mother-in-law is enchanted by the prospect of taking the niece of her beloved cousin under her wing for the Season and indeed I think it will do her the world of good after the sadness of the past couple of years."

"My wife and I are most appreciative of all your kindness and that of your family, Duchess," Jack said sincerely.

"We find her delightful. You are a fortunate man, Mr Rembleton."

"I know," he murmured.

She favoured them with a glittering smile and moved on, leaving her ladyship remembering how she and her daughter had preened themselves on the Gracechurch invitations earlier in the day. Beset by the lowering suspicion that they owed them to her despised sister-in-law, she did not hesitate to vent her mortification upon that lady's husband. "Really, Jack, you might have informed us of the Gracechurch connection. We thought she was just a provincial nobody."

"Beneath your notice, I know." He regarded her with distaste. "I didn't marry her for her pedigree or her connections, Hannah. And you are not to think you may take advantage of them to help you finally turn Lydia off. How old is she now? She must be at least twenty."

This was too much for her ladyship and she stormed away.

Olivia rested her head against the squabs of the carriage and thankfully wriggled her toes. "I have never danced so much in my life."

"You were the belle of the ball, according to Hannah. She was not very happy at the idea."

"She came up to talk to me after supper. She was so sweet it was sour, if you understand me."

He laughed. "I can well imagine."

"She invited me to drive in the park with her and Lydia tomorrow."

He groaned. "I was afraid of that. This must be the chit's third season. You need not go if you do not want to."

"I accepted, for I wish to be on good terms with them, but do not intend to be drawn into her net. The dowager asked me to call tomorrow—to plot our strategy for the Season, she said."

"I'll leave it to the two of you, then. Just tell me when my presence is required."

Although tired from dancing, Olivia was still elated. It had been a heady experience to be so sought after. None of her partners had discommoded her in any way; she had enjoyed their mild flirting and had also met several pleasant young matrons who had been pleased to welcome her to their ranks.

She looked over at her husband. They had danced together again later in the evening. He had come to her bed frequently, but this was the first time she found herself wishing for his visit. Perhaps the pleasure, the closeness of the dance might also be experienced there.

The carriage stopped. "Home at last," he said and sprang out but did not wait to hand her down, relinquishing that office to the footman. Disappointed, she mounted the steps. Jack stood back to permit her to enter the house first. He lit two of the candles waiting on the hall table and handed her one.

"Good night, Olivia," he said briskly. "Do not feel you must join me for breakfast tomorrow, you must be tired."

"Good night, Jack." Disheartened, she mounted the stairs beside him, parting from him at her door without another word. She had been dismissed.

Jack whistled softly as he toed off his pumps and stripped off his cravat. The evening had surpassed all his expectations. Olivia was well and truly launched and the duchesses' interest would spare him a vast number of society engagements. He had the additional satisfaction of having annoyed his sister-in-law. He stirred up the logs of the dying fire and sat back in his armchair, stretching his toes to the blaze and sipping a glass of brandy. If he could only get his wife with child soon! Then he would have a long respite from the necessity of bedding her.

It had been an instructive few weeks, Luke decided, as he returned to Cambridge on a wet and windy spring day. He had recovered his equilibrium after the contretemps with Mrs Rembleton, who had nodded civilly to him in the park two days later. While no other girl had attracted his interest, he had been sought out the following week by a married lady who had indicated she would not be averse to indulging in a little dalliance. The resulting encounters had been satisfying enough but he was not sorry to have the excuse of his return to his studies to terminate the connection.

He stared out of the carriage window. The massive inequalities that, he had come to realise, underpinned English society, made him uneasy. Why did no one else see it? He had devoured the copy of Mr Paine's *Rights of Man* that he had found in the library at Needham House. While he didn't agree with Paine's extreme views on the taxation and redistribution of income, he could not but recognise the inequity of the present system. Worst of all, he thought, was the innate feeling of superiority and entitlement that, for example, required a gentleman to pay a so-called debt of honour to his peers while permitting him to ignore the bill of an honest tradesman who had supplied him with goods and services. He recalled one young sprig of an aristocratic tree scribbling vowels for five hundred guineas, having lost a bet as to which of two raindrops would roll down the window faster. "My boot-maker will have to wait again," he had remarked, laughing. "I'll order another pair to keep him sweet."

"How long have you owed him?" Luke had enquired curiously

"Forever. I tip him some of the ready every so often, if he whines too loud."

"He should be honoured to have a gentleman's patronage," the one who had won the bet said lazily. "Let the cits pay." He waved at the waiter. "Another bottle here!"

An older gentleman sitting near the group caught Luke's eye. "Don't follow their example, sir. I've known more than one man lose his livelihood, having gambled away his estates and others imprisoned for their debts, with their wives and children left to fend for themselves."

If they could see themselves as a stranger might, Luke thought as the carriage pulled in at the *Bell* in Puckeridge to the cries of ostlers shouting for fresh horses. Supposing one were to write a letter purporting to be from a visitor to these shores, perhaps an oriental envoy reporting to his master and remarking on the idiosyncrasies of English life. It would have to be incog. Not *Spectator* or *Observer*, they had already been used, something more exotic. Addison had written about the vision of Mirza. Herodotus? No. Who was that Persian companion of Darius who had not wanted to be king? Otanes! That was it. He put his feet on the seat opposite, rested his notebook against his raised knee and began.

I departed France on the second day of March, arriving in England some two days later due to the storms which I am told are not uncommon in these waters at this time of the year. Since 1800, when the parliament in Ireland was abolished, the state in which I find myself is called the United Kingdom of Great Britain (a large island divided into the countries of England, Scotland and Wales) and Ireland (a neighbouring island to which England lays claim). This union of the two islands which is dominated by England has come about more by conquest than collaboration. While this is particularly true of Ireland, which sees constant rebellions, most recently last year, it is less than sixty years since Scotland last rose in arms.

Book two

Chapter Ten

Hertfordshire, England, April 1814

Stanton, 6 April 1814

Dearest Olivia,

So we have won and after over ten years of war are at last to have peace! It hardly seems possible. Let us hope that this will not be a false peace like that of Amiens, but will endure. At times I have feared that the best we could hope for would be some sort of interminable stalemate where we would have to remain constantly vigilant, for Bonaparte could never be contained, only defeated.

Now we must celebrate. I am determined that our May Day festivities here at Stanton will be truly splendid this year, with victory fireworks in the evening. You are coming with your family as usual, I trust, and Mr Rembleton is very welcome should he chuse to join us. He has been a favourite of Stanton's ever since that first evening when they played with the Noah's Ark. You will be surprised when you see him (Stanton, I mean), for he has shot up over the winter and is now more man than boy. He looks down on me now and frowns when I call him Rowland—it is not manly enough for him—but to me he is still my boy.

I hear the waltz is to be danced regularly at Almack's this Season. I have not yet decided whether I wish to learn the steps. I saw Countess Lieven dance it last year and thought she presented a most "off" appearance. There is so much to tell you, but I must close now, dearest Olivia. Pray let me know when we may expect you.

Your affectionate friend
Flora Gracechurch

Postscriptum: Mr Harte continues to enjoy good health, as does Mamma-in-law and they remain as happy a married couple as ever I have seen. They beg me to send their fond remembrances and to say they eagerly await your arrival and that of the children. F.G.

Olivia put down her letter and walked to the window. Her heart lifted at the sight of the bright beds of tulips in the garden below. In the park beyond, trees were breaking into leaf and daffodils trumpeted the defeat of one of the most severe winters in living memory. Here at Southrode Manor she had been able to put down roots for the first time in her life and she savoured each new spring. The old Jacobean house was truly her home. Here she had borne her children and created a satisfactory life for herself, even if it was not the life she had hoped for ten years previously.

She was long since resigned to the lack of any loving connection between Jack and herself. One might as well fault a blind man for being unable to see, she thought. Jack lived by reason. There was no problem that could not be resolved by the application of rational thought, he claimed, and was wont to act according to this maxim willy-nilly, insensible of any counter claims that might be made by the emotions. Although rarely wittingly unkind, his was at best a passive consideration for others. He did unto them as he would have done unto himself. He did not see that his golden rule was self-centred and it never occurred to him that others might have different needs and wishes.

Olivia had been very willing for love to grow between them, as Mrs Carr had suggested. But from the beginning their marriage had been rooted in arid soil. It had soon become apparent that his interest in her was limited to her child-bearing abilities, and her burgeoning interest in what might exist between a man and a woman had withered and died. At least their second child proved to be a girl, otherwise she might never have had a daughter. All intimacy had ceased with the conception of their third child and second son, Samuel, almost five years previously.

Sometimes she wondered what it would be like to exchange the love that flowed through her parents' letters to one another, to experience the closeness she observed between her uncle and Lady Ottilia, to know passion—just once to deny the lark and claim it nightingale. Oh, there were men enough who were only too happy to indulge bored or neglected wives with an amorous tryst, but what good would such a connection be without a loving commitment, a commitment she was not free to make?

Why was she so blue-devilled? She should be rejoicing at the fall of Paris. England had been ecstatic; church bells had pealed, houses were decked with greenery and people sang and danced in the streets. But she could not help remembering those families who must, as she did, in the midst of these celebrations silently count the cost of a war that, it had seemed, would never end. Her father had given his life at Trafalgar and she had prayed nightly for her brother's safety for a further nine years.

"Are you not ready, Mamma?" her elder son's voice interrupted Olivia's musings. "Pray hurry, today's Good Friday. Mrs Carstairs always gives us hot cross buns and afterwards we may watch the men play marbles on the green."

"So it's not eagerness for your books that has you so prompt, John," Olivia teased but obediently went in search of her bonnet and redingote.

"May I take the ribbons, Mamma?" the boy begged. "Henry says I'm coming on prime."

She raised an eyebrow at this cant. "I beg your pardon?"

John hastily recast his statement. "Henry says my driving skills are improving."

"Very well, but only until we reach the south gate. And the same applies to the drive home. You are not to pester Henry to let you take the reins in the village. You may drive only once you have entered the park."

He looked downcast at this restriction but was soon chattering happily as the bay gelding trotted down the avenue.

"I wonder will Papa be there when I come home. What do you think he has planned for us this time?"

"I don't know. If the weather stays fine, perhaps to look for frog spawn or even tadpoles tomorrow." Olivia suggested.

The boy's eyes gleamed. "I declare you are the best of mothers, Mamma," he said lavishly. "Other chaps get a jobation or their jackets dusted if they get dirty or muddy but you never complain as long as we remove our boots as soon as we come in."

She laughed. "Papa's addiction to the pursuit of the knowledge of nature meant that I either had to learn to tolerate mud or be constantly scolding."

She drew up outside the vicarage. "Be good and obey Mr Carstairs, especially if he is kind enough to let you watch the marbles."

"Yes, Mamma," the boy said submissively, but his broad grin as he jumped down from the gig and ran to join his fellow pupils had his mother smile and shake her head.

When Olivia turned in again through the gates of the manor, she could see another carriage ahead of her. Curious, she flicked her whip. When she reached the house, her husband had just alighted from a post-chaise.

He turned at the sound of the approaching gig and waited for her. "Good day, Olivia."

He looked happy, almost exuberant, she thought and remarked with a smile, "I never expected to see you travel in such state."

"I had too much to bring with me to ride. There are some parcels in the chaise," he called to the footman who had descended the steps . "Bring them to the library and pay off the boy."

"Have you had breakfast?" Olivia asked as they entered the hall.

"Just a cup of coffee before I left. I trust you have something for me."

"I'm sure we have," she said with an amused glance at her butler, who made an abbreviated bow in acknowledgement.

The footman returned carrying four large parcels and Jack went ahead to the library.

"Put them here," he pointed to the table and went to pick up a paper knife.

"The fruit of my labours," he said triumphantly, opening the first parcel to display three heavy quarto volumes handsomely bound in calfskin and tooled in gold.

"Your encyclopaedia! How wonderful. Congratulations, Jack."

"This copy is for you. I also had sets specially bound for each of the children, so that when they grow up each will have one of their own. Who knows, our grandchildren may find it of interest."

Olivia was touched. "This is your real legacy, is it not?"

"Yes. It is my own achievement, not that of some ancestor."

He opened the first volume to display the dedication to his sons and daughter, expressing his hope that they would never cease to explore and discover the wonders of nature.

"They will be so proud, at least John and Miranda will. Samuel is perhaps a little too young to appreciate it now. You must present it to them this afternoon when John has returned from his lessons." She turned the pages. "The plates are magnificent. I see they are by Mr Wilkins. I had no idea he was so talented."

"They are taken from his sketches and paintings. This morocco edition has more coloured plates—in the cheaper one there is just a coloured frontispiece in each volume."

"The duchess enquires whether you wish to join us at Stanton for May Day."

Jack poured himself another cup of coffee. "No, not this year; in fact, I'm considering something else entirely."

"Oh?"

"I had a letter from Sir Humphrey Davy." He grinned suddenly. "At least he managed to collect his medal from Bonaparte before it was too late. He's now in Italy—he was still in Rome when he wrote but planning to go on to Naples. I thought of joining him. Now that the encyclopaedia's finished and through the press, Bart and I need to find new inspiration. And I confess I long to escape this island, to hear the wind in the sails again."

Olivia tried to conceal her shock. "How long would you be gone?"

"I have no idea. I never did the Grand Tour but headed straight for India and I should like to experience the natural wonders of Europe; the great rivers, the Alps, Mount Vesuvius and the relics of Pompeii. Perhaps we might visit Herr von Goethe in Weimar. We have been corresponding these many years as best we could—his theory of colours is most intriguing." He became more excited as he listed all these possibilities. Then the light died in his face.

"Should you object, Olivia?" He ran his fingers through his short, grey hair. "I acknowledge that I am not as free as I once was; that I have an obligation to you. If you wish me to remain here, I will."

He meant it sincerely, Olivia knew, for Jack never said anything he didn't mean. However, she had long since learned not to look for a deeper sense in what he said. An obligation? If truth were told, she was not an obligation but the price her husband had paid for his—or more precisely—his family's heirs. If she were to disappear from his life, he would not miss her except as the woman who cared for his children.

"Object that Rambling Jack wishes to ramble once more?" she said lightly. "I understand it all too well. Pray do not remain here on my account. However, I expect you to keep me informed of your whereabouts and write to the children from time to time."

"Yes, yes, of course," he agreed hastily, tugging his notebook from his pocket to begin scribbling hectically.

He barely looked up from his notes when she left the room. It was as if the frail, invisible thread that linked them had suddenly snapped.

"Well?" Bart raised his head from the microscope and looked eagerly at his companion.

"She made no objection," Jack announced triumphantly. "We may go!"

"Any stipulations; how long you may remain abroad, for example?"

"Nary a one. I'm as free as air!" Grinning from ear to ear, Jack tugged open his cravat and stripped off his coat. "Can we be ready by the end of the month?"

"I don't see why not." Bart cleared a space on his worktable and grabbed a pencil and paper. "I was afraid to make proper plans before now."

Jack laughed and pulled up a chair. "As was I. But now!" He flourished his notebook. "If we go up the Rhine, it will be deuced slow. The boats are towed by horses from Cologne and it is against the current. Perhaps it would be better to return that way, taking a boat downstream, which would be much faster. What do you think?"

"He left the manor on Tuesday," Olivia said. "He was to spend the night in town and leave early the next morning to catch the tide."

"Were the children very distressed?" Flora enquired.

"They didn't seem to be. They are used to seeing him at irregular intervals which have got longer in recent years, so they were surprised when he reappeared less than two weeks after his visit at Easter to say good-bye."

"That sounds as if he will be away a good many months at the least." Flora looked at her friend. "What is it, Olivia? Something troubles you."

"I don't know, Flora. I just have a feeling it may be years before he returns. I have never seen him look as happy as when I gave him leave to go."

"Leave?"

"Yes. He would have remained here if I had insisted."

"And you didn't think of setting a limit to his travels—six months or a year?"

"No."

"So what troubles you?" Flora repeated.

"It's just—where does it leave me?" Olivia demanded. "I know ours was not a conventional marriage, but it was really no more unusual than those of many others of our class. The only difference is that Jack spent his time in pursuit of science instead of gambling or hunting or bedding his latest mistress. I thought we were content. And he was there in the background—people respect him, even if they think him eccentric. The critical acclaim of the encyclopaedia has been immense. He put in enough appearances during the Season and at the manor that it was clear we were on good terms. But now it feels as if he has deserted me."

"He has answered the call of his profession, like any soldier or sailor," Flora suggested.

"They must go," Olivia argued. "This is his choice."

"Yet you didn't stop him."

"He was so keen, Flora. If you had heard him speak of his plans, what they might do, he and Mr Wilkins. Call it pride if you will, but I could not endure his remaining just because he felt he owed it to me."

"Yes, I can see that," Flora said slowly. "Sometimes our pride is all we have."

Chapter Eleven

*L*uke gracefully placed his right arm across his partner's shoulders while she mirrored his movement with her left. Their free hands joined in a gentle curve in front of their bodies, they stood side by side in the fifth position and glided into the initial march steps before embarking on the first series *of pas de bourée* of the slow French waltz. These shoals successfully negotiated, he felt the girl's intense concentration relax a little and he smiled down at her encouragingly.

"You're doing splendidly, Clare. We'll have you dancing the *valse sauteuse* next."

"Just let me feel comfortable with this one," she begged. "Lord Hayley requested the supper dance, but it is to be a waltz and I thought to—,"

"Have a practice one with me first," he finished understandingly.

She smiled up at him. "You are the kindest of brothers! And thank you for arranging for Lady Needham to chaperon me this evening. I don't wish to be unsympathetic, but it seems that Mamma suffers from the headache whenever she is disinclined to do something. She has been complaining about the heat all day, although it is only the first week in May and not at all warm, and how she was sure tonight would be a horrid crush. How Ann ever managed to get married, I don't know."

He laughed as he turned her under their joined hands. "Lady Needham more or less brought her out with Lady Mary. Mamma did come to London but from what Ann said, she went to very few of the parties."

"Are you so anxious to marry?" he enquired as they left the dance floor.

"Ssssh!" she hissed, "someone will hear."

He drew her into a little alcove. "Now," he asked quietly, "what's wrong?"

"I do want to marry in general," Clare admitted, "but not yet in particular, if you understand me."

"You mean that no one has yet caught your eye?"

"Precisely—but I should like the opportunity to find out if one does. Mamma clings so and is already saying she doesn't know what she will do when Ephraim goes up to Oxford, although when you recall that he's been at Eton these past three years, you'd think she'd be accustomed to his absence. And now she's telling everyone she knows she may depend upon me to stay with her. Honestly Luke, I vow I'll go mad if I have to dwindle into an unmarried daughter forever at her beck and call, and an object of pity in the neighbourhood to boot."

He had to laugh at this gloomy prophecy. "I'm sure it won't come to that. I'll take you about as much as I can, and I'll have a word with Lady Needham as well."

"Would you, Luke? Thank you!"

She smiled so brightly at him that the young man bowing in front of her was quite dazzled. "This is our dance, I believe, Miss Adams."

"Lord Hall." She curtsied demurely and went off on the viscount's arm to join the next set.

Satisfied that his sister was in safe hands, Luke went in search of refreshment. Daughters were even worse off than younger sons, he reflected, with marriage the only respectable future open to them. But had he really fared any better? Granted Otanes was not without his following, and had even on occasion been quoted in the House, but as the war with Napoleon dragged on and reports came back from the Peninsula of defeats, retreats and finally victories, Luke had felt more and more worthless. *What am I? A frivolous butterfly as Mrs Rembleton is reported to have described me? An adornment of society, skilled in dance and flirtation, a useless fribble? It's what I often feel like, God knows. How am I to look the veterans in the eye when they return?*

Draining his glass, he headed back to the ballroom. Clare was chatting to Lady Needham and Mrs Tamrisk, a recent bride, so no need to intervene there. The elegant Mrs Grettan smiled invitingly when their eyes met across the room and he went languidly to solicit her hand for the supper dance. After exchanging a few more pleasantries, he moved on.

"Congratulations, my dear," one of the other ladies said enviously.

"He dances so well that he makes the clumsiest partner seem accomplished," another commented, to which spiteful remark Mrs Grettan only replied "Miaou".

There she is! It was an involuntary response, more sensed than thought, fired by a familiar prickle of excitement and it irritated Luke hugely. *Why, after ten years, did he still feel that instant tug of attraction when he caught sight of Mrs Rembleton for the first time each Season? It's not as though she's ever given you the slightest indication that she thinks even kindly of you*, he told himself. *In fact, she seems to have no interest in dalliance at all. When you consider that her husband spends the best part of his time at his own residence and refers openly to their place in Hertfordshire as 'my wife's home', you might expect her to indulge elsewhere. But no.*

Or perhaps she has a bucolic swain, he thought idly, one who never sets foot in town. Perhaps she is fooling us all with an appearance of chastity. The idea annoyed him. His lips firmed and then quirked upwards. He had to admit it was amusing to ruffle her feathers. It was a private game he played, to see if he could shake her composure. She always seemed so aloof, as if she considered herself above the throng, her cool smile underlining her superiority.

An hour later Luke strolled over to the alcove where Mrs Rembleton stood with Mrs Dunford, a young matron and Mrs Tamrisk. They greeted him civilly but immediately resumed their intense conversation about governesses of all things. He had not thought Mrs Rembleton to be so solicitous of her children as to have strong opinions regarding their education. But apparently it was something she and her husband had discussed at length.

"I agree with him completely about developing their minds, but am adamant that it is as important to develop their hearts so that logic and judgment may be tempered by mercy and charity," she said.

"What was it Horace Walpole said?" he interjected idly. " *'Life is a comedy to those that think, a tragedy to those that feel'*?"

"Very witty, Mr Fitzmaurice," and there came that disdainful look down her arrogant nose. He took that trick.

"I agree that we must aim to balance the demands of the heart and the mind," Mrs Tamrisk said quietly, before enquiring if Mrs Rembleton's children were in town with her. "I miss my younger sisters," she confided.

"If you wish to forego the pleasures of Hyde Park for Grosvenor Square, do call, Mrs Tamrisk. I am staying at Gracechurch House and the Duchess and I take the children into the square about four o'clock most afternoons. We can always use another pair of hands at bat and ball."

Intrigued by this remark, Luke made it his business to pass the square a couple of days later, where he saw a merry group of mothers and children with hoops and balls. He didn't think his mother had ever played with him. Her role in her children's upbringing had been restricted to fleeting visits to the nursery or schoolroom and a formal half hour each evening when they were brought down to the drawing-room with warnings to be on their best behaviour and not tire Mamma.

On Wednesday evening, having fulfilled his fraternal duty by taking his sister driving in the park, Luke did not change into the silk knee-breeches required of a gentleman destined for Almack's—this was the one engagement his mother could be counted upon to fulfil—but, clad in more comfortable trousers, headed towards Covent Garden. Neither drama nor dissipation were on his mind. As he walked his stride lengthened, his pace became brisker and his whole demeanour less languid. In Maiden Lane he turned into the *Crossed Swords*. Ignoring the few patrons sitting at the tables, he nodded to the stout man behind the counter and went through the door beside it, then took the narrow stairs two at a time. A long, sparsely furnished room took up the whole of this floor. Several men in their shirtsleeves sat on benches around the walls critically appraising every thrust, slash and parry of the sword-fight in the middle of the floor.

The clash and slither of steel on steel, the intent faces of participants and on-lookers, the tang of male sweat mingled with tobacco, ale and oil all bore witness that this was no modish academy of politeness such as Angelo's where gentlemen displayed their skill with the foils, but rather the refuge of those who appreciated an honest bout with sabres. Those who found their way here, and few came by chance, were a mixture of retired military and fencing masters enjoying the absence of their pupils. They bowed to their indoor location by removing their coats but otherwise fought fully-clad, boots and all. 'For,' as one *habitué* remarked, 'the enemy ain't going to wait while your valet tugs them off for you'.

It was the sergeant who had furnished Luke with the direction of the *Crossed Swords* when he first took lodgings in London, saying gruffly 'Tell Bill Jones Ned Quant sent you, and mind you don't disgrace me. Or you can go to that Angelo's if you prefer, sir,' had been his final, disparaging sally.

"No, sergeant, thank you, sergeant," Luke had said meekly.

Although in those first years, he had still occasionally accompanied Lord Needham to Angelo's, he had stopped visiting the Bond Street salon once his lordship's health failed. He preferred the less rarefied atmosphere here, where the only rank that mattered was that of skill and politeness was based on mutual respect rather than standing in society. Young Mr Fitzmaurice had been welcomed cautiously but was soon recognised to be a good swordsman and a decent fellow, one who could stand up to his opponent, take his heavy wet and blow a cloud as well as any man. After some time, he had told a few of the fellows about the dashing of his hopes of buying a pair of colours and found their macabre humour easier to deal with than outright sympathy.

'Best give us the name of your physician in case you drop dead on us,' one had remarked while another added, 'Rest assured, lad, we'll keep the resurrection men away from your lovely corpse'.

Now Luke raised a hand to salute the spectators but said nothing until the bout was brought to an end by one of the combatants disarming the other to a murmur of, "Well done, sir".

The victor grinned, acknowledged the applause and offered his hand to his opponent. "A good bout, Murray. You made me sweat for it."

"That was a neat trick at the end," Mr Murray complimented him. He took out his handkerchief and mopped his brow theatrically. "You're not the only one who had to sweat."

They moved to a table where jugs of beer waited invitingly.

"Not doing the pretty tonight, Fitzmaurice?" Luke's neighbour enquired good-humouredly.

"No, thank God. My mother tried to convince me to accompany them to Almack's but I cried off." He stripped off his coat and stretched. "Who's up next?"

"O'Connor and Warren." The speaker was an older man who suffered badly from rheumatism that prevented him from fighting and acted as the unofficial chairman of the gathering. "Are you acquainted with the new Lord Franklin?" He nodded across the room. "His brother died last year, you may remember and he is now the heir. With the peace, he felt he could no longer remain with the army."

Luke looked at a man of about his own age who exuded a nervous energy even while participating in the conversation around him. "We haven't met."

"Let me introduce you. I think you'd be a good match for him."

The viscount greeted him amicably and readily agreed to a bout.

"Are you long returned home?" Luke asked as they waited their turn.

"Just a fortnight."

"How did you find your way here so quickly?" Luke asked, wondering dismally if they were going to be overrun by former soldiers.

"That was pure luck, I tell you," Franklin sighed. "My family are in town for the Season and my mother insisted I join them. But it's too quick—the change, I mean; just two months since, we were entering Bordeaux. I've not been home these five years—and to return here—you'd think we had never been at war. My father insisted I sell out. He would have had me do so last year, but I was adamant that I remain with the army until

Boney was defeated. Once that happened—why, he even wrote to old Douro to have me released as early as possible. And now they're pestering me to choose a bride. So I've been playing least in sight and happened to pass here the other evening, got talking to Jones—he has the look of an old soldier—and he suggested I pop my head in upstairs."

He turned to look critically at the fight on the floor that was reaching its climax. "Here provides some sort of a connection between the military and the civil lives, I suppose. When I see the pinks on Rotten Row and think of the shabby state we were in after crossing the Pyrenees! Many a night I wake up sweating, thinking I've forgotten to post sentries. Not that it ever happened," he added hastily. "I never lost a piquet, I'm happy to say."

"You'll feel more the thing once you can get out of London," Luke said sympathetically. "There are ways of surviving the Season. You must have your sanctuaries so that you can get away from the females and plan your campaign, as you might say. This is one, and then there are the clubs and coffee houses. Some hostesses are more amenable than others when it comes to a chap slipping away to the card-room and if you make up a party at supper it is less particular than taking a girl in on her own, which she might read to mean more than you intend. And never engage to take your female relatives home from a party. Accompany them there if you must, but say you'll be going on somewhere later and will leave them the carriage."

"I see you are a dab at this, Fitzmaurice," his lordship said appreciatively.

"Dine with me on Friday and I'll put you in the way of things, introduce you to some of the others."

"That's deuced kind of you, sir."

"Eight o'clock at Stephen's Hotel in Bond Street," Luke said as the floor was cleared and he and Lord Franklin went to don their masks.

"Good evening, Miss Gregg."

Olivia smiled at the young woman who was companion to Jack's eldest niece. An orphan whose only brother was a lieutenant in the 1st/52nd, she had been forced from a young age to earn her living and for the past seven years had been employed by Mrs Frome to fetch and carry and in general take care of all the little tasks which that lady found to be tedious, irksome or beneath her consequence. This evening she accompanied Lady Rembleton who, refusing to employ a companion herself, had no compunction in demanding the services of her daughter's.

"Good evening, Mrs Rembleton." The young woman looked around cautiously and then said, "Pray forgive my temerity, but would you be so kind as to present me to Lord Franklin?"

"I don't have the pleasure of his lordship's acquaintance," Olivia replied, surprised at the usually so unassuming companion putting herself forward in this way.

"I understand that is he talking to Mr Fitzmaurice." Miss Gregg looked discreetly to where a thin man of unusually dark complexion tapped his fingers restlessly against his thigh as he spoke. "I do not like to be so bold, but it may the only opportunity I get and my brother has charged me most particularly with expressing his gratitude and sense of obligation if I can. Captain, or I should say Lord Franklin resigned his commission and insisted my brother get the promotion, waiving any payment." Her eyes shone and Olivia, knowing how devoted she was to her brother, turned slightly to catch Mr Fitzmaurice's eye and gesture subtly with her fan.

It was unheard of for Mrs Rembleton to favour him with her notice and Luke was initially inclined to ignore her summons, but curiosity got the better of him and he crossed the floor to her side. He suspected her interest was more in his companion and, even more intrigued by this, duly steered him to where the two ladies were standing. All was made clear when Miss Gregg simply but eloquently repeated her brother's message. There was nothing of the coquette in her manner and no suggestion that she had seized on the opportunity to attract the attention of either gentleman beyond fulfilling her brother's wishes.

"Gregg's sister?" Lord Franklin displayed more enthusiasm than Luke had seen in him up to now. "I am very happy to meet you, ma'am. He has frequently diverted us while on campaign with extracts from your letters which admirably transported us back to England."

Miss Gregg blushed at this and demurred. "I cannot think my humdrum life can have been of much interest, my lord,"

"You don't understand how valuable a faithful correspondent is to a soldier and how much we like to hear of what I may venture to call normal life; the description of a cricket match or an April shower, or the report of the first cuckoo call. It takes us out of our weary existence, you see. The Peninsula was a deuced hard slog with little comfort while we were on the march and we were all grateful to be able to sit around a campfire listening to tales of home. You have an unusual gift of description, Miss Gregg and your anecdotes brought our home nearer to us."

"Then I am glad you were able to find some comfort in my letters," she said gently.

"As for the captaincy, there is no need for thanks and so I wrote to Gregg. I should hate to see it go to a Hyde Park soldier. Just imagine," he turned to include the other two in the conversation, "at Bayonne some of the guards were observed using umbrellas to protect themselves against the rain. Afraid they would melt, I suppose! The duke was not pleased and soon put a stop to it. Their colonel received a real wigging after the battle for permitting his officers such unmilitary behaviour."

A new set was forming and Lord Franklin turned to Miss Gregg. "May I have the pleasure of dancing this next with you, Miss Gregg?"

She went white and then red, turning appealing eyes to Mrs Rembleton before stammering "I am honoured, my lord, but you misunderstand. I would not so presume—I am not here as a guest. Oh, pray excuse me!" She hurried away leaving his lordship looking astonished.

"Miss Gregg is companion to my husband's niece Mrs Frome and here tonight with my sister-in-law Lady Rembleton," Mrs Rembleton explained. "You would not be doing her a favour by standing up with her, my lord."

"You may rely on Mrs Rembleton to know what is proper," Luke said dismissively. Why should the chit not enjoy a dance if invited?

"It is easy to disdain propriety, sir, when one is not dependant on its observance for one's livelihood," she snapped. "If Lady Rembleton were to hear that her companion had stood up with one of the guests, she might have her dismissed." She turned to Lord Franklin. "I am sure you would not have wished that, my lord."

"You are quite right, ma'am and I should be grateful if you could convey my apologies to the lady. But I confess I should like to further my acquaintance with her."

"I collect you are not long returned home after an absence of many years with the army. I beg you will forgive me if I speak as directly to you as I would to my own brother, a naval officer, who also has been out of society these many years." She paused and when he did not poker up but nodded encouragingly, continued, "You must be wary of paying attentions to Miss Gregg that might raise unfounded hopes or cause her to be the object of unwarranted speculation as to the nature of your interest. A single lady, especially one who is obliged to earn her bread, must, like Caesar's wife, be above suspicion. You need not assure me," she added earnestly, "that you would never seek to bring dishonour or shame on Miss Gregg, but sadly there are plenty of idle tongues in society whose favourite pastime is speculation and whose currency is the perceived misdeeds of others."

"Mrs Rembleton is right, Franklin," Luke said reluctantly. "Were you to single Miss Gregg out in any way, they would have her set up as your *chère amie* in a trice—or at least be betting on the possibility in the clubs."

"Thank you for your frankness, ma'am," Lord Franklin answered. "I understand that you spoke out of concern for the lady's welfare and am grateful to you."

Mrs Rembleton smiled approvingly at him. "Not at all, my lord. Now if you will excuse me, gentlemen, I must go and talk to Lady Faulkner."

"An admirable woman," his lordship commented, his gaze following the erect, elegant figure.

"'*Nobly planned, to warn, to comfort and command*' as Mr Wordsworth has it," Luke agreed with a grin. "I prefer my women to be more—yielding." He had to admit that she had faced up to a delicate and difficult situation bravely, just as she had on their first encounter, he recalled. He supposed she had won tonight's hand, for even if he had provoked her into giving him a magnificent set-down, he had had to acknowledge she was in the right. It looked as if his next task would be to educate Franklin in the niceties of female attire so that in future he could distinguish the companion from her employer.

Are you enjoying the Season, Miss Adams?" Olivia enquired the following evening at Lady Neary's musicale.

"Yes. It has been truly splendid, ma'am."

Mr Fitzmaurice's sister was a pretty girl, dark where her brother was fair, her open eager features contrasting with his habitual polite expression that was never varied by anything other than a slight smile. We all have our company faces, she thought, the gentlemen even more than the ladies. And how many of the people here tonight are genuinely interested in music? At least Jack had never pretended to be anything other than himself. If he attended an event such as this, he listened intently to the music, at the theatre he watched the play and became irritated if addressed during it. And any conversation sooner or later turned to questions of natural philosophy.

Almost as if he had picked up her thoughts, Mr Fitzmaurice said, "I hear Mr Rembleton is off rambling again."

"When the news of the peace came, nothing could hold him here," Olivia answered calmly.

"Have you seen the Emperor of Russia and his Cossacks, Mrs Rembleton?" Miss Adams asked.

"Yes, at the Opera."

"Aren't they vastly romantic?" the girl sighed.

"Did you see Prinnie bow to his wife?" her brother asked, intrigued.

"The Emperor and the King of Prussia bowed to the Princess, it is true. The Prince bowed as well, but whether to her or to acknowledge the applause of the house, which he appropriated to himself, I cannot say. She certainly took it as meant for her and made a magnificent curtsey in return."

"She has been treated abominably," another lady said heatedly. "The Queen will not permit her to attend a drawing room, even for her daughter's presentation—the Duchess of Oldenburgh did the honours then—or to meet the King of Prussia, even though her father fell in his service at Jena. Whatever her failings as a wife, she should receive her dues as a mother and daughter. It is not as if the Prince is a paragon among husbands."

"Why, my lady, next you will be saying that we men are to be held to the same exalted standards as apply to the fairer sex," a gentleman exclaimed.

"And why not?" she retorted. "I hear that Princess Charlotte has quite rightly given the Prince of Orange his *congé* because he was noticeably in his cups at Ascot."

At the babble of demands for more details this *on-dit* provoked, Olivia eased away from the group, accompanied, to her astonishment, by Mr Fitzmaurice who smiled ruefully and said, "I take the blame for drawing attention to palace matters. They are extremely tedious, aren't they?"

She could only agree. Miss Swift moved just then to the pianoforte and he pulled out a chair for Olivia, remaining correctly beside her during an outstanding rendition of a Beethoven sonata.

"Do you play yourself, Mrs Rembleton?" he enquired during the applause.

"No, or no more than competently," Olivia replied, conscious of the short little finger that made it impossible for her to achieve the evenness and fluidity necessary in some passages. "But that does not mean that I cannot appreciate and applaud excellence."

"You are generous as well as discerning, ma'am," he remarked before they were joined by another couple.

Well, Olivia thought when he finally departed, how unlike Fitzmaurice to pay such a sincere compliment. He generally delights to provoke.

Chapter Twelve

"General Blücher was positively persecuted by his female admirers in the park yesterday. In the end he had to set his back against a tree to defend himself," Charlotte Faulkner said. "Poor man—I'm sure he would have much preferred to be on the battlefield."

The Duchess of Gracechurch laughed. "I vow if I had known the Sovereigns had intended to descend upon us, I would not have come to town until they had safely departed these shores. Although it was vastly entertaining the other evening to see Prinnie trying to force Lady Hertford on the Emperor's notice. He introduced her twice, but the Czar would not speak to her but merely bowed."

She had invited her particular friends to an al fresco breakfast. The nine ladies now toying with strawberry ice sat around a table set up on the lawn in the shade of a copper beech where they had enjoyed an array of light delicacies including cucumber and pea soup, delicately poached trout and asparagus dressed the Italian way.

"This is wonderful, Flora," Anne Heriot sighed.

"Have another lemon biscuit and I think we need some more champagne." She beckoned to the footman to refill the glasses and then dismissed him. Once he was out of earshot, she announced, "Watier's are to give a big masquerade at Burlington

House on the first of July in honour of Wellington. Admission is by ticket only and I am determined we shall all go."

Olivia wasn't sure if she wished to attend. It was bound to be a sad crush and the company would be mixed to say the least. She looked around the table at the smiling faces. The idea of disguising herself was intriguing—for one evening not to be staid, sensible Mrs Rembleton. Why must I always play spoilsport? If we are masked, no one will know who we are. She took a deep breath.

"Supposing we dress identically? It would be more difficult for the individual to be recognised. We would have everyone guessing."

"Surely that would be impossible," Lallie Tamrisk looked around the group. "We are all different sizes."

"Not if we are properly costumed," Anne contradicted her. "We were used to put on a lot of private theatricals at home. Much can be done to alter appearances and if we use full masks, our features will be obscured. But we must decide quickly if we are to have the costumes ready in less than three weeks. Perhaps we could arrange for help from one of the theatres."

"Not if we wish to remain *incognita*, which I, for one, would wish to do," Olivia said firmly. "Just think of the scandal if we were recognised."

"Surely with the help of our maids, we could contrive to make the costumes ourselves, especially if we select a pattern that is not too complicated," Lallie volunteered.

"What comes in groups of nine?" Charlotte asked to a sudden silence.

"A cat has nine lives," Flora said to general laughter.

"There are nine circles of hell, according to Dante," Olivia offered.

"Too grim," Flora decided.

"Nine Worthies?" Anne suggested.

"Too tedious," Charlotte decreed to a chorus of agreement.

"The only other nine I can think of is the pins in skittles," Anne sighed, "though I suppose the costumes might not be too difficult."

"You mean we may just put a sack over our heads, cut holes for eyes and mouth, and tie it at the neck?" Flora retorted. "I should like something a little more flattering."

Anthea Lovell had been silent up to now. "What about the nine muses? If we have Grecian gowns and white wigs in the Grecian style—."

Now they were all talking at once.

"And masks bearing the attribute of our muse—that will be the only way to distinguish us—."

"We could use the white *maquillage* that was popular last century. If we apply it to our arms and *décolletages* it would hide any little moles, like this one at my throat. It would give me away to anyone who knows me well."

"If we're not wearing gloves, we must take off or disguise our wedding rings."

A large bedroom in Gracechurch House was turned into a workroom. Anne had procured the wigs and the white paint under the pretext that they were for a summer production of *A Midsummer's Night's Dream*. It was easy to purchase nine plain white masks and Anthea and Lallie undertook the gold ornamentation.

Amid much laughter, they spent hours lined up in front of a row of cheval glasses trying to achieve as uniform an appearance as possible and identifying idiosyncrasies that might give away the one or the other.

"If we bind your hair flat to your head, *Madame*, make your wig less bouffant than those of the other ladies and you wear absolutely flat sandals while the others have a heel, then we may even out much of the height," Martin pronounced.

"And it is not as if it will be broad daylight," Flora pointed out.

"We must make a grand entrance," Charlotte declared, "not just slip in meekly."

"Perhaps hand in hand, dancing as if we were on a Greek vase, slightly turning so that our draperies float properly."

There was a babble of suggestions.

"Nothing too fast. Perhaps minuet steps at a slow, stately pace."

"We need a flautist to lead us."

"Dressed as Pan."

"Should it not be Apollo with his lyre?"

"Where should we find a lyre player?"

"Come in in a long line, then form a circle—. It need not be for long."

"You excel at the minuet, Flora. What do you think?"

"Perhaps something like a sarabande might be better. Let me see what music I have."

"Where will we get a flautist?"

"I think I'll be able to arrange the music," Anthea said mysteriously. "We'll need to practise every day if we are not to make fools of ourselves."

Anthea clapped her hands. "Excellent, ladies. I defy anyone to know who we are. We shall cause quite a stir, I am convinced of it."

"How are we to manage that?" Anne asked. "They expect there to be such a crush that people are advised to be in their carriages by five if they wish to gain entrance by nine or ten o'clock."

"We shall enter via a side door and have been promised a room where we can make ready," Anthea said. "It is all in hand."

"What about going home?" Anne asked. "I don't want to stay much beyond midnight."

After much argument, Flora decreed, "A carriage will be available at midnight and after that it will wait at the side entrance. I believe breakfast is to be served at eight o'clock, if anyone wishes to see it out to the bitter end."

Flora put her head around the door of Olivia's bedchamber. "Will you keep an eye on Lallie, or Clio, I must say? I want to be sure she doesn't miss the midnight carriage."

"Of course."

"I'll look after the other Cinderellas. What about you, Thalia? Have you made up your mind yet?"

Olivia shook her head. "I'll wait and see."

"We're meeting in the workroom in twenty minutes for the final touches."

When the door had closed behind her friend, Olivia went to stand in front of her looking-glass. She already wore Thalia's gown. Martin had plaited her hair tightly and wrapped the braids close around her head so that the wig would fit easily over it. She had thought the style would make her look even more severe but the mischievous sparkle in her eyes made her look years younger. The gown was cut lower than she usually wore, with a broad vee that went from her shoulders to the top of the valley between her breasts. Thank goodness all that exposed skin was whitened. Perfume! She picked up the vial of *Les Fleurs de Parnasse*, the scent that had been created especially for tonight and touched it behind her ears, to her throat, between her breasts and to her wrists. It seemed particularly daring not to be wearing gloves.

She suddenly smiled at her reflection and turned in a quick pirouette. She felt lighter, a girl again, the girl she might have been if fate and Mr Rembleton had not intervened. She picked up her mask from the dressing table and held it in front of her face. Her eyes gleamed through it and it was cunningly cut out around the mouth to reveal the curve of her lips. Thalia, Muse of Comedy. She had chosen to be Thalia. Mr Fitzmaurice's quip about comedy and tragedy had resonated deeply within her. For Jack, she had thought, life was a comedy. But at what price? Did he not feel, or for some reason did he not permit himself to feel? Earlier in their marriage she had wondered, but then she had come to accept him as he was.

And what of her? Was her tragedy not that she felt but that she sought to repress her feelings? Austere, aloof, straitlaced, haughty, an icicle—they were all terms she had heard applied to her. Initially her calm air of superiority had been a mask she donned when confronted with the ton, but she had also found it useful, she had to admit, when dealing with her husband's lack of sensibility. It helped her meet him on a more equal footing.

A tap on the door heralded Martin. "We are ready below, *Madame*."

Smiling, Olivia picked up Thalia's mask. It was strange to use a mask to remove a mask, she thought, but who knew? Tonight she might release the tight hold she kept on her dreams and her desires.

The guests at Burlington House turned at the flute's haunting melody. Supported by a rhythm beaten on two tambourines, it evoked a mysterious past and stilled conversation as they strained to listen.

"Pan. 'Tis Pan with attendant nymphs," a voice cried.

"What now?" Luke asked himself, but moved back with the crowd to permit the musicians to pace out a large circle.

The music changed, became quicker, and a file of women appeared, hand in hand, each facing in the direction opposite to that of her neighbours. They were all in white, their finely pleated, flowing garments bound under the breast and at the waist with gold cords. They wore identical wigs and their masks matched apart from a small emblem delicately delineated in gold on the right cheek. Their movements were studied, hieratic, slight turns causing their hems to flutter above golden sandals.

"The Nine Muses!" someone announced.

Their arms gracefully outstretched, the nine formed a circle and moved into a flowing dance, their draperies stirring with the lissom motion to hint at a pretty breast, display the swell of womanly curves or reveal a bare ankle, all made more exciting by the expressionless masks above.

Who are they? Luke wondered. Probably opera dancers, they're so uniform in size and so well-rehearsed. As the pace quickened, he noticed the quick rise and fall of their bosoms, could hear the catch of their breath and the beat of their leather sandals on the floor. As one, they released their clasped hands and those who had been facing out turned to the centre of the circle. They clasped hands again and stepped in close together, raising their joined hands high as if in invocation. The beat of the tambourines ceased but the flute melody continued for several moments until ending suddenly on an unresolved phrase. The women lowered their hands, bowed to the centre of their circle and, upright once more, quickly pivoted so that they faced outwards.

The rapt silence was broken by a storm of applause accompanied by an undercurrent of male voices trying to recall the names of the muses and at the same time demanding to know who the dancers were.

"Damme, if they had appeared so at school, I'd have marked their names better," one disgruntled gentleman complained.

The Duke of Devonshire, who together with the Duke of Leinster acted as host, came forward and bowed low. "Divine ones, we are honoured that you deign to mingle with us poor mortals. It is known that '*the words of Mercury are harsh after the songs of Apollo,*' but dare we hope that you will linger with us a while?"

"Why not, good sir?" one replied.

Her voice broke the spell and the Muses were surrounded by a press of gentlemen offering their arms, soliciting a dance, begging to be permitted to fetch refreshments.

Elated by their success and liberated by her disguise, Olivia parried these approaches almost instinctively while she looked about her. There were all sorts of costumes; flower-girls and nuns, rustics of all nationalities, a Spanish grandee, Marie Antoinette, with a scarlet ribbon around her throat; Olivia's nose wrinkled beneath the mask at the sight. Some were heavily veiled or masked, while others made little or no effort to conceal their identity. Mr Fitzmaurice, for example, whose burnished gold hair was admirably set off by Hamlet's black, carried a narrow mask on a stick which he raised from time to time to his eyes. Like a dowager with a lorgnette, she thought, amused. What had led him to represent such a brooding, melancholic figure? And surely that peasant boy who stared so boldly was really a girl?

As the clamour of voices subsided slightly, a gentleman dressed as Apollo seized his chance to proclaim, "Each divine muse will select her partner for the *valse sauteuse.* Strike up, musicians!"

Olivia felt a little trickle of excitement down her spine. She was not often invited to dance in London, although at home she rarely sat out a dance at the assemblies and local festivities. Along with the others, she had learnt how to waltz but had not yet had the opportunity to try her prowess outside the classroom. And for once to have the power to select any gentleman she chose! The memory of all the years she had had to watch Luke Fitzmaurice dance with other women rose to taunt her. After that disastrous first invitation, he had never again asked her to stand up with him. Her lips curved and she stretched out an imperious hand. "Prince Hamlet!"

He walked forward, tucking his mask into the girdle at his waist and bowed elaborately. "You honour me, fair Thalia," he said and immediately led her into the first position, turning her to face him, his hands on her waist. She was wearing the lightest of stays and his clasp seemed unbearably intimate. She raised her hands and placed them lightly on his shoulders, hoping fleetingly that the white paint would not mark his black velvet doublet.

He was indeed a most accomplished partner. He held her firmly but allowed her all the freedom she needed to make her turns. His hands tightened slightly when she should spring into the step and he seemed to lift her but still held her securely. It was exhilarating, like flying, Olivia thought. Above all, there was a unity between them that lent their steps a thrilling harmony so that they moved as one, each able utterly to rely on the other.

Who was she? Luke was sure he had never danced with her before. He had come to the masquerade expecting to be bored, as he was nearly all the time nowadays. His sister's innocent pleasure in her first Season, her honest aspiration to love and be loved, had opened his eyes to how jaded he had become. He found himself spending more time with Clare, using her as a protection against the lonely matrons who sought to assuage the emptiness of their marriages in secret assignations. In previous years he had been very willing to oblige them, but this year they were unable to appease his desire.

His partner had initially been a little unsure of her steps but she had soon gained confidence and matched his every move-ment with innate grace. Smiling to himself, he gathered her more closely to him than would usually be permitted so that their bodies brushed each other. Her infinitesimal hesitation made her later yielding all the sweeter. An exotic scent, something new that suggested hot sun, flowers and pines mixed with a faint, salty tang, wove itself about his charmed senses.

She was taller than most ladies and it made waltzing all the more seductive. He did not have to bend to put his hands on her waist or arch his arm uncomfortably when they clasped hands above their heads. When he held her closely, they were torso to torso and he could see the shady valley between two rounded breasts. Her eyes sparkled behind her mask. The quick steps and turns of the dance made conversation difficult and they tacitly gave themselves up to the pleasure of the movement, so attuned to each other that they stepped and turned as one. The music stopped too soon.

"A pleasure indeed, Thalia," Luke bowed, "but no less that I would expect from the sister of Terpsichore."

She curtsied gracefully. "Thank you, Prince. You are not as melancholy as you are reputed to be, but moved admirably by 'concord of sweet sounds'."

He laughed. "Is that what is meant by that passage, do you think? I had understood it to concern the internal appreciation of music, not its external expression."

"I think the one must lead to the other. I have frequently known music, and particularly dance, to chase away the blue devils."

"Music can also make one melancholy," he remarked. "Walk with me, Thalia?"

"Comedy escorted by the tragic prince?" she asked lightly. "I wonder who would prevail—would she succeed in making him laugh or would he subdue her raillery?"

"Let us put it to the test." He angled his arm invitingly and she slipped her hand into the crook of his elbow.

By now the excitement caused by the appearance of the Muses had waned, although they were still besieged by suitors. Luke did not stop when his companion was addressed, but continued strolling. On being challenged by one gentleman, he merely responded, "No, no sir. You may not mar this strange conjunction of tragedy and comedy," and swept her on.

"How high-handed of you," she commented.

"He's a bore and a dullard, Thalia. You should be thanking me, not reproving me."

Some four yards from them a couple had withdrawn into a window embrasure and were conversing, no, it looked more like arguing vigorously. One was wearing a dark brown robe like that of a monk, belted at the waist and falling to his ankles. He was extremely handsome with a fine profile and a high forehead set off by artfully arranged locks. His companion was slighter, a boyish figure wearing green pantaloons under his domino. He made a hasty movement and his hood fell back, to reveal a mask and short dark curls. The monk jerked it up again.

"Surely that's Caro Lamb—"

"and Byron," Luke completed. As they looked on, Lady Caroline made another extravagant gesture and the poet seized her, tugging her away presumably to continue their dispute in a more private place.

"Tell me, Thalia," Luke enquired, "do they more properly belong to you or to your sister Melpomene?"

"She, poor lady, I think to my sister, for she is a tragic figure, but he to all of us."

"I never thought to envy him, but if he is beloved of you all—." He ran his finger down her bare arm and felt her shiver.

"It is not love but more a claiming and not entirely to be envied, Prince. Our gifts come at a price."

He smiled and dropped his arm to put it around her waist. "We are becoming too serious, Thalia." He took two glasses of champagne from a passing waiter. "Smile at me, or better, kiss me." He touched his lips to hers before handing her a glass. "To life, to love!"

She raised her glass and drank as a clock struck midnight.

"I must leave you, Prince."

He caught her to him. "You will not desert me at the '*very witching time of night*'?"

"I must. I am called." She eased out of his embrace. "Perhaps we will meet again."

"Another kiss, Thalia" he begged. "The Muses' blessing!"

Smiling, she raised her head to kiss him as swiftly as he had kissed her and slipped away.

Luke watched as she flitted across the room, her skirts swirling to expose golden straps that encircled pretty ankles and calves.

"You lucky dog, Fitzmaurice," a male voice said behind him, "to have captured one of the Goddesses."

"But beware" another put in, "they are not always kind to their favourites."

Luke finished his champagne, smiling as he watched Thalia murmur in a sister's ear. She drew the other muse away from her partner and the two left the room.

"The carriage is outside if you still wish to leave. It has just struck midnight," Olivia whispered to Lallie.

"I do. And you?"

"I'll stay awhile."

Arm in arm they strolled through the huge suite of rooms and turned into the passage that led to the side entrance. Suddenly Lord Byron bowed low before them.

"You leave us, Divine Ones. The Muses' kiss was ever fleeting but no less welcome."

"Then take our blessing." Olivia kissed his cheek and Lallie shyly did the same.

"That was Byron," Olivia hissed in her friend's ear once she was sure he had left them, rendering Lallie speechless.

Chapter Thirteen

*O*nce Lallie was safely in the carriage, Olivia returned to the Muses' parlour. She was glad of a moment's repose. *Better check that everything is still in place*, she thought and went to the overmantle mirror only to stop, spellbound by the mysterious, alluring creature whose golden eyes gleamed from behind the mask. The deep vees front and back of her gown drew the gaze to hidden curves and the bare throat and arms invited seduction. She moved differently, she realised, less reserved, more aware of her body. A secret smile caressed her lips. *What would he say if he knew it had been her first kiss?*

A tide of some two thousand people surged within the mansion. Supper had been announced and the drawing of the lottery had commenced. A quadrille followed another waltz in the ballroom. Olivia wandered from room to room but was disinclined to linger longer than a few minutes with any group. A cavalier invited her to take supper with him but she declined gracefully. She exchanged a smile and a wave with Melpomene across a room, but felt no inclination to join her. Between the press of bodies and the hundreds of candles, the rooms had got very warm and she went to an open window in search of some refreshing breaths of cooler air. As she stood looking out into the night, an arm slipped around her waist.

"Well-met by moonlight, fairest Thalia."

Her pulse quickened. This was what she had hoped for. She looked down at the black, fur-trimmed sleeve. "Well-met, Prince," she said and turned within his arm to face him. His other arm came around her.

"You are my captive and must pay the forfeit."

"Must I?" She raised an eyebrow and then chuckled, remembering that it was concealed by the mask.

"If you wish to be released."

"That will depend on how well you care for your prisoners," she told him, with a challenging little smile. "I have not yet had any supper."

"Nor have I. But you will not wish to brave the supper-room. It surpasses the worst crush imaginable. Let me see if I can arrange something better." As he spoke he urged her gently to the door of the ballroom where he murmured to a footman. She heard the chink of coins.

"If you will follow me, sir."

The servant led them from the brightly illuminated rooms to a small parlour dimly lit by two branches of candles, one on the mantelpiece and one on the round table in front of a canopied daybed.

"I'll return instantly with your supper, sir."

The man was back in less than ten minutes, bearing a tray with a platter of delicacies, a bottle of champagne and two glasses. He set it on the table and withdrew, Mr Fitzmaurice hard on his heels to lock the door behind him.

"We don't want anyone else stumbling on this little retreat."

Olivia, who was standing at the window looking out, turned to regard him gravely.

"You might have stepped down from a Grecian vase" he said huskily, "or be a marble statue come to life." He held out his hand, walking towards her as he spoke. "Will you sup with me, Thalia?"

He was not merely inviting her to share a meal with him; an intent appeal in his eyes spoke eloquently of his desire. It was a look Olivia had never seen on her husband's face. Luke Fitzmaurice was reputed to know all about pleasure. If he was happy to sport with an unknown lady, why should she not indulge? It was an opportunity that would never be repeated.

Taking a deep breath, she took a few steps to meet him and placed her hand in his.

Curse that mask, Luke thought. How am I to know what she thinks when I can't see her face? She seems uneasy, as if she's not used to this type of *tête-à-tête*. He linked his fingers with hers and bent to kiss her, letting his lips linger until hers softened, but did not press his advantage further.

"Come, sweetheart." He drew her to sit with him on the daybed and took a finger of toast spread with a salmon paste. He held it to her lips.

She seemed startled but then took a bite and he popped the other half into his own mouth.

"More?"

She nodded and he presented her with a spear of asparagus. This took four bites between them. To his pleasure, she seized the initiative and held the next one to his mouth. He gently nipped at her fingers as he bit and she gave an intriguing little giggle. He poured a glass of champagne and held it so she could sip from it, then turned it to put his lips where hers had been. Dipping a ripe strawberry in the wine, he held it to her mouth, then leaned forward to lick the juice from her lips before presenting her with the second half so that the tip of her tongue must just touch his finger-tips.

She giggled again.

Enchanted, he moved nearer to press a kiss on her half-open lips, his tongue just venturing between them. There, again, was that slight hesitation. She seemed very inexperienced.

"You are unused to dalliance, Thalia?" Luke murmured against her mouth.

"Dalliance? Yes," she admitted.

He drew back. "I don't despoil women," he said. "My partners all know what they are about; they seek a pleasant interlude and no more."

"That is all I may seek," she answered, a note of sadness in her voice. "For once, I would like to lie with a man not out of duty but for pleasure."

"Duty?"

"Yes. His and mine. But that is over now—he has his heirs and I have my children." Her voice cooled. "But, Prince, I will not compel you. You may unlock that door if you please." She sat up and leaned away from him.

Luke swore to himself. "I need no compelling, sweetheart. I just want to be sure that you won't regret this." He took her hand and pressed a kiss in the palm. "You honour me with your trust. Are you sure, Thalia?"

She stiffened for a moment and then subsided against him. "Yes. Are you? I will not be an obligation, Prince. I would rather you walk out of that door than you remain because you feel obliged to do so."

She spoke in a low voice but with a feverish vehemence that struck him to the heart. He stood abruptly, unfastened his cloak and dropped it to the floor before stripping off the short tunic that hung in soft folds to his thighs.

Clad only in a fine cambric shirt and clinging black pantaloons that left nothing to the imagination, he moved directly in front of her, planted his feet either side of hers, and took her hand to press it firmly to the proud bulge at his crotch. "This does not speak of obligation, Thalia."

He groaned softly when her fingers closed almost instinctively around the hard column. "That's right, sweetheart, but not yet. Let me make some preparations." He quickly felt in his pocket for a cundum. She seemed so innocent it might not have occurred to her to take precautions against getting with child. But if her husband, as she had implied, no longer came to her bed, it was better to be safe than sorry. He put the little packet on the table and went to take her in his arms again, kissing her more deeply, his hands going to the ties of her mask. He was burning to see her face—he could not put a name to her but somehow was sure he would recognise her.

She raised her hands to cover his, stopping him with a whispered, "No."

"I want to see you, sweetheart."

"No."

"Don't you trust me?"

"It's not that." Her voice faltered. "I, I just can't."

He heard the note of desperation. Was she so afraid of discovery? "I don't want to make love to a mask." He put his fingers on her lips to prevent a response. "If I were blindfolded would you take it off? And the wig? Could you easily don them again?"

There was a moment's silence and then she whispered. "Very well, but you must snuff the candles on the table.

He blew them out at once.

"What will you use?"

With a flourish Luke handed her the tray-cloth. "Take this." He sat on the edge of the daybed while she folded the cloth and bound it tightly about his eyes.

"What a strange game of blind-man's buff," he murmured. "Now where are you?" She had slipped away from him.

"Here, fulfilling my part of our bargain."

She must have taken off her mask, for her voice sounded different. He could hear she was smiling and she placed something, presumably the mask, on the table. There was an odd soft sound, followed by a sigh of relief. Had she removed the wig? Then he heard her footsteps and the rustle of her skirts as she moved towards him. He held out his hand and, when she put hers in it, drew her down to lie with him on the daybed.

Very gently he raised his hand to trace her features, lingering over each one as if he were learning her by touch. His hand moved down the side of her neck towards her shoulder and she stooped her head sideways to caress his hand with her cheek. His fingers tightened on her shoulder and he raised his other hand to her face, holding her still while he took her lips, his kiss more insistent, his tongue probing deeply into her mouth. He felt her hand curve around his cheek, holding him to her, as if she did not wish to let him go.

This tender response vanquished Luke. He had never known anything like it. His usual partners were very experienced, at times demanding and always aware of the possibilities of their sensual bouts. Clearly the exchange of pleasure was new to Thalia and the more she yielded to him, the more determined he became to serve her in every possible way. To indulge her was his reward and he resumed his slow exploration, pushing down the shoulders of her gown so that he could explore her breasts, waiting breathlessly to feel her next caress.

"Can we take off your gown?" he muttered.

"I would never manage to tie the cords again."

He could hear the regret in her voice.

She gasped when his searching fingers reached her nipples and stilled when he replaced his fingers with his mouth, his hair brushing the tops of her breasts. With one hand she held him to her, while with the other she pulled open the laces at the neck of his shirt so that she could stroke inside.

"A moment, Thalia." He sat up and offered his wrists. "Unlace me, madam."

With a soft laugh, she complied.

"Help me take it off without disturbing the blindfold," he commanded.

She carefully helped gather the shirt together and lifted it over his head, both of them gasping when her fingers brushed his torso. She paused and then feathered her fingers through his chest hair and shaped his muscles with her hand. Her hand drifted lower and hovered at his waistband.

"Wait." He toed off his pumps, then flicked open buttons and pushed down his pantaloons and drawers, kicking them off before bending to strip off his stockings.

"Come here, Thalia." He pulled her to him again and carefully began to push up her skirts, shaping her bare calves with his hands. "Drawers, how dashing," he approved, letting the palm of his hand fondle her through the fine silk.

She chuckled huskily. "With no stockings, it seemed too daring to be completely bare under the gown."

"It is unkind of you, Thalia, to deny me sight," he murmured as he explored her.

"Our gifts come at a price," she reminded him.

"And I pay it, but unwillingly."

She became more adventurous, putting her arms around him so she could run her hands down his back to cup his buttocks and—at last—closed her hand around his cock.

Luke had felt like shouting in triumph when she stopped merely accepting his attentions, although it was very sweet how she gasped and sighed, even purred under his lips and hands. But to feel her reciprocal touch as she determined the difference between male and female was immensely arousing. He slipped the silk drawers down her legs, easing them over the sandals he had neglected to remove and gently touched her hidden flesh, skin to skin for the first time.

This slow exploration had Olivia savouring each stroke and longing for the next. She didn't know whether it was better to close her eyes and concentrate on the exquisite sensations his caresses aroused in her or open them so she could feast her eyes on his male body, savour the concentration that had his features taut beneath the blindfold. He would come into her now, she thought and tensed against the invasion. There was no vial of oil such as Jack had used to ease his way. But no, he continued his exploration, first with almost feather-like touches and then more insistent until she felt she had never really known her own body. She felt wet, but before she had time to become embarrassed, he had murmured in approval and she realised that her body could prepare itself. His fingers slipped inside her and she felt her hips rise, seeking—something, she didn't know what. His touch became stronger, more rhythmical and she moved with him until she attained a strange peak and quivering release.

"What?" she sobbed.

"Don't be frightened, Thalia," he hushed her with a tender kiss. "This is the pleasure that can exist between men and women."

He looked strained and was still hugely erect. "And you?"

He smiled. "Now you must be my eyes, sweetheart. Do you see the little packet on the table?"

"Yes." She leaned over to retrieve it.

"It's a cundum. You must put it on my member."

She opened the packet and curiously examined the contents. "Why?"

He pressed a kiss to her breast. "So that you do not get with child."

"Oh!" She had not thought of that. What a disaster that would have been. "And this will prevent it?"

"It will catch my seed," he said matter-of-factly. "You must ease it down over me."

By the time she had completed this exercise he was breathing hard.

"Now, sweetheart." With a last kiss he moved between her legs and thrust into her.

To Olivia, his sigh of relief as he settled within her, his head resting for a moment on her breast, was as intoxicating as his caresses. She caught him to her and, when he began to move, eagerly matched him. That strange feeling built again but now, even better, she registered a similar tension rise in him and when she tumbled over the cliff, he followed her on a long groan before collapsing on her. She could feel his heart thrumming against her and wanted to protest when he lifted himself from her, but he just slipped to the side and rested his head again on her breast.

"My God, Thalia," he gasped. "You've killed me. But I die a happy man."

She smoothed his hair back from his forehead. "We have both died then, Prince."

They lay quietly together, exchanging lazy caresses until she raised her head from the cushion. "Was that two o' clock?"

"I think the clock struck twice, sweetheart, but as to the time—I can't see, remember?"

She eased away from him and stood, her skirts rustling as they settled around her. She padded over to peer at the clock. "It's after three! I must go."

"Are you sure, Thalia? I don't want this night to end."

"Nor do I," she said regretfully. "But it is best. Stay where you are until I say otherwise."

"As you wish."

She carried the second branch of candles to the mantelpiece and lit them so she could inspect her reflection. She looked different, all swollen lips and languorous smile. No one else would ever see her like that, she thought with a pang. The white paint was not too smudged and she evened it out as best she could. Spreading out her arms, she spun rapidly in a circle.

"What are you doing?" A lazy voice came from the daybed.

"Putting my gown to rights. If I turn around quickly so that the skirts flare out, they will fall into the original folds." She carefully put on the wig. It was a pity to cover that glowing, vibrantly happy face with the mask, but she had no choice. She tied it behind her head and, unable to resist, went over to undo his blindfold, bending to press a kiss on each eye.

"Thank you," she whispered.

"You don't have to thank me, Thalia," he said, shocked.

"Not for that," she explained, "although it was worthy of thanks. For indulging me and agreeing to have your eyes covered."

"It was strangely exciting," he answered with a smile.

Luke took the cloth from her and discreetly removed the cundum. When he turned back, she was perched on the edge of a chair, just about to insert her feet into her drawers. She first drew them up to her knees, then stood to pull them up her thighs and over her round bottom, her skirts caught over one arm.

"Show me," he ordered. "Slowly. Don't drop your skirts— lift them higher."

She complied with a smile.

"Now turn around." He waved a lordly hand. "Play the whirligig with your gown again."

She let her skirts fall, extended her arms to the side and spun in increasingly faster circles, her skirts flying round her, lifting and opening out to display the laces of her sandals winding up her legs to very pretty knees and hinting at the silk drawers above.

Suddenly she stumbled and sat down hard, gasping, "If you do it too long, it makes you dizzy."

Alarmed, he knelt hastily beside her, holding a glass to her lips "Here. Have some champagne."

She sipped and then said, "You must put yourself to rights. Wait a minute." She took a napkin, moistened a corner with champagne and carefully blotted the white tints from around his mouth. "Show me your hands." He held them up obediently and she wiped his fingers.

The clock struck again.

"I must go."

"Wait, Thalia, I'll see you to your carriage."

He would not permit any discussion but dressed quickly, thrusting his hand through his hair in a vain attempt to tidy it.

"Let me. Sit here."

She combed his hair with her fingers and gently smoothed it into shape.

"You'll do."

He grinned up at her. "You make a very pretty valet."

She laughed back and held his cloak for him. "At your service, Prince."

"My lady!" He offered her his arm.

"This way."

Olivia dreamily led him to a small staircase that gave onto a side entrance where the carriage waited. They didn't speak as they went. At the door, he bent and kissed first her hands and then, for the last time, her mouth.

"Adieu," she said.

He handed her into the conveyance and waited until it had pulled away. Looking back, she saw him go slowly back into the house. Luke Fitzmaurice. Her lover.

Chapter Fourteen

Who was she? In all his years of sexual encounters, Luke had never experienced anything like it. She had made it clear that she was not a virgin and there had been no virginal barrier, but she had been so innocent, ignorant even of how a man and woman might please each other that it was clear that her husband had exercised his marital privileges in the most basic and selfish manner. It made him angry to think of her submitting out of duty, perhaps hurt, certainly unfulfilled. And how she had blossomed under his attentions!

Instead of writing, he spent hours languorously recalling each moment they had spent together, trying to create a picture of her. Her eyes had been more or less level with the tip of his nose. She had soft feminine curves, but was— sturdy was the wrong word—not overly delicate, he decided. You needn't be afraid of cracking her ribs if you held her too tightly. Her voice was warm, but occasionally had a cooler tone that had seemed familiar, but he couldn't place it. She had a beautiful laugh and the most seductive little giggle he had ever heard. Her eyebrows had felt finely arched under his exploring fingers and her nose well-defined. Her face was oval. Her eyes were dark rather than pale, but he had been able to see no more beneath the mask, especially in the dim light. Her breasts swelled plumply above the neckline of her gown and filled his hands perfectly. Her sweet arse had been high and proud beneath the silk drawers.

He assumed her hair was long—he had felt the ridges of tight plaits wound around her head. Her ears lay close to her skull but with full, free lobes. The upper rim of the right ear was slightly uneven, as if there had been a previous injury. Her hands were more square than long and the little finger of her left hand was unusually short, coming only to the top of the first joint of the ring finger beside it. He knew of no lady with such an imperfection and, if there were one, he could not identify her by this unless she happened to be sitting to his right at dinner, the only time one saw a lady without her gloves. She had at least two sons, for she had spoken of heirs, but that was all she had revealed of her private life.

Perhaps she had only been in London for a couple of weeks and had already returned home. But if she were a provincial nobody, how would she have managed not only to acquire one of the coveted tickets to the masquerade, but also to take part in the Muses' tantalizing performance? Harriette Wilson and her familiars had been at Burlington House. Perhaps they or others of the *demi-monde* had grouped together to play the Muses? No. Thalia was certainly *bon ton,* just not well known to him.

Leaving yet another insipid ball where he had again failed to discover her among the guests, he returned home to brood over a glass of brandy. What good would it do to unmask her? She had made it clear that there could only be that one night. It would be hell to be in her company but unable to acknowledge what had been between them. Or, what would be worse, to see her neglected by her husband and be unable to intervene or comfort her. Gloomily, he refilled his glass. Was he cursed to fall in love with unattainable women—first Miss—Mrs Rembleton all those years ago and now Thalia? Thalia was not as tall as Mrs R., he thought, and her voice was different, warmer. And he could not imagine Mrs R giggling!

Olivia stared unseeing at her weekly accounts. She only had to close her eyes to lie again in Luke Fitzmaurice's arms. I never dreamt how exciting it could be to be with a man, she thought longingly, how together you could climb unknown heights only to fall in dizzy rapture. And how he would cherish you, create a special connection between you so that you were the only inhabitants of a strange, new world. Afterwards, when he lay in my arms, his head on my breast, I felt whole. He didn't make me feel clumsy or untutored, but desirable, a woman.

She smiled fondly at the memory of the tender intimacy.

I suppose I should feel guilty but I can't. If I have nothing else, I will have had that one night. How must it be to be able to indulge frankly, perhaps even lovingly, whenever you wish? But for me, that cannot be. I'm bound to Jack and there's no escape. I must think of the children. They should not have to blush for their mother; her name should not be bandied about in the clubs and Miranda must be able to dance at Almack's.

She pushed the heavy ledger away. Fitzmaurice must never learn I was his muse. I exposed so many of my innermost secrets to him that night. It would be so mortifying if he found out! And how would he react? He might be shocked or, worse, laugh. I couldn't bear it if he made one of his mocking remarks.

She rose, sighing. Perhaps when the children no longer need me, when there is no further risk of pregnancy, I might find a loving companion in the autumn of my life. I don't think Jack would care as long as we were discreet. And maybe, one day when we are very old, I might tell my Prince Hamlet who Thalia was and we might smile and remember.

Her eyes stung and she blinked tears away. Life must go on. Today was Samuel's birthday. He was four and would finally put off his petticoats for his first breeches. He would no longer be her baby. Smiling resolutely, she went up to the nursery for the great occasion.

"A Captain Frobisher has called to see you, ma'am, the butler said, adding disapprovingly, "He insisted he be announced at once despite the early hour."

Olivia looked up from the *Morning Chronicle*. "Captain Frobisher, you say, Hinks?"

"Yes, madam."

She jumped to her feet. "Where is he?"

"In the hall, madam."

She rushed past him and hurried down the stairs towards the naval gentleman who was pacing up and down as if the hall were his own quarterdeck.

"Robert? It is indeed you, Robert!"

"Who else should it be, Livvie?"

He strode towards her holding out his arms and Olivia collapsed into them in a flood of tears.

"Livvie! What's this? You never cry."

"I thought I would never see you again," she sobbed.

"Aye, there were times when I thought the same," the captain said ruefully, as he handed her his handkerchief.

She wiped her eyes and looked at him, shaking her head. "You have grown so like Papa. For a moment, it might have been he who stood there. But come up to my sitting-room."

"When did you arrive in England?"

"We made port in Southampton two weeks ago. The men have been paid off. That was a sad thing, Livvie. They are a terrible bunch of rogues, but they've been my rogues this past six years and we've been through thick and thin together. But the *Pride* had taken such a battering that she is beyond repairing."

"Are you now on half-pay?" Olivia asked hopefully.

He shook his head. "I'm bound for America next month. I have four weeks leave before I must report. I must kit myself out afresh; I have just the one good uniform left to me, but I wanted to see you too. It's a great good fortune that you are still in town."

"We leave next week. Can you come with us? I'll write to Uncle Samuel and invite him and Lady Ottilia to join us as soon as possible. They usually come to us in August."

"I still haven't got used to the idea of Uncle Samuel as a married man," he said with a grin.

"They're very devoted to one another. I'm glad they have found such happiness in later life."

"Maybe there's hope for me yet," he said cheerfully.

And me, she thought, but said aloud, "You must not leave it too long."

"I suppose not." He changed the subject. "Now, you must tell me all your news. What of Rembleton? Is he staying here too?"

"No, he never has, but he always used to visit the children, take them on outings and such. He's not in England at the moment however, but somewhere on the continent. I don't know when we'll see him again."

Robert frowned at this news but just said, "Perhaps the children would like to show an old tar something of London. I hardly know it, hardly know England if it comes to that."

"I'm sure they would be delighted. Tomorrow we go to Hampton Court, if you would like to accompany us."

Captain Frobisher made himself comfortable under the awning of the Duke of Gracechurch's private barge and accepted a glass of iced punch. "I didn't think you'd have me on the water again so quickly, Livvie, but this is something like, I must say."

They had boarded the shallop above London Bridge and soon were moving briskly up-river, propelled by the efforts of eight liveried oarsmen and assisted by a rising tide.

He was very happy to sit back and let the panorama of London unfold as they passed. "I'm ashamed how little I know of my own country," he remarked as he admired the classical façade of St Paul's cathedral, surmounted by its dome and twin spires.

"You cannot be blamed for that, Captain," the duchess assured him. "It was your duty to your country that has kept you from these shores."

"But must it continue to do so," his sister asked quietly, "especially now that the war is over?"

"The war with Napoleon is over," he reminded her. "There is still America—and the general defence of our realm."

"You have given over a quarter of a century to it," she cried. "Isn't it time you thought of yourself—and your family?"

She has also paid a price, he thought. And what do her children know of their mother's family? But what would he do without the navy? He would not want for money, but how would he occupy himself?

"I am committed to this voyage to America, but then we'll see," he temporised.

"We're passing Somerset House," the duchess announced. "Should you not salute, Captain Frobisher?"

"Not today, Duchess. Today is a holiday and the Navy Office can go to the devil as far as I'm concerned."

Olivia frowned at him and looked meaningfully at the little girls. He felt his face grow warm. "I beg your pardon for my intemperate language, ladies. I fear I must become re-accustomed to polite society. My mother would have rapped my knuckles, I may tell you."

"What did you say?" his nephew demanded.

The captain laughed. "You won't catch me out that easily, John."

They left the Palace of Westminster behind them and moved into the more open reaches of the Thames, past Vauxhall Pleasure Gardens and the Royal Hospital at Chelsea. Miranda came to sit on her uncle's knee and Tabitha leaned against her mother.

Flora put her arm around her. "Are you enjoying yourself, sweeting?"

The child nodded. "It's better than a stuffy carriage." She pointed. "Look, there are swans with their babies."

"Cygnets," her elder brother corrected her loftily.

"It's not the same without Father," John Rembleton, who had been very quiet up to now, declared.

"I know," Olivia agreed sympathetically, "but if you write up your journal as usual, we'll send it to him."

"How long will it take to reach him?" John grumbled. "We don't even know if he received the packet we sent to Rome and by now he may have left for Naples."

"Naples?" Captain Frobisher was immediately alert. "If you entrust it to me, my boy, I'll have it on the next ship out."

"Oh, would you, uncle?" The boy beamed. "That would be famous."

"There's Kew Palace," Flora's elder son broke the silence. "It won't be long now."

The company relapsed into silence, lulled by the rhythmic sweep of the oars and the wash of water against the boat. The air was fresher here, away from London's noxious vapours and the scent of sweet water diluted the salty tang of the tide.

"There's Teddington Lock," Rowland announced eagerly. The three boys rushed to the side of the barge as the rowers skilfully manoeuvred it into the chamber but the two girls looked uneasy as they saw the steep sides rise above them and the gates close behind their boat.

"Don't worry. We'll soon be lifted to the top, just watch," Flora said.

Water flooded in and gradually the shallop rose with it until it was able to leave the lock and continue up river. Above the lock, the Thames was much calmer. Soon they rounded the Hampton Court peninsula and it wasn't long before they pulled in at the landing stage below the main entrance to the palace.

"You say the King doesn't live here now?" Robert enquired.

"No, apparently he took a dislike to it as a young man," Flora replied. "They say he hasn't set foot here since he came to the throne and has permitted it to be divided into grace and favour apartments for old retainers."

"We come here for the tilt-yard and the maze," Olivia told him. "The boys like to imagine they are knights jousting and they love getting lost in the maze. It's the girls' first time," she added. "Until now we thought they were too young for the river journey."

"Lost, Mamma?" Miranda interrupted. "I don't want to be lost."

"It's not really lost, more like trying to solve a puzzle. But rest assured that Mamma knows the answer."

Relieved, the child ran after her brother and their friends.

"It's ingenious, isn't it?" Clare Adams remarked as they reached the centre chamber of the maze. "If you think to take the shortest, most obvious way, you soon find yourself at a standstill."

"A metaphor for life, perhaps," Lord Franklin suggested. He and Luke had agreed to drive their sisters out to Hampton Court to escape the heat of the city. None of them had been there before and it had taken several wrong turns and much retracing of steps before they found their way. Now they sat peacefully beneath the two tall trees that marked the centre. The silence was broken abruptly by children's voices.

"Bet I get there first!"

"Hah! I'm faster than you!"

"Line up to race properly," commanded a male voice that was clearly used to being obeyed. A man stooped at the end of the path and then stood back and waved two boys to him. "Toe the mark! Ready, steady, go!"

At the word, the boys raced towards the trees, followed more sedately by the rest of their party; two smaller girls, an older boy and the gentleman escorting two ladies.

The first boy burst into the space crying, "Victory" and raised his arms in triumph. When he saw the four people sitting there, he stumbled to a stop and made a very creditable bow to the two ladies.

"Beg pardon," he said gruffly.

"Well done," Lady Alys commended him. "That last stretch just cries out for a race, doesn't it?"

Olivia felt a little self-conscious when Mr Fitzmaurice rose to his feet as she and Flora entered the outdoor room. It would be the first time she had spoken to him since the masquerade; while she had not precisely avoided him, neither had she sought his company and whenever she looked, he was dancing with a different lady. After a flurry of greetings she gratefully accepted Lord Franklin's offer of his seat and chatted quietly to Miss Adams.

"I own I shall be glad to leave London," the girl said after a while, "In the heat it is quite unpleasant, but I'm sorry my first Season is at an end. I enjoyed it beyond anything, especially once my brother arranged for Lady Needham to chaperon me. Mamma is inclined to be delicate and was unable to attend many of the parties." She smiled affectionately. "He has always been a wonderful brother. He is ten years older than I and until now I have only known him at home." She laughed suddenly. "Just imagine, Mrs Rembleton, the first time I saw him in a London ballroom, I didn't recognise him. He is very different here in town, much more reserved." She nodded over to where her brother was talking to the two little girls. His face was alight with interest as he listened to their account of their river journey and how they had found their way through the maze. "That's the way I know him."

"Mamma knew, of course, but we wouldn't let her tell us," Miranda was saying importantly and Mr Fitzmaurice chuckled.

"You're going to be just like her when you grow up, I see."

Lord Franklin, who had been looking fixedly at Captain Frobisher, now exclaimed, "Corunna—that's where I know you from, sir. You took us off. You were a lieutenant then, as I was."

"Were you with Moore? That was a sad business. Aye, and the voyage home, the holds crammed with your poor wretches and a south-westerly to hurry us through the Bay of Biscay is one I've no wish to repeat."

The three boys immediately clamoured to hear more.

"Is there an inn near to which we may adjourn, Fitzmaurice?" his lordship enquired. "I'm sure we would all enjoy some refreshment—especially if Captain Frobisher and I are to answer all these questions."

"The *Kings Arms* is at the Lion Gate. Your Grace, Mrs Rembleton, may we have the pleasure of your company?"

"We should be delighted, Mr Fitzmaurice," Flora replied. "But we have reserved a private parlour for a late nuncheon. Perhaps you and your companions would care to join us?"

There was no gainsaying the duchess's invitation and together they began to make their way out of the maze, Luke bringing up the rear with Mrs Rembleton. She was more approachable today, he thought. She looked younger somehow.

"How old is your son?" he enquired.

"He'll be ten in December. He and Lord Jasper are of an age, as are Lady Tabitha and Miranda. Stanton is elder brother to all four, and to my Samuel. He is only four and too young for such an expedition." Her affection shone in her face when she spoke of her children.

Luke looked ahead to where his sister, Lady Alys and the two little girls walked together in matching couples, a blonde head close to a dark one. He caught his breath at the sight. It was odd how a memory could suddenly rise to haunt one.

"Is something the matter, Mr Fitzmaurice?"

Mrs Rembleton had tilted her head and dark golden eyes regarded him enquiringly from beneath the brim of her bonnet.

"Clare—my sister—had a twin, Cecily," he said abruptly.

"Had? I am so sorry."

"She died when they were seven. Clare is fair like me, but Cecily was dark. When I saw the two little ones together with my sister and Lady Alys—for a moment the happy past and an impossible present were before my eyes."

He felt her fingers clasp his arm more firmly. "I understand," she said sympathetically. "It must have been a shock."

He shook his head as if to clear it. "She stood before me again in that instant. But I am glad to have been reminded of her."

She pressed his arm again. "To remember them lovingly and joyfully is the best possible memorial to those we have lost. But it takes time, does it not, to achieve the tranquillity of mind that permits us to do so?"

"Yes."

They walked on in silence. By the time they turned the next corner, the others had vanished.

"Mrs Rembleton, your daughter assured me that you know the way through the maze. I hope she is right or we may be trapped here for ever."

"Fear not, Mr Fitzmaurice, I may not be Ariadne, but I have something better than a ball of thread." She fished in her reticule and triumphantly brandished a plan. "I never tell the boys I have this, for half the fun for them is in going astray. Now, we go right here and then left."

151

'To guide, to comfort and command,' Luke misquoted to himself with an inward grin as he obediently followed her instructions.

Olivia scolded herself as they rounded the hedge. You are altogether too aware of his changes of expression. Remember, while you are aware of what passed between you, he is not.

"Mamma!" Miranda called and ran to deposit a blood-stained handkerchief in her mother's outstretched hand. "Another tooth fell out."

"Did it, dearest? Let me see."

She blotted the child's mouth and inspected the new gap. "You can rinse your mouth when we are at the inn," she said comfortingly. "Does it hurt?"

"No. Will you mind the tooth for me? We must save it for Papa. I promised."

"Of course, dear." Olivia folded the handkerchief around the tooth and slipped it into her reticule. Miranda took her mother's hand and they walked on together.

"She's not at all like Mamma," Clare murmured to her brother as they fell in behind. "Her sensibilities were always too refined for such things."

"And yet she has given birth five times, once to twins," Luke responded before recollecting with horror that that was not a suitable comment for any lady's ears, let alone his sister's. "I beg your pardon, Clare."

To his relief, she laughed and tucked her hand into his arm. "Now I know I am truly grown-up, Luke, when you say such a thing to me. You'll be telling me warm stories next."

"Still, I shouldn't have said it—it's disrespectful to our mother as well as to you."

Chapter Fifteen

"What are your plans for the summer, Fitzmaurice?" Lord Franklin enquired. He and Luke, feeling they had done their fraternal duty for the day, had retreated to the *Crossed Swords* for a bout. There were few others there and the two men had gone down afterwards to the taproom where they were addressing a beef and kidney pie.

Luke waved for more ale. "I'm considering popping over to Brussels, maybe go on to Paris. Unlike you, I've been trapped here for the last ten years. And you?"

"I'm looking forward to going home," the viscount admitted. "I hadn't reckoned with being pitchforked into the Season immediately on my return. Now I'm the heir, I must get acquainted with the estate in a different way."

"What about your bride?" Luke enquired with a grin.

Franklin rolled his eyes. "I know I must marry but to be candid, the only lady I would like to get to know better is Miss Gregg, if only I knew how to go about it. I met her again at Mrs Frome's musicale. My mother asked me to escort her and my sisters."

"And for once you didn't complain?"

"Complain? A dutiful son and brother like me?" He sighed. "She was there and run off her feet. It annoyed me to see her so."

"Did you speak to her?"

"Very briefly. I was conscious of Mrs Rembleton's remarks and careful not to single Miss Gregg out, especially as Mrs Frome made a point of seating me beside Miss Frome."

"There would be hell to pay if you were thought to favour the companion over the daughter," Luke agreed. "Maybe it's because she provides a connection to your old life. The attraction might fade once you become more reconciled to your new one. Could you tell your parents you need some time to adjust, to make sure you don't make the wrong choice?"

"I could try. The next heir after me is a cousin. I don't really know him, but my father says he's a wastrel."

"See if you can hold out until next Season. Then, if you are still interested in Miss Gregg, I think you should make a push for it. Her family is respectable, I take it?"

"Perfectly," his lordship said shortly. "What of you? Have you never thought of matrimony?"

"No. There is no imperative as in your case and I've never met a female I want to be leg-shackled to. There are plenty of unsatisfied wives to keep me amused," he added with a reminiscent smile.

"Another reason not to make a ton marriage," Franklin agreed. "Not many ladies follow the drum, but most who do are in every sense help-meets. They are real, Fitzmaurice, as your society ladies are not. Oddly, Mrs Rembleton and the duchess are different—they are good mothers at least. But where are their husbands? Have they no place in their lives?"

"If not, the fault is most likely to be laid at the gentlemen's doors," Luke said fairly. "The duchess is known to look out for young wives whose husbands are—distant, shall we say? She encourages them to be independent, to make their own lives. They're known as Flora's fillies."

"I'm not sure I would want to have my wife included in their ranks."

"Then she will have to be someone you are not inclined to neglect."

His lordship threw up his hands at this. "And so we're come full circle! Landlord, more ale!"

Once back at home Olivia was quickly absorbed by her usual rounds. Thoughts of routs and masquerades yielded to discussions of the harvest and memories of Prince Hamlet were superseded by the news that John was feverish and had broken out in a rash. This proved to be the chicken-pox, which he generously passed on to his sister and brother as well as two young maids and a footman. It took four weeks for the infection to pass from the manor and another two for the parish to be declared free of it. Olivia was worn out between nursing her children and doing the best she could for her stricken tenants and was delighted to accept Anne Heriot's invitation to bring the children to stay for a fortnight.

I'm sure the sea-air can only do them good, Anne wrote. *Our land runs down to a very sheltered cove so they may bathe if they wish; indeed Charles swims twice a week. He swears by the sea-water, we even bring it up to the house for him when the weather is too inclement to go in.*

Although she knew he was only forty, Mr Heriot seemed to Olivia to be nearer fifty, with the worn look of one who has suffered a life-time of illness. He had a weak chest and could not tolerate the city air which provoked prolonged, debilitating paroxysms of coughing that frequently led to an inflammation of the lungs. Each time he took longer to recover and in the end had bowed to his doctor's strongly worded advice that he remain at home, although he insisted that his wife continue to enjoy her annual visit.

"Welcome, Mrs Rembleton," he said, courteously coming to his feet when they entered the parlour. He solemnly shook hands with the three children.

"So you've been out of sorts, have you? We'll soon put that right. You'll feel much more the thing once you've had a few days of our fine sea air."

"Do you think we might find some fossils, sir?" John enquired hopefully, "perhaps some snake-stones or devils' fingers?"

"You might indeed. But how do you know this is a good place for them?"

"I consulted my father's encyclopaedia regarding the natural phenomena of the area," the boy explained proudly.

At this, Mr Heriot exclaimed "Rembleton? Never say that you are Rambling Jack's son! Why did you not tell me, Anne?"

"I suppose I thought you knew, dear."

"Do you know my father, sir?" John enquired.

"I heard some of his lectures at the Royal Society. It is a pity he is not with you."

"He's looking at volcanoes in Italy," Miranda explained.

Olivia sat on a rock looking out to sea. Beside her, Anne's two-year-old son Ned slept in the shade of a large parasol that had been planted in the sand. He was weary from helping the older children build a sandcastle. Now they were busy digging a channel so that the moat would be filled by the incoming tide.

"This was a wonderful idea, Anne," Olivia sighed. "I can't thank you enough."

"I'm enjoying having some of my London life here. I don't know why I never thought of it before. At times, I think I'm two people. That month in London does so much for me, Olivia. We live very quietly here, as you see, and my London sojourn provides welcome stimulation for all of us. Charles must hear of all my doings while his mother loves to hear the ton gossip and the descriptions of the latest modes, the more extravagant the better, although you would never think it to look at her. I keep a journal cum scrapbook for him and bring the latest books and music back with me, not to mention some new gowns."

"Do you tell him everything?" Olivia asked enviously, unable to imagine having such a connection with Jack.

"Most of it, but nothing hurtful or malicious—neither of us is that way inclined. He likes to know about the latest plays and operas. He reads the reviews, but it's not the same, he says."

"Did you tell him about the masquerade?" Olivia felt uneasy at the thought.

"Yes, but not all about the muses," Anne reassured her. "That was not only my secret, after all. I described them, but as if I had seen them, for it was reported everywhere, remember, and it would have been odd if I hadn't mentioned them. I said I went with some friends but he was not to press me as to who they were."

"He must trust you very much," Olivia remarked.

"He knows he may," Anne said simply. She lowered her voice. "I didn't have a chance to talk to you before I left town. I saw you dancing with Luke Fitzmaurice. My mother-in-law is his stepfather's sister so we are in a sort of a way connected. His sister Miss Adams is Charles' cousin."

Olivia stared at her, appalled. "You will not give me away, Anne?"

"Of course not. But do you mean he doesn't know who you were? Surely you have danced together before?"

"Once, a very long time ago, before there were any waltzes. I was just married. Since then he has never asked me to stand up with him."

"So you took matters into your own hands. He's an excellent dancer, isn't he?"

Olivia felt her cheeks grow warm. "Yes," she agreed.

A jubilant shout from the children heralded the flood of water into the moat and Olivia, glad of the opportunity to break off the conversation, went down to admire this great feat of engineering. The week had done wonders for the children who had lost the pasty complexion of illness and, despite her best efforts to make them wear their hats, glowed from the effects of the wind and the sun.

"Look, we've made boats from mussel shells." Miranda carefully launched one. It floated for a few seconds before it tilted and took in water.

"See if you can find one that is more evenly shaped," Olivia recommended. "That one is too lop-sided."

"It's time we went back to the house," Anne decreed when a pitiful wail announced that Ned had woken fractious from his nap.

Olivia surveyed her damp, sandy offspring and shook her head in mock disapproval. "You're unfit for society at present. We'll have to take you in through the back door."

"Send nurse down to collect Ned," Anne called after the children as they ran ahead.

At the house she gratefully handed over her son and continued towards the door to the hall where the butler was apparently addressing a new arrival.

"Mr Heriot is in the library, sir."

Conscious of her unkempt appearance, Anne peeped to see who the caller might be, then hurried forward. "Luke! I thought you still in Brussels. Charles will be so pleased to have a report from the continent."

"I came home a couple of weeks ago." He took her outstretched hands. "You look blooming, Anne."

"Untidy, you mean. We were down at the sea-shore with the children."

He released her hands and sketched a bow to Olivia. "We meet in the most unusual places, Mrs Rembleton."

Anne's eyes flew to Olivia at this comment. To her surprise her friend was not in the least flustered but replied, "The last time was the centre of Hampton Court Maze, as I recall, sir."

"Go in to Charles while we make ourselves respectable," Anne ordered Luke. "His mother will be delighted to see you, too. I have told her what I know of Clare's Season, but I was only in town for the one month."

"I am charged with all sorts of messages from my mother and stepfather. When they heard I would be in the vicinity, they insisted I must call."

"I should hope so. You'll stay for a few days, I hope."

"If you have a bed for me."

"I daresay we'll find a straw pallet somewhere," she retorted and headed for the stairs.

Grinning, Luke stood back to let the ladies pass. Who would have thought austere Mrs Rembleton could look so deliciously dishevelled? Her bonnet sat askew on tousled curls. A streak of pink on her nose suggested she had been overlong in the sun and the hem of her muslin gown was sandy. As she went up the stairs, she revealed bare legs with prettily turned ankles and, with a reminiscent pang, he recalled Thalia's seductive sandals.

As usual, the children came to the drawing-room for the hour before dinner. It was a merry, informal gathering. Miranda went to show Mr Heriot the latest additions to her collection of seashells while John played beggar-my-neighbour with old Mrs Heriot. The two smaller boys wandered from group to group, Samuel astride a hobby-horse and Ned pulling a little dog on wheels. Tiring of this, he raised his arms to Mrs Rembleton.

"Rant an' Roar," he demanded.

"I told you you'd be sorry you ever started it," Anne remarked.

"Rant an' Roar," Ned insisted and Mrs Rembleton stood up.

To Luke's fascinated amusement, she began to sing '*Spanish Ladies*'. When she came to the chorus, she picked Ned up and, holding him under his arms, swung him exuberantly from side to side in time to, '*We'll rant and we'll roar like true British sailors*'. Her children joined in the singing, swaying and stamping around the room. At the final line, '*And here's to the health of each true-hearted lass*,' her sons gave a smacking buss each to their mother and sister, while Mrs Rembleton lifted Ned so that he could kiss Anne.

Mr Heriot brushed a kiss on his own mother's cheek. "We can't leave you out, Mamma."

"Again," Ned commanded from his mother's arms.

Olivia shook her head. "I've no breath left."

"It's a sailors' song, isn't it?" Luke asked. "Where did you learn it?"

"You ask that of the daughter and sister of naval officers, Mr Fitzmaurice?" The warm smile in Olivia's voice belied her reproof. "My father was used to sing it with us and kiss Mamma and me like that, but my brother, who is ten years older, told me that Papa staggered round the room with him as if he were trying to maintain his footing in a rolling sea. I did it with my children, too, but even Samuel is too big for me to lift now. As you see, they manage to rant and roar very well by themselves," she added, laughing. "Papa used sing '*Come away, Fellow Sailors*' as well and Mamma would shake her finger at him and respond with '*Sigh No More Ladies*'."

"You must sing them for us after dinner," Anne said. "Here are nurse and Miss Carstairs to take the children back upstairs."

Talk at dinner was mainly of Miss Adam's Season and Olivia, having commended Luke's sister as both pretty and accomplished, was content to listen. Mr Fitzmaurice sat beside Mrs

Heriot, with Olivia taking the opposite side of the table and she had to discipline her thoughts to stop them straying back to Burlington House. When the ladies withdrew, she slipped up to the nursery. Samuel was asleep already, exhausted from his day, but the other two were awake.

John yawned hugely. "It must be nice to have your father living with you all the time like Ned does. You didn't have that either when you were a child, did you, Mamma?"

"No. Your grandfather was away for years at a time. Much longer than Papa. But it didn't stop him loving me, and I loved him."

"Maybe there will be a letter waiting for us when we get home," the boy said wistfully.

"I'm sure he'll write soon and tell you all about Vesuvius," Olivia consoled him. "You have a lot to put into your journal, too."

"I hope you will sing those two songs for us, Mrs Rembleton," Mrs Heriot said when the gentlemen had joined them.

Olivia complied, and was instantly transported back to her childhood. Despite all the time her parents spent apart, they had truly loved one another. They were richer than they knew.

"You gentlemen may not leave the entertainment solely to us ladies." Anne declared afterwards. "Will you read to us, Luke?"

"What would you like to hear?"

"Some Shakespeare," her mother-in-law said. "When Hamlet spies the ghost, perhaps."

"If Charles will join me, we could do the ghost scenes from the first act. What say you, Charles?"

"Why not?"

Mr Heriot read well in a gentlemanly fashion, but Mr Fitzmaurice's reading was of a different order entirely. You couldn't call it acting, precisely; he remained seated and was not given to gesticulation, but his intensity, his varied tone and the euphony of his voice together with his subtle changes of position and expression all served to make his characters live.

It awoke bitter-sweet memories in Olivia, who could so readily conjure his image in the garb of Hamlet and from there it took but a moment to see him naked and blindfolded in her arms or reclining on his cushions afterwards like a pasha assessing a new odalisque as he told her to lift her skirts higher. Her face grew hot as she remembered how she had enjoyed obeying his command. She felt a dull ache at the base of her stomach and had to bite the inside of her cheek to distract herself from these tempting memories. Fortunately the others were so engrossed in the performance that they noticed nothing and by the time it was over, she had regained her composure.

"Thank you, Luke." Mrs Heriot broke the rapt silence. "I vow Mr Garrick could not have done it better. I only saw him the once, when I was sixteen, but have never forgotten it." She smiled. "He had a special wig made for Hamlet so that he could make his hair stand on end when he saw the ghost."

"You had no need of that to convince us of your horror, Mr Fitzmaurice," Olivia said, "and Mr Heriot was most effective as the ghost."

"Can you imagine Edmund Kean with such a wig?" Anne asked and the conversation turned to the actor who had burst onto the London scene earlier in the year with an ecstatically received performance of Shylock at the Drury Lane Theatre.

Chapter Sixteen

"We're going for a nature walk, Mrs Rembleton," the governess said when Olivia visited the old schoolroom the next morning. "Little Ned had a disturbed night; Nurse said he's cutting his back teeth. He is not used to other children on this floor and we might disturb him if we remain here."

"Will you come too, Mamma?" Samuel asked.

"We'll see. There may be something I can do for Mrs Heriot."

"Mr Heriot said there's a splendid chestnut tree in the park," John said thoughtfully. "I wonder can you play conqueror with chestnuts."

Olivia smiled at him. "What would your father say?"

The boy grinned. "There's only one way to find out," he quoted, just as Miranda announced, "Try it and see."

Anne showed signs of a wakeful night. "He's asleep now," she replied in answer to Olivia's enquiry. "His poor cheek is very red and hot and he is a little feverish, I think."

"You could try bathing it with a cool infusion of chamomile and see if he will take a little on a spoon. It should reduce the inflammation," Olivia suggested.

"I'll try anything now," Anne sighed.

"Is there anything I can do to help you?"

"In fact there is. I'm long overdue to visit to Charles' old nurse who lives with her daughter about eight miles away. I had been going to suggest we go over this morning—it's a pleasant drive—but I don't like to leave Ned. Would you mind going on your own? Take Martin with you, of course. I would suggest my mother-in-law accompany you, but she and Nurse don't always agree and if they start to argue—well, you will wish you were anywhere else but there."

Mr Fitzmaurice laughed. "I have once had the privilege of observing such a battle, Mrs Rembleton. You are well advised to avoid the possibility. Why don't I drive you?"

"I would escort you myself ma'am, but am committed to my land-steward today," Mr Heriot put in. "Take the phaeton, Luke, it will do better on those roads than your curricle and you may give your pair a rest."

"If you really don't mind, Mr Fitzmaurice," Olivia said, "then I accept your kind offer with pleasure."

Mrs Legg was more than pleased to receive Mrs Rembleton and Mr Fitzmaurice. She clucked sympathetically when told of Ned's distress and immediately went to fetch a little bottle of a potion she swore by in such cases. "A drop or two rubbed into the gums and he'll sleep all night," she said.

Luke sniffed at it when their hostess had left the room to store the contents of the basket Anne had sent and murmured to Olivia, "I've no doubt he will. Pure moonshine, I would say."

"Moonshine?" she whispered.

"Illicit liquor," he explained.

"Hush, she's coming."

"You'll take a glass of my daughter's cowslip wine, sir, madam?" Mrs Legg bustled back into the room carrying a tray with a dusty bottle and three glasses.

Olivia had to repress a giggle at the look on her companion's face when he tasted the sweet liquid. Luke noticed her dancing eyes and had his revenge when, upon being pressed to another glass, he declined piously. "Not for me, ma'am, not when I have charge of a strange team, but I know Mrs Rembleton would greatly appreciate another." He met her dagger-look over the old woman's head with a bland smirk and she rewarded him by swapping remedies for childish ailments with the old woman for quite half an hour until he rose purposefully to his feet saying, "We must be on our way, ma'am".

Clouds scudded overhead as they left the cottage and Luke cast an anxious glance to the south-west where a darker line in the sky foreshadowed rain. I hope it holds off, he thought, setting the team to as fast a pace as he dared along the narrow, wind-ing country lane. They were protected to some degree by high hedges and it was only when they turned south onto the wider toll-road that he realised the extent to which the south-west wind had increased. It now drove the clouds before it and already he could feel on his face the prickle of not yet visible rain. He swore to himself and pulled up the horses.

"Hold them steady while I put up the hood," he ordered, transferring the reins to Mrs Rembleton. He noted approvingly her competent grasp of them—no need to worry there—and jumped down just as the squall hit them.

The first strong gust lifted her bonnet, whipping it over the hedge and across a field where she could see it lodge in a tall tree. Luke managed to clap a hand to his own hat in time to pre-vent it following. He handed it to his passenger for safe-keeping, deeming it useless to try to wear it despite the tempestuous rain. Swearing to himself, he struggled with the fastenings on either side of the carriage, but by the time the hood was up and he could regain his seat, they were both drenched.

"I can turn so that the rain comes from behind us—the hood will afford us more protection that way—and we can try and wait it out, or we can head for the *Two Pheasants* a mile or so down the road."

"Let's do that," she decided. "We can hardly get any wetter."

He flashed a quick grin. "Hold tight, Mrs Rembleton."

He concentrated on guiding his team along the wet road but was briefly distracted by his passenger who unfolded the rug he had earlier laid over her knees and extended it to cover his also. He did not protest but merely said, "Thank you. We're nearly there."

A groom ran to the horses' heads when they clattered into the small yard and a side door was held hospitably open.

"Come this way sir, ma'am," a buxom landlady directed. "You have had a soaking to be sure. We saw you from upstairs, so I've had fires lit in the two bedchambers and I'll send up hot water as soon as may be. Barton," she instructed her husband, "do you see to the gentleman and I'll look after his lady."

He saw Mrs Rembleton blink at this last but she said nothing. It was a natural assumption, he supposed and better to leave it stand.

"Mary," Mrs Barton called into the kitchen. "Make an egg flip quickly, there's a good girl. There's nothing like it for warming a body up." As she spoke, she chivvied her unexpected guests up a narrow stairs to two small bedrooms under the eaves where fires blazed cheerfully.

"There, ma'am." The landlady helped Olivia remove her carriage dress. "We can spread it across this chair towards the fire. Here are towels for your hair."

"Thank you, ma'am, you are very kind." Olivia took the pins out of the hair that had all but tumbled down in the wind and blotted it with the towels.

"I'll just fetch you a shawl, ma'am, and if you would accept a comb? It's quite new. I bought it from a pedlar only yesterday."

Before Olivia knew it, she was wrapped in a warm shawl over her petticoat and sitting on the floor by the fire, combing her hair to help it dry. A generous mug of egg flip on top of the cowslip wine left her warm and muzzy-headed, content to drift in the moment. She felt her dress and turned it, spreading another section of the skirt towards the flames.

Clad only in shirt and buckskins, Luke tapped on the door beside his and after a moment pushed it open a crack, only to be transfixed by the sight of Mrs Rembleton veiled in a luxurious fall of vibrant hair of all shades from palest gold to dark brown, spread over a rich green shawl that reached to the skirts of a lawn petticoat. She was singing softly to herself, swaying slightly as she worked on a recalcitrant tangle at the back of her head.

" 'Now let ev'ry man drink off his full bumper,
And let ev'ry man drink off his full glass,
We'll drink and be jolly and drown melancholy,
And here's to the health of each true-hearted lass.' "

As Luke watched, she dropped her arms and shook her shoulders as if to ease them, causing the shawl to slip a little.

"Let me," he said, crossing the room towards her.

"Mr Fitzmaurice!" She turned her head and tried to scramble to her feet.

"Pray don't get up, ma'am. I just came to see if you had everything you wanted and note you are in need of a lady's maid." He took the comb from her hand and dropped to his knees behind her.

"This is most improper," she scolded.

"None of it is proper, Mrs Rembleton, but who's to know? There's no one here but us and the Bartons assume we are man and wife."

As he spoke, Luke gently drew the comb through the long tresses, patiently unravelling the tangles. She did not protest any more but resumed humming '*Spanish Ladies*'.

"Is your father still at sea?" he asked casually, gently lifting another strand of hair and resisting the temptation to drop a quick kiss on the white nape that was bared to him. He had always admired the way her proud head was poised on her neck.

"He was killed at Trafalgar," she answered softly.

"I'm sorry," he said gently.

"It's almost ten years ago now. Like you and your sister, I'm glad to remember him."

Her face was turned away from him and he was reminded suddenly of another lady whom he hadn't been permitted to see. He shifted uneasily, too aware of the scent of orange-blossom rising from her hair and the way the shawl threatened to slip from her sloping shoulder.

He finished the strand of hair he was working on and carefully drew all her hair back from her forehead to hang down her back almost to her waist. Now that it was completely dry it formed a cloud of curl.

"I never realised you had so much hair," he murmured. "It's magnificent. How do you manage it?"

"With difficulty," she admitted. "How many hair pins are there? On the table," she added.

He glanced over. "At least a dozen."

"That will have to do. I wish I had a hairbrush." She began to gather her hair together at the nape of her neck. "I wonder if Mrs Barton has a spare bonnet she could lend me."

"I'm sure she does." He absently stroked his hand down the beautiful curve of her neck towards her shoulder and was stunned when she stooped her cheek to it in a fleeting caress. Only one other woman had ever done that. She did not seem to realise what she had done, but dropped her hair to turn and feel the dress that was spread out towards the fire.

"It's dry," she said, "and the rain has stopped. We can go."

Luke did not reply but remained kneeling, his eyes fixed on the little wavy scar on the edge of her right ear. Holding his breath, he reached out and touched it lightly.

"Mr Fitzmaurice?" She turned to face him and he gently lifted her left hand to inspect the little finger. His hand shook.

"You're Thalia," he accused her.

Even if she had thought to deny it, she was betrayed by the deep blush that rose from the top of her breasts to flood her neck and face.

"You're Thalia," he repeated. "The last woman I would have imagined."

The wave of red receded leaving her completely white, but she was apparently unable or unwilling to respond.

"Don't be frightened," Luke said, amused. "I'm not going to post it in the *Gazette*." He was pleased he could speak so nonchalantly, for if truth were told, he was as shocked as she was. More perhaps, for she did not seem surprised that he had been her partner.

But then she knew who I was. I made no attempt at concealment, he realised. Why had that never occurred to him before? It changed things somehow. While he had been dallying with a stranger, she had not. Did that make things better or worse? He stood, lifted her dress off the chair and spread it on the bed.

"Come, sweetheart."

She blinked at the endearment but let him help her first to stand and then to sit on the chair.

He peered into the saucepan of flip that had been set on a trivet beside the fire. "Will you take a little more?"

She suddenly found her tongue. "I had better not, I think, sir. It is stronger than I supposed."

"Some coffee then and perhaps a sandwich. We can't delay much longer."

He left the room and by the time he returned, accompanied by the landlady bearing a tray, Thalia had contrived to put up her hair and don her gown.

"Would you do up my gown please, Mrs Barton?" she asked calmly.

"Certainly, madam." She put the tray down and nimbly fastened the laces. "Your husband says you're in need of a bonnet. It won't be anything fancy, mind."

She did not repudiate him, but just said, "I should be very grateful if you can help me."

Mrs Barton disappeared, returning five minutes later with a simple straw bonnet that was trimmed with black ribbons and a small black rose. "Should I remove the veil, ma'am?"

"No, no. It will do admirably. I'll send it back first thing in the morning. And I hope you'll accept this as thanks for all your kindness, Mrs Barton."

The landlady allowed a guinea to be pressed into her hand. "Not at all, ma'am. I'm only too glad to have been of service."

"Anne will be wondering where we are." Luke's passenger broke the uneasy silence that had prevailed since they had left the *Two Pheasants*.

He glanced sideways, irritated that he couldn't see her face under the deep brim of the bonnet and frustrated that she apparently wished to obliterate the memory of that passionate encounter in Burlington House.

"You can't pretend it didn't happen, Thalia."

"Mrs Rembleton, if you please sir," she corrected him coolly. "And nothing happened. You were content not to know then and I cannot see how it matters that you know now."

How could she fob him off like that? Had those hours in truth meant nothing to her? Incensed and wounded, he enquired in his most sardonic drawl, "Tell me, Mrs Rembleton is it a favourite amusement of yours to blindfold your partners, as if they are unworthy to behold you?"

She did not reply, but despite being seated beside him in a moving carriage, contrived to cut him as directly as if she had crossed the street to avoid passing him too nearly. Carefully edging towards the side of the phaeton, so that not even an inch of her sleeve or skirts touched him, she reached up to lower her veil. A slight turn of her head and shoulder was all she needed to dismiss him from her notice.

He was still debating inwardly whether to ignore her just as comprehensively or goad her into response when his team was thrown into disarray by a flurry of hens chased by a barking dog. Controlling the horses with an iron hand, he skirted around the fowl, flicking his whip at the dog to ensure he kept his distance from the wheels. Damn all women and particularly her, he thought wrathfully, remembering the delirium of the weeks when he had been unable to expel Thalia from his mind. Sometime it is better if our wishes remain unfulfilled.

A ray of sun pierced the clouds as he cast another sidelong glance. To his horror, tiny drops sparkled on her black veil. It's only a sprinkling of raindrops shaken from the leaves, he assured himself, unable to bear the thought that they might be tears.

Olivia sat upright, her gaze fixed on the horizon to her right, one hand pressed against her stomach and one against her compressed lips. She blinked furiously and prayed that she would make it back to the Grange without disgracing herself either by giving in to the nausea that threatened to overwhelm her or losing control of the tears that filled her eyes and were at risk of spilling down her cheeks.

She jumped down from the carriage immediately they pulled up, almost stumbling in her haste to get inside the house before Fitzmaurice could hand his team to a groom and accompany her. She reached her bedchamber in safety and rang for Martin.

"*Mon Dieu, Madame.* What has happened?"

"We were caught in a heavy shower of rain," Olivia replied drearily. "I want a bath and then I'm going to bed. I don't feel at all the thing. Please make my excuses to Mrs Heriot."

Anne stood beside Olivia's bed, looking down anxiously at her friend. "Luke tells me you were caught in a downpour."

"Yes. Between him and Mrs Barton at the *Two Pheasants*, I was admirably looked after, but despite it all I have the headache. Pray excuse me, Anne, but I would prefer not to come down to dinner tonight."

"Of course. You must do just as you like and Martin should tell Cook what you feel like eating."

Olivia made a face. "Some tea and a slice of toast, perhaps. Nothing more. But later."

"What shall I say to the children?"

"Just tell them I have a migraine. It doesn't happen very often, but when it does, it lays me low. Miss Carstairs may bring them in to say goodnight when it's their bedtime." She smiled wanly. "It will amuse them to tuck me in for a change."

Anne nodded. "I'll tell her to bring them down to the drawing-room as usual."

"Thank you."

Martin returned to Olivia's bedside once she had closed the door behind Anne. "Should you like tea now, *Madame*?"

"No thank you, Martin. Look in in an hour, please and see how I feel then. I'll try to sleep."

"Very good, *Madame*. I'll refresh the lavender compress first. That one is almost dry."

Olivia felt the linen handkerchief lifted from her forehead and another one, soaked in lavender water, replace it. The cool liquid and aromatic astringency of the lavender soothed her and eased the tension in her temples.

"Thank you."

The maid tiptoed out and Olivia sighed with relief to be alone. But behind her closed eyelids she saw Mr Fitzmaurice's disdainful face. His derisive query rang in her ears. '*Is it a favourite amusement of yours to blindfold your partners, as if they are unworthy to behold you?*' A sob escaped her. The blindfold had been his idea. It would never have occurred to her. Did he have to spoil the memory of that night for her? She had so little. What had he expected? Was she to fall into his arms and take advantage of the bed that was so conveniently in the room? The thoughts swarmed in her head like wasps from a nest and in trying to evade one sting she must suffer another until at last she could drop into a fitful sleep.

"Leave them with us, Miss Carstairs," Anne said to the governess. "You will be glad of the respite, I have no doubt."

"Thank you, ma'am. But they have been very good," the young woman added before she departed.

"Is Mrs Rembleton not joining us?" Luke enquired from the window where he had been brooding silently.

"She has the megrim," John explained.

"Poor Mamma," Miranda said. "She's hardly ever ill. I'm sad when she's not well."

This made Luke feel even more guilty. How could he have said that to her? He had not doubted Thalia's inexperience that night for one moment. He remembered silently cursing her anonymous husband as a clumsy and insensitive oaf and now that he knew who that gentleman was, he renewed his maledictions. He couldn't imagine what had induced her to break the chaste habit of years, but he should feel honoured and protective of her. He had no excuse for lashing out at her like that. Having been privileged to awaken her passion and, more recently, seen how warmly maternal she was, he could only imagine how she felt, trapped in a joyless marriage to an indifferent fool who had all but abandoned her and his children. She had been right to point out that the circumstances had not changed.

Her sons were showing a collection of chestnuts to Mr Heriot while trying to prevent Ned from grabbing one and stuffing it into his mouth. With an effort, Luke smiled down at Miranda. "Are you too old for stories?" he asked her.

She shook her head.

"Would you like me to tell you one I used to tell my sister when she was a little girl?"

"And Mr Fitzmaurice told us stories," Miranda told her mother. "First Cinderella, just for me, and then Puss in Boots for the boys as well."

"That was very kind of him."

"Are you indeed better, Mamma?"

"I am, darling," Olivia assured her. "Come, kiss me goodnight."

"First I'll tuck you in." Miranda had to climb on the bed to achieve this and took the opportunity to half-strangle her mother with a hug.

"Goodnight, Mamma. Sleep well."

John helped Samuel down from the bed and then kissed his mother's cheek. "Should I blow out the candle?"

"No darling, thank you. Good night."

It was noon. He could delay no longer. Luke had hoped to attempt some sort of an apology before departing, but apparently Mrs Rembleton had not yet left her room. Almost as if she had been waiting for the right moment, she came down the stairs just as he was making his final farewells to his hosts in the hall. As remote as ever he had seen her, she met his gaze without flinching. She did not offer her hand and her distant nod and polite smile cut him to the quick.

"I wish you a safe journey, Mr Fitzmaurice."

He bowed briefly. "Thank you, Mrs Rembleton." He hesitated. "I trust you took no harm from your drenching yesterday?"

"No, I thank you."

Her voice was so frosty that there was clearly no more to be said. Luke bowed again and picked up his hat and gloves. When he turned for a final farewell to Charles and Anne at the front door, Thalia, no, Mrs Rembleton had already retreated up the stairs. Somehow he managed to repress the urge to follow her and shake a response from her. He mechanically mouthed the final platitudes and five minutes later whipped up his team, barely holding them in check until he had rounded the bend in the drive and was out of sight of the house.

Fitzmaurice, you're an arrant clodpoll if ever there was one, he said to himself. You finally find her and the first thing you do is insult her! He smiled wryly at the echo of his first meeting with the lady. She had been kinder then, but that time he had blundered unintentionally while yesterday he had burned to prick that damned composure of hers. It was ironic that he should feel that immediate attraction, that compulsion towards a female, only twice in his life and each time for the same, unattainable lady. Now he had spoiled not only those memories but also the easy amity they had enjoyed during the past few days with Charles and Anne.

It had started in the maze, he realised. She was less prickly, more at ease with you then. She noticed your upset when you saw the four girls together and you were able to talk to her about Cecily. She must have felt a connection between you, even if you weren't aware of it. Obscurely comforted, he drove on.

Chapter Seventeen

My Lord and Sovereign Master,

More than ten years ago you entrusted to me the task of describing to you the habits and customs of the Britons, and more particularly of the English and longer ago than that I left my home at your behest. I begin to feel the weight of my years and, regretfully, must humbly beg you to recall me to your side. I would die on my native soil. However, while awaiting your august reply, I remain wholly at your service and shall continue to furnish you with my observations to the best of my ability.

Luke raised his pen. Where had that come from? But, yes, it was time Otanes took his leave. He had been a useful vessel but after ten years, he was no longer a novelty. Besides, was it not cowardly to hide behind a pseudonym? Other, braver writers had taken up their pens. He had no wish to share the fate of the Hunt brothers, imprisoned and fined for libelling the Prince Regent, but it must be possible to work openly for reform. Hearing Franklin's voice in the hallway, he carefully blotted his page and put it into his desk.

"So keen to see the new Juliet?" he asked his friend as he took his hat and gloves from his manservant.

"One hears great things of her from Dublin."

"As long as she doesn't speak with that terrible brogue," Luke commented, accepting his cane and going to the hall door. "After you, my lord!"

There was a buzz of excitement from the pit and the tiers of boxes were fuller than one might expect in October, especially with Parliament still in recess.

"She really is exquisite isn't she?" Olivia remarked to Flora.

"Miss O'Neill? Yes and how well she portrays a girl half her age just coming out into society. There was no brashness or forwardness, just maidenly modesty."

"Although Juliet is forward enough later on," Olivia could not help pointing out. "Poor Romeo; one evening of flirtation and she demands marriage!"

"Have you no heart for romance, oh proper Mrs Rembleton?" Flora teased, just as a light tap on the door of the box announced a visitor.

It was Mr Fitzmaurice. Olivia stiffened but did not shrink and offered her hand when he turned to her having greeted the duchess. He bowed gravely over it.

"Lady Benton has charged me to convey her invitation to a supper party after the play. She begs you will excuse the short notice, Duchess, but she was not aware you and Mrs Rembleton were in town."

"We only came up today," Flora said. "We shall be delighted to accept, shall we not, Mrs Rembleton? Mr Fitzmaurice, may we impose upon you to let the countess know?"

"It will be my pleasure, Duchess."

"May I beg the favour of five minutes conversation with you, Mrs Rembleton?" Mr Fitzmaurice asked quietly when they met again at Lady Benton's.

Olivia felt suddenly hot and then very cold as if someone had thrown a bucket of water over her. She glanced around quickly but nobody appeared to take any notice of them. She felt ill. There could only be one subject he wished to discuss with her. Was he going to sneer at her again, or worse, press her to repeat their encounter? He had always seemed to delight in provoking her and she had handed him a fine weapon that night at Burlington House. She tried to remain impassive as these barely formed thoughts tumbled through her mind, but he must have noticed something of her inner turmoil.

"I swear I will do or say nothing to distress you," he murmured. "If anyone should comment, we may say that you brought me news of my cousin Heriot."

She scanned his face. He appeared to be sincere; he was pale and unusually solemn.

"Very well." She put her hand on his arm and strolled with him towards the door of the drawing-room. "Indeed, poor Mr Heriot was quite unwell when we left."

"He gets weaker every year. It seems that each winter takes its toll. It is such a pity, for he is an excellent fellow."

"Most charming and not at all invalidish," Olivia agreed. "It must take a particular courage to remain in good spirits all the time, as Mrs Heriot tells me he does. And he insists she come to town every year."

I'm sure he knows of a secluded room in every house in London, she thought disparagingly when he guided her to a quiet parlour. Leaving the door ajar, he led her to the window where they could not be overheard and turned to face her.

"Mrs Rembleton, I am so very sorry for what I said to you on the way back from the *Two Pheasants*. I deeply regret having insulted you with such an unfair and uncalled for insinuation. I beg you will accept my heartfelt apology." He spoke simply and without any of his usual nonchalance; his eyes fixed on hers in almost painful anticipation of her answer.

How could she not soften towards him, Olivia wondered, when he spoke so in earnest? "I accept your apology," she said with equal simplicity.

His tense features eased and a sigh escaped him. "You are very gracious, Thalia."

"Let us forget it, sir—all of it," she added meaningfully, but not unkindly.

He took her hand and kissed it. She looked at the fair head bent before her and longed to run her fingers through his hair.

"I will never refer to it again," he vowed, "but believe me, Thalia, I shall cherish the memory of our hours together to my dying day." Almost involuntarily, it seemed, his hand rose to touch her cheek and she could not resist letting it rest fleetingly in his palm.

"I too, sir," she whispered and stepped back. "I must go."

Luke curled his fingers to retain her caress, grateful beyond measure for this parting gift. His gaze followed her, but he made no effort to stop her leaving. Even if he could breach her defences, he would not, for ultimately it could only cause her pain. He waited a discreet few minutes before following but, once back in the drawing-room, could not refrain from scanning the crowd for her. She was talking animatedly to Lady Neary and her daughter Mrs Dunford and, reassured of her well-being, he turned to Stephen Naughton, who was suggesting a hand of cards.

"I need something to wash the taste of all that sentiment out of my mouth. Did you hear Ferdie Foster boasting that he was moved to swooning by Miss O'Neill's Juliet? Faugh!"

Luke snorted. "He was moved—or unable to move—by tight lacing if you ask me. He'll be emulating Prinnie next and require a hoist to mount his horse."

"I saw you go apart with Mr Fitzmaurice," Flora said lightly as she and Olivia sat in the Gracechurch carriage. "I never thought you would fall for his wiles."

"I didn't," Olivia lied calmly. She and Flora had never discussed the masquerade beyond agreeing that their entrance had been a resounding success and neither had enquired of the other at what hour she had returned home. "Anne's husband is his cousin—or step-cousin to be precise—and he was looking for news of them."

"Have you heard from Mr Rembleton lately?"

Olivia shook her head. "The last letters we had were dispatched from Naples at the beginning of September. There may be more waiting when we return home. The children are looking forward to his account of Vesuvius. They'll send him a fair copy of their Dorset journals in return."

"He isn't the worst of fathers," Flora remarked.

"No. The children miss him."

"Do you?"

"There is very little to miss, just his occasional visits. I don't know why I was so disturbed at his departure. It's not as though I haven't been managing on my own these many years."

"Would you do it again? Marry him, I mean?"

"I doubt it. At times I can't help wondering how things might have been if he had not proposed or if I had not accepted or if Uncle Samuel had not agreed to the match." Olivia smiled wryly. "I learnt long ago that there is no point in repining; what's done is done. I do know that I love my children and am fortunate in my friends; I am at no one's beck and call and am financially secure. It must suffice. I must be content."

"Yes," Flora agreed quietly.

Olivia sat at her bedroom window, looking out into the moonlit garden of Gracechurch House. She had dismissed Martin but was too restless to sleep. Yes, she repeated to herself, I must be content.

Mr Fitzmaurice had not been compelled to seek her out tonight. She hadn't expected his apology, despite the hurt he had caused her by reducing what had been between them to one sordid encounter of many. But tonight's short conversation had drawn the poison from the wound. Perhaps now she might heal. And there was something more. His parting words had given her an assurance she had not realised she lacked—the assurance that a man could desire her. There had been no mistaking the look in his eyes. Jack's lack of interest in her other than for breeding had led her to consider herself unfeminine, unlovable even as a man loves a woman. Even if I have no more tenderness in my life, I have this, she thought.

"Supposing," she whispered into the night, "supposing I had been unmarried, as he thought I was, at my first ball when he asked me to dance? We were both very young, but where might it have led us?" For a moment she allowed herself to dream and then practical Mrs Rembleton put away such foolish thoughts and went to bed.

Chapter Eighteen

"His Grace the Duke of Gracechurch has called, madam."

"His Grace?" Shocked, Olivia leaped to her feet. It was unheard of for the duke to call at Southrode Manor. Something must be gravely wrong. "Where is he?"

"In the drawing-room, madam."

She darted out of the room and ran down the stairs, arriving at the drawing-room panting. The duke stood at the window but before he could say anything, she gasped, "Pray, your Grace, tell me. Is it Flora or one of the children? Does she need me?"

He crossed the floor and took her hands. A reserved man, he was clearly not without sensibility, for he did not attempt the usual courtesies but said, "I fear, Mrs Rembleton, my bad news does not relate to my family, but to yours."

"Mine?" she faltered. "Uncle Samuel?"

He smiled sadly at her. "No, Mrs Rembleton. It is of your husband that I speak."

"Jack? I don't understand."

"Might we sit down?" he asked gently.

"Oh! Please forgive me."

He led her to the sopha and sat beside her.

"I have received word that your husband met with a serious accident while descending from the crater of Mount Vesuvius."

"Was he badly hurt? Where is he now?"

"Mrs Rembleton, I grieve to tell you that in falling he suffered a severe blow to his head, an injury that proved to be mortal. He is no more."

Olivia stilled, her mind a blank. A faint echo of the duke's words beat against her consciousness like rain at a windowpane and with as little meaning. She did not react when, alarmed by her marble countenance, her visitor went to the tray of refreshments but started when she felt him fold her fingers around a glass.

"Come, ma'am," he said implacably, "drink this."

He raised the glass to her lips and tilted it so that she must swallow. The sweet burst of madeira against her tongue unlocked the paralysis that gripped her and she took the glass from him, sipping at it while he went to pour one for himself. He returned to sit beside her but said nothing more. Finally she broke the silence.

"What happened? And, forgive me, Duke, if I seem ungrateful, but I don't understand why you should be charged with bringing me this news."

He looked into his glass. "Apart from the connection between our families due to the marriage of my mother to your uncle, and the friendship between you and my wife, your husband and I are acquainted through the Royal Society. He came to see me just before he left for the continent. He is—was—a very practical man, as you know and wished to make arrangements for precisely such an event as has occurred. We agreed that in the unlikely event of such an occasion arising, for he had no reason other than normal prudence for these plans, his amanuensis Mr Wilkins would send or bring word to me and I would then inform you." He paused before continuing, "Mr Rembleton expressed the opinion that you might find my support useful in dealing with his brother, whose heir presumptive your elder son now is."

Olivia had come to herself while listening to Gracechurch's measured tones. "I thank you most sincerely, sir, for accepting my husband's commission. Poor Jack! He was so excited to be able to travel again. I wonder did he have a premonition he would not return." She thought for a moment. "The children! How am I to tell them? They sent a letter off only yesterday." She gave a funny little laugh, almost a giggle, and the duke looked at her warily. "Get the facts first, Jack would say. Pray tell me what you know."

"Mr Wilkins called to see me late last night. He had just arrived in London."

"He is here in England? Then it must have happened some time ago."

Gracechurch nodded. "The fall occurred on the fifteenth of September and the unhappy end came three days later."

"While we were in Dorset," Olivia whispered. "What happened to—him?"

"Mr Wilkins arranged for Mr Rembleton's mortal remains to be brought by boat to Rome where he was buried in the Protestant cemetery. He then returned to Naples where he packed their belongings and took ship for England, but not without taking care to have the death registered at the Embassy. He will be happy to call upon you himself and give you a first-hand account of these events, but I insisted he rest first and recover from his journey."

"Of course. Poor man," Olivia said. "I suppose I must write to my brother-in-law and notify Jack's solicitor. But first I must tell the children."

The duke agreed. "I took the liberty, Mrs Rembleton, of sending a message to your uncle, requesting him to tell my mother and my wife, so I daresay you may expect more visitors today." He hesitated. "Might I make a suggestion?"

"Please do, sir. I was just wondering how to go on," Olivia admitted. "The necessity of making arrangements generally tides one over the first horror, does it not? And then there is always a doctor or clergyman on hand to advise one."

"It is strange how our customs and rituals sustain us at such time, but the circumstances are unusual in that there can be no funeral," he agreed. "If you request your husband's solicitor to attend you here in a day or so for the reading of the will, you may advise Lord Rembleton of this. As head of the family, he will wish to be present."

"I'm sure the rector would read the service for Jack, even if there can be no interment."

"You could also hold a memorial in London at a later date. There are many in the scientific community who will be shocked by the news and wish to honour him."

She smiled gratefully at him. "Thank you, Duke. You are a support indeed."

"I am glad to be of service, ma'am. I shall be happy to frank any letters you may have and take them to London with me tonight. I shall return for the reading of the will, if you permit, as Mr Rembleton proposed to add a codicil appointing me joint guardian of the children and trustee for you and them."

"He what?" Olivia demanded inelegantly. How could Jack have done that without consulting her? They had agreed from the beginning that she would be sole guardian if he died before her. Why change things now?

"Pray do not be concerned, ma'am," the duke reassured her. "I don't know what gave rise to this, but he instructed me that I was not to meddle with you or your decisions in any way, but rather stand buff between you and any possible interference." He smiled faintly. "He said, '*I don't trust my brother not to make difficulties out of spite. Duke trumps viscount any day*'."

Olivia smiled. "I can just hear him say it. Very well, you may raise your banner in our defence, your Grace."

She stood and he rose with her. "I must go to the children. Will you take a nuncheon with us in an hour or so? They will have questions and it will be easier for them if they may talk directly to you."

"I shall be happy to join you."

A picture of charming industry met Olivia's eyes in the schoolroom where Miranda was helping her brother read *The Tragical Death of an Apple-Pye*, he identifying the initial letters and she completing the phrase for him. She broke off at 'L longed for it' to enquire severely, "Why are you here, Mamma? It is not yet one o'clock."

Olivia repressed a smile. Her daughter liked matters to be ordered and was proud that she had recently mastered the art of reading the clock.

"Really, Miranda! Your mother does not require your permission to visit the schoolroom," Miss Carstairs reproved the child.

Miranda hung her head. "I beg your pardon, Mamma."

Olivia held out her hand. "You did not mean it the way it sounded, I know. But come, there is something I must tell you, and Samuel too." She sat down and lifted the little boy to her knee, putting an arm around Miranda, who came to stand beside her.

"Would you like me to leave, Mrs Rembleton?" the governess asked quietly.

"No, Miss Carstairs, please remain. I shall need your support." There was no way to soften the blow. "The Duke of Gracechurch has called. He came to bring us word that Papa suffered a bad accident while on Mount Vesuvius."

"Did he break his leg?" Miranda demanded. "Is that why he hasn't come home yet?"

"No, my darling." Olivia's eyes met Miss Carstairs' over the child's head and an awful realisation dawned on the governess's face. "He hurt his head so badly that he could not get better."

"Is he dead, like Miss Carstairs' grandmother?" Samuel enquired.

"I'm afraid so, dearest."

"Did they put him in the ground?"

"Yes, dearest. He lies in a graveyard in Rome."

Miranda began to cry. "We'll never see him again."

Olivia hugged her daughter to her. "No, sweetheart, we won't"

"Or write to him. Samuel is just learning to write. It's not fair."

"No, it's not," her mother agreed as her own tears fell. After some moments, she fished for a handkerchief and dried first the child's eyes and then her own. "We must fetch John. Miss Carstairs, would you please ask Henry to collect him—tell him we are expecting a visit from my uncle and Lady Ottilia. But don't say anything of what has occurred—I want to tell John myself. Once he knows, I'll inform Mrs Hawley and the other upper servants. And perhaps you would pen a note to your father, asking him to call this afternoon?"

"Certainly, Mrs Rembleton. May I tell Papa in confidence what has happened?"

"Yes. Tell Henry to send John up to me immediately he arrives."

Her elder son arrived some twenty minutes later and Olivia had to break the news again. Having to repeat it made it more real, she found.

The boy was stunned. "And he was dead and buried while we were writing to him about Dorset? It doesn't bear thinking about, Mamma!"

"I know, darling."

"What will happen? There can't be a funeral."

"There can be no burial, but I'm sure the rector will read the service for him. I have asked him to call this afternoon."

"He'll know what to do. When soldiers are killed, they aren't brought home either."

"No," Olivia agreed, thinking of her father who had been buried at sea. "In fact, Mr Carstairs read the service for your grandfather after Trafalgar."

John's face cleared. "And you put up a memorial tablet in the church. Can we do the same for Papa? Perhaps beside grandfather's."

"That's an excellent suggestion." Olivia was relieved to see some colour return to the boy's face. "Shall we go and join the duke? I thought you would like to talk to him yourself. I was so shocked that I could hardly take in what he was saying."

"Did Papa's head hurt him very much?" Samuel asked the duke.

"They are their father's children, sir," Olivia said to him quietly when he hesitated to reply. "They have been taught to seek the facts and we attempt to answer their questions as respectfully as if they were put by an adult. In fact, Jack was accustomed to say it was a useful discipline, for it forced him to put matters simply without obfuscation. Children are merciless and will not pretend to understand so as to save face, as an adult might." She turned to the boy. "I'm sure it hurt, Samuel. Just remember how sore your head was when you bumped it crawling under the table. But Mr Wilkins was with Papa and we may be sure he looked after him most carefully."

"That is correct," the duke said. "He had doctors and nurses and everything was done to make him comfortable. But he lost consciousness the next day—"

"It's as if he went to sleep," Olivia interjected when the two younger children looked puzzled.

"And didn't wake up again," Gracechurch finished.

"If he was asleep, it can't have hurt," Miranda announced. "Thank you, sir."

Olivia collapsed onto the cushions of the sopha in her boudoir. A tea-tray was set on the table in front of her and she leaned forward to pick up the pot.

Flora waved her back. "You rest, I'll pour."

"I had forgotten what a stir is caused by death, especially when it is unexpected. There is such a coming and going. I must finish those letters. The duke will wish to leave soon. He has been very kind. Jack appointed him co-guardian in a codicil just before he left."

Flora raised an eyebrow. "Why did he do that?"

"Apparently he was afraid Rembleton might cut up rough about some of the provisions of the will. He will take it hard that Jack's son and not his own grandson is now the heir presumptive."

"Presumptive? Oh, if your sister-in-law were to die, he might marry again and beget a son. Do you think he would?"

"Jack always said he would take an example from Hamlet's mother."

The duchess wrinkled her nose distastefully. "'*The funeral baked meats coldly furnishing forth the marriage tables*'? How old is Rembleton?"

"They are both seventy-two."

"What a prospect for a young bride! One can only hope that her ladyship outlives him."

Two days later, broad-chested and short-necked, a square, aging bull of a man who was a head shorter than his deceased brother, Lord Rembleton swaggered into Southrode Manor as if it were his property and his brother's family occupants by his grace and favour. Some half-dozen carriages had followed the Rembleton coach and spilled out a retinue comprised of his wife, three daughters, their husbands, children, companion, governesses and his solicitor, all of whom followed him into the hall while the conveyances went round to the back to deposit the accompanying servants and the luggage.

Olivia exchanged glances with her butler and housekeeper as the procession grew ever longer. They had planned for the worst, and the worst they had got!

"Well, madam," Rembleton proclaimed, shrugging out of his coat and letting it fall from his shoulders, "this is a sorry mess, but no more than I might have expected from Jack."

Olivia, fortified by a new black bombazine gown trimmed with Norwich crepe and a matching turban that gave her additional height and gravity did not respond to this remark but made the stiffest of curtsies, more a suggestion of genuflection than anything else, while uttering in arctic tones, "Good afternoon, my lord, my lady."

Lord Rembleton responded to the unvoiced disapproval despite himself, making an abbreviated bow before replying equally stiffly, "My condolences, Mrs Rembleton." He surveyed the hall through his quizzing glass. "I assumed my heir would be here to greet me."

"My son is in the schoolroom," Olivia replied. "He and the other children will join us in the drawing-room before dinner. You may meet him then."

She ignored his grunted response and went to greet her other guests, graciously accepting their murmurs of sympathy.

"Pray come into the drawing-room while the luggage is seen to," she invited her sister-in-law and her family and then smiled at the two governesses who stood to one side with their pupils. "James will take you to the schoolroom—James, my compliments to Miss Carstairs and I should be grateful if she would look after our guests—and Mrs Hawley will show you your rooms later." As the footman led his charges away, Olivia added, "and James, tell Mr Phelps that Mr Cartwright had accompanied his lordship."

"Very good, madam."

Lord Rembleton had not waited for these domestic matters to be resolved but gone on ahead followed by his family. The butler stepped forward to intercept the solicitor when he made to follow his employer, saying frigidly, "If you will remain here, sir, while the arrangements are made."

"I wish you could have seen Rembleton's face when he caught sight of us," Flora told Olivia later. "His entrance was more royal than that of Prinnie at Brighton and he was utterly deflated when he spied mamma-in-law and me on the sopha, not to mention Gracechurch and Uncle Samuel."

"He brought his solicitor," Olivia told her.

"What impertinence."

"And then to demand the will be read immediately instead of tomorrow after the service! But the duke withered him with one look."

"Where have you put the solicitor? Have you a room left? I had not thought so many would come."

"Nor I. There is a very small bedroom on the second floor, just beside the backstairs and opposite a housemaid's closet. I've put him there. I didn't want to wish him on my land steward, who was happy to take the other two solicitors and Mr Wilkins. Mrs Hawley has sent down another maid to help his housekeeper."

"They'll probably have a more pleasant evening of it than we shall," Flora said with a grin.

Olivia put down her cup. "We must change for dinner. What are we to do afterwards? We can hardly play cards or make music."

"Tell your uncle to keep the gentlemen in the dining-room for as long as possible. You may rely upon mamma-in-law to set the tone in the drawing-room and no-one will expect you to remain for long after the tea-tray is removed."

Chapter Nineteen

" ' I heard a voice from heaven saying unto me, Write; from hence-forth blessed are the dead which die in the Lord; even so saith the Spirit; for they rest from their labours'."

Under cover of the congregation reciting the Lord's Prayer, John leaned towards his mother and whispered, "Papa won't like that, he loved his labours."

Olivia touched his hand and smiled while her brother-in-law in the pew behind them cleared his throat harshly in admonishment. Poor Jack, she thought. But John was right. He had loved his labours and perhaps it was fitting that he died while enjoying them. And he had seen the encyclopaedia published to great acclaim. His hadn't been a wasted life and she must be grateful for that. While not the best of husbands, he certainly was not the worst. The children mourned him sincerely and she felt for their loss. But what of herself? It was hard to put a name to what she felt. Shock at his sudden death, certainly; at the thought of a life snuffed out. She would miss him as a sort of colleague or partner, she supposed, especially when it came to making plans for their children but, if she mourned, it was not so much for the end of a marriage, but more for one that had never flourished.

The final *Amen* jerked her out of her musings. She hoped they would get through the reading of the will without any upset and that once it was over Lord Rembleton would remove himself and his family. Poor John, she thought, to be heir to such a man. I wonder does he understand the full implications for him. Jack never put much value on his position as heir and it was never a subject of conversation within the family.

"Miranda, you are to go up to Miss Carstairs in the schoolroom, John, please stay with me."

"What's wrong, Mamma?"

"Nothing. I just need to explain some things to you. Papa's will is to be read shortly and I think you are old enough to attend, especially as you are so nearly affected by it."

"How affected?"

Olivia pondered this question, annoyed with herself for not having mentioned the matter to him sooner. "Come into the library for a moment," she said finally. Two neatly dressed men who had been working at the desk rose at their entrance.

"John, I wish to introduce Mr Soames and Mr Phelps. Mr Soames is your father's solicitor and will advise us presently of the terms of his will. Mr Phelps is also a solicitor. He has looked after my interests for more than ten years. Gentlemen, my son John."

The men bowed and John made his best bow in return.

Olivia sat on the settee. "Come, sit beside me." When the boy obeyed, she took a breath and began. "Your uncle Rembleton has three daughters but no sons and because generally women may not inherit titles,"

"Why not?" John interrupted. "After all, there have been several Queens of England, have there not?"

Olivia had to smile. "You are so like your father," she said. "That is all too long to go into now. Perhaps Mr Soames would explain the laws relating to the peerage, entails and life estates to you later?" She raised an enquiring eyebrow and the solicitor nodded.

"Certainly, Master John."

"For the moment, all you need to know is that Papa was your uncle's heir; that is he would have been the next Lord Rembleton if your uncle had died before him. Now that Papa is dead, you are the heir."

"Not Theo Frome? After all, he is my uncle's own grandson."

Olivia sighed. "Mr Soames—"

"—will explain it to me later," the boy finished. "But this doesn't mean I have to go and live at Rembleton Place, does it?"

"No, no. But we may have to visit there more frequently so that you get to know the people—the tenants, I mean. And you must learn about being responsible for such a large estate. Papa has arranged that the Duke of Gracechurch will help me decide what is best for you. But that is all set out in his will and that is why I wish you to be here when it is read."

"I see. Nothing else is going to change, is it?"

"No. We'll live here and you'll go to school at Shrewsbury when you are old enough, just as Papa planned."

"My uncle is much older than Papa was. What happens when he dies?"

"We hope it won't be for very many more years, not until you are grown up."

"But if something should happen?" John persisted. "Like with Papa."

"We'll cross that bridge if and when we come to it," Olivia said firmly. "Much would depend on how old you were at the time. You may rest assured that nothing will interfere with your education. But now we'll join the others in the drawing-room. We shall be with you in an hour or so, gentlemen."

As soon as the last of the neighbours who had returned with them to the manor to drink a glass of wine had left, Olivia addressed her guests.

"Mr Soames is ready for us in the library. Uncle, your Grace, my lord, Mr Wilkins, would you be so good as to come with John and me, please."

Lord Rembleton immediately protested. "Mrs Rembleton, you cannot exclude my brother's family from the reading of his will. My wife, daughters and their families will accompany us."

"This is not an after-dinner entertainment, sir. I see no reason for anyone other than those most immediately affected to attend. My other children are too young." She moved towards the door which John opened for her.

The duke waved him on. "Go with your mother, my boy," he said, and then gestured to the other men to precede him, bringing up the rear in so decided a manner that no-one else dared follow.

"Tell Cartwright to attend me in the library," the viscount snapped as he passed the butler in the hall.

Gracechurch looked mockingly at him but said no more, herding him along to the library where Olivia took a seat on the settee beside her son. She waved her uncle to a chair beside John and the duke to the one beside her, placing Lord Rembleton and Mr Wilkins at the edges of the semi-circle.

"Mr Soames, if you please," she said.

The solicitor had just picked up his sheaf of paper when Lord Rembleton's man of law hurried in, pausing inside the door when he saw the assembled company.

"You sent for me, my lord?"

"Yes. I wish you to take note of the details of my brother's will," Rembleton growled. Olivia raised her eyebrows at this and was gratified to see her brother-in-law flush and run a finger around the top of his cravat as if it were suddenly too tight. He glowered around the room, his fringe of iron-grey curls making him look more bull-like than ever, she thought,.

"That will not be necessary," she advised him. "Mr Soames will be happy to furnish you with a copy of any relevant clauses. Is that not so, Mr Soames?"

Mr Soames bowed gallantly. "I am at your service, madam."

The silence continued until the viscount flapped a hand at his retainer. "What are you waiting for, man? Go! Go!"

"Yes, my lord." The solicitor scuttled to the door. Mr Soames waited for it to close behind him, then settled his pince-nez more firmly on his nose and cleared his throat to signal he was about to begin.

"'This is the last will and testament of me John William Emmanuel Rembleton'."

It was a simple enough will, Olivia thought, especially for someone like Jack who had devoted himself to exploring the minutiae of things. The terms of their marriage settlement and her ownership of the manor and its appurtenances, which were listed in exhaustive detail, were confirmed 'to avoid any doubt or possible dispute' and anything purchased since for the Southrode house or estate, including all furnishing and fittings, works of art etc. etc. were left to her, as were all items loaned or given to her by him over the years.

Hayes Farm and its contents were left to Mr Wilkins, with the exception of the contents of the safe which were left to Olivia.

Each servant or employee either at Southrode Manor or Hayes Farm who was still employed without notice having been given on either side at the date of the reading of the will was to receive one month's wages or one twelfth of their salary for each year of service, "'Which I think will be of more real use to them than a mourning ring which would serve either to promote my posthumous consequence or enrich the jewellers and pawnbrokers'." Olivia had to smile at this and she could see Mr Wilkins stifle a grin.

His scientific notes, collections etc. were left to his long-time friend and collaborator Bartholomew Wilkins in the hope that he would continue their joint work.

A copy of his *Encyclopaedia of Nature* was left to his brother and each of his nieces, "*'As they have apparently been prevented from subscribing to this work. Should any of them prove to my executors that they have purchased this encyclopaedia before the date when my will is read, in lieu of a second copy I leave each such person the sum of one thousand pounds.'*" Olivia was surprised and gratified on Jack's behalf to discover later that his two younger nieces Sophia and Lydia were able to claim the benefit of this clause.

"*'My children John Emmanuel, Miranda Margaret and Samuel Robert I leave to the loving care of my wife Olivia Anne née Frobisher whom I appoint as their guardian in the knowledge that they could not be in better hands.'*"

The residuary estate was to be divided into four equal parts, one of which was left to Olivia outright and the other three in trust, one for each of the children.

"*'Signed and delivered this fourteenth day of April 1814*
John William Emmanuel Rembleton'"

The solicitor took a breath but before he was able to continue, Lord Rembleton exploded into speech.

"Outrageous! What of his duty to his brother and his house? My heir to be treated equally with his brother and sister and a woman to be his guardian! The bulk of the property to be left to his wife and my estate-manager's son! I won't have it! I made it clear to Jack the last day I met him—it was just before he sailed—that I would not have it. And that boy must be taught to be a man, do you hear me? No namby-pamby is going to succeed me!"

Olivia glanced down at John who was watching his uncle as if he were in a raree-show.

"I think he's going to have an apoplexy," he whispered dispassionately. "Old Bert looked just like that before he fell down with one. I do hope he doesn't die."

"Hush," she reproved him before murmuring to the duke, "Now we know why he made that codicil."

He nodded. Lord Rembleton finally spluttered to a halt and Mr Soames cleared his throat again.

"There is a codicil to the will, made on the twenty-ninth of April 1814."

"Why didn't you say so directly?" Lord Rembleton grunted. "That's more like it."

" 'I, John William Emmanuel Rembleton do hereby appoint Jeffrey George Rowland, 4th Duke of Gracechurch etc. etc. to be guardian jointly with my wife Olivia Anne of my children, John, Miranda and Samuel and co-trustee of their estates until they reach the age of twenty-five, with the exception that my daughter Miranda's marriage portion may be released sooner if she marries with her mother's and the duke's consent. I commend my children to his grace's good offices, confident that they will be advised and guided wisely by him.' "

The solicitor's voice faded away. The viscount was snapping at the air, apparently too irate to be able to give voice to his sentiments.

The duke rose to his feet and bowed to Olivia. "Mrs Rembleton, I am honoured by the confidence your husband placed in me and shall endeavour to give you no cause to regret it."

"I'm sure I won't, your Grace. I need not present John to you, I know."

"No, indeed. We shall deal well together, I am sure."

Mr Harte looked closely at his great-nephew. "I think he's had enough for the moment. I'm sure you'll excuse him, my dear."

Olivia nodded. "Go to the schoolroom, John. I'll come up in a moment."

"Yes, Mamma. But don't let Mr Soames leave—"

"Before he explains to you? I won't"

"Come, lad. I'll go up with you," Mr Harte said.

"Thank you, Uncle," Olivia said gratefully.

Lord Rembleton, who sat slumped in his seat, shook his head as the door closed behind them. "I have never understood why my wife could only present me with daughters while Jack, whom I always held to be a molly, sired two sons, the first born within a year of his marriage." He glared balefully at his brother's companion-in-arms, "As for you, Wilkins!—"

There was an ominous pause. Olivia looked from one man to the other, puzzled by the frozen silence. The faces of Gracechurch and the two solicitors were oddly expressionless while Mr Wilkins' bronzed colour had faded to a pale, almost sickly hue. He seemed to brace himself.

"My lord! You forget yourself!" The duke's rebuke cracked whip-like through the room.

"Eh?" Lord Rembleton seemed to come to himself. "I beg your pardon, ma'am," he muttered to Olivia, pressing heavily on the arms of his chair to heave himself to his feet. "See that you give Cartwright that copy within the hour," he ordered Mr Soames and lumbered out of the room.

Olivia collapsed limply against the back of the settee. "Oh dear," was all she could say.

The four men regarded her cautiously.

"What was he expecting? That Jack would leave everything to him?" she asked, exasperated. "What did he think?"

"He doesn't think, ma'am," Mr Wilkins said unexpectedly. "Forgive me, but I've known him all my life." His colour returned with a rush and he grinned suddenly. "Jack was wont to say his brother was proof that the family's antecedents reached back to the brutish, British mire. He described him as operating on instinct and an inchoate sense of entitlement, allied to brute strength and unrefined by even a veneer of civilisation and culture."

Even the solicitors had to smile at this comprehensive indictment.

"John can't understand why he is the heir and not Rembleton's own grandson. I must admit to having some sympathy for his lordship's feelings but I cannot condone his behaviour." She sighed. "I must go to my son."

"I'll follow Rembleton, ensure he is not subjecting the ladies to his ravings," the duke announced.

"I would back both the duchess and Lady Ottilia against him any day," Olivia assured him, "but perhaps it would be as well if you join them."

John sat on the window-seat in the schoolroom, his feet pulled up and his head resting on his drawn-up knees. He looks so forlorn, Olivia thought, her heart aching, and went to kneel on the floor beside him. She gently put her hand on his shoulder and he looked at her from reddened eyes.

"Doesn't he care that Papa is dead?" he burst out. "It's all him and his damned heir."

She ignored his unseemly language. He knew that he should not use such expressions and that he had done so while talking to her was a measure of his upset.

"I'm so sorry. I never thought he would behave so badly. If I had, I would not have suggested you be present. But I wanted you to hear for yourself the provisions Papa had made for you."

"The duke's quite the thing, isn't he? I don't really know him—he never does things with us when we stay with them, like Papa was used to. Even Rowland loved it when he planned an excursion and he's fifteen. But I felt safe with him. Papa made a good choice."

"Try not to judge your uncle too harshly. It is perhaps unfair that you and not Theo will succeed him, inheriting the Place one day. Your aunt, if she is still alive, will have no further right to live there but must remove to the dower house, which is a much smaller house meant for the last lord's widow. She has lived in the Place for almost fifty years and would find that hard."

"But I could say she should stay, couldn't I?"

"Yes. We must hope her husband doesn't die for many years, not until you're a man, but you're a kind boy to think of it." She hugged John and brushed his hair out of his eyes. "Have you had your nuncheon?"

"They had just finished when I came up. Miss Carstairs would have rung for more, but I didn't want anything. She took the others for a walk." He looked at his mother. "I'm hungry now."

"Why don't we go down to the kitchen and see what Cook has?"

"Mamma? That about the encyclopaedia—it wasn't very kind of Papa, was it?"

"Not very."

"It's not sporting to put something like that into your will, I think. It's like kicking a man when he's down, for the other may not reply."

"The encyclopaedia was very important to Papa. It was his life's work, you might say, and very many notable people subscribed to it. I suppose he felt his brother didn't respect him enough to do so."

"So this was a sort of retal—retal—"

"Retaliation," Olivia supplied.

"I can see that, I mean I understand why he did it, but I still don't think it was right."

"Papa would have been so proud of you!" she exclaimed.

"Why? Because I don't agree with him?"

"Because you have considered it fairly and come to your own conclusion."

"Do you think he was right?"

"No. I agree with you," she told her son, "but because I understand him, I can forgive him for doing it."

"Mr Carstairs says that if we won't forgive somebody, we hurt ourselves as much if not more than that person. I asked if he meant that God won't forgive us—you know, '*forgive us our trespasses, as we forgive them that trespass against us*', but he said that clinging to our resentments poisons us. If Papa had been able to forgive his brother, he wouldn't have done that about the encyclopaedia."

"No," Olivia said again. She felt like weeping but managed to smile at her wise child. "Now, let's see what Cook has for you—perhaps she'll have time to make you some apple fritters."

"Good afternoon, Miss Gregg." Olivia met the companion at the top of the stairs. "I trust they are looking after you."

"Very well indeed thank you, Mrs Rembleton."

"How is your brother?"

The young woman's face lit up. "In excellent health, thank you, ma'am. And he is to have two months' furlough soon. Mrs Frome has been so kind as to permit me two weeks' holiday and my brother has said he will take me to Bath. We have no home now, so if we wish to spend time together we must take rooms somewhere and he said I might choose where to go."

Somewhere she could be a guest herself, an equal participant in all the entertainments, Olivia realised and said impulsively, "Miss Gregg, I imagine you will be going into society in Bath. I must wear mourning for the next year. Would you be offended if I were to offer you some of my coloured gowns? We are more or less of a size and it would not take much for my maid to alter them to fit you. If she takes your measurements while you are here, I can send them on to you when they are ready. When do you go to Bath?"

"The first fortnight of December." Miss Gregg replied. "That is extremely kind of you, ma'am."

"Not at all. Come into my bedroom; I'll ring for Martin."

"Oh, but I mustn't tarry. His lordship has decided we are to leave today and I must help with the packing."

"It will only take ten minutes to measure you," Olivia said firmly. "A nuncheon will be served shortly and that will take up some time. And the governesses have gone for a walk with the children and that will cause additional delay."

"Alone in the drawing-room, Duke?" Olivia asked lightly. She had said goodbye to her brother-in-law and his family and now came to see how her remaining guests fared.

"My wife took my mother and your uncle off to rest. You should emulate them, but first there is one last duty for me to fulfil."

"What is that?" She sat down and gestured for him to do the same.

"To convey a last message from your husband," he informed her gently. "As he was leaving me that day, he suddenly stopped at the door to my library and said, 'If it should come to it, tell her I am sorry I couldn't be the husband she deserved'."

Olivia stared into space for a long minute. "Perhaps he wasn't," she acknowledged, "but he did his best, I think. Only consider how he secured your support for me. And he was a good father too in his own way. He didn't seek marriage and fatherhood; it was forced upon him because of the succession. And our marriage brought me many advantages. I will always think kindly of him, I assure you."

The duke smiled at her. "Mr Rembleton was fortunate in his choice of wife," he said simply. "He said no more to me, but hurried out almost as if he was discomfited by what he had said." He rose. "I'll leave you to your rest, ma'am."

Olivia felt as weary as she ever had been in her life. It was similar to the exhaustion one felt after giving birth, she thought, but without the euphoria that accompanied it. She dragged herself to her feet and slowly climbed the stairs, hoping that she could gain the sanctuary of her bedchamber without being accosted by anyone, be it family, guest or servant.

Chapter Twenty

We are saddened to report the untimely demise in Naples of one of our most distinguished natural philosophers, the Honble. John Rembleton, who succumbed on 18 September to the injuries he incurred in a fall on Mount Vesuvius three days previously.

Shocked, Luke put down the *Times*. 'She is free', was his first, instinctive thought and his lip curled in self-disgust that this should be his reaction to the death of a man and the orphaning of his children.

"Lord Franklin, sir."

"What tears you away from the shires?" Luke exclaimed. "I thought you were celebrating the start of the hunting season."

"And so I would be if Parliament hadn't finally been recalled to debate the army estimates. I want to be sure my father votes and the right way. He has even agreed to speak if I tell him what to say, but it's damned hard going, I may tell you. It's all here," he tapped his head, "but getting it onto paper is a different matter. What's more, it's not done to read a speech, he tells me, so I'll have to din the contents into him."

Luke laughed. "What do you want him to say?"

"I want him to stand up for the men who fight, not the man-milliners who parade in Hyde Park; describe what it's like to be stranded on a mountainside in Spain and the commissary miles away. Or how, when they have meat, the men have to scavenge to get enough fuel to cook it in those kettles they must lug around. Frequently the meat was half-raw because they could not get it hot enough. Or how it is to see the ragged wretches as good as barefoot, yet determined not to fall out on the longest march. I tell you, Fitzmaurice, when I think of those well-fed, prosy politicians daring to sneer at the army it makes my blood boil."

While he was speaking, Luke had thrown the *Times* onto the floor and started making notes. Now he rang the bell.

"Coffee or ale?" he asked when his manservant appeared.

"Ale," declared his lordship.

"And coffee for me," Luke ordered. "Now Franklin, you continue talking and I'll shape what you say into something for your sire."

Two hours later, his reminiscences having been fuelled by judicious questions and copious draughts of ale, Lord Franklin came to a halt. He looked dubiously at the stack of scribbled sheets at Luke's elbow. "Can you really make something useful of that?"

"When do you need it?"

"He should speak tomorrow."

Luke sighed. "Go away and leave this to me. Will it suit your parent if he has it early in the morning?"

"Come to breakfast," his lordship invited promptly. "We're a bachelor household—my mother is in Bath with my sister. She wants to take the waters, she says, can't imagine why. She even tried to convince me to go with her." He shuddered. "She's still trying to marry me off as quickly as possible."

Lord Lutterworth was astounded the next morning to be presented first with a neatly inscribed quarto sheet and then with a small slip of paper on which a few words were listed clearly.

"These are different points you may wish to make, my Lord," Luke explained. "The larger sheet summarises the thoughts and experiences that led your son to suggest them. Once you are thoroughly familiar with them, the other will serve to jog your memory discreetly if necessary.

His lordship picked up the sheet and read it carefully, glancing from time to time at the smaller slip. "A very clever method, Mr Fitzmaurice," he said approvingly.

"It was a trick of the late Lord Needham," Luke told him

"I see I have work to do," Lutterworth exclaimed. "I beg you will excuse me, sir. Franklin, you will accompany me. Mr Fitzmaurice, I hope to speak this evening. If you wish to listen in the gallery, I shall make the necessary arrangements. I should be pleased if you would sup with me afterwards."

Lord Franklin seized Luke's arm when his father rose to speak. His grip eased as the older man spoke simply yet eloquently of the need, "For those of us at home to support the men who risk their lives for us abroad". After some minutes, he paused and looked around the house. "My lords, I know that many of your sons, brothers and nephews have made the ultimate sacrifice. Others may have not been privileged, as I have been, to hear at first-hand of the privations our soldiers must suffer when campaigning. You may say that that is the price we—and they—pay for victory. Perhaps it is, but let it not be because we are too stingy to provide them with the funds they need or too careless to ensure these are properly spent."

Franklin put his face in his hands but at the cries of "Hear him, hear him" lifted it to grin sheepishly at his neighbour who muttered, "That was his own. Too maudlin for me, but very effective".

"Mr Fitzmaurice, I am considerably in your debt," Lord Lutterworth said later. They had adjourned to Boodles where he had been the recipient of sincere if sometimes astonished congratulations. Franklin had excused himself to talk to someone at another table and for the moment his father and Luke were alone. "Not only for your assistance today," the earl continued, "but more importantly, for the first time my son has spoken to me of his military experiences." He sighed. "He came home this year and I found I hardly knew him. I couldn't reconcile the man who returned to us with the boy just out of school who was mad for a pair of colours. You have broken down the barrier that separated us and I am eternally grateful to you."

"I may have helped dismantle it, my lord, but you started the process when you agreed to speak in the debate," Luke pointed out.

The earl brightened. "That is true, I suppose. I don't usually speak in the House, but when he asked me to, I couldn't refuse."

"Coming home can't have been easy for him," Luke ventured. "From what he tells me, he has spent little time among the ton and must learn its ways, just as we would have to find our way in the army. Each society has its own way of doing things and the unwritten rules and codes are the hardest to fathom. Or the tricks that are necessary for survival, for example, in the ballrooms," he added with a knowing grin.

"I hadn't thought of that," Lutterworth admitted. "Both mothers and daughters will be setting snares for him, especially now that he is Franklin. His brother was so completely up to snuff—too much so, if I am honest—that it never occurred to me that Vernon might be different. That is another lesson for me! I'll have a word with his mother; tell her not to press him so hard. But he must marry; if his brother had done his duty, we would not find ourselves in this predicament today."

"Give him a year to find his feet," Luke suggested. "By the end of next Season, he may feel quite differently about it—some lady will very likely have caught his eye."

Flanked by her brother and elder son, Olivia took her leave of Sir Joseph Banks at the entrance to the Royal Society. She had visited Somerset House before for the Academy's summer exhibitions, but had never previously set foot in the Society's hallowed rooms. John had stunned her by declaring his intention of writing to Gracechurch to see if he might not attend the commemorative symposium the Society proposed to hold in honour of his father. To her surprise, the duke had not only arranged for the boy to be present, but also for her to accompany him—a rare honour indeed for a female. She had been greatly moved when Sir Joseph, as President, had welcomed them formally and announced that the Society had accepted an anonymous endowment for the John Rembleton medal, which in future would be awarded annually to the author of the best work published each year with the aim of familiarising the youth of both sexes with scientific principles and thought.

Captain Frobisher paused as they left the house to exchange brief greetings with a couple of naval men on their way into the Admiralty.

"You don't feel the urge to set sail again?" she asked him as they walked on.

"No. It's time I settled to civilian life," he admitted.

"I still can't believe that you have never learnt to ride or to drive a team," John said.

His uncle laughed. "I was always destined for the navy, and what good is a horse to a sailor, tell me that? But I am grateful to you for your lessons, my lad."

The boy flushed with pleasure. He greatly enjoyed instructing his imposing uncle under Henry's watchful eye.

Boot heels rang purposefully on the flagstones behind them, as if someone was trying to catch up with them.

"Pray forgive us for accosting you in this way, Mrs Rembleton," Lord Franklin said. "We had hoped to be able to express our condolences within but you slipped away too quickly."

"Thank you, my lord, you are very kind," she murmured and turned to hold out her hand to his companion.

"Mr Fitzmaurice."

"Pray accept my deepest sympathy, ma'am."

"Thank you," she said again.

"May we walk on with you?" he asked.

She wasn't sure whether his company would be too unsettling, but found herself saying, "Please do." However, as the little group re-formed, she was happy to accept the offer of Lord Franklin's arm.

"I think your father would have been pleased about the medal," she heard Mr Fitzmaurice say seriously to John behind them.

"Yes. I wonder who the anonymous donor is."

"Certainly somebody who admired and valued his work."

"Have you heard that Captain Gregg is to be in England soon, is perhaps here already?" Olivia asked his lordship quietly.

"No. Did you learn of it from his sister?" he asked eagerly.

"Yes. I understand he is taking her to Bath next month."

He looked piercingly at her. "Why are you telling me this, ma'am?" he asked bluntly. "I was under the impression that you disapproved of my interest in the lady."

"Should that interest still persist, my lord, and if it is an honourable one, it would be quite unexceptional for you to pursue her acquaintance while she is in the company of her brother, a fellow-officer. In Bath she will attend the assemblies and other entertainments on an equal footing with you and you may invite her to stand up with you without causing undue speculation."

An appreciative smile lit his features. "I see you are a mistress of tactics, ma'am. When are they to be in Bath?"

"I believe the first fortnight of December."

"Splendid! My mother is there at present and plans to remain until a week before Christmas. I think a devoted son would visit his afflicted parent, don't you?"

"You are no mean tactician yourself, my lord," Olivia commended him.

She turned back to the others just in time to hear her brother say, "Mr Fitzmaurice, if you would offer my sister your escort, I'll take this young fellow for a walk—shake the fidgets out of him after sitting still for so long." He grinned down at his nephew as he spoke. "I noticed a shop that sells kites—what say you, John?"

John grinned back. "Maybe you'll be better at flying one than you are at driving," he retorted.

"Insubordination!" his uncle exclaimed. "It'll be mutiny next."

"Matchmaking, Mrs Rembleton?" Luke asked as the carriage moved off. "Franklin will be greatly obliged to you."

She shrugged. "It will very likely come to nothing. It would be quite an unequal match, wouldn't it? But it will give him the opportunity to explore his interest and it will do her consequence no harm if an earl's son asks her to dance."

"You are a strange mixture of sense and sensibility," he teased, revelling in this unhoped for opportunity to spend some time with her privately. "Where are you staying?"

"At the Pulteney Hotel," she replied absently, folding back her black veil.

She had got thinner since he had last seen her and the dull weeds emphasized her stark pallor. He saw her take a deep breath.

"Mr Fitzmaurice, there is something I wish to know and you are the only gentleman I can think of whom I would feel comfortable in asking and who might answer me truthfully. I know too you would keep my confidence."

Luke considered her thoughtfully. Under other circumstances, such a request from a woman might have been coquettish or even seductive, but she was too serious for that.

"Shall we take a turn around the park?" he suggested. "At this time of day it will be almost deserted and we may talk undisturbed."

She nodded and instructed the coachman.

"Now," he smiled encouragingly at her. "What is it you wish to know?"

She twisted her fingers together. Distracted, he looked at her left hand and realised that she must have had the little finger of the glove stiffened by some means.

"Mrs Rembleton?" he prompted her.

She took another deep breath and said in a rush, "What does a gentleman mean when he says of another that he is 'a molly'?"

Luke stared at her. Who could have used such a term in her presence? "Where did you hear it?" he asked carefully.

Haltingly, she described the little scene after the reading of her husband's will. "When I thought about it afterwards—the other gentlemen were clearly shocked and if you had heard the duke's reprimand! It was so cutting, and this to a man twice his age. I thought there had to be more to my brother-in-law's remark than just a diatribe about Jack siring sons. After all, I had borne them," she finished with a glint of a smile. "It was not news to me."

His mind raced. How was he to answer her? He couldn't, wouldn't lie to her. He had too much respect for her for that. And she clearly suspected something disreputable or derogatory at the least. Finally he said, "I will tell you if you insist, but it will pain you, I fear. Are you sure you want to know?"

She swallowed. "I think I must," she said sadly. "It's a bit like Pandora's Box—once it's opened, there's no closing it. It would be worse not to know and always be wondering."

"I understand," Luke murmured and then said as matter-of-factly as he could, "A molly is what some call a man whose sexual preference is not for women but for other men."

She said nothing, her eyebrows meeting in a puzzled frown.

"It is the sin of Sodom, Mrs Rembleton," Luke elaborated, praying silently, please don't, don't ask me for details.

"I see," she said slowly. "He meant that Jack—?"

"Yes, or so he thought."

"But they hang sodomites, don't they?"

"If they are caught in the act, yes."

"I see," she said again. "And that might be why he married so late in life?"

"It is possible."

She said nothing more for some time, clearly wrestling with her memories of her husband and her marriage. Suddenly her eyes flashed. "Sexual preference, you said. You mean that he would prefer to lie with a man than with a woman? And perhaps find pleasure and, and even love with him that he could not with her?"

Luke hesitated, remembering how uninitiated she had been at Burlington House. Rembleton had clearly not been incapable with a woman, but it seemed to have been a mechanical exercise that had certainly left his wife unfulfilled. He hated to hurt her further, but sometimes a wound had to be cauterized.

"Yes," he answered steadfastly.

Her anger flared. "And he would have known this when he married me?"

"If what we assume was indeed the case—and remember that we only have your brother-in-law's rantings as evidence,—I think it is unlikely that he was unaware of his true nature when he married you. If so, he was understandably discreet. I for one never suspected it, but I only knew him as a married man."

"So the marriage would have afforded him some protection?"

"Certainly, especially after your children were born. How did you come to marry?"

Luke listened intently as she recounted the events of ten years ago.

"Mrs Carr said love may grow afterwards," she finished. "But that would require a, a willing disposition on both sides, would it not?"

"I should think so," he agreed sympathetically.

Suddenly she exploded in fury. "That dastard! All this time he had Bart! Mr Wilkins," she explained curtly in answer to his questioning look. "He spoke today. They have known each other for ever. He was at the reading of the will too—Rembleton rounded on him, which struck me as odd because Wilkin's father was land-steward on the Rembleton estate and Rembleton is the sort to be flattered by the thought of such a loyal servant. But if Wilkins is not really a servant, that would explain it. Jack even told me they shared a home, but I was too stupid to understand. They were very close. I hadn't met him until the funeral, but it was apparent in the affectionate way he spoke about Jack." She laughed harshly. "I see it all, now. Why, he's just as much—or more—a widow as I am. And to think I invited him into my home! Even when I learnt Jack was leaving Haye Farm to 'his long-time friend and collaborator', I didn't guess."

"If you have never met him, never seen them together, I don't know how you should have guessed," Luke soothed her.

She didn't respond, but stared out the carriage window, her beautiful lips compressed to a thin, iron line.

"Mrs Rembleton." He leaned forward to take her hands. "Thalia,"

"Olivia," she snapped. "After this, I think you are entitled to use my name."

"Olivia," he repeated softly.

"I was stupid," she said again, clinging to his hands. "At first I wondered if there was something lacking in me but later, when he displayed so little warmth towards the children, I thought it must be an innate failing in him, that he had none of the finer feelings; that that side of his nature was stunted. I did try in the beginning to establish a deeper connection between us, but I was young and shy and he was so much older that I was easily daunted. But it wasn't that. His affections were reserved for his paramour." She spat the word out as if it had soured in her mouth. "And he knew. He entered into our marriage wittingly." She laughed bitterly. "He told me I need not fear there would be other women." Her voice broke on the word and she began to sob. "He deceived me from the beginning."

"He did." Luke moved to sit beside her. He gathered her into his arms, rocking her while she wept. "Ssh, my darling, ssh, Olivia, ssh."

After some time, she shuddered and sat up. "I'm sorry, Mr Fitzmaurice."

"Luke," he said, drying her eyes tenderly. He touched his lips to hers. "After this, I think you are entitled to use my name."

She gave him a watery smile and rested her head on his shoulder.

"I thought he was honest," she said bleakly, "true to himself, as Polonius has it."

"He probably was in all things but this, and we must not forget that concealing his true nature was a matter of life and death for him. I suppose it became a habit with him to suppress all feeling," Luke reflected. "But don't misunderstand me, Olivia; if I had him before me, I would personally hang, draw and quarter him for what he did to you. Regardless of the truth of the relationship between him and Wilkins, he clearly should never have married and especially not a girl as vulnerable as you were then. He took most unfair advantage of your situation. He called the tune and was content for you to pay the piper." He brushed a kiss against her temple. "Worst of all, he seems to have denied you an intimacy he enjoyed elsewhere himself. He made you feel you were an obligation, a burden, didn't he?"

A faint flush tinged Olivia's cheek at this reminder of Burlington House. "Yes. I don't deny that I married him for security, but he did conceal his true circumstances from me. If I had known that his desire was not directed towards females and that his affections were engaged elsewhere, I would never have accepted him nor, I am sure, would my uncle have supported the match."

"Your husband should have had the spunk to stand up to his brother," Luke grunted. "He could hardly drag him to the altar."

"I suppose not. Jack did leave me a message saying he was sorry," she added, telling Luke of her husband's parting words to Gracechurch.

Much good that was, he thought contemptuously, but said "Then try and forgive him Olivia, for your sake if not for his. You have the rest of your life ahead of you. Don't let him poison that too."

She lay back against him, closing her eyes. Luke bent down to kiss the soft eyelids that fluttered beneath his lips like butter-flies' wings. "Olivia? Sweetheart?"

Her eyes opened. "What if he hadn't died? I would still be trapped, wouldn't I? And, Luke?" She sat up, turned in his arms to face him and cried despairingly, "I don't want to be glad my children's father is dead,"

"You aren't," he assured her firmly. "To be relieved that you have been freed from an abominable situation doesn't mean you rejoice in his death. He was considerably older than you, after all, and you must have expected, even hoped to outlive him. That would have been only natural. But not so soon, I think?"

"No, I would have liked the children to have had him lon-ger. Even if he was more a teacher than a father, they loved him."

She sighed. "I hope his brother manages at least ten more years so that John can complete his education before he inherits."

"We can't live our lives by ifs and buts, Olivia, but must deal as best we can with whatever fate throws at us. You have done admirably so far, I think."

"Thank you, Luke." She smiled weakly at him. "I must go back—they'll be wondering where I am."

"Yes," he agreed, resting his brow against hers. He glanced out the window. "We're getting near the more frequented areas." He straightened her bonnet and began to unfold her veil, pausing to kiss her tenderly before it covered her mouth. "Now you are the proper Mrs Rembleton again," he said, adding with a smile, "and I must behave more decorously," as he moved back to his own seat.

She returned his smile wearily. "I can't thank you enough."

"I am glad you felt you could ask me. You were very brave, Olivia. Another woman would have ignored her suspicions."

"Many would say that was the correct thing to do. But I could not."

"No. You are too courageous for that."

She looked drained. He longed to carry her off to his bed where he could love her and care for her. She would probably not demur if he coaxed her, but he would not exploit her defence-lessness as that bastard Rembleton had. She needed time to heal. Next Season, sweetheart, he vowed silently, next Season we shall explore all that could be between us.

By the time she returned home the following day, Olivia's initial anger had been replaced by cold mortification and resentment. In the succeeding weeks old cuts bled again as she recalled her innocent efforts to develop a closer connection with Jack in those first months. Then she had cherished a girl's naïve hope for love, now she must recognise that he had already found love elsewhere and in any event would never have looked for it with her. Bit by bit, his mute rejection had pushed her to the fringes of his life. It had been a slow, subtle repudiation until that day when he had made it clear that he only had one purpose in coming to her bed. Had he done it deliberately, she asked herself or had it been an instinctive reflection of his true nature? She didn't know which would be worse.

How foolish she had been to have hurried into the marriage! You have no-one to blame but yourself, she told herself bitterly in the depths of another sleepless night.

Book three

Chapter Twenty-One

England, March 1815

"Here's an advertisement for a fine estate near Southampton," Olivia said to her brother.

He held out his hand for the newspaper. "I have been hoping to find something nearer here. Having been so long away from my only family, I am reluctant to give you up so soon and," he reddened slightly, "Abigail would prefer to be closer to her parents, I am sure."

"Abigail?"

His flush deepened. "Miss Carstairs, I should say."

Olivia gaped at him. She had noticed nothing that might suggest a more intimate connection between Captain Frobisher and her children's governess. "Am I to understand that you and she have come to an understanding?"

"No, but I am seriously considering making her an offer. Over the winter I have come to have the highest regard for her and as we may expect news of the ratification of the Peace Treaty with America any day now, I can leave the navy in all honour."

"Does she return your regard?"

"I haven't yet ventured to say anything, but we have become good friends, I think. You must admit I have had a singular opportunity to get to know her that is afforded to few suitors."

There could be no denying that Robert was enjoying his immersion in family life to the full. Olivia knew he frequently joined the children on their afternoon walks with their governess. The three adults made a comfortable company at dinner and somehow it had become usual for Miss Carstairs to join them in the drawing-room afterwards to play three-handed domino or loo. Sometimes the captain challenged her to chess, a game for which Olivia had never acquired a taste while other evenings she accompanied their song on the pianoforte or played a sonata while brother and sister chatted quietly.

Olivia felt a pang. If they were to marry, they would both leave the manor. She would miss their pleasant family evenings and have to find a new governess as well—a double loss. But then she looked at her brother's hopeful countenance and went to kiss his cheek. "I'm sure I wish you both every happiness. I think it a splendid idea that you would remain in the neighbourhood."

He caught her around the waist. "Do you think I've a chance, then?"

"She is very reserved, but I don't see why not. Now that I think of it, you have become very comfortable together."

"Mamma! Uncle!"

At John's shouts, Olivia hurried to the parlour door. As soon as he saw her, the boy gasped, "Mamma, the mail coachman! Boney!"

The door from the back regions opened and the housekeeper and butler emerged, the other servants clustered behind them.

"Ma'am!"

"Henry says!"

"Boney!"

Miss Carstairs, about to go for a walk with the other children, stopped to ask, "What has happened?"

"Quiet!" Captain Frobisher's quarter-deck honed voice silenced the hubbub.

"Thank you," Olivia said. "Now, John, and slowly if you please."

John took a breath. "When the coachman pulled up to exchange the mailbags today, he shouted at the top of his voice, 'the monster Bonaparte has escaped from Elba'."

"What?"

"How?"

"Well I never!"

"Where is he?"

Olivia held up her hand for silence. "John?"

"That's all he said, Mamma. You know the mail may not tarry. He immediately whipped up his horses and off they went."

A hush fell on the little group. Eyes dimmed and faces grew solemn as they recalled the long war and its sacrifices. Had it all been for nothing? Was it all to do again?

"I must report to the Admiralty," the captain announced abruptly. His sister paled and Miss Carstairs put her hand to her mouth.

"Would it not be better to wait until we have seen tomorrow's *Times*?" Olivia asked. "At present we know nothing. Who knows—by tomorrow he may have been recaptured."

Dr Ferguson listened attentively to Luke's account of his youthful illness and long recuperation and the resultant dashing of his military hopes.

"What did you do then, sir? Take to a chaise-longue clutching a vinaigrette, I have no doubt," he asked, the twinkle in his eye belying this assumption.

Luke grinned. "I've always had a stubborn streak, sir. However, I did consult an old soldier who made me see that I might not be able to stand up to the rigours of a long, hard campaign. But that was ten years ago and I don't think it's what will be called for now. Bonaparte is likely to risk all on one throw of the dice. His troops have been scattered and there is a new king on the throne of France. If he can manage to crush the allies with a sudden blow, he will. I cannot see why I shouldn't be fit for such a contest. I haven't had a day's illness since my youth, I practise regularly with the sabre, ride to hounds and can walk all day when I take out a gun."

"Hmm. Let's have a look at you."

The doctor took his time over the examination, carefully feeling Luke's pulse at different points and listening to his heart, first with his ear against his naked back and chest, then using a strange wooden instrument.

"My father's old ear trumpet," he explained. "It amplifies the sound. Now, Mr Fitzmaurice, I want you to stand with your feet together and then jump them apart while at the same time spreading your arms wide. Like a jumping-jack when its string is pulled" he clarified at Luke's puzzled look. "Very good. Now repeat twenty times, as energetically as you can."

"Smarter, faster!" Dr Ferguson said after the first ten and at twenty, "now another ten! This time, clap your hands briskly over your head as you jump. Continue until you can do no more."

Feeling every sort of a fool, Luke jumped and clapped until, red-faced and gasping for breath, he was forced to halt.

"Stand still," the doctor ordered and repeated his previous examination. "Hmm. You may get dressed, sir."

"Well, Mr Fitzmaurice," he began when Luke was comfortably seated in the chair opposite his desk. "I can find nothing to suggest you are unfit for the army. There is no murmur or any strange sounds or rhythms and your heart reacted well to the bout of violent exercise, accelerating and then slowing again in the normal fashion. I will not say that your family physician was overly cautious ten years ago; the illness was much more recent when he advised you and your physique was very likely not yet fully developed. But now? You are no more at risk than any other man, in my opinion. If you wish to serve your country, there is nothing to stop you."

"There he sits in Paris, Emperor again," Franklin said some days later. "At least it put an end to the riots against the Corn Laws. The Englishman is a patriot when all is said and done."

Luke looked at him, exasperated. "Yes, when his country is under threat he may risk his life in its defence and when it is at peace, he may starve to protect the landowners' interests! You insisted your father speak up for the fighting man. Is his brother who labours at home not also worthy of your protection? Should he not be able to afford bread to feed his wife and children?"

"I had not thought you to be so radical, but must admit you have a point. Have you ever thought of standing for Parliament?"

"I've considered it," Luke admitted, "but between party politics and the rotten boroughs, most MPs are marionettes whose strings are pulled by their leader, their patron or both. Once inside the house, they are allowed neither free speech nor a free vote. Essentially the Lords control the Commons as well, something that is not surprising when you consider that only about five per cent of the population may vote—"

Lord Franklin interrupted this rant to enquire, "Would you consent to represent a pocket borough if you were assured that you may speak and vote as your conscience directed you?"

Luke laughed. "And who is going to offer me such a prize?"

"My father might," the other said slowly. "The member for Lutterworth wishes to apply for the Chiltern Hundreds at the end of this session. He had not wanted to stand again in '12, but my father persuaded him. He had some idea he would be keeping the seat warm for me—that was before my brother died."

"Are you not interested?"

"I need to come to grips with the management of the estate; time enough for me to engage in politics when I come into the title." He looked at Luke. "My father was very impressed by you. He might be willing to make the experiment and give you a free hand."

"It would be tempting," Luke acknowledged. "I could work for reform from within as well as without, I suppose."

"As long as you don't find yourself incarcerated in the Tower, like Sir Francis Burdett," Franklin said with a grin. "May I suggest it to my father?"

"If you wish. But, Franklin, he must not feel under any sense of obligation or hesitate to say no if he would rather not. There would have to be a by-election, I suppose. But first, there is something else I want to discuss with you."

"Luke!" Clare came running down the steps to greet her brother. "Welcome home."

He caught her in a hug. "I need not ask how you are, Clare. I can see that you are in great looks."

She smiled ecstatically. "Oh Luke, Hayley has spoken to Papa."

"Has he indeed? What did he say?"

"Don't tease! He offered for me of course."

"Did you accept him?"

She nodded. "I didn't know you could be so happy. He loves me, Luke and I love him."

She said this with such simple certainty that he could tease no more but stooped to kiss her cheek. "I wish you may always be as happy as you are now."

"Thank you." She tucked her hand into the crook of his arm and urged him into the house.

"How is Mamma taking it?" he enquired.

"She alternates between being over the moon with joy at such a triumph, as she puts it, and lamenting that she will be bereft of all her children."

"When is the wedding?"

"We haven't decided yet, but most likely this year. The countess wishes to give a betrothal ball next month at Marwood House."

"The man is to wait for your reply, ma'am."

Surprised and a little worried at this urgency, Olivia opened Flora's note.

Stanton, 27 March 1815

Dearest Olivia,

I write in haste to tell you that I plan to remove to town this day week. With all this upset over Bonaparte, I will feel more comfortable there than waiting here for the news to trickle through. We shall return for the May Day celebrations but they will be much more muted than last year. I do hope you and the children will be able to join us for both as usual.

Fondly,
Flora

Olivia picked up again the Countess of Marwood's invitation to a ball to mark the betrothal of her son Viscount Hayley to Miss Adams. What an excellent match. She felt the two would deal extremely well together. She had not yet decided whether she wished to go to town this year, but now thought, why not? Her period of strict mourning was over and, although she would not dance while in half-mourning, she could go into society. She might hear of a governess who was looking for a new situation. Miss Carstairs had accepted Robert's offer, but, given the uncertainty surrounding his possible recall to duty, they had been unable to make any further plans. However, she did not feel that he would wish to postpone the wedding indefinitely.

"I've had a letter from Colonel Sir John Colborne," Lord Franklin told Luke over a heavy wet at the *Crossed Swords*. "He has agreed to take you. You should at once lodge the purchase money for an ensigncy in the 52nd but not wait for it to be gazetted—rather go out immediately and join the first battalion as a volunteer. Then you will be able to remain with them once your commission comes through. Otherwise you would very likely be sent to the second battalion at Dover for the first six months."

Luke was electrified by this news. He seized his friend's hand and shook it. "Thank you, Franklin. I'm much obliged to you— and the Colonel. I'll go round to the Horse Guards first thing in the morning, but I can hardly leave before my sister's betrothal ball on Tuesday."

"Oh, it will take you that long to get your kit together. I'll take you round all the tradesmen—you'll have to have your uniforms made and all the rest. You have your sabre, at least. And you'll need a couple of horses."

"I thought it was an infantry regiment."

"Colborne insists that an infantry officer on active service should have a riding horse. Mounted, they are more useful, he says. Believe me, you'll be much less tired after a long march if you have covered the stretch on horseback."

"I'm sure you're right," Luke replied, exhilarated by these intimations of a completely different life.

"I tell you what; I'll see if my groom would like to accompany you. He was my servant when I was with the regiment and was complaining only the other day about not being able to have another go at Boney. He knows his way about and will make sure you don't fall for any of the tricks that might be played on a Johnny Raw."

"That's very good of you."

"Nonsense! I'd go myself, but Lutterworth would have a fit."

"You've done your bit," Luke said firmly.

"So have many other fellows who are still there," his lordship answered ruefully.

He wouldn't say anything to his family until after the ball. He knew all too well what response he might expect from his mother and there was no point is dimming his sister's happiness. He had been surprised but pleased when she had requested that Mrs Rembleton be invited. He had not dared hope to see Olivia so soon; in fact he had feared that if his plans worked out, he might not meet her at all this Season.

"The countess has no objection, especially as her husband's sister is married to Mrs Rembleton's uncle, Mr Harte," Clare had explained. "The thing is she, Mrs Rembleton, I mean, is always kind to girls, not like some of the older women who seem to delight in being disapproving. And we all knew that if we needed," she pondered for a moment, "shelter, we could always look to her."

"Shelter?"

"There are some ladies whom one may always seek out if a gentleman is becoming over-familiar or making you uncomfortable in any way and you are not near your chaperon. In addition, they are aware of what is happening around them and will intervene tactfully if necessary. Lady Needham is like that too, but Mamma is not."

Now that he thought about it, it was men who had given Olivia the reputation of being aloof and standoffish. She must have been very alone after she married, he realised. And a neglected wife was the favourite prey of many rakes. It was no wonder she had quickly learnt to distance herself and so protect herself from unwanted approaches. But she had lowered the drawbridge for him, he remembered triumphantly.

Luke lingered near the foot of the staircase that led down to Lady Marwood's ballroom. He was to partner Hayley's sister in the opening quadrille. This was the first ball of the Season and avid greetings were exchanged as the *haut ton* gathered the latest intelligence in preparation for the new social campaign.

A knot of gentlemen on the other side of the dance floor parted to reveal Olivia sharing a settee with Anne Heriot. To Luke's astonishment, Charles stood behind his wife. So he had braved the metropolis in Clare's honour. He caught his cousin's eye and raised a hand in greeting. Charles bent and murmured something to the ladies and they looked over, acknowledging Luke with friendly nods and smiles. He bowed back automatically, his gaze fixed on Olivia. She was exquisitely gowned in white satin with an overdress of black net. Narrow vertical bands of black ribbon ran from her high waist to the flounced hem, emphasizing her willowy figure. Her hair was crowned by a delicate black and white confection adorned with egret's feathers.

A stir behind him announced the descent of the betrothed couple and he offered his arm to Lady Maud to lead her onto the dance floor.

How many times have I stood at the side of a ballroom and watched Luke Fitzmaurice dance, Olivia wondered as she admired the elegance of the dancers. Will I ever dance with him again? Not this Season; Jack wouldn't have cared one way or another, I know, but I'm not ready yet. I hadn't thought the rakes would descend so quickly, either, or the men looking for a complaisant wife who has demonstrated her aptitude for bearing sons. She frowned at the memory of the crass remarks of one widower seeking a new wife with indelicate haste and turned to Mr Heriot.

"How long do you remain in town?"

"Only a week. I dare not stay longer."

Inspired by the prospect of an excuse to return home, she enquired, "Is it only town air that you find so noxious? Would you consider coming to stay in Hertfordshire for a while? Our climate is very pleasant."

"That's a wonderful notion, Olivia," Anne interjected. "We could then accept the duchess's invitation to Stanton for the May Day revels." She looked at her husband. "What do you think, sir?"

"I think it's a delightful idea. I don't know that part of the country at all."

"That's settled then," Olivia said briskly.

"Charmed to see you restored to us, Mrs Rembleton. Your presence adds lustre to the evening," purred a well-corseted *roué*, bowing plumply as he raised his quizzing glass halfway to his eye, his gaze lingering on Olivia's bosom.

This bodice is far too low, she thought, resisting the temptation to tug at it. Martin must add some lace before I wear the gown again. "Thank you, sir," she returned frostily, then smiled at Lord Franklin whose approach enabled her to turn a cold shoulder to her would-be *inamorato*.

"Did you enjoy your visit to Bath?"

"It went splendidly, ma'am. I am most grateful to you for the hint. I didn't like to monopolise Miss Gregg, for she had not seen her brother these many years, but was able to stand up with her regularly and the three of us and my sister undertook some outings together. My mother says she is a prettily behaved girl," he finished with obvious satisfaction.

"I met Miss Gregg at Rembleton Place at Christmas. She told me you had been so obliging as to dance with her," Olivia remarked, recalling the young woman's shining eyes. 'It was like a dream come true, Mrs Rembleton,' she had said, 'for I have often regretted having been obliged to deny him last Season. And the countess was everything that is gracious.'

"Is Mrs Frome in town, ma'am?" was his lordship's next query.

"Not yet. They are at Frome Court, I understand."

To her surprise, he smiled hugely. "My parents and sister are there as well. My mother came out the same year as the countess. I understand there is a party in honour of her birthday."

"Miss Gregg mentioned that she is in some sort a protégée of Lady Frome. There is some distant connection, I believe."

This information seemed to please Lord Franklin even more.

"Mrs Rembleton."

Olivia smiled as Luke bowed before her. She had wondered what she would feel when she next encountered him; would the memory of her confidences in the Park embarrass her. But no, she felt perfectly comfortable with him. Her heart missed a beat when Mr Heriot had pointed him out earlier and now his warm smile sent a little trickle of excitement down her spine.

Luke feasted his eyes on her. She had lost some weight, but not too much, he decided. Her gown was cut deliciously low to display lustrous pearls gleaming against her skin like sugar grated onto cream. He wanted to lick it. Her little puffed sleeves reminded him of flowers, with cunningly fashioned petals of black and white satin layered on black net cuffs under which he longed to ease a finger. Her white kid gloves came to her elbow, exposing tantalising inches of bare skin. He felt his cheeks crease in an unusually open smile and was heartened when she returned one that contained none of her former aloofness.

"Do you dance this evening?" he enquired.

"No. It is too soon."

"Then perhaps you will stroll a little with me?" He crooked his arm invitingly and she slipped her hand into it.

"Miss Adams looks so happy," she commented.

"Yes. Hayley is a good fellow. I have no qualms about entrusting her to him."

"I was surprised to see Mr Heriot."

"So was I. Clare was so pleased that they came. I believe his mother insisted on being here. Clare is her only niece and, 'to make such a splendid match, my dear. I could not but come'."

Olivia laughed as he mimicked the old lady's tones. "She will be company for your mother."

"Who is savouring her triumph," he said solemnly.

As they talked he led her out onto a wide terrace where glowing lanterns created pools of warm light and seductive shade. Several other guests had come out to enjoy the evening air, but they returned to the ballroom when the musicians struck up again, leaving Luke and Olivia to look up at the dark sky spangled with glittering stars.

Entranced, she quoted softly,

" 'There's not the smallest orb which thou behold'st,
But in his motion like an angel sings,
Still quiring to the young-eyed cherubins',"

"Sometimes I think that if we could only be still enough and attentive enough, we might hear them. But our lives are too busy—perhaps deliberately so, to distract ourselves from the verities."

"Come down the steps with me—we may sit there for a while and listen."

She shook her head. "It is an internal stillness that is lacking in me."

He looked down at her. "Why do you say that, Olivia?"

She stirred in a seductive rustle of silk, releasing a subtle fragrance that suggested sunny summer days. "I'm still puzzling everything out. I understand Jack better—it all fits together somehow. I need no longer wonder was there anything more I could have done to make things better between us. I can accept that the fault was his, but won't forget that he is the children's father and I wouldn't spoil their memories for all the world. They must be able to talk of him as they always have."

"You are very wise and kind," he said admiringly. "I don't know if I could hold so little resentment against someone who treated me so badly."

She smiled ruefully. "If I understand him better, I understand myself even less."

"In what way?"

"I constantly ask myself why I rushed headlong into marriage."

"You must be kind to yourself too," he said gently, "and not judge the girl you were then with the knowledge and experience of the woman you are now."

"But if I don't know where I went wrong, how can I be sure I won't make another terrible mistake?"

Her voice shook and he covered her hand with his, turning slightly so that his body shielded the sight of their clasped hands from the inquisitive.

"Olivia, nobody could have expected a young girl to suspect the truth about Rembleton. You did your best at the time. If it is important to you to look back, perhaps you should try to find that inner stillness. It might help you to know yourself, as the ancients put it. There is a place I ride to in the hills above my parents' home. There is never anyone there and I can sit and think. Perhaps you need somewhere like that or even just to allow yourself time for contemplation."

"Perhaps you're right," she said slowly. "Thank you, Luke."

"Do you remain in town for the whole Season?"

"The Heriots come to Hertfordshire with me next week and remain until we go to Stanton for May Day."

"I don't know how Charles will stand such dissipation," he said with a grin, inwardly cursing the fact that he could not take advantage of such a fine opportunity. "I would request your permission to call while they are there, but I leave England the day after tomorrow." His heart beat faster as he spoke. Apart from Franklin, she was the first person to learn of his plans. "I'm going to join the army in Brussels."

"Luke!" Her hand turned and gripped his. "Why now?" she asked after a few moments.

"It's long overdue," he confided, describing the thwarting of his boyhood dreams.

"But you're quite well now?" she asked anxiously.

"So Ferguson assures me."

"He is said to be very competent," she conceded.

"You would have laughed to see me jumping like a confounded Jack-on-a-string, not to mention him and his ear trumpet. He has a real enquiring mind—made me promise I'd come back to see him when I return from the army so he can examine me again."

"I won't tell you to be careful," she said. "It is a foolish thing to say to a soldier. But I wish you the best of good fortune, Luke. You will be in my prayers," she finished softly.

"'*Nymph, in thy orisons be all my sins remembered*'," he murmured, lifting her hand to kiss it. "I hate gloves," he complained and quickly ran his finger down the side of her neck in a remembered caress. She smiled at him and inclined her head to his hand.

"I wish I could kiss you properly," he said longingly.

"Not here."

"No, not here."

"And not today, Luke."

"You need time. I understand. Is your brother still with you?"

"Yes and no. He has been recalled to the Navy and is patrolling the channel. He plans to deprive me of my governess at the earliest possible opportunity. They are having the banns called so that they may marry as soon as he can get a couple of days' furlough."

"Is this your new governess?"

"How on earth did you know that I had a new governess?"

"I remember being shocked to hear you and Mrs Dunford talking about governesses at some ball last year."

"Shocked?" She raised her eyebrows.

"It didn't match my perception of the haughty Mrs Rembleton."

He was amused to see the return of her old arrogant expression. "There she is again," he whispered, "staring at me down her charmingly superior nose." He stroked the organ in question and Olivia had to laugh despite herself.

Chapter twenty-two

"Have you a moment, sir?"

Mr Adams seemed surprised to be sought out in his study by his younger stepson. But then, Luke thought, his visits home had become seldom and in town there was rarely the opportunity for a serious discussion.

"Come in, Luke. Ring for coffee. I had to forego my last cup at breakfast—could no longer stomach the feminine rhapsodies on gowns and the discussions of who had danced how often with whom last night. You were right to avoid it."

"Jer and I went riding and looked in at Boodles afterwards. He said he might as well get some value for his subscription. I had something to tell Jer. And now you."

"You seem very serious. Are you about to follow in Clare's footsteps?"

"What? Announce my betrothal? Not I, sir." Luke accepted a cup of coffee from the footman and waited for the man to leave the room. "I haven't yet told my mother, but I leave for Brussels tomorrow."

Mr Adam's brows jerked together. "Not escaping your creditors, are you?"

"No sir, nothing like that. I shall join the 1st/52nd, initially as a gentleman volunteer, but shall soon be gazetted as ensign."

His stepfather slapped his hand on his desk, rattling his cup in its saucer. "What the devil are you about, sir?"

"I'm joining the 1st/52nd, first as a volunteer and then as ensign," Luke repeated patiently.

"This will kill your mother."

"I sincerely doubt it, sir," Luke answered drily. "I look to you to prevent her from over-indulging in hysterics. My mind is made up and cannot be altered. I have purchased my commission and my arrangements are all in place. With so much of his former army overseas or disbanded, Wellington has need of every man he can get. I could never look myself in the eye again if I failed to serve now."

"But your health? Surely the reasons are just as compelling now as they were ten years ago?"

"On the contrary, sir. I am not so foolish that I did not first consult a physician. According to Dr Ferguson, it need not cause me any concern."

Mr Adams seemed unsure how to respond. That he was not happy with the idea was evident, but he clearly understood that neither his approval nor his permission were sought. After some minutes silence, he cleared his throat. "I see you are determined to go. I find it hard to argue with you, I own. Tell me what this doctor of yours said and let me break it to your mother. Just promise me you won't put any ideas into Ephraim's head."

"I promise," Luke said, relieved. "Thank you, sir."

Mr Adams listened to the account of Dr Ferguson's examination and grunted, "He seems to have been very thorough. I'll go up to Eliza now and send for you when she is able to see you. Help yourself to a glass of madeira while you're waiting."

"Won't you have one with me to fortify yourself?" Luke suggested with a grin.

"A good idea." Mr Adams went to the decanters and handed his stepson a glass. "To your continued good health and good fortune, my boy."

"Thank you, Father."

Luke hoped his mother would be able to respond in the same generous spirit.

Some fifteen minutes later he entered her sitting-room. The air was redolent of smelling-salts. Supported by her husband, she lay half-reclined on the chaise-longue, dabbing at her eyes with a lace handkerchief. She held out a wavering hand.

"Luke! My son!"

Repressing the urge to point out that he was but one of three, Luke went over and gently clasped it.

"Your father says you are determined to do this."

"Yes, Mother. I cannot honourably hold back."

"Then I shall not try to dissuade you." Her voice quivered. "But you must promise me to take every care."

"I will, Mother," he pledged solemnly, while his eyes met those of his stepfather in helpless masculine understanding.

Shrouded in a boat cloak that concealed the unfamiliar short scarlet jacket and grey overalls of the 52nd Regiment of Foot, Luke stood at the railing of the packet boat and watched the Belgian coast draw near. He felt curiously unsettled in a way he had not experienced since he first donned cap and gown at Cambridge. It was the sense of being in transition, he recognised, of having assumed a character to which he had not yet earned the right. Once he had joined the regiment and been acknowledged as one of theirs, he would recover his tranquillity.

His spirits improved on the journey by canal boat from Ostend to Ghent where he was readily accepted by a motley assortment of young officers also travelling to join their regiments.

His first action must be to call on his commanding officer. From Ghent it was a morning's ride to Brussels, where Colonel Sir John Colborne still served as Military Secretary to the Prince of Orange. Luke was lucky to find a room; the hotels were full of English pleasure-seekers and a stranger walking through the streets of the city would never have thought that a vast army was assembling on its doorstep.

A tall man in his late forties, his dark hair streaked with grey, Colborne was no Byronic hero, but a practical and experienced soldier whose sharp eyes promised that he would neither tolerate nor condone any sort of obfuscation.

"I confess, Mr Fitzmaurice, that it is the first time I have known a gentleman of your advanced years to join as ensign," he said mildly. "However, Lord Franklin pled your case well enough to convince me to take you."

"For which I am very grateful, sir."

"What is your object in this? I doubt that you seek a military career."

"No, sir. Rather to serve my country in a way that was not permitted to me ten years ago when I had to bow to medical advice."

The colonel's brows rose. "I take it that is no longer an issue," he snapped.

"I have been assured so, sir, else I would not have taken this course. As to your first question, I am resolved to remain with the army until Bonaparte has been defeated, but do not propose to serve longer than that. In confidence I may tell you that I have been offered a seat in Parliament, but have requested that the incumbent defer his request to retire from politics for the moment. However, should he do so while Boney is still at large, I would not sell out but forego the opportunity if necessary."

Colborne nodded. "Let us hope we can deal with him quickly and it does not come to a lengthy pursuit into France.

Very well. The regiment is at Lessines. I'll make you known to Lieutenant Jaspers, who returns there tomorrow. If you travel with him, he'll soon put you in the way of things." He inspected Luke critically. "Strictly speaking, as a volunteer you should replace those wings on your shoulders with straps to hold the crossed-belts that the men wear but you may leave them as your commission is probably already gazetted. I'll send Colonel Rowan a note to that effect"

Lieutenant Jaspers was a dark, intense young man, not yet twenty. Despite his tender age, he had spent over nine years in the military and had served with distinction in the Peninsula. He did not blink when presented with a raw ensign some eleven years his senior but made Luke welcome.

"Glad to have you," he said cheerfully. "We had a stroke of luck, I can tell you. We set out for America twice, but each time were forced back as the wind was against us. Imagine missing the chance of another crack at Boney! Now what do you say to a bite of dinner followed by a stroll in the park? Then we may see how we shall spend the evening."

After the hectic scramble to make everything ready in England, it seemed somehow ridiculous to saunter in the sunshine exchanging greetings with the very same ladies to whom he had bowed a year previously in London.

"I say, Mr Fitzmaurice, do you know everyone?" his companion asked, awed by the flutter Luke's appearance had caused among the fair sex.

"I've been on the town longer than you have been in the military," Luke replied, amused, halting beside Lady Holton's landau.

"Whatever are you doing here, Mr Fitzmaurice?" she cried after the exchange of greetings and introductions. "And in regimentals, too! Are you free this evening? You must come to my ball. And Lieutenant Jaspers as well," she added kindly. "Where are you staying? I shall have cards sent round instanter with my direction."

She drove off leaving the lieutenant in as hapless a state as Luke had been on the boat to Ostende.

"I know how to behave at the various hops we had in the Peninsula and attended some assemblies at home last winter, but I've never been to what you might call a ton ball," he said frankly.

"You won't find it very different," Luke consoled him. "Wear your dress uniform and be on your best behaviour. It's more than likely you will know some of the other officers who will be among the guests and as long as you do not consider yourself too proud to dance, you will do very well. We may go together if you like."

"I should indeed," the other said gratefully.

The lieutenant proved very much in demand among the young ladies, his tough, wiry physique, set off by features that had been refined and hardened by the rigours of the Peninsula campaign, proving a dangerous attraction to girls more used to pampered young officers who had barely seen service.

"Your friend has all our young maidens in a flutter," Lady Holton remarked to Luke as they took a glass of champagne together. They were old companions; she had been one of his flirts some years ago and while their more intimate connection had ceased, a warm friendship remained."

"I only met him today," Luke answered. "You wouldn't think it to look at him, but he was at Badajoz when the 52nd stormed it."

"I am very grateful to him, for his dancing of every dance has, I think, spurred others on so as not to be cut out with their current interests."

Luke was having a similar effect among the matrons; several officers who had set up flirts among the married women being quite put out at this ensign who was greeted with such warmth and clearly had his choice of partners.

"Who the devil is he?" a major muttered to a captain. "Damned dandy," he added rather unfairly as Luke led out a lady of whom he himself had great hopes. "Here, sir," he said to Mr Jaspers who was about to take the floor with Lady Holton's niece. "Who's your friend?"

"Oh, that's Mr Fitzmaurice of ours," the lieutenant responded coolly. "A capital fellow."

All in all, Luke was happy to leave the next day for the quieter environs of Lessines, some thirty miles south-west of Brussels and about half-way between it and the French border. As they approached the town they heard the sound of bugles and the tramp of feet. Luke was gripped by a mixture of awe and pride when he saw the long column of more than a thousand men proudly march by. Later that evening he was formally put in orders as Volunteer Fitzmaurice and five days later news of his gazetting made the rounds.

He was soon immersed in practising his drill, getting to know the men of the company to which he had been assigned and familiarising himself with the Articles of War and other Regulations and Orders as expected of every officer. He had had his sword sharpened in London but now took it to have the edges and tip refined.

"A fine blade, sir," the man looked up from his grindstone," but not standard."

Captain Gregg who was standing nearby, held out his hand. "May I?" He took the weapon and examined it carefully.

"You didn't purchase that last week."

"No. It was made for me some eight years ago. It's based on the 1803 light infantry design."

Gregg's curiosity was pricked. "Why did you need it? It's been well kept but obviously used."

Luke nodded. "I like sword work, but have no taste for the modish fencing salons. There are other places in London if you know where to look. Lord Franklin strayed into ours one evening—that's how I made his acquaintance."

"If we ever meet in London, I should be glad of an introduction," Captain Gregg exclaimed, handing the sword back to the grinder. "But if you have only used it for sport—," he hesitated for a moment, "it's a different thing when you must continue your thrust into your opponent's body. It may seem macabre, but it would be to your advantage if you could find a carcase—some old nag, perhaps, and experience the resistance."

Chapter Twenty-three

Robert Frobisher leaped out of the post-chaise, hurriedly paid off the postilion and hastened into Southrode Manor, followed more slowly by another naval officer.

"My sister? Miss Carstairs?" he flung at the butler who greeted him in the hall.

"Madam is not at home but is expected shortly. Miss Carstairs is in the schoolroom, Captain."

"Thank you," the captain tossed over his shoulder. "Look after my friend." He took the stairs two at a time and burst into the schoolroom to the astonishment of his niece, nephew and their governess, whose rebuke withered on her lips when she saw who disturbed them.

"Robert!"

"Abbie! My dearest girl." He bent to kiss her, spied the fascinated children and pressed a chaste salute on her cheek.

"Miranda, Samuel, pray excuse us for a moment. I must speak to Miss Carstairs in private." He tugged his betrothed outside the door where he could indulge himself with a deeper, more intimate embrace, his hands cradling her face. He felt her lips part and smiled against her mouth before sinking into her.

"What a welcome, my darling," he whispered at last. "Abbie, I've got five days leave. Will you marry me tomorrow morning? The banns have been called, haven't they?"

"Yes, Sunday was the last time. But tomorrow?"

"Is it too soon?"

"No," she said resolutely. "Although I don't know what Mamma will say. And Olivia."

"She should be back soon. We'll tell her and go down to the Rectory. I've left my first lieutenant downstairs. He'll stand up with me."

"Where did you come from today?"

"Chatham. We had to put in for some minor repairs. We left before dawn."

"You want your breakfast, I suppose," she said with a smile.

"See what an excellent wife you will be," he teased her and stole another kiss.

Olivia's hand went to her heart when she found a strange naval officer standing in her hall.

"Mrs Rembleton?"

"Yes."

The man bowed. "Lieutenant Redfearn, *HMS Minotaur,* at your service, ma'am."

The *Minotaur* was Robert's ship. "My brother?" she asked sharply.

"The captain is with me, ma'am. He went to seek out the lady to whom he is betrothed."

The breath rushed out of her and she sank into a chair.

"Ma'am?" the lieutenant asked, concerned.

"Pay no attention, sir. Are they looking after you?"

Before he could answer, her butler appeared from the kitchen regions. "I understand the officers have not yet broken their fast, madam. A repast will be served in the breakfast parlour in ten minutes."

"Excellent, Smith." She glanced at the valise at her visitor's feet. "Have Lieutenant Redfearn shown to the green bedchamber. I shall see you later, Lieutenant."

"Thank you, ma'am."

The lieutenant watched his hostess ascend the staircase, his lips curling in male appreciation of the sway of curved hips and rounded arse beneath her muslin skirts. She was a widow, he remembered, and considerably younger than the old man. A neat little property, too. A chap could do worse.

Robert and Abbie moved apart when they heard Olivia's footsteps. He picked his sister up and exuberantly whirled her around. "Livvie, can you take the children for the rest of the day?" he enquired as he set her back on her feet. "Abbie has agreed to marry me tomorrow morning and she'll need some time to prepare."

Olivia stared at him before demanding, "Are you happy to wed so precipitously, Abbie?"

"Oh, yes." The younger woman blushed. "But I should like to spend a last night at home."

"You must do just as you like, my dear. Your poor mother won't know whether she's on her head or her heels. Perhaps it would be best if I give the wedding breakfast here. Then she may concentrate on you. I'll write her a note. You are going to see her now, I presume?"

"After breakfast," her brother said decisively.

"It will be served in the breakfast parlour in a few minutes. Abbie, why don't we go to my sitting-room and make plans while the gentlemen have their meal? The children may come with us and work quietly."

Half an hour later, the captain strolled in to collect his betrothed. "What am I to do with Redfearn, Livvie? He'll only be here tonight—he is to stand up with me in the morning, but must be back on board by the end of the first dog watch."

Resisting the temptation to reply, 'He's your guest', she handed him that morning's *Times*. "He might like to have a look at the newspaper or stroll in the garden if he prefers. I'll see if Mr Heriot is willing to take him out this afternoon, to Hitchin perhaps."

"Heriot?"

"My friends the Heriots are staying with me at the moment."

"I'll leave it in your hands then. Come, my dear." He offered his arm to Abbie who looked apologetically at Olivia as she allowed herself to be steered out of the room.

"I hope she took him to task for being so high-handed," Olivia said later to the Heriots. "The sooner he finds a house of his own the better."

"You must make allowance for a man in love," Mr Heriot said. "I'll take this lieutenant off your hands for the rest of the day."

"And you may safely entrust the children to Mrs Heriot and me," Anne said. "You will have enough to do."

"Mrs Heriot would like a word, *Madame*."

"Come in, Anne," Olivia called. "That will be all, Martin."

"I wanted to catch you before we go down for dinner," Anne said. "Charles asked me to mention something to you. He hopes you will forgive him for interfering," she added.

"What's wrong?" Mr Heriot was not usually given to sudden starts and tended to leave the distaff side to its own devices.

"It's Lieutenant Redfearn. Charles felt he went over the line today in quizzing him about Mr Rembleton's will and in particular how this estate was left. First it was casual comments—he supposed your eldest son was the heir and assumed you had been left comfortably off as well—but when Charles didn't respond he moved to direct questions, which at least enabled Charles to give him a sharp set-down. However, he thought you should be warned."

"Thank him for me and beg him not to say anything to my brother. Redfearn leaves at midday tomorrow in any event and I shall be able to keep him in check until then."

"I have no doubt of it," Anne said with a grin. "Shall we go down together? That way he won't be able to get you to himself."

The lieutenant went out of his way to make himself pleasant and if Olivia had not been fore-warned, she might well have taken his attentiveness at face value. She had no alternative but to seat him on her left but did her best to keep the conversation general. In this she was ably abetted by her guests, in particular old Mrs Heriot whose genuine interest in the countries visited by the naval gentlemen led to a flood of reminiscences.

"We shall leave you gentlemen to your port," Olivia said at last.

When the men returned to the drawing-room, Mr Redfearn successfully claimed the seat beside his hostess. "I must thank you for your hospitality, ma'am especially at such a time. You have a very welcoming home, if I may say so." He looked around the room. "This is what we dream of in our long months at sea."

This statement was accompanied by such a lost puppy look that Anne intervened to enquire, "Where is your own home, Lieutenant Redfearn?"

"Lancashire, ma'am."

"Are you far from the Lakes, sir? We visited them on our wedding journey. I have never seen more sublime landscapes."

The topic lasted them until the arrival of the tea-tray and afterwards Captain Frobisher challenged the other men to a game of billiards.

"Then I wish you all a very good night," Olivia said thankfully.

Olivia looked out into the quiet night. The stars wouldn't sing for her tonight, she thought and sighed. The little episode had left her dispirited. Was no man to be trusted? Even where they appeared to deal honestly with one, as Jack had done when he proposed, the honesty was frequently superficial.

She felt no eagerness to remarry and the thought of Lieutenant Redfearn silently assessing whether he could install himself as master of her house strengthened this resolve. What of the alternatives to marriage? Luke had wanted to kiss her in Lady Marwood's garden. Was he hoping she would agree to an *affaire de coeur*? But did she want a lover, or lovers; wish to embark on those precarious waters cruised by so many ton matrons and widows? Would such an odyssey not ultimately be as unsatisfying as her marriage had been? She could not expect to find the tender passion of Burlington House in a hasty rendezvous at a ball or a rout.

Sighing, she drew the curtains and got into bed. As usual, her last thought before she fell asleep was a heartfelt 'keep him safe'.

"I apologise for the hasty departure," Olivia said to Anne the following afternoon.

Anne laughed. "There's no need to apologise. You are quite right to leave the lovebirds to themselves and Flora won't mind if we come a day or two early."

Miranda pouted. "I don't see why Miss Carstairs and Uncle Robert can't come too."

"She is Mrs Frobisher now, and your Aunt Abigail," Olivia corrected her. "She and Uncle Robert prefer to remain here."

"I don't see why she had to marry him," the child grumbled. "Now I shall have to have yet another governess. That will be the third in a year."

Olivia was mortified by her daughter's display of egotism. Jack's principle of encouraging the children to speak their mind was not always a good one. Certainly, Miranda seemed to have inherited something of his self-centredness.

"Miranda, the world does not revolve around you and people are not obliged to make their decisions according to that which would suit you best. You will return to the schoolroom and write twenty times in your best hand '*I should not think only of myself but must also consider the wishes of others*'." She seated herself at a little writing-desk. "I shall write it out for you to copy."

"Yes, Mamma. I am sorry." Miranda took the sheet of paper, scarlet at this public rebuke.

"And do not dawdle. We leave in half-an-hour," her mother added sternly.

"What do you think of Mr Fitzmaurice being gazetted as ensign in the 52nd?" Flora asked some nights later over dinner. "It is the sensation of the Season. I had thought him past the age of seeking military glory."

"What, Luke?" Charles Heriot exclaimed and then, "I beg your pardon, Duchess."

"I received a letter from my brother earlier," his mother said. "I'm sorry, Charles, I did not have an opportunity to mention it to you. My sister-in-law is in great distress but determined to be brave, he says."

Olivia smiled inwardly at this, but forbore mentioning that Luke had told her of his intention the night of his sister's betrothal ball. "What news of Bonaparte?" she asked.

The duke shook his head. "Nobody seems to have any idea what his plans may be. Or Wellington's either, if it comes to that. I'm told he has complained to the Horse Guards that they should send him more troops instead of more generals, so I suppose Mr Fitzmaurice will not be too unwelcome."

It was several more hours before Olivia regained the privacy of her own room and could look at the post that had been sent over from the manor. She sorted through the usual business letters—they could wait until the morning; glanced quickly at the invitations—she must decide whether she wished to return to town with Flora—and then picked up a letter in an unknown hand. It was firm yet fluid, the writing of someone well accustomed to the pen. She didn't recognise the seal. She broke it carefully and unfolded the page only to drop the letter, stunned. It was from Luke.

Lessines, May 1815

My dear Olivia,

I beg you will forgive my impertinence in writing to you without so much as by your leave. I feel the need to tease out the differences between my old and my new life. I could do so in a journal, of course, or write to Franklin, who also has experience of both worlds, but when I finally set pen to paper, I discovered you to be the one who occupies my thoughts, the one to whom I feel I can address my reflections and musings without fear of their being given any disproportionate weight or other reception beyond that of an intelligent and understanding reader. I don't know yet whether I shall send this to you, but for now shall write as if we were sitting on the steps of Lady Marwood's terrace.

It is almost dark outside, that late dusk which seems to struggle more successfully against candlelight than full darkness does. I am sitting at the open window, enjoying a rare moment of solitude while smoking a cigar, an unsavoury habit I have acquired from some of the Peninsula veterans.

I have never seen a more fertile countryside than here; the husbandry appears to be modern and of a high standard and the crops are already well up. It is odd to be preparing for battle among such bounty. The old hands tell the new recruits it is more like a holiday than a war, and yet war must come.

I have been received here with great kindness. There are some sixty officers; we 'mess' or dine in the same hotel but need two rooms because of our numbers. After mess, we amuse ourselves with racing our horses in a sort of steeplechase through the meadows and over the brooks that cross them. Wine is plentiful and cheap; four shillings a bottle for champagne for example, while one can obtain a good hock for two shillings and threepence. This can lead to the most curious occurrences; one evening I found myself instructing sixteen fellow-officers (half of whom were perfectly willing to try the lady's steps) in the latest quadrilles. Despite our exertions, we were all fit for parade the next morning, I assure you. The odd thing was that the following night, when someone arranged an impromptu hop, they proved to have remembered most of the steps, even those who had never before attempted a quadrille. I suppose the habit of drill is so engrained in them that they can easily commit a series of movements to memory.

I have to say that I have had more honest fun here than in ten years at the entertainments of la haute societée. When did it become desirable for us to exhibit no more amusement than a polite smile? Why must we always hide what we are thinking from others? And why is the ton's amusement so frequently at the expense of others? What an artificial society we have created for ourselves! Is it lack of occupation, do you think? Nature abhors a vacuum, they say, and if we will not or must not work, why then we make our play our work and take it far too seriously. Only think how many times each day a tonnish lady changes her gown or of the dreadful blunder if she appears at the opera in a dinner dress!

My dearest Olivia, I have come to the end of my sheet. I believe I shall cast my bread upon the waters or at least entrust this letter to the mails and hope that you will look kindly on one who has the honour to be your obedient servant,

Luke Fitzmaurice.

Olivia clutched the letter to her breast, tears in her eyes and a smile trembling on her lips. She didn't know this Luke, although she had seen glimpses of him that day they drove in the Park. She glanced again at the close of his letter. It was a minor variant of a very usual phrase, but immediately conjured up the image of him lolling naked on the day-bed in Burlington House, his eyes still bound and his satisfied member resting against his thigh. She pressed her hands to her hot cheeks for a moment and then picked up the letter to read it again more slowly before refolding it carefully and secreting it in her writing box.

Luke shook his head. Sir Henry Clinton's division had marched twenty miles towards Quevres-au-Camps, near the frontier with France and now attempted to set up an encampment of tents using large blankets that had been fitted with loops at each corner for this purpose. Cursing and swearing, the men wrestled with blankets, bayonets and firelocks. One veteran earned particular opprobrium by remarking in superior tones, "ah, that's how we camped when we chased the Frogs after Salamanca," but it was noticed that his efforts met with little more success than those of the newest recruits. As the best results achievable resulted in a hot, stuffy enclosure, many said that they would prefer to sleep rolled in their blankets, especially if the night was dry.

"What's the point of this?" Luke asked Captain Gregg.

"A show of strength, I think." The captain nodded towards the woods surrounding them. "There's a French fortress at Condé, some seven miles from here."

After a few uncomfortable days bivouac, they were all relieved when orders came to return to Lessines. The regiment dismissed, Luke left his horse with his groom and headed for his quarters where he at once removed the tight shako, rubbing the mark it had left on his forehead. He supposed it would ease with time. He stripped off his red coat and splashed some water onto his face. It would do for the moment.

A little bundle of letters, the first he had received since leaving England, had been left on top of his campaign chest and he flicked through them, recognising those from his mother and brother by the handwriting and one from Lord Franklin by his father's frank. The fourth letter had 'Gracechurch' scrawled across the corner and he held his breath as he carefully broke the seal and unfolded it. She had written! He was doubly gratified that she had had the duke frank it. She had clearly decided not to make a secret of their correspondence—or was she so unworldly that it had not occurred to her that it might be prudent to do so. For his part, he would be discreet until she indicated there was no need for it. He poured himself a glass of the excellent cognac it was so easy to obtain here and sat down with an anticipatory sigh.

Gracechurch House, London, May 1815

My dear Luke,

What a surprise it was to receive your letter and how interesting to have a personal report from Belgium. Here all is speculation and rumour. You will say that by and large that is all you have to go by too, but you are nearer the font of knowledge that we at home are.

You cannot imagine the stir caused by the appearance of your name in the Gazette. *You would be vastly diverted if not necessarily flattered by the peculiar mixture of speculative and laudatory comments it launched. Some ill-natured souls such as young Norris suggested you were fleeing your creditors, but unfortunately no amount of enquiry could reveal who these might be, so their remarks rebounded on them as others hinted that this possibility first sprang to mind because they themselves are but a short step away from the spunging-house. A few young ladies considered you might be suffering from unrequited love, but this was repudiated by others who point out that no girl could resist you. (Are you blushing or laughing when you read this, I wonder?) Your sister simply said when appealed to, as she recently was in my presence, that you felt it to be your duty and your mother murmured, 'So brave, so brave' with a little flourish of her lace handkerchief. Lord Franklin finds it (I mean the tittle-tattle) amusing, I think, at least to judge from his expression.*

You will be relieved to know all the talk died down as soon the next on-dit (Mrs S. C. discovered in flagrante delicto with Sir M. F.) made the rounds. The lady's husband was not amused and we understand that she has been banished to the wilds of Yorkshire while Mr C, or so I am told, continues to consort with his latest interest, a young protégée of Harriette Wilson. At least Mrs C and Sir M have been true to each other these past ten years and, indeed, he left town not long after the lady did. Perhaps they will be able to enjoy a rustic, summer idyll. I'm sure I wish it for them and that Mr C is not so hypocritical as to sue for Criminal Conversation. How unfair it is that such redress is not open to females, but I suppose the courts would break down under the pressure of all the cases brought.

Luke grinned appreciatively at this tart remark.

My brother contrived to get five days furlough and married Miss Carstairs out of hand. He has now returned to duty and the duchess and I are distracting the bride by arranging for her presentation at court. I am engaged in negotiations with my modiste regarding the width of my hoops and the level of my waist, for if the one is too broad and the other too high, I shall resemble a partially inflated balloon and must be wary of the slightest breeze lest I be wafted away. As Napoleon did not require the return of the hoop at his court, I can only suppose that her Majesty considers it her patriotic duty to insist on its retention here. Another example of your artificial society!

It was that tedious Lord Chesterfield who declared that there was 'Nothing so illiberal and so ill-bred as audible laughter', a maxim that has been impressed on generations of children ever since. That reminds me that I have acquired a new governess, a Miss Mullins who has just handed over the youngest of the Kerswell sons to his tutor. A highly qualified lady, of whom Lady K has only the highest praise, she likes the idea of having a female pupil whom she will not lose at as young an age. She accompanied me on a walk with the children and each side approved of the other. She is spending two weeks with her elderly parents and will come to us on the first of June.

John was thrilled to learn that you are now a military man while Miranda, who fondly remembers your skills as a story-teller—nobody does the cat in Puss in Boots as well as Mr Fitzmaurice, she says and Samuel nods solemnly in agreement—hopes that you will not be hurt, a wish in which she is joined by her mother.

Luke put down the letter, moved by the thought that she had spoken to her children of him. He had expected to be the subject of ton gossip and conjecture but had not dreamt he might be mentioned in Olivia's private family conversations.

My dear Luke, I pray that you remain safe and well despite all the alarums and excursions to which you are now exposed and that your military experiences continue to enliven and inspire you. If you have time to write again, this reader will strive to be as understanding and intelligent as you wish.

Your sincere friend,
Olivia Rembleton

Chapter Twenty-Four

"We're off again in the morning, I hear." Major Carew's announcement was greeted by a chorus of groans and calls for more champagne.

"Where to this time?" Captain Gregg enquired with a marked lack of enthusiasm.

"Ellignies-St-Anne—back towards Quevres-au-Camps and Condé."

"Not blanket tents again, I trust," another officer put in languidly.

"How long is this to continue?" Gregg demanded impatiently. "What's today? The eleventh of June? That's three and a half months since Bonaparte escaped."

"He might wait to move until the harvest is in," the major pondered.

"Can he afford to? The longer he leaves it, the more time the allies have to amass on his borders. He's hardly going to risk an attack on all frontiers."

"He's still in Paris, isn't he?" Luke asked. "We won't know what way the cat is going to jump until he leaves. He might decide to sit tight, let us come to him."

"He'd be risking a lot; there is still a royalist faction to contend with, a faction that has already had a new taste of power," Gregg said. "Don't forget that his forces are more accustomed to attack than defend. Apart from last year, when Wellington already had them on the run, they are not used to fighting on home soil."

"No more than we are," the major reflected. "Thank providence we are an island nation."

Would we be as keen to wage war abroad if we were exposed at land frontiers, Luke wondered cynically but said nothing.

Luke tugged his jacket to sit correctly, buckled his sword-belt and set his shako on his head. They had been kept busy drilling these past four days and he was about to put his company through their final exercises in advance of the division field day that had been announced for the morrow. As he waited on the improvised parade ground, a clatter of hooves signalled the brisk approach of the general's aide de camp who did not pause to exchange civilities but instructed crisply, "Your company, sir, is to be a mile on the Ath road in twenty minutes."

"Yes, sir." Luke acknowledged the order and turned to his bugler. "Sound the assembly!"

The men fell in immediately. Luke had initially been mildly astonished and relieved that his commands were obeyed unquestioningly and without hesitation, but that was before he came to appreciate the training and discipline that instilled instant obedience in the British soldier. He was not too proud to learn from the sergeants, one of whom reminded him of his own mentor and now felt completely comfortable in taking command.

Where were they off to this time? He had already learnt that all longer marches were subject to the delays and hindrances caused by the movement of baggage. Today was no different and it was two o'clock before they halted at Enghien. Wood and water parties were dispatched, rations issued and the men settled to cooking their meat. As they sat in the afternoon sun, waiting for their meal to be ready, a new recruit cocked his head.

"Thunder," he nodded towards the east where a rumbling could be heard. "That's odd—the sky don't have the appearance of it."

"Here's hoping we're not in for a downpour," another said. "There's nothing worse than a wet march."

"That's not thunder. Boney's shaking his blankets again."

"Blankets?" The youngster was puzzled by the veteran's comment.

The other laughed. " 'Tis cannon, lad. From the distance they sound as if someone is shaking blankets." He listened for a moment. "Sounds like someone's getting a hard pounding, too."

It's begun, Luke thought. While we're eating our dinner here, others are killing and being killed. It will be our turn next. Don't let me disgrace myself, he prayed, but let me stand up to the enemy like a man.

This was war? Masses of soldiers marched and countermarched with little or no idea why they were sent first in one direction and then suddenly about-turned to retrace their steps. Grateful that he was on horseback, Luke could only appreciate the equanimity of the men who stopped, started, and waited while carrying their full kit including blanket, musket, bayonet and, on Colborne's instructions, a hundred and twenty rounds of ball—double the usual issue.

Ravenous by midnight, he counted himself fortunate to secure a meagre meal in a little *auberge* at Braine-le-Comte. Afterwards he prowled through the small rooms in search of a bed, finally throwing himself down to doze for two hours beside a snoring Highlander who remained oblivious of his temporary companion. Then it was off again through the night, picking his way in torrential rain on a road that was quickly churned to mud. At last the sky lightened a little and they could see where they were going. It was seven o'clock when they reached Nivelles. Here they were directed to a large orchard where they could break their fast and rest as best they could.

"At least the rain has stopped and at this time of the year there's some heat in the sun," one man said, draping his blanket to dry on an apple-tree. "Did you see all those cavalry horses? They'll have to move on before us; the streets are too narrow for us to pass them."

"I hope the locals are keen gardeners and remove the muck quickly," his companion said gloomily. "Otherwise we'll be marching through it."

At noon the 52nd fell in again, heading directly towards Brussels but impeded from time to time by Dutch-Belgian troops trying to cross their line to go towards Genappe. To the right and left, British cavalry and artillery plodded through the fields. The men were tired and progress was slow and weary. Once they had to stop to make way for several waggons carrying the wounded from the previous day's fighting.

"Mr Fitzmaurice, go back along the road and bring up any stragglers, if you please."

Glad to have something else to do, Luke trotted back the way they had come, scrutinising the figures lining the road for a glimpse of the familiar uniform. Some men had stopped exhausted while others had slipped away, perhaps to answer nature's call or to scrounge a drink or something to eat. A young drummer, pale with fatigue, sat hunched on a stone. Luke rode over and the boy climbed wearily to his feet.

"I'm sorry, sir. I just couldn't go on."

Luke handed him his flask. "Have a swig of that and wait here until I return. You'll feel more the thing then and we'll go on together."

"Yessir."

The boy drank and Luke was relieved to see a little colour return to the white face.

By the time he came up to the boy again, he had a group of some twenty men and a few women, camp-followers who had also fallen out. "Now, lad," he instructed, "give us a good rat-tat to set us on our way."

With a flourish of his sticks, the drummer rapped out the familiar rhythm of the British Grenadiers and before long one of the men began to sing, soon joined by the others in a version Luke hadn't heard before.

Eyes right, my jolly field boys,
Who British bayonets bear,
To teach your foes to yield boys,
When British steel they dare!
Now fill the glass, for the toast of toasts
Shall be drunk with the cheer of cheers,
Hurrah, hurrah, hurrah, hurrah!
For the British bayoneteers.

"There they are!"

"Who?"

"The Frenchies." A corporal pointed to the right where a long column could be seen moving north on the road from Charleroi. His sleeve was adorned by a VS framed by laurels, the proud Valiant Stormer badge awarded by the 52nd to survivors of a forlorn hope, and he spoke with the satisfaction of a hunter who has spied his prey.

"About bloody time!" his neighbour grunted. "We must've marched fifty miles since yesterday. The sun'll be setting soon and I don't want another night march."

"You've got soft. This is nothing to what we did in the Peninsula," the corporal scoffed.

"I know. And I've no wish to do it again," his friend retorted. "At least there are no bloody mountains here!"

"What a cheek!" a third man exclaimed. Two French officers had ridden towards the British column. "Look at 'im—making notes as cool as you please."

"You can be sure old Douro has someone doing the same for us," the second man remarked placidly.

As night fell, they were allowed a brief respite to bivouac on a wet, ploughed field. "Take to your blankets, men and make yourselves comfortable," the major said to general laughter, but soon the field was covered with cocoon-like bundles lying on straw that had somehow been acquired by the fatigue parties. Luke wrapped himself in his boat cloak, pulling the hood over his head so as to avoid the pricking of the wet straw. Despite the rain, he managed to fall into a heavy doze, but it seemed that he had no sooner done so than they were roused again and told to move on, taking their straw with them.

At last they reached their final halting place and could pile arms before settling down for the night, huddled in cloaks and blankets against the persistent rain and bedded on muddy straw that contrived to find any weak spot in their protective wrappings, scratching and dripping through any gaps. After two days of constant movement in purposeful, organised confusion, with arbitrary stops for random meals and no proper rest, Luke felt completely disoriented. He managed to fall asleep, only to be woken roughly when some picketed horses tore themselves loose and hurtled wildly through the lines, causing additional mayhem as men scrambled to get out of their way.

Afterwards he slept only in fits and starts, plagued by dreams of cavalry charges interspersed with tranquil glimpses of his family at home. Once he dreamt of Olivia. They were in the parlour at Burlington House, but his eyes were no longer bound and she lay in his arms as trustingly as she had that day in the carriage in

Hyde Park. He raised a hand to unpin her hair only to be jerked awake by the bugles sounding 'rouse'.

Cold, dirty and unshaven, the 52nd shook the stiffness from their limbs, rubbed the sleep from their eyes and foraged in their knapsacks for something to break their fast. This done, they turned their attention to the day ahead, checking equipment and ensuring that their arms were clean and dry. Haunted by stories of swords rusted fast in their scabbards, Luke drew his and polished it to remove any trace of damp that might have seeped down, then swabbed dry the inside of the scabbard as best he could with the aid of a borrowed ramrod. Satisfied, he sheathed his weapon and, having checked his pistol, took the opportunity to stretch his legs a little.

Wellington's troops were disposed along a ridge some two and a half miles wide. Below them stretched a wide valley, on the opposite side of which, Luke presumed, Bonaparte's army was also arrayed for battle. It was a fertile area, the ground still richly covered with heavy crops despite the arrival over night of tens of thousands of soldiers, horses, and guns. Some houses and farms stood dotted among the fields; he could see British forces reinforcing the defences of a handsome walled property nearby. Luke wondered idly what compensation, if any, the owners would receive for their damaged home and ruined harvest. Would this land ever be farmed again? When he looked at the vast multitude preparing to fight; to kill and be killed here, he had to doubt it.

"Mr Fitzmaurice, sir, there's a bit of breakfast for the officers of your company over yonder."

Luke joined his fellows who were sharing some biscuit and a little broth. Thin as it was, the warm drink dispersed the last vestiges of his disturbed night. The rain had stopped some time earlier and the ground was steaming in the heat of the June sun. An ADC rode up with instructions for the regiment to withdraw to form part of the reserve forces on the plateau behind the ridge.

Here we are, Luke thought, pieces set out on a giant chess-board, waiting for the game to begin, dependent on the hand of the player to pick us up and move us forward to attack or defend or perhaps even be sacrificed so he may gain a tactical advantage.

His reverie was interrupted by the strident bray of the enemy trumpets. A battery of drums challenged with unfamiliar rhythms and supported thousands of male voices raised in defiant song.

"It's their *Chant du Depart*," Major Carew said:

" *'La République nous appelle, Sachons vaincre ou sachons périr*
Un Français doit vivre pour elle; Pour elle un Français doit mourir'."

"The Republic calls us; let us know how to conquer or to perish. A Frenchman must live for her, for her a Frenchman must die'," Luke translated reflectively. "Stirring stuff."

"Bonaparte's putting on a grand spectacle for us," an ADC riding by called across to them. "He's reviewing his army as if it were the victory parade; a magnificent display, if a trifle premature."

Captain Gregg snorted dismissively. "If he thinks his troops need to be fired up in such a way, it won't be long now. Imagine the Peer wasting his energies so."

The roar of French cannon proclaimed that the time for postur-ing was over. Battle had commenced, but only indirectly for the 52nd who soon were lying down to avoid the shells and round shot that reached their position, having passed over the heads of the troops to their front. The old hands made themselves as comfortable as they could, some even snatching a little sleep. Luke tried his best to emulate the sang-froid of his fellow officers who appeared to pride themselves on ignoring the boom of guns and the shrill whine of shells as they chatted beneath the shade of a large elm tree.

The contrast between the rural landscape and its military encampment was rendered all the more startling when a round shot from a cannon cut a swathe through the standing corn before burying itself in the soft earth.

"It's a good thing we had so much rain," a lieutenant observed, "the damn things are less likely to bounce."

Luke was unable to say afterwards how long they had remained there on the plateau but, judging by the sun, it must have been for several hours. Frequently enveloped in clouds of dark smoke that wafted up to impose their fumes of gunpowder and burning on the more pleasant scents of wet ground and crushed crops, his ears battered by the awful sound of war, seeing now two men killed by another cannon-ball and later small convoys of wounded being ferried back through the ranks to the rear, he felt transported to a different universe where time shifted and stretched and his awareness altered so that there was no past, no future, just this interminable, infinite moment. Within this strange sphere, men attempted to rest or divert themselves—he saw one group at cards and another was gathered around one of their comrades who recited some bawdy verses to great acclaim.

He remembered how all those years ago he had found consolation in Milton's *They also serve who stand and wait*. He had never envisaged anything like this waiting. And yet, the comradeship of the mess held. The officers gathered in little clusters, drifting from one to the other in an attempt to find out what might be happening, passing on the information garnered from ADCs.

"The battalion will form up in companies to the left!"

Eager for action after the immobility of the previous hours, the 52nd hurried to respond to the bugles' call. To one side,

Major Carew drew a miniature from within his jacket and touched it to his lips before carefully replacing it. Luke pressed his hand to his own jacket, over the inside pocket where he kept Olivia's letter. As soon as this was over, he would write to her.

On cresting the brow of the ridge, even the most hardened veteran was awed by the fury raging below, their ears brutally assailed by the massive roar of artillery, the sharp crack of muskets and the clash of swords on cuirasses and casques. The two properties nearest the ridge were smoking ruins where allied forces still held their position, steadfastly repulsing the repeated efforts of the *Grande Armée* to drive them from it. The regiment advanced through churned up mud reddened with blood, avoiding as best they could the mangled corpses of Brunswickers and Frenchmen slain in the earlier onslaught.

Luke sat proudly in the saddle, at once observer and participant in this crucial moment when the fate of Europe would be decided. The valley was swathed in a drifting fog of smoke shot through with vegetable particles from the trampled crops and other, denser material that didn't bear thinking about. As the billows swirled and lightened, he saw here an advancing column of cuirassiers, their metal breastplates gleaming in the sun, a squat golden eagle carried proudly above them, there a British square, unfaltering in the face of the oncoming cavalry charge, the colours fluttering defiantly in the centre. A horse-drawn gun-carriage dashed to a new position, regardless of the dead and dying caught beneath the hooves and wheels. Bugle and trumpet calls duelled for supremacy and in the distance he could hear the wild shriek of highland war pipes. A small figure in a cocked hat cantered on a bay horse along the ridge. It was Wellington and Luke's heart thrilled at the sight.

Now it was the turn of the 52nd's squares to stand up to the French artillery. Pressed shoulder to shoulder, facing outwards, four deep, the men closed ranks and endured, for there could be no overt resistance to a cannonade where a round shot might kill or wound a score of them. If one fell, he was dragged back into the centre hollow of the square, as the ranks closed again. Roughly bandaged and propped against one another the wounded attempted to stifle their groans while beside them others were quiet in their last sleep.

With a piercing crack a shrapnel shell burst overhead, showering the square with shot. "What the devil!" Major Carew barked, wiping blood from his face. "That's from our lines. Mr Fitzmaurice, my compliments to the Artillery and request them to fire somewhere else."

Luke wheeled his horse. The rear side of the square opened to let him through and he headed up the slope to the battery of guns, bent low over Crusader's neck. Black smoke blinded him, stinging his eyes and throat. Fervently hoping that he had not inadvertently fixed on the trajectory of the next shot for his ascent, he listened desperately for the initial explosion and the whistling whine of a shell.

"Where the hell did you come from?" the battery captain demanded when Luke emerged from the grim mists.

"Down there," Luke pointed back.

"Good Lord! I suppose you'd prefer us to aim elsewhere."

"It would be appreciated," Luke answered with a grin.

"Explain the dispositions below, if you would. It's deuced hard for us to see what's happening." The captain listened carefully, nodded and said, "Thank you, sir."

Luke lifted his hand to his shako. "Good luck," he said and touched his heels to his horse's sides. Back in the square, he dismounted and knelt to speak to a young recruit, one of his company, who had suffered a long, deep gash at the back of his arm. A bandsman did his best to staunch the blood, packing the wound before bandaging the arm tightly.

Luke took the man's free hand. "Hold tight, now. It looks worse than it is," he added consolingly.

"I'm sure I hope so, sir," the young man said. "I didn't know I had that much blood in me."

"How did it happen?"

The wounded man rolled his eyes. "Fred was hit. I was in front of him and his bayonet caught my arm when he fell."

"Keep it still now, Billy," the bandsman admonished him. "Undo your middle buttons and tuck your arm in to support it."

"Just like Boney," Luke encouraged him and stood. "Devil take it!" An almost spent cannon-ball that had already brought down several men had rolled in and rapped him painfully on the ankle. It hurt like hell and, supported by one of the sergeants, he hopped on the other leg for a few minutes, before he gingerly put his foot to the ground again. It was sore but not impossible to walk on it. Fortunately the injury was to his right foot and he was able to hobble to his horse and remount so he could rest the foot in the stirrup. After another ten minutes or so, the pain settled to a dull ache that he managed to ignore. What was a bruised ankle compared with a shattered leg or the horror of a belly-wound?

The bugles' metallic sound rose above the dull roar of the cannon: "Tah-tata-rah, tah-tata-rah."

" '*The enemy is cavalry*'," an old hand grunted. "That'll stop those bloody guns for a bit! They can't continue to shell us if their horse is in the way."

While he spoke, the front rank knelt so that their bayonets and those of the rank standing behind them formed a sort *of cheval de frise.*

There was an abrupt silence when the cannon bombardment stopped and then they could hear the thud of hooves and the jingling of harness as the cuirassiers attacked. Breastplates gleaming and sabres extended, they thundered at full gallop, each man searching for the vulnerable spot where he might break the square.

"Hold your fire," the major commanded, "Hold steady now. Let them come near enough that it will do most good."

"Rank two, make ready, fire!"

The muskets barked as one. Riders and horses crashed to the ground, while others tried to escape being caught in their fall. Luke winced to see one poor devil, his foot still caught in the stirrup, dragged painfully over the ground, his head bouncing helplessly among the maelstrom of hooves. The succeeding ranks pressed on, to be met by another devastating volley. Unable to penetrate on this front, they swerved to ride round the square, searching for a weak point on one of the other sides.

"Close up there!"

"Hold shoulder to shoulder!"

"Don't give them an opening!"

Tirelessly exhorted by their officers, the 52nd held firm, driving the encircling enemy back with successive volleys as they were challenged on all sides of the square.

"They're retreating. Well done!" Luke exclaimed, seeing the cuirassiers wheel and gallop away.

The charge rebuffed, it was back to the merciless bombardment. "How long can they keep it up?" one man muttered. "What are our boys doing?"

At last the order came for the 52nd to relinquish their static position and move out of reach of the French artillery. Seeing their prey escape them, the French subjected them to a ferocious hail of fire, pouring round shot at their squares so that it seemed a miracle that anyone could escape unscathed. About forty paces past the crest, they found themselves almost out of range, although still subject to the barrage of sound that had assailed them for the past seven hours. Even when the artillery paused, Luke's ears still rang—whether with the last reverberations of the shots or through some internal tintinnabulary echo he didn't know. His right leg ached, but apart from that he seemed to have escaped with a couple of scratches.

They took the opportunity of a brief lull to move the more seriously injured to the shelter of a hedge and bank, where they lay covered by blankets. How long would they be left there, Luke wondered. The reek of gunpowder combined with the insidious stench of slaughter crept into his nose, stung his eyes and soured his parched mouth with a foul, acrid taste. Nearby, wounded horses ate the downtrodden wheat within their reach while others struggled, trying to stand despite fractured legs. Poor beasts, he thought compassionately. They did not ask for this.

"Vive le Roi! Vive le Roi!"

An officer of the cuirassiers was suddenly among them, leaning forward over his horse's withers and shouting at the top of his voice. A quick glance around and he rode up to Sir John Colborne.

"Ce coquin Napoléon est là avec les Gardes. Voilà l'attaque qui se fait."

"Sergeant," Sir John said abruptly, "take this gentleman to the Duke."

"What did he say?" Lieutenant Jaspers asked Luke as the Frenchman was escorted up the ridge.

" 'This rascal Napoleon is there with the Guards. This will be the attack that does it'."

"Hmph! And he chooses to desert now? That's like having your cake and eating it, if you ask me."

Not long afterwards, Wellington himself rode across quite alone to speak to Colonel Colborne. He did not wear regimentals, but was attired in a blue coat, white pantaloons and hessians.

If it were not for his sword and the small telescope he carried, he might have been any middle-aged gentleman taking a sedate turn in the evening air. They spoke briefly and the duke left as unobtrusively as he had come. In later years, Luke was to say that this quiet conversation between two gentlemen was one of his most abiding memories of the battle of Waterloo.

'Tarumtum, tarumtum, ta-rummadum dumadum, dum, dum,'
    "Vive l'Empereur!"
    The impassioned cries punctuated the pulsating drumbeat of the *pas de charge*, rolling on and on, swelling in an ominous, menacing, growling tide that propelled the entire French army forward. Luke felt the incessant rhythm reverberate through his spine.

"No. 5 Company extend and engage!" Colonel Colborne ordered as a mass of French skirmishers attacked.

"The regiment will advance in quick time!"

'Ta-ratata, ta-ratata, ta-ra-ta-ra'. British bugles soared above the French drums.

As he crested the low rise, Luke saw two vast columns, per-haps ten thousand men in all, of the Imperial Guard advance at right angles to the 52nd's position. This is it, he thought. If we can't beat them back now, we're done for. His heart thumped and he settled more firmly in his saddle, his sword held *en garde*.

"Hip hip hurrah! Hip hip hurrah! Hip hip hurrah!"

Three tremendous British cheers were flung at the approach-ing French column. Soon it was so near that the 52nd's front ranks had to mark time to avoid being outflanked. Almost instinctively, the men touched in to their left.

"Right shoulders forward!"

Colborne's command sped down the line, picked up and repeated by each mounted officer. The din of battle was so fero-cious that it was as much by instinct and touch that, section by section, as smoothly as if such an unprecedented manoeuvre had been refined in a hundred exercises on the parade ground, the entire battalion of one thousand men wheeled to become a four-deep line parallel to the left flank of the leading French column. The mounted officers, Luke among them, rode to the front of the line.

"Now, 52nd!"

A continuous fusillade raked the entire French flank, who tried desperately to turn their left files so that they could return fire.

"Sound the advance!"

At the plangent bugle call the 52nd lowered bayonets and charged. The leading French column did not stand to receive them but broke and fled in a wild, disorganised retreat, mercilessly harried by the 52nd who subjected their enemies to running fire at point blank distance, advancing over dead and wounded heaped so thickly on the ground that at times they had to leap over the fallen foe.

"'Ware Cavalry!"

Mounted horsemen emerged from the smoke and charged through the ranks, riderless horses careering among them, so that the men had to leap out of their way to avoid being ridden down willy-nilly or having their faces sliced open by a sabre or flying stirrup. French cuirassiers were in hot pursuit of British and German Dragoons and one of them, perhaps judging the mounted infantry officer easier prey, swerved to ride at Luke, his sabre raised ready to slash down viciously. Luke furiously pulled his horse up on its haunches and pivoted to evade the charge. Arm extended, his enemy turned to hack at him and, quick as lightening, Luke lunged to skewer him through the unprotected armpit, the shock of the thrust travelling up his own arm. With a twist and a jerk, he withdrew his weapon and the Frenchman toppled from the saddle.

A soldier yelled, "Well done, Mr Fitzmaurice, sir!" and Luke raised his bloody sword in acknowledgement as he galloped on.

A hail of grapeshot hit them from the right. Luke touched his hand to his stinging cheek and his glove came away bloody. But he pressed on, exhilarated by his defeat of his assailant and buoyed up by the common endeavour and the knowledge of hard duty done. This was what it was to be a man! To his left, he saw Captain Gregg tumble to the ground and lie still. But the advance could not be halted. The enemy were in full flight. Another burst of grapeshot struck both Luke and his mount. His grasp on the reins loosened and he felt Crusader collapse under him. With his last strength, Luke pulled his leg from beneath the animal to lie beside him.

High on the ridge above them, the Duke of Wellington waved his hat to signal the general advance of the allied troops who stormed down into the valley, rushing over the bodies of their fallen comrades to pursue the defeated French. But Luke knew none of this. As he lay gasping for breath, a horseshoe clipped the side of his head and the world darkened around him.

Chapter Twenty-Five

Where was he? Not in bed—too uncomfortable and no blankets. A dull light filtered through his closed eyes. In the distance he could hear the bark of a gun. Luke stretched out his hand. It met something warm, hairy, large. He moved his hand and felt leather—a saddle. He must have fallen while out hunting. His body hurt with the general ache you felt after taking a tumble, but there were more specific pains in his shoulder and leg. It was an effort, but he managed to lift his heavy eyelids. That was Crusader, right enough, his eyes dull in death. Puzzled, Luke looked around. What had caused them to fall? He could see neither fence nor wall nor ditch. A rabbit-hole, perhaps? He shook his head to clear it, but stopped when a sharp pain darted through it. He must have hit his head.

He could hear movement and faint voices. Struggling, supporting himself with a hand on the saddle, he managed to pull himself up to a sitting position. His sword lay beside him. A battle! That was it! There had been a great battle. His haversack was still slung across his chest and he reached into it for his flask. It gurgled promisingly when he shook it. Not empty then. He carefully opened it and put it to his lips. Brandy and water. Nectar.

Luke swallowed another mouthful and cautiously moved his arms and legs. He appeared to have the use of his limbs.

He stowed his flask away and got to his knees. So far, so good. Holding on to the saddle, he got his right foot under him. Bad idea! He switched to the left. It took his weight and he was able to drag himself to his feet.

The setting sun hung in the west, turning the haze of smoke that hung over the battlefield a virulent, sulphurous yellow. Beneath it, body was piled on body, friend and foe heaped together in unholy communion as far as the eye could see. Riderless horses roamed among them causing further injury to the wounded and damage to the dead. Other steeds, dead or injured, lay beside their masters, the cries and groans of man and beast uniting in unceasing clamour that reverberated through the valley. As far as Luke could recall, they had had the French on the run, but when he looked around he could see no difference between victor and defeated.

It was unlikely that anyone would come to help the wounded before nightfall. How to get out of here? They had been near a road, he thought. Perhaps he could find it? Swaying a little, he picked up his sword and sheathed it and unstrapped his boat-cloak from behind his saddle. Then, very gingerly, he began to pick his way over the ground, stepping cautiously between the living and the dead, avoiding muskets and bayonets, skirting around horses and abandoned guns. Gregg had fallen just before he had. Perhaps he could find him. Luke stumbled on, ignoring the outstretched hands and pleas of the wounded. In the distance he could see other figures moving, stooping to the fallen men. Perhaps they would know what to do, what was usual.

Was that Gregg's horse? He struggled over. Its rider lay motionless beside it. Luke knelt painfully beside the captain. He must have sustained a serious wound to his head; his eyes were closed and his face was covered in blood. Sadly, for it was the last thing he could do for his friend, Luke moistened his handkerchief from his flask and gently wiped the pale face. As he cleaned the lips of caked blood, he thought he felt them move. Had he imagined it? Hands trembling, he soaked the cloth and pressed more firmly. This time the lips moved as if sucking in the liquid.

"Gregg! Captain Gregg!" he said urgently, tapping the man's cheek. There was no response. Luke tore open the Captain's collar, loosened the black stock and put his fingers against his throat. There was a pulse. It was very faint, but it was there. Instinctively he raised his head to seek help, only to realise despairingly that there was no one he could call upon. It was almost dark. There would be no help before morning.

"Sir!"

The voice came from beside a gun-carriage that had been abandoned when its horses were shot.

"Sir!"

The call was more insistent and Luke looked over to where he could dimly make out a man leaning awkwardly against the wheel.

"My leg's smashed, sir. I can't get up."

"What can I do for you?"

"Not much, I suppose, except, sir, if we stay together it'll be safer. There's no doing anything in the dark and the scavengers and plunderers will be out. They always are after a battle. Some of 'em'll finish you off soon as look at you, especially officers. But if we're together, we can each look out for the other. If we have a couple of bayonets, that will help."

Luke looked at him, horrified. Was this the glory of victory?

"Can you get your captain over here?"

"I'll try."

Inspired by the gunner's words, Luke went looking for blankets. The dead had no further need of them, poor souls. He handed two to the wounded man and then spread another on the ground. His leg and shoulder hurt like the devil and bending intensified the ache in his head. But what must be done must be done. Fortunately his injuries were both on his right side and Gregg was not a big man. Going down on his left knee, he carefully turned the captain and managed to ease him over his shoulder. He straightened slowly and stood, staggering slightly but able to regain his balance. Covering the three yards to the gun carriage was less easy with a man over his shoulder, especially as he could not put his full weight on his right foot. It was getting darker by the minute and difficult to see where he was going. But he managed it and gently lowered Gregg onto the blanket, making sure he was not lying on his wound. He felt his pulse again. Was it weaker? Luke couldn't be sure. He slowly trickled a few drops of liquid between the captain's lips and the injured man seemed to swallow it. With a sigh Luke spread another blanket over him before handing the flask to the wounded gunner.

"There isn't much left, I'm afraid."

"You could try them Frenchy saddlebags, sir."

"You're an old hand I see," Luke answered, not without respect.

"Twenty years, sir, but it's over now. All through the Peninsula, I was."

A rummage through some saddlebags yielded a bottle of wine and one of cognac as well as bread and cheese.

"Luxury," Luke announced, handing a tin cup of wine and a hunk of bread and cheese to the gunner. "What's your name?"

"Bombardier Sawyer, Jeb Sawyer of the Royal Artillery. And yours, sir?"

"Ensign Fitzmaurice of the 52nd. This is Captain Gregg. We'll leave him between us, I think. Oh, and I found these as well." He displayed a pair of pistols with balls and powder.

"That's the barber," the bombardier said contentedly. "If we have these as well as the bayonets we'll be safe."

Exhausted, Luke dropped onto a blanket and poured himself some wine. There was still a dark silver streak in the western sky, but that would soon vanish. The moon was almost full and its pale, cold light had turned the valley floor into a crazed chessboard of blacks and greys, the pieces tumbled anyhow over the squares. He rested his throbbing head against the gun carriage.

"What usually happens with the wounded after a battle, Sawyer?"

"They'll send out fatigue parties in the morning, I expect, sir, to look for us. But I've never seen anything like this. It'll take days to find everyone."

Luke rubbed his jaw, feeling the rasp of over two days' stubble. "When you read about it at home, you don't think of the before and after," he said reflectively.

"Your first action, sir?" the bombardier asked, surprised.

Luke shrugged. "I joined in April." He drank again and, unable to see clearly enough to risk putting his cup to the captain's mouth, wet his handkerchief to moisten his lips again.

"What happened to him?"

"I don't precisely know. A head injury, at any rate."

Luke's companion seemed eager to talk, perhaps to drown the unsettling sounds they could hear. A susurration of groans and rustlings suggested that the very battle-field was alive. Once there was a loud clatter, as if something had been knocked over or had fallen. Sometimes they heard voices, but it was impossible to say from where they came. The distraught horses had calmed a little with the coming of darkness; they too must be exhausted.

After some time, Sawyer began to recite the twenty-third psalm. Luke joined in. "My mother made me promise I'd say it every night and I've never missed," the bombardier said when they were finished. "I reckon we walked through the valley of the shadow of death today, sir."

We're not out of it yet, Luke thought sombrely, but he just replied, "Yes", and leaned over to moisten Gregg's lips again.

Their desultory conversation ceased and the two men dozed fitfully. In the distance, the haunting cry of an owl presaged a small, natural death amid the man-made carnage, a paradoxical reminder that life continues in the face of utter destruction. Gradually Luke felt the tension in his body relax and his head grew heavy.

Sawyer sat up suddenly. "Hsst!"

Luke had also heard the jangle of accoutrements. Two forms loomed out of the darkness. They went from one huddled figure to another, stooping to each body, the chink of coin betraying their purpose.

"Over there," one of the looters said and then turned to see Luke and Sawyer eying them grimly, their pistols cocked and aimed. He raised his hands. "No 'arm done. Come on, 'Enry." He nudged his companion who obediently departed with him.

"They were—." Luke was too shocked to continue.

"Our lads," Sawyer completed for him. "I know. Scum—the lowest of the low. There's many a man has been finished by the likes of them. But there's no proving it, sir." He looked eastwards. "The sky's beginning to lighten. Any military will go soon, as they'll have to be with their regiments for roll-call at latest. But there'll be others, locals maybe, after the same thing."

As the sun climbed higher in the sky, the full extent of yesterday's slaughter became apparent. Luke climbed painfully to his feet, clinging to the gun-carriage for support. A sea of bodies covered the devastated valley, many in the same formation they had defended in life, rank and file lying symmetrically as if in some macabre drill. Is anyone left alive? he wondered. Now he could see his companion, a stocky, ginger-haired man whose freckles stood out above the stubble on a deathly-white face. His left leg, which was shattered below the knee, had been crudely bandaged.

He greeted Luke cheerfully enough. "Morning, sir."

"Good morning. We've still some wine or would you prefer brandy?"

"The brandy, I think. It'll warm my bones. And if we have an empty bottle, I've another use for it, seeing as how I can't move. I'd prefer not to be lying in my own piss."

Luke grinned sympathetically and, having filled their cups, emptied the bottle into his own flask. He handed it over before he made his way to the other side of the gun-carriage where he could relieve his own bladder in as seemly a fashion as possible.

Captain Gregg was breathing quite regularly now, but still hadn't opened his eyes or displayed any other awareness of his surroundings. The June sun was hot and Luke used a blanket and some bayonets to rig an awning over the two wounded men using the gun-carriage as a support.

He felt very shaky. If I sit down again, I'll never get up, he thought, and propped himself against the gun-carriage. He saw groups of soldiers who were clearly searching for the wounded. But among so many, how were they to decide whom to help? Each regiment, it appeared, sought its own.

"The 52nd?" a sergeant said as he passed. "I saw them behind you, sir."

Luke turned and spied the familiar uniform. He put his hands around his mouth and trumpeted, "52nd!". The little party stopped and Luke waved vigorously. "52nd! Here! To me!"

To his huge relief, they made their way over to him.

"Mr Fitzmaurice!" The corporal saluted.

"And Captain Gregg." Luke gestured to the man on the ground. "He's alive but unconscious. And this is Bombardier Sawyer, thanks to whose sage advice we survived the night."

"We've some carts on the road. We'll carry the captain. If you can mount a horse, we'll lift Sawyer up behind you, sir."

"Find me a neat animal, corporal, nothing too large, and I'll try."

One of men captured a roving stray and steadied it while Luke climbed creakily into the saddle.

"I feel like my own grandsire," he muttered. "Is all right behind, Sawyer?"

"Yessir. And thank you, sir, for not leaving me here."

Luke gripped the reins grimly. As they trudged through the carnage, wounded men raised pleading hands and voices, begging for water and aid. United in one desperate quest, distraught ladies and camp-followers knelt in the foul mud, attempting to trace beloved features beneath masks of blood and dust. At the edge of the battlefield, a group of dandified fops, handkerchiefs raised fastidiously against the all-pervasive stench, inspected the scene in fascinated horror.

"Bloody sods," Sawyer grunted. "Too fine to fight or even to help, they are."

"Here we are, sir."

Luke was not too proud to disdain assistance both in dismounting and awkwardly clambering into the cart.

"Can you steady the captain, sir?"

Luke braced himself at the back of the cart and they laid Gregg so that Luke could support his head. Three other soldiers were helped up, the driver cracked his whip and they plodded off to join the jerking, jolting procession of wounded towards Brussels. The torrential rain of the night before last together with days of heavy, military movement had turned the road into a quagmire that sucked at the wheels and caked the horses' legs with mud.

The men in the cart didn't speak. Now and then, a particularly violent jerk elicited groans and curses, but otherwise they seemed to have relapsed into apathetic silence. Relieved to have escaped the field, they now faced the rough care of the army surgeons. Luke's head throbbed. He hadn't retrieved his shako after his fall and now had to close his eyes against the sun's glare. He dozed as best he could, rousing himself at intervals to trickle more liquid between Gregg's lips. The captain seemed to sleep peacefully, but it could not be a natural sleep.

A canopy of leaves provided welcome shade, but the going through the forest was more difficult and several times the convoy was halted.

"A dead horse," the driver reported once and later, "some poor soul's had it. They're burying him before we go on."

"It's not far to Brussels now, but we'll be here some time," he announced at the entrance to a little village. "A wheel's come off one of the big waggons up front. How's the captain holding up, sir?"

"I don't like the way his breathing has changed," Luke answered. "Do you think there might be room in one of those houses? Let us see if we can get him into a bed."

Luke was stretched out on a mattress hoping he might finally get some sleep when Sir John Colborne walked into the room.

"Sir!" He struggled to sit up.

"What's the damage, Mr Fitzmaurice?" the colonel asked, eyeing Luke's splinted right leg and array of bandages.

"The bone-setter thinks it's most likely cracked, sir. I took a knock from a round shot early on that caused a massive contusion and then I fell on it later. My boot held it together, he said."

"And the rest?"

"A musket ball through my arm and, judging by the cut, it seems as if a horse clipped me on the head, but no great harm done, I think"

"What of Captain Gregg?" Colborne looked over to where the other man lay.

"A head-wound from a ball. It didn't penetrate the skull but stunned him severely. He hasn't come round yet. And multiple bruises—it looks as if he was trampled on while lying there. He's breathing easier since we got him out of that damned cart."

The colonel looked grave. "What does the bone-setter say?"

Luke grimaced. "Nothing sir, except that it's in God's hands."

"Is there nothing to be done for him?"

"Our host here has supplied us with poultices and embrocations to ease the bruising. I suppose they can't do any harm. I've been keeping his lips moist with brandy and water. He seems to take a little, but that's all."

"Stay with him," the colonel said abruptly. "The regiment moves on into France tomorrow."

"I'll re-join as soon as I can, sir."

"Very good. Is there anything I can do for you, Mr Fitzmaurice?"

"If it were possible to have a letter sent to Lord Franklin, sir? He is acquainted with Miss Gregg, Captain Gregg's sister. She should be told how it stands with him. He has no other family, I understand."

"If you can scribble it now, I'll see if I can get it off tonight. You've no paper, I suppose." Colborne tore a sheet out of his notebook and handed it to Luke together with a pencil. "If we can find your baggage, I'll have it sent on, but half of the waggons are missing."

Luke hastily scribbled a few lines, folded the paper and addressed it.

"I'll seal it for you," Sir John said. "I must go."

"Goodbye, sir."

Chapter Twenty-Six

*I*n a sunny morning-room at Gracechurch House, the duchess and Mrs Rembleton eagerly perused the newspapers. Olivia glanced up from the Duke of Wellington's dispatch to Earl Bathurst, the Principal Secretary of State to the War Office, issued that morning in a *London Gazette Extraordinary*. She bit her lip. Had Luke survived?

"The fighting continued over three days. Wellington says our losses were immense."

"And he only mentions the most senior officers," Flora's tone was sombre. "It will be days before they have the lists together."

"Lord Franklin requests the honour of a word with Mrs Rembleton."

Olivia rose at the butler's announcement. It could hardly be good news that brought his lordship here so early.

Flora looked curiously at her friend who had gone white but merely said, "Show him up here, Hinks."

Franklin hurried into the room, his features taut with distress. He bowed perfunctorily but immediately announced, "Mrs Rembleton, I have come to beg your assistance."

"Why, what is wrong, my lord?"

"It is Captain Gregg. I had a brief note from Fitzmaurice—I don't know how he contrived to get it here so soon—telling me that Gregg has been seriously injured. There is very little hope, he says."

Even as Olivia registered the shocking news, she was guiltily conscious of her relief that Luke was clearly still alive,

"He requests me to inform Miss Gregg," Lord Franklin continued. "Do you happen to know where your sister-in-law is at present, ma'am?"

"She is staying at Rembleton House for a few days before going on to Rembleton Place."

"Is Miss Gregg with her?"

"I assume so. I haven't heard to the contrary."

"Mrs Rembleton, may I impose upon you to come with me to Rembleton House? My mother and sister have returned to Leicestershire, so I cannot call on them for support."

"Of course I'll come, my lord, if you just give me five minutes to get ready."

Olivia paced nervously while they waited for Miss Gregg. Finally she could restrain herself no longer and whirled to demand, "Did Mr Fitzmaurice say anything else? Of himself, for example?"

"Only that they are in a house in Ixelles, a village just south of Brussels."

Miss Gregg stopped on the threshold of the library at Rembleton House when she saw Lord Franklin. "Good morning, Mrs Rembleton. My lord?"

Olivia took her hand. "I fear we bear bad news, Miss Gregg."

"Jonah! Tell me he is not dead!"

"All we know is that he was very gravely wounded," Lord Franklin said. "Mr Fitzmaurice wrote to ask me to tell you."

A painful hope lit her eyes. "But he's still alive?"

"He still lived on the evening of the nineteenth, but was unconscious since the previous day."

"The nineteenth? That's three days ago." The young woman swayed, her hand to her mouth.

Lord Franklin hurried to put his arm around her and lead her to a chair. He knelt beside her and took her hands. "I am sorry to be so brutal, but it is best that you know the truth."

"Who is looking after him?"

"A local bone-setter has been treating him."

"What did he say?"

"That it is in God's hands," Lord Franklin repeated reluctantly.

"Who is nursing him?"

His lordship hedged. "Presumably the housewife where he is billeted will do her best."

She clutched his hand. "I could nurse him. If you took me there, I could nurse him. Please," she implored.

He cast a beseeching look at Olivia.

"My dear Miss Gregg, even if you were able to make the journey, it would take several days and you may well arrive too late," Olivia said compassionately.

"I don't care," came the anguished reply. "I must try at least. He is all I have—and I am all he has," she added quietly as tears spilled down her cheeks. "Even if I am too late, I could lay flowers on his grave."

Lord Franklin released her hands. He sat on the arm of the chair and drew her in his arms. She rested her head on his shoulder for a moment but then pushed him away. "If you won't take me, I'll go by myself," she said determinedly. "I can travel by stage and packet boat." She scrambled to her feet. "I must pack."

"No! I forbid it. A lady to travel unescorted through a countryside roamed by the remnants of two armies. It's unthinkable."

"I have no choice," she snapped at him. "And you have no say in what I may or may not do. If it were your brother, would you not go to him?"

"Lord Franklin is right," Olivia intervened reluctantly. "Even with a maid, it would be most unadvisable. Surely your brother would not wish it?"

Miss Gregg sank into the chair again and buried her face in her hands. Franklin drew Olivia over to the window.

"Mrs Rembleton, even if I were to agree, it would be the ruin of her if we were to travel together. I don't wish to force an offer on her in such circumstances—she might construe it as the price of my compliance. Unless—would you consider accompanying us with your maid? That would make it all right, I think."

Olivia looked at Miss Gregg who had dried her tears and sat unmoving, a look of absolute desolation on her face.

"It depends on whether I may leave my children with the duchess. But I cannot imagine that being a problem," she added honestly.

He seized her hand. "You are an angel!"

"I thought there would be more military to be seen," Olivia remarked as the carriage clattered along the *chaussée* from Ghent to Brussels.

"I understand that Wellington is in hot pursuit into France," Lord Franklin replied. "He won't want to give Bonaparte the opportunity to regroup."

She sighed and rested her head against the squabs. They had left Dover on the evening tide of the twenty-third of June. Lord Franklin had contrived to borrow a private yacht, so the crossing to Ostend had been comfortable if slow and they had not arrived until the following morning. They had spent last night at Ghent and were now on the final stage of their journey, hoping to reach Ixelles by mid-afternoon.

"That's the last change of horses," Lord Franklin said.

During the intervening days, Miss Gregg had made a valiant effort to conceal her terror of arriving too late, but now she paled and grew tense. He smiled sympathetically at her from across the carriage, saying softly, "Courage, my dear."

"It will be better to know," she said resolutely. "I can't thank the two of you enough."

"I thought you had agreed not to thank us anymore," Olivia said, her teasing smile coaxing an answering one from Miss Gregg.

"It's like one huge infirmary," Olivia said in hushed tones, as she read the chalked words on the doors of the Brussels houses, recording the number of wounded soldiers and officers cared for in each one. A few men could be seen through the open windows, as pale as the pillows on which they lay. Straw had been laid down in front of some buildings to muffle the sound of passing traffic. Could this be the gay city to which the British had flocked after the peace? Last year's frivolous ladies and cheerful officers had flown. Here and there a man made his painful way along the street or a woman hurried by, clearly on an urgent errand. As they crossed the city, they had to halt several times to allow a soldier's simple funeral procession to pass. Finally they could pass through the ramparts and leave the stricken city behind them. The chaussée onto which they emerged was muddy and deeply rutted, the roadsides littered with the dismal relics of the thousands of soldiers who had passed that way.

"That must be Ixelles." Lord Franklin broke the apprehensive silence.

The little village was beautifully situated among verdant woods and gleaming ponds, but the visitors had no eyes for the beauties of nature where every house and cottage bore chalked witness to those who suffered beneath its roof. They made their way slowly down the street.

Suddenly Olivia gasped, "Look—in that window!"

The others' gaze followed her pointing finger to where Luke Fitzmaurice sat reading at the open casement, in a state of *deshabillé* that would have raised eyebrows sky high at home. His fair hair was tousled, his shirt was open at the neck and he wore neither cravat nor coat, just a waistcoat over his shirt. At that moment he looked up to see Lord Franklin step down into the street.

"Good God!" Luke exclaimed. Before he could hail his friend, the latter turned back to the carriage and held out his hand to assist someone to alight. A lady appeared in the door and Luke's heart took flight. She's done it again, he told himself, a broad smile creasing his cheeks. The very last person I expected to see here! Her carriage dress of soft lavender was trimmed with silver-grey ribbons. The colours were reversed in her bonnet, to which she had attached a posy of dark violets. No black at all, he noticed happily. She fastidiously lifted her skirts away from the mud, displaying her pretty ankles.

"Ol—Mrs Rembleton," he stuttered.

"Good day, Mr Fitzmaurice," she replied. "We had not realised you would still be here." Despite her warm smile, he felt a sharp disappointment that this unexpected visit was not on his account.

Lord Franklin had not relinquished his post at the carriage door and all became clear when Miss Gregg alighted carefully. Luke called into the room, "You'll never guess who has come to call on you!"

A surprised voice answered, "Call on me?"

"Jonah?" Miss Gregg's voice broke on a sob.

"Sally?" they heard from within and then, "Give me my coat".

Suddenly remembering his own state of undress, Luke hastily left the window.

"He's awake!" Miss Gregg exclaimed tearfully and ecstatically hugged first Lord Franklin and then Olivia before heading purposefully to rap the knocker smartly. The door was opened by a maidservant. Behind her, Luke stood in a doorway, leaning heavily on a walking stick. He had hastily draped his jacket around his shoulders and knotted a Belcher handkerchief around his throat. Beneath his buckskin breeches, his left leg was properly stockinged while the right one was splinted to the knee.

"Pray forgive my attire," he said, "My choices are somewhat limited at present. But please come in."

Miss Gregg sailed straight past him, eyes only for her brother who sat propped up against his pillows. He was as white as the bandages wrapped around his head, still gaunt and hollow-eyed from his ordeal. She dropped to her knees beside his narrow bed and threw her arms around him. "Oh, Jonah, I was so afraid," she gulped.

"Now, Sally, you know I'm as tough as an ox," he said, patting her shoulder. "There's no need to take on so."

Luke took Olivia's hand. "I can't express how overjoyed I am to see you," he said quietly.

"And I you, Luke. But you were hurt too. Should you be standing? It's not only your leg, is it? Your arm is bandaged as well."

He shrugged it off. "It's just a scratch and a cracked leg, more inconvenient than anything else. He smiled happily at her. "I beg you won't think me ungrateful or ungracious if I ask what brings you here."

"I'm just the chaperon. Miss Gregg was determined to come and Lord Franklin asked me to accompany them," Olivia explained. "You seem to be well looked after."

The small room was bright and cheerful. Pale yellow walls had been over-painted with the soft greens and pinks of wreathing sweetbriar so that one had the impression of being in a summer garden, an impression that was heightened by the scent of lavender from the linen sheets and the pewter vase of aromatic flowers and herbs that stood on the rectangular table that had been pushed right up to the wall between the windows to provide more space. There were four chairs at the table while the officers' campaign chests stood between the beds, with some personal belongings arranged on top. A green and white tiled stove stood in one corner, its country scenes so much more appealing than England's cold, summer fireplaces. The furnishings were completed by a screen that presumably concealed a close stool and wash-stand.

Looking around, Olivia was impressed both by the generosity of the owners in making over what was clearly a favourite parlour to the two foreign officers and also by the practical mind that had made it an airy, pleasant sick room. A tray with two earthenware goblets and a moisture-beaded jug that was covered with a square of muslin suggested that the hosts were assiduous in caring for their unexpected guests.

"The Michels have been very good to us," Luke agreed, pulling out a chair for her. "Franklin?" he asked and his lordship, who had remained in the door, came to join them. He nodded over towards the brother and sister.

"How did that come about?"

"God alone knows." Luke's comment was not irreverent. "Two days ago, he suddenly opened his eyes. He must have the hardest skull in the army. The ball apparently bounced off it, causing a long furrow of a flesh wound and a massive concussion of the brain, but it didn't fracture the skull. The local bone-setter has been attending him. All we could really do was trickle liquid into him, but the bone-setter said that the fact that he was able to swallow was a good sign. He's still inclined to dizziness, but it will pass."

"And your leg?"

"In six weeks, five now, it should be as good as new."

"Five people in the room are probably too much for Captain Gregg," Olivia observed. "Lord Franklin, perhaps we should go to the inn and see if we can get some rooms. Everywhere is very full. I hope we won't have to return to Brussels."

"You are not going to desert us, I hope, Mrs Rembleton," Luke pleaded.

"Of course not," she replied briskly. "If necessary, we shall return each day."

They were fortunate to find rooms under the roof of the little inn.

"You see the bend in the narrow staircase, milord—we could not carry the injured up," the innkeeper explained, "but the rooms themselves are spacious as you will see."

"Have you many wounded here, sir?" Olivia enquired.

"Now only ten, *Madame*; two English and two Prussian officers and six soldiers."

"Who is nursing them?"

"We all do what we can," he said simply.

"We must see if there is anything we can do to help," Olivia said to Franklin after the innkeeper had left them.

He nodded. "I'll do the rounds later, call on the officers and see how the men are. I wonder how they are fixed for supplies."

By the evening of the second day, the intimacy resulting from the necessity of the wounded men receiving their visitors in their bedchamber and the subtle relaxation of the proprieties that occurs when a small group of people spend considerable time together in unwonted surroundings had the company agreeing to dispense with formality and generally use Christian names. But, much to Luke's chagrin, Olivia treated all three men in the same sisterly manner and did not seem to recognise or accept any closer connection to him.

Chapter Twenty-Seven

Delighted as Olivia was to find Captain Gregg on the mend, the discovery that their headlong journey had been unnecessary had thrown her into a state of uncertainty that was compounded by Luke's unexpected presence. Sally could not have stayed alone at the inn with Lord Franklin, so Olivia's role as chaperon must be maintained in public. But in the privacy of the Michels' house there was no need to act the duenna; in fact it would have been both foolish and impertinent for her to do so, for there Sally had the protection of her brother. If anything, Olivia's presence was more likely to cause raised eyebrows especially if it became known that she spent several hours each day alone with Luke.

With Jonah Gregg still confined to bed, it had seemed natural for the other four to split into two couples, one of which remained with him while the other took the air, and she was well aware that it was not her company that Lord Franklin sought. As a result, she had taken refuge in a neutral friendliness towards all three men which enabled her to conceal both her general disquiet and her simple enjoyment of Luke's company. Although not permitted to walk far, he was able to hobble about the Michels' property with the aid of his stick. The unsettled weather of the previous week had cleared and he led Olivia to the old orchard where pears, apples, cherries and plums grew

296

in cheerful profusion. Fans of apricots and nectarines had been trained against the south-facing brick wall, while the others were lined with bushes of lavender and rosemary.

"What a heavenly place," she observed. Through a gate in the rear wall she could see a large field and strolled down to see what grew there. "It's a magnificent herb garden, the best I've ever seen," she reported on her return to where Luke sat, his injured leg stretched out in front of him.

"I understand M. Michel is well versed in plant-lore and renowned for all manner of simples, tinctures and tisanes. Indeed, I am convinced that they helped our recovery." He patted the smooth bench beside him. "Come and sit down. Tell me all the news from home."

"Apart from that of the battle itself, and you probably know more about it than I do, there is little to report. There were to be public illuminations on the twenty-third and the twenty-fourth, but we had left by then." She thought for a moment. "Oh yes! Lord Cochrane was released from prison last week. He took his seat in the Commons on the very same day."

"I'm glad he is free and is holding his head up. That was the oddest business," Luke remarked.

"My brother never believed him guilty. It was all circumstantial, he said. He had sailed under Cochrane some years ago and said being involved in such a conspiracy to manipulate funds was completely contrary to his character. And he would never have been party to creating a false rumour about the war."

"It's hard to imagine an Admiral doing so."

"Omnium rose eight and a half per cent after Major Percy's news was made public," she reflected.

"All sorts of scavengers chase the spoils of war," Luke growled. He was suddenly back on the battlefield with Bombardier Sawyer, their pistols cocked as the two plunderers approached.

Olivia was astounded by this savage snarl and alarmed by his sudden pallor. He stared past her, his eyes fixed on something only he could see. She touched his hand. "Luke? Luke, what is it?"

His fierce gaze softened and he dragged in a shuddering breath, his hand turning to grip hers. "After the battle," he began haltingly, "help only came the next morning. I had found Gregg; he was unconscious. It was almost dark and it seemed as if the field was just one immense pile of bodies; friend and foe, living and dead, all heaped one upon the other. There were horses too. You had to work your way around them, through the churned soil that was mixed with—everything you could possible imagine." His voice faded.

"What did you do?" she asked quietly after a moment, holding his hand comfortingly.

"I could still just about see where I was going, but it would have been impossible to move once night fell. I knew I would have to wait out the darkness. What I didn't know was that the first to return to the field would come not to aid us but to steal what they could—whether from comrade or enemy, it didn't matter to them. And if you resisted, well, what was one more dead man in such a place?"

"Dear God! But you were able to protect yourself—and Jonah?"

He nodded. "If it were not for a veteran who lay near a gun-carriage, Sawyer, his name was, I don't know what would have happened. His leg had been smashed so he couldn't move at all. He said we should stay together and told me to bring Gregg to him."

"How did you manage that? You were wounded too."

He shook his head. "I don't know. I suppose because I had to. We put Gregg on the ground between us and we had the gun-carriage at our backs. Sawyer told me to get some bayonets and I found a pair of pistols too, so we were prepared when they came. They turned tail immediately, like the cowards they are."

"So you got safely through the night. What happened then?"

"The 52nd sent out fatigue parties the next day to collect their wounded. We were lucky. I heard later that others were left for days, without water even, some trapped under the carcases of horses. When boys dream of battle, they never think of that sort of thing, Olivia." He looked around the sunny orchard. "If a week ago, someone had told me I would be sitting here with you today, I would not have believed them. I am so glad you came. I couldn't talk to anyone else about it. Gregg was unaware of what happened, but there is also a huge conspiracy of silence among the survivors."

"I suppose it's the only way they can bear it," Olivia said compassionately. "And men are prone to make light of things. How do the Lambs put it? A boy must *'Keep his voice and visage steady, Brace his eyeballs stiff as drum, That a tear may never come'.*"

"Do you agree with the sentiment? Do you scold your sons if they cry?"

"No, at least not if they are genuinely upset or otherwise in pain. Although as John got older, he was much less inclined to weep. I think he heard other boys call it girlish. But I never encouraged any of the three to cry from temper or in an attempt to get their way as some children, especially girls, are inclined to. Miranda doesn't. But she essentially grew up without a father, just as I did, so she had no-one to work her wiles upon. It is generally the gentlemen who melt at a female tear, I find."

"They terrify us," he agreed with a smile, then remembered little drops sparkling in a black veil. But she had forgiven him for that.

"Alone at last." Lord Franklin placed a glass of port on the chest beside Captain Gregg's bed. The ladies had remained at the inn after dinner to rest and later drink tea and he had seized on the opportunity to get the full story of the battle.

"It was unlike anything you've ever experienced," Gregg began. "Just hard pounding, hours and hours of it. Douro didn't attack until the very end. We were in the rear for the first half; so far back we had very little idea of was happening. And then we had to stand fast in squares—you know what it's like. Colborne was superb, especially when we advanced. You should have seen him pivot the whole regiment—no-one has ever done anything like it before. 'Right shoulders forward' he says and away they go, turning as the command was passed on as neatly as a line of dominoes falling. You could only be proud to command such men."

"Tell me from the beginning," Franklin commanded.

"Give me my pencil and notebook," Gregg said and began to sketch.

Luke was as fascinated as his lordship. "It's completely different when you see it spelled out like that."

"That's always the way," Franklin agreed.

"This is only our end of things," Gregg added. "I have no idea what happened elsewhere."

"I brought the *Gazette* with Wellington's despatch with me," Franklin remembered. "I'll bring it later when I collect the ladies."

"Tell us what happened afterwards, Fitzmaurice," Gregg demanded. "I have no idea about anything from the moment I was hit to when I woke up in this room."

Luke began reluctantly. He had no wish to overemphasize what he had done to help the captain, but between his incisive questions and both his and Franklin's experience of war, Gregg soon extracted the whole story.

"I have to thank you for my life," Gregg observed.

Luke waved this away. "Say rather that we both should thank Sawyer."

"Perhaps, but if it weren't for your efforts, it's unlikely I would have been brought off the field so soon. Do you know what happened to him?"

"He most likely lost his leg. I've asked Phibbs to try and track him down, see if he needs any assistance."

Luke looked much happier, Olivia thought, when she and Sally joined the gentlemen. The conversation turned to their evening entertainment. "Luke could read to us," she suggested.

He beamed at her and asked, "What would you like?"

"Something to make us laugh," she said spontaneously.

"Your wish is my command." He made an elaborate bow and snatched up the copy of Miss Burney's *Evelina* that Sally had been reading.

"Letter Fourteen" he intoned and curtsied, fluttering his eyelashes wildly as he did so, before embarking in thrilling tones on the heroine's account of how she made the acquaintance of her grandmother. He threw himself into every part; out-braggadocio'd the captain in his exchanges with Mme. Duval and gifted that lady with such an exaggeratedly French pronunciation of her English that he soon had his audience in stitches. At the end of the letter, he laid the book aside and rested the back of a limp wrist against his brow.

"I vow I am exhausted," he simpered in response to their applause and demands for more.

"So am I," Sally said. She pressed her hand to her ribs. "I ache from laughter, but it did me good. You must read again tomorrow."

"Not before these two shirkers have done their bit," he declared, waving at the other two men.

Luke rested his cane against his favourite bench and stretched out his arms, breathing deeply. "This is better than the last time I was laid up. I spent a whole summer and more unable to leave my bed."

"The last time? Oh, when you were a boy." Olivia looked at him. "That was what stopped you buying a pair of colours ten years ago, wasn't it? Did you find it odd to join now at such an advanced age?"

"A bit."

"It must have been like—oh—putting away the most recent volume of your life and starting again at the end of the previous one."

"Except that you can't erase your memories or return to the person you were then. I discovered that. To be honest, Olivia, I have no idea why I was so insistent on coming."

"Are you sorry you did?"

"No, yes, no." He scrubbed his hands over his face. "I was so keen. It was as if I was nineteen again. Perhaps that part of me hadn't grown up."

"Or an opportunity you had thought lost suddenly presented itself again?"

"Exactly! And I rushed to seize it, as if I had learnt nothing in the intervening period."

"Learnt nothing?" she repeated. "What should you have learnt?"

"A lot," he retorted. "Have you not changed and developed in the past ten years?"

"Of course I have. I had to."

"So have I. After all, it's only when we are in our twenties that we begin to consolidate our values and opinions, to test what we were taught against our own experience. I questioned a lot, but I never questioned the need for war. It is literally drummed into us, isn't it, from our earliest age?"

"I suppose it is," she agreed, startled.

"And yet we claim to be Christians."

"Do you think war is wrong, then?"

"I think there are very few occasions when it is right," he answered. "One has the right to defend oneself if one is attacked. We are taught to love our neighbour as ourselves. Perhaps we should go to his assistance if he is attacked. But to go to war for profit, to protect trade, ensure monopolies or extend one's territory—that is wrong. We don't need any more empires, Olivia."

"I suppose not."

"What will be the outcome of last week's battle, do you think? Sooner or later, Bonaparte must either surrender or be captured. What will happen then?"

"I expect there will be another peace treaty and the Congress of Vienna will reconvene."

"And for that to happen, thousands of good men had to kill each other and tens of thousands were wounded. But supposing countries could bring themselves to talk first instead of fighting?"

"That sounds very utopian," she answered with a little smile. "I doubt if talking would have done any good in this case," she added dryly. "Bonaparte has shown that he is no respecter of frontiers."

He shrugged. "We'll never know. The Congress refused to speak to him. This time, he might have agreed to remain within France. And if Louis can only keep his throne with the support of his neighbours against his fellow countrymen, how long can he survive?"

"You sound very radical," she said uneasily.

"Do I? Imagine a world where countries agree to respect each other's borders and allow trade to flourish freely. Would we be any worse off? Think of the cost of war; not only the monetary cost, but what we pay in human suffering. Why can't countries accept what they have? Why do they always want more?"

"Perhaps because women are excluded from all decision-making," Olivia suggested. "It leads to a very lopsided way of looking at things."

"That may well be true." He sighed. "It was only when I saw the horror of war that I began to question it."

"I never thought you took these things so seriously, Luke. You always seemed so—," she paused, wondering how to put it without offending him.

"Superficial?" he offered. "Frivolous? A butterfly? I believe that's what you called me."

She blushed but defended herself. "I may well have. You went to great pains to ensure no one thought otherwise."

"That's true," he conceded.

"It's a sort of disguise, isn't it? I suppose we all wear them to some extent."

He gently touched her cheek. "Did you find it hard to be unmasked, Thalia?"

He held his breath until she smiled at him. "Yes," she said, "but afterwards I was glad. I could not have spoken to you the way I did last November otherwise."

"The truth shall make you free," he murmured, delighted that she had not fobbed him off.

She nodded. "Even with Jack. Knowing the truth helped me understand him. I thought a lot about him in the succeeding months. It was not his fault that he was as he was or that he had to hide it. In the end I could forgive him for his deceit."

"*Monsieur!*" Marie called from the side gate. "M. Jean wishes to see you."

"That's the bonesetter." Luke struggled to his feet.

"Go on in. I'll wait and come later." She watched fondly as he limped away. He used to move so beautifully. Would he be able to dance again?

At the gate he turned and lifted a hand in farewell. She waved in return and leaned against the back of the bench, lifting her face to the sun that pierced the leaves above her.

Olivia returned to the house to find Captain Gregg seated triumphantly at the table. "I shall be able to eat my dinner like a Christian," he announced.

"But you must rest again afterwards, Jonah," his sister warned him. "Remember what M. Jean said—today you may sit up twice for up to an hour each time, provided you don't feel dizzy."

"Now Sal, don't fuss."

"Promise you will not attempt to play the hero," she begged.

"I swear." He held up his hand as if taking the oath.

"How long do you wish to remain here, Sally?" Olivia enquired over tea the following evening.

"I hadn't thought," she said. "Jonah doesn't really need me, does he?"

"He is very well looked after and clearly on the mend, but I'm sure he is delighted to have your company. There is nothing more tedious than being confined to bed. However I cannot stay here indefinitely."

"I understand. I am so grateful to you for agreeing to come, and at such short notice."

"What arrangement did you make with my sister-in-law?"

"She said to take whatever time I needed. She is going to stay with her own sister next month and will not really require me there. I'll talk to Vernon tomorrow and see what he thinks. He will have things to do at home as well."

"Congratulate me," Lord Franklin said. "Sally has agreed to be my wife." He smiled blissfully as he watched his new betrothed being passed from arm to arm.

"About time," Luke said as he shook his hand. "I thought you'd never get round to popping the question."

Franklin grinned ruefully. "She's stopped worrying about her brother now."

"When is the wedding to be?" Jonah Gregg asked. "I'd like to be able to give you in marriage, Sally."

"As it happens, I have a special license with me," Lord Franklin announced. "We could be married at the Embassy, or perhaps the chaplain would agree to come here to perform the ceremony."

"Tell me about your plans, Luke," Olivia invited the next day in the orchard. "I don't think you will stay long in the army."

"No. I told Colborne I would remain until Bonaparte was finally defeated and that can now only be a matter of weeks if not days. I wish to work more openly for change, for reform. Lord Lutterworth has offered me a seat in parliament. There is to be a by-election as soon as may be convenient."

"Would you be able to speak your mind? Will you not have to comply with your patron's wishes?"

"He has said that he will not seek to influence me. I must try it, Olivia," Luke said earnestly. "With the final end of the war, so much will be different in England. If we allow the mercantile system to prevail, as with the Corn Laws, we are heading for disaster. And we must also look at parliamentary reform and catholic emancipation. We have seen in France and in America what happens when the people are not treated fairly or given a voice."

"So you propose to lend them yours?"

"Until they have their own."

"What did you mean by working more openly," she asked curiously. "Have you been involved in politics behind the scenes?"

It was time to remove another mask. "Not exactly," Luke answered. "Have you read any of the letters of Otanes?"

"I have, and found them both entertaining and enlightening. In fact, I have kept some of them in an album. I thought the children could usefully read them when they are a little older. They are less prosy and more thought-provoking than many texts that are considered suitable for young people. He holds up a mirror to society and encourages us to consider our reflection."

Her words filled Luke with an enormous sense of pride and achievement.

"Why do you ask?" Olivia enquired and then read the answer in his glowing face. "He's you! I never would have guessed it. Oh Luke, how clever of you. And to fool us all too!" She held out her hands to him and he slipped his arm around and hugged her to his side.

Completely comfortable with him, she kissed his cheek in congratulation. "You should consider publishing them all in one volume," she suggested.

"I've never thought of that. But I would prefer to remain anonymous."

"It might be better if you intend to go into politics," she agreed.

Chapter Twenty-Eight

livia sat beside Luke on 'their' bench in the orchard, lulled by the buzzing of the bees that probed the spikes of lavender and rosemary. She knew so much more about him now. His manner towards her had changed as well—he was neither acerbic nor flirtatious, a friend if not a brother, but certainly not a lover. As the days progressed, the three men and two women had gradually coalesced to a sort of family. It's as if we each play our own instrument, she thought whimsically, sometimes solo, sometimes together with one or more of the others, but always conscious of the overarching melody and underlying harmony. She had never before had male friends. The fraternal affection of the Greggs, the honest love between Vernon and Sally and the frank comradeship of the three men all revealed different aspects of masculine behaviour and sentiment to those displayed within the artificial confines of the *haut ton*. They were more direct, less affected, prone to teasing women they liked and disguising their affection for one another in robust banter.

An involuntary sigh escaped her. She would miss them when she returned home. She had her children, but that relationship was still very unequal. However, it would improve as they got older.

"Luke?" Olivia's voice broke the contented silence.

"What is it?" he asked lazily, his arms spread along the back of the bench, his eyes half-closed and his hat tipped forward to shade them.

"Could you spare Phibbs for a day or so?"

"Of course. Is there some errand he could do for you?"

"I wish him to escort me to Ostend."

He bolted upright. "What? Why?"

"It's time for me to go home. I came as Sally's chaperon, but she won't need me once she is married. What reason could I give for my continued presence?"

"To comfort the afflicted?" he suggested.

She smiled and shook her head. "You are both doing very well."

"When were you thinking of leaving?"

"Tomorrow, after the ceremony. After that, I shall just be sitting bodkin between the newly-weds."

"Tomorrow?" He felt stabbed to the heart. Why must she leave so soon? What of him? His world had suddenly righted itself when he saw her step down from Franklin's carriage. Until then he had been trapped in a haze of battle memories, intensified by the pain from his injuries and his worry for his friend. But she had come. It hadn't even signified that she had not come for him. She was there and that was all that mattered. She couldn't go.

"If we were to marry as well, you could stay. Nobody could question the propriety of it." He spoke lightly, the words out before he could stop them, the proposal rising from the hidden depths of his soul. Even as he made it, Luke knew how right it was. But what a way to do it! He turned to look at Olivia, his heart in his mouth.

Her eyes brimmed with rueful amusement. "It's a tempting idea to remain in this paradise, but we can't shut the world out indefinitely. You will soon re-join your regiment or take up your new life in politics and I must return to my children." She spoke indulgently, almost as if to a child.

He forced himself to smile and say what had to be said. "I know you must. Of course you may have Phibbs."

"Thank you. My maid is with me but I would prefer to have a male escort as far as the yacht. Franklin was able to borrow Lord Rastleigh's, so we shall be in excellent hands once we are on board. If I send Phibbs to you, would you explain matters to him?"

"As you wish," Luke said dully, inwardly cursing the injury that prevented him from accompanying her.

"I must go in. There is a lot to be arranged before tomorrow. You stay here and enjoy the fine morning."

He watched her walk gracefully to the gate in the orchard wall. She turned and smiled as she went through, lifting her hand in a brief farewell. He smiled back mechanically. He felt as if he had missed a step on a dark stairs. It would have been unrealistic to expect her to accept such an inept proposal, but he hadn't been able to suppress a wild hope that she would simply put her hand in his. But to her, his suggestion had clearly been made in jest and, worse, her blithe response had been devoid of any hint of a more intimate attachment between them. Burlington House might never have happened—she had somehow transmuted and neutered their encounter so that she could now treat him as a brother. But incapacitated as he was, and given their confined situation, what chance had he had of playing the lover?

"How old is Olivia?" Captain Gregg asked over the port that evening.

"About our age, I think," Luke said. "When I first met her I was still up at Cambridge. She was not long married then."

"Is that all? At first I thought she was nearly forty, but she seems to have got younger as the days went by."

"The reverse is happening now," Franklin said with a grin. "She's snapped back. She reminded me of a commanding officer, the way she sat at the table drawing up her lists and writing her notes, ordering us to think of any commissions we might have or letters we wanted her to deliver."

"And she has three children?" Gregg asked.

"Yes." Luke didn't elaborate but refilled the glasses. Couldn't they discuss something else?

"Her eldest is Rembleton's heir," Franklin said. "What is he? About ten?"

"About that."

"And the other two?" Gregg enquired.

"I'm not sure. I think she's around eight and he four or five. But why all the questions, Gregg?" Luke carped sourly. "Thinking of following your sister into parson's mousetrap?"

"Good God, no. Certainly not with Olivia."

This categorical denial irritated Luke even more.

"You could do a lot worse."

Franklin's intervention didn't improve matters.

"Don't misunderstand me," Gregg said hastily. "I have the highest possible regard for her, but it would be like marrying your elder sister, wouldn't it? She would always know what was best for you."

"I imagine she had no choice but to be that way," Franklin said unexpectedly. "All mothers do to some extent and by all accounts her husband wasn't much of a support to her."

"No," Luke answered. "His life was his work." She never had a chance to enjoy her girlhood, he thought, not like Clare and Ann.

The Michels had kindly offered the use of their family parlour, a sunny apartment at the rear of the house, for the wedding ceremony. Sally looked charming in a pale pink satin gown over which she wore the robe of exquisite Brussels lace that her bridegroom had insisted on buying for her. It outlined her pretty bosom like a spencer but fell away from the high waist in a deep oval that dipped at the back to the hem of her gown. A delicate lace veil was thrown lightly over her dark curls to frame her radiant face. Standing by her side, Olivia could not but remember her own wedding and deliberately shut away her envious thoughts.

Afterwards she clasped the hands of the newly-married couple. "You have found the greatest treasure of all," she said. "Guard it well. And may you always remember how happy you are today; it will be your beacon in times to come."

"You have been our beacon, Olivia," Lord Franklin smiled down at her. "Thank you, dear friend, for your help and support."

"Yes," Sally said, throwing her arms around Olivia. "If you hadn't sent him to Bath!"

"I think he would have found his own way," Olivia said, laughing.

At twelve o'clock she made her farewells, leaving Luke until last. She held out her hand. "Goodbye, Luke. I hope you continue to make a good recovery."

He took her hand to tuck it into his arm, saying, "I'll walk out with you."

Phibbs stood at the open carriage door and Luke jerked his head to send him away. "Olivia." He took a breath and found he could not say goodbye to her—the word would not pass his lips. Lifting her hands, he kissed them and murmured, "Safe journey and *au revoir* in England. Will you write to say you have arrived safely?"

Her eyes clung to his for a moment before she blinked and lowered her head. "If you wish."

"Please."

She nodded. "*Au revoir*, Luke," she said quietly and climbed into the carriage. He closed the door, shutting her away from him.

Phibbs, who was to ride beside the carriage, swung up into the saddle.

"If any harm comes to her, I'll skin you alive," Luke snarled at him and stood back to watch until the carriage was out of sight. Unwilling to return to the wedding party, he limped out to the orchard. High in an apple tree a blackbird sang mockingly above him as he dropped onto the bench and put his face in his hands.

They stopped briefly at the inn so that Olivia could change into a carriage dress and make herself comfortable before the journey.

"Have you the headache, *Madame*?" Martin asked solicitously

"A little." Olivia forced a smile. "I'm not used to champagne in the morning."

"I'll put some lavender water on your handkerchief and soak another one. I'll sit beside the coachman and you may cover your eyes and rest."

"You must tell him to stop at any time if you wish to sit inside," Olivia said. "The sun is hot today."

"I'll wear a wide-brimmed hat and throw a veil over it," the maid assured her. "That will help."

Olivia had hardly slept the previous night and the effort of concealing her heartache had grown greater by the hour. To think that such a fatal blow could be dealt so light-heartedly! Luke hadn't meant to wound her, she knew, when he suggested they marry. It was a silly joke, or at best a sort of wishful thinking that their little society should not be broken up. But to be offered in a casual quip the fulfilment of her most secret hopes, desires that she had only recognised when he had given voice to them, had hurt bitterly. It's too late for foolish girlish dreams of love and happiness, she thought drearily. Sally had the courage to turn down a respectable match because she didn't love the man, but you made a different decision and there is no going back.

Don't think of him. Think of the children. They will be glad to have me back at home. I must find some little gifts for them in Ghent. What would they like? Is Miranda too young for lace?"

"What has you so blue-devilled?" Franklin demanded.

Luke was glad of the interruption. He couldn't keep away from the orchard where he had spent so many happy hours with Olivia but when there he only seemed to hear echoes of his own foolishness.

"I'm bored, I suppose, tied to the house for another week. Jean is insistent that if I use the leg too much, it won't heal properly."

"You're halfway there," Franklin said encouragingly

"Hmph. Has Phibbs brought the mail?"

"Not yet. Are you expecting something?"

"I asked Olivia to write once she was home."

"You sound worried," Franklin observed.

Luke shrugged. "It's foolish, I know. Phibbs saw her safely on board, but—."

"You grew very close while she was here," Franklin said,

Luke looked at his hands and said nothing.

His friend inspected him more closely. "I'll be damned! You're in love with her."

Luke didn't deny it.

"Well?" Franklin urged impatiently. "What are you going to do about it?"

"I don't know. I could hardly have made a worse botch of things if I tried."

"Why, what did you do?"

"Only made the clumsiest, most frivolous proposal you could imagine."

"You? The elegant Fitzmaurice, the darling of the ladies of the ton? I don't believe it."

Luke nodded, too miserable to think up a suitable rejoinder to this sally.

"And she declined, I take it?" Lord Franklin asked more gently.

Luke nodded again. "She didn't even take it seriously—thought it was a joke. I didn't know I was going to make her an offer until it was said—and it came out all wrong."

"Is that why she went home so suddenly?"

Luke shook his head. "It was the opposite. She told me she planned to leave the next day and I lost my head."

Franklin sat down beside him. "You're not going to give it in, are you?"

"I don't know what to do. I'm committed to the regiment as long as Bonaparte is at large. Once I see her letter, I'll have a better idea of her sentiments towards me."

"This time last year, I should have been delighted to have had the possibility of corresponding with Sally," Franklin pointed out. "My case seemed hopeless then."

Luke was faintly cheered by this observation. "True enough. If I can establish a regular correspondence, it should help smooth things over."

"From what you say, she didn't take it to heart, so it's not as if you offended her," his friend encouraged him. "As for the boredom—now that Gregg is so much better, why don't the two of you dine with us at the inn? I'll send the carriage. You must be sick of living in one room."

Chapter Twenty-Nine

Southrode Manor, July 1815

Dear Luke,

I write as promised to tell you that I am returned home safe and well. After a tediously slow crossing, we arrived in Dover yesterday in the forenoon and proceeded directly to London, where I posted all the letters that were entrusted to me. Pray tell Vernon that his packet was also delivered to his solicitor.

Early this morning, I left for Stanton to collect the children. The duchess pressed me to stay but we were all eager for our own beds and so came on home this evening. These long summer days make travelling so much easier, don't they? All is well here. I had never left the children before and you may picture our joyful reunion. Miranda confessed afterwards that she had been afraid that something would happen to me, just as it had to her Papa when he went abroad. You may imagine how guilty I felt on hearing this.

Luke put down the letter, frowning. Was this a subtle reproach? Probably not. Olivia was not given to insinuation. If offended, she either reproved or withdrew. But now he too felt guilty. He had not really considered her children or her other responsibilities, only his own selfish desire to keep her with him. Unlike him, she could not simply let go of her old life and take up a new one.

She is very sorry that you were hurt and hopes that your leg will soon be mended. John, on the other hand, was most impressed that you had

316

been wounded in battle—and is quite annoyed that I couldn't describe the action to him. He clearly thinks I wasted my time with two 'heroes of Waterloo'. I do see what you mean when you say that notions of military glory are drummed into us from an early age—dulce et decorum est, *etc. I didn't know what to say to him. He is very proud of his grandfather, who was killed at Trafalgar. It is difficult to know how to deplore war without making light of those who have given their lives for their country.*

Luke smiled to himself. He felt they were still sitting on their bench. If he married Olivia, he would become stepfather to her children. He knew something about that relationship, if only from the other side. And perhaps she would welcome a masculine perspective on some things, especially as her sons got older.

I imagine that you have heard that Bonaparte declares his political life terminated and has again proclaimed his son Emperor Napoleon II. Poor little eaglet, to be just a pawn on his father's chessboard.

Pray remember me to your companions. I hope that Captain Gregg continues to improve and that Lord and Lady Franklin find some time for their rather unusual honeymoon. With best wishes for your own speedy recovery,

Your friend
Olivia Rembleton

Luke sighed with relief. She had not cut him off. Indeed, her remarks positively demanded a response. She signed herself his friend. He wanted more, but the time for that would be later. He must preserve the understanding that had grown between them in the orchard. 'A marriage of true minds', he thought sentimentally. For a real marriage, it was as important as physical intimacy. Friends shared their joys and sorrows, whether trivial or significant, they sought and gave advice, truly talked to each other. He could do that.

Brussels, July 1815

My dear Olivia,

Thank you for your letter. I like to think of you and your children safely at home. It is an antidote to the confusion and horror that still reigns in Brussels. Once Gregg was pronounced well enough to withstand the carriage ride, we removed here to the house the Franklins have taken. It is certainly more convenient to have an adequate number of apartments so that we need no longer share one room for everything, but I admit to missing the tranquillity of our orchard. And your company. I must make do with pen and ink when I want to talk to you.

They say that the number of wounded in Brussels has diminished rapidly over the last week or so, but even still one sees evidence everywhere of the destruction wrought by the battle. Franklin recently visited the battlefield. This has become a favourite outing for many visitors here and I am told that there is quite a trade in souvenirs such as caps, badges and all sorts of bits and pieces. I will not distress you with his depiction of the scene but will only say that he was greatly shaken by it.

He is able to divert his thoughts by introducing his bride to the society that remains in Brussels. Sally has generally been welcomed although there are, as always, some ladies who consider that such a prize as he should not have been wasted on a mere companion. I heard similar comments made about Clare and told Sally that she should ignore such spite which serves only to explain why the purveyors of it are destined to be ape-leaders. However, she is too happy and too sensible to be pricked by their claws.

Wellington has left for Paris, but many English remain including the Richmonds. The Uxbridges (he lost a leg) and the Fitzroy Somersets (he lost his right arm) have returned to England, as has poor Lady de Lancey.

Franklin managed to hire an ancient landau in which Gregg and I are perambulated like a pair of dowagers in the Park each day to the amusement of the passing populace. We present a slightly off appearance, as his shako is a size too large so as to accommodate his bandage—much reduced it is true, and no longer turban-like—and the leg of my overalls has been opened to accommodate the splint, the volume of which is also reduced because the swelling has gone down considerably. The more I learn how others have fared, the more I realise how fortunate we were to have fallen into the hands of M. Jean and M. Michel rather than those of the army butchers, who after a first visit left us to recover—or not—as best we might.

We took an affectionate leave of the Michels and were put to shame by the modest amount they requested for our care. They could not be persuaded to accept more. Fortunately Sally hit upon the happy notion of painting a small portrait of Gregg and me in our regimentals (but without bandages) which we inscribed appropriately. Franklin has had it framed and we were assured that it shall have a permanent home in 'our' room.

Olivia, I can imagine how puzzled you were as to how to answer John. How can one disapprove of war without denigrating the fallen, you ask. Perhaps you could say to him that it is precisely because we place such a value on them and their lives, that we consider they should only be asked to make the supreme sacrifice when all else has failed. War must not be our first, but our last resort. You quote Horace, and indeed that line has sent God knows how many men to die. It may well be sweet and fitting to die for one's country, but to my mind the French put it better when they call upon their children also to live for it, to devote their best endeavours for the welfare of all.

Unfortunately, the Englishman (and woman) is taught to know his place and remain there, to submit to all masters and order himself lowly and reverently towards his betters. The divine right of kings has somehow been expanded to encompass the privileges and prerogatives of the aristocracy and nobility, whose chief aim in life is to preserve them. I have heard of soldiers promoted out of the ranks for valour and exceptional service who begged to be returned to their former status because their new fellow-officers would have nothing to do with them. Compare this with Bonaparte's much-vaunted comment that every soldier carries a marshal's baton in his knapsack.

Our most recent news of Bonaparte is that he is on board a French frigate at Rochefort, north of Bordeaux but prevented from leaving port by our men-of-war who maintain their blockade. Rumour has it that he hopes to get to America. That would be all we need! I don't know which would be worse—the United States or Canada. He would certainly do us no good in either.

By the time you receive this letter, I will, I hope, be about to leave for Paris to join my regiment. I shall write again as soon as I arrive there to inform you of my plans.

My dear Olivia, I have missed you immensely since you left us and sincerely hope that this farce will soon be at an end so that I shall not be detained too long abroad. In the meantime, I beg that you will continue to favour me with your letters.

Yours,
Luke

P. S. I remember I never thanked you for the most entertaining and informative lines you sent me at the beginning of June. I trust that in the circumstances you will forgive this omission.

P.P.S. Pray thank Miss Miranda for her good wishes and tell her my leg no longer hurts.

Southrode Manor, August 1815

Dear Luke,

Well, Bonaparte departed these shores on the Northumberland *last week, bound for St Helena. And high time too! My brother told me that the scenes during his final days at Plymouth were disgraceful, with up to one thousand boats putting out, all wishing to get a glimpse of him walking the deck of the* Bellerophon, *whose seamen actually chalked details of his activities on a board and held it up for the edification of the masses. At least one man is reported drowned in Plymouth Sound.*

While I have little sympathy for Bonaparte, I feel for those who must accompany him to that remote island, in particular the soldiers who are to provide the garrison there. However it is consoling to know that he will finally be placed where he can do no more harm. When one thinks of how premature our great rejoicings of last year were and how bitterly they were brought to an end, it is perhaps understandable that our celebrations this year are much more muted. There is no talk yet of an official Thanksgiving, although countless unofficial prayers have been said.

After all the upsets of the past year, I am content to spend a quiet summer here at home. There is very little to tell you. The hay has been gathered in safely and we prepare for the harvest. We still hear the cuckoo, but not as often and I suppose he will soon depart. The children had been used to keep a record of his calls for their father. This year they were not sure what to do and, in the end, John decided he would write to Mr Wilkins and enquire whether he proposed to continue their father's work. Mr Wilkins replied very civilly that he did and should be most obliged if they would send on their notes at the end of the summer. I suppose I must be grateful to him.

My uncle Harte and Lady Ottilia come next week on their annual visit. My brother and his wife are still with me; she much more than he, but I imagine he will resign his commission as soon as practicable. He has his eye on an estate not too far from here and if all goes according to plan, they will remove there at Michaelmas.

Olivia lifted her pen. It would be strange to have the house to herself again, she admitted. Part of her longed for it and part feared it. And yet, there was no going back. Her mourning would be up in a month. Had she truly mourned Jack? Her initial grief had been mixed with guilty resentment about her interlude with Luke at Burlington House. She had kept her vows for so long; why could she not have kept them to the end? Later, after the revelations regarding her husband's deception, she had been fiercely glad that she had stolen that evening of pleasure. It seemed to balance the scales between them somehow. She bent again to her letter.

Have you given any further thought to issuing a volume of your alter ego's *letters? I am sure it would be well received. I am directing this letter to you c/o the 1st/52nd, Paris and trust that it will reach you sooner or later. I am sure you will find the French capital fascinating, especially at such a time. Keep well, Luke,*

Your friend,
Olivia Rembleton

Paris, September 1815

My dear Olivia,

Colborne has confirmed that he will have no further need of me after the end of the month and I am already making my preparations to return to England. I shall not be sorry to forego the amenities of my tent, I assure you. It remains strange to be encamped in the Champs Elysées; imagine our feelings if the French were similarly ensconced in Hyde Park! I can hear you remind me that as one sows so shall one reap and the French have only themselves to blame. You are right, of course, but still!

Wellington has had the Louvre cleared of all its spoils of war, which are to be returned to their original owners. The other day we were marched up to the Place Louis Quinze *to secure the peace while the Austrians removed the four magnificent horses that had been taken from Venice.*

We spend our days in an odd mixture of drill and idleness. You would be amused to see the men playing cricket here, as if they were on their own village green. The gambling at the former Palais Royale is as excessive as anything I have seen and unfortunately some of the young pigeons must needs demonstrate their 'pluck' here by risking more than they can afford. I know of one officer of the Grenadiers who spent his entire leave there, saying he found there everything he could possible require and indeed every masculine whim is catered for, I am told.

But all in all, occupied Paris is not a pleasant place to be and Franklin had the right of it when he refused to entertain the notion of bringing Sally here. Although the worst excesses of Prussian retaliation for the injuries inflicted on their country by Bonaparte's troops ceased with Blucher's departure, there is still a very uneasy mix of royalist and bonapartist, Prussian and British here, with many prone to provocation and reaction.

Oh dear, Olivia, I am become very prosy, am I not? I long for more civilised society. On my return, I must first visit my parents, but hope it will not be too long before I have the pleasure of talking directly to you rather than relying on my poor pen. As ever,

Yours,
Luke

You will probably see me sooner than you think, Olivia thought as she folded the letter. She was sure Luke was also bidden to Lutterworth for the celebration of Lord Franklin's marriage; indeed she would not be surprised to learn that it had been delayed until his return. She blew out the candles on her writing table and started to hum a seductive little melody. It was in waltz time and she couldn't resist spreading out her arms to turn in a series of airy dance steps. She stopped at the door, laughing at herself and picked up the remaining candle to light herself to her bedchamber.

Chapter Thirty

"Mamma! Is that where we are to stay? In that castle? It's really prime, isn't it?"

The horses had already turned in under the gate tower and were trotting up the approach. John couldn't look around fast enough and slid across the seat from one window to another in an attempt to drink in the crenelated glories of curtain wall and keep. As soon as the carriage stopped, he pressed down the handle and jumped out.

"Come, Mamma!" He offered his hand to assist first her and then his sister. He knew better than to try and help Samuel, but stood protectively by as his brother hopped down. At last he could turn and gaze in awe at the imposing structure.

"John," Olivia prompted him, "come and make your bow to Lord and Lady Franklin."

John blinked and came to himself. "I beg your pardon," he said very correctly and bowed before exclaiming, "What a truly splendid castle. Used you play at knights when you were a boy?"

Lord Franklin laughed. "Yes. We even have a tiltyard and an old quintain. Can you ride?"

John's eyes grew even bigger. "Of course I can."

"My father had a small quintain built for us boys as well. I must see if it's still there."

"What about the girls?" Miranda wanted to know.

Olivia smiled. "We may bestow a favour on our gallant knight."

"A favour? You mean they may play and we have to do them a favour as well? I call that shabby."

Her mother tried not to laugh. "We give them a ribbon, say, which they tie around their arm to show that they are braving danger to win our love."

"Hmm." Miranda didn't seem convinced.

"The other guests come tomorrow," Sally explained to Olivia. "We invited just you and Luke to come today. Jonah is here as well."

"How is he?"

"Very much improved, but he still has difficulties with his balance, especially on horseback."

"I shouldn't worry," Olivia consoled her. "These things take time."

The subject was inevitably changed by the entrance of Captain Gregg himself.

"I need not ask how you are, for I can see the improvement," Olivia said cheerfully

He smiled and stooped to kiss her cheek as if she were another sister. "You are blooming. I like the brighter colours."

"So do I. That periwinkle blue is ravishing with the silver ribbons," Sally agreed.

"Thank you both. Who else is coming?"

"The Fromes for one. I thought it only proper, especially as she wrote very cordially to felicitate me on my marriage."

"I wish she would not refer to me as 'my Aunt Rembleton' in that odious way," Olivia complained. "I cannot forbid it, but it is quite ridiculous, especially when she is at least fifteen years older than I."

"She is the one it makes ridiculous," a voice said from behind her.

"Luke!" Sally jumped up. "Welcome home!"

"Thank you." He kissed first her cheek and then Olivia's before shaking hands with the two gentlemen.

"Well, here we are again, and in much better shape than when we were last together." He accepted a glass of madeira and sat, stretching his legs towards the fire.

"You're not in uniform," Gregg remarked.

"No. Should I be? I have notified the authorities of my desire to sell out. My military days are behind me." He raised his glass. "Here's to the bride."

"A double bride," Sally said with a wry grin. "Lord Lutterworth insisted we marry again here."

"Why was that?" Luke enquired lazily. "The first marriage was perfectly orthodox. I was there."

"Apparently there is no provision here at home to register an Anglican marriage which took place abroad," Franklin explained. "My father wished to ensure that the legitimacy of our children could not be challenged in the future. I didn't mind. I would marry Sally a dozen times if I could."

His wife blushed and smiled back at him before saying, "Olivia, Lady Lutterworth likes to have the children join us for the hour before dinner."

"Mamma loves children," Franklin agreed. "My sister comes tomorrow with her three and there will be numerous cousins of all ages as well."

"I had better have a word with Miss Mullins." Olivia got to her feet.

Luke went with her to the door. "Are you well?" he murmured as he opened it.

She nodded. "Yes. And you?"

"All the better for seeing you." He opened the door and stood back to let her pass.

"And that is as close as I've got to having a private conversation with her," Luke said wrathfully to Franklin two days later.

"The fault is yours, with your talk of jousts and quintains. That led the ladies to decide to have a mediaeval tourney and fair, with all manner of games, so everyone, including the children, must practise and they've been milling around at archery and bowls and quoits and marbles ever since. Then, to crown everything, some idiot of a woman thought it would be charming if everyone dressed in medieval costume. What a frenzy that caused," he reminded his friend glumly. "First they turned the place upside down and went rummaging in the attics, then they had to visit every draper, milliner and haberdasher within fifteen miles—that's where they are today—and from tomorrow they'll be closeted somewhere making gowns and what-not to out-do each other. And they move about in little gaggles and it's impossible to cut a particular lady out without creating a stir."

He flung himself into a chair. "It's all very well for you to laugh; you may retire with your wife each evening and need only say you must have a word with her to get her to yourself during the day."

"I'll talk to Sally; see if she can think up something that will throw you and Olivia together. You'll see her at dinner, at least."

"And that's another thing. This damned castle of yours has no convenient doors to terraces or balconies where one might slip away unnoticed. The only way out is through that bloody great door and down the front steps. Even if I can cut her out, where can I take her?"

"Come with me," Franklin said solemnly and led Luke down the passage to a narrow arched door that he opened with a flourish. "That useful medieval invention, the turret stair," he intoned. "And here," he went down a couple of steps and opened another door, "the turret chamber."

It was a small room, lit by two long mullioned windows. The stone walls were hung with tapestries and a rich carpet covered the floor. The only furniture was a small oak table and a high-backed chair.

"No-one comes here now," Franklin said. "My grandmother used to retreat here. It soothed her, she said, to sit and look out into the distance. If you continue down the stairs, there is a door that opens into a walled garden. Cross it and you reach the stable yard."

"Franklin, you are a true comrade." Luke slapped him on the shoulder. "I thank you, my friend."

"Mr Fitzmaurice?"

Luke smiled down at the child. "Yes, Miranda?"

"Do you think you could tell us some stories? The boys are all playing their noisy games but we girls are not allowed to join them."

"We're not either," Samuel piped up. "Tell us about Puss in Boots again."

Luke looked at Miss Mullins. "What does your governess say?"

"She would be most grateful," that lady answered promptly.

"Well, I never would have thought it," Lady Lutterworth exclaimed, stopping on the threshold of the Great Hall,

"Thought what, Mamma?"

Her ladyship turned, a finger to her lips. "Ssh. Don't disturb them. Only look." She moved quietly aside and gestured to where Mr Fitzmaurice sat on a settle beside the fire, surrounded by children. The two smallest sat on his knees.

"And what do you think Jack did then?" he asked.

"He stabbed the giant with his sword."

"No, he cut off his head."

"He hid," a little girl offered.

The boys immediately pooh-poohed this cowardly suggestion but Luke nodded. "She's right. He wanted to see what the giant would do next. But before he hid, Jack took a log from the basket beside the fire and put his cap on it. He then tucked it into his bed, with the cap on the pillow so that it looked as if he were lying there asleep."

"Clever," a small boy approved.

The countess moved forward. Luke saw the group of ladies and broke off, making as if rise but she gestured to him to remain seated. "Pray continue, Mr Fitzmaurice."

As Olivia passed the group, she could see her own children among the rapt audience. Miranda sat proprietorially close to the story-teller. He met Olivia's eyes with a sweet smile but did not interrupt his narrative.

"Sally says she will ask Olivia to go to Leicester for her tomorrow. Something to do with their fancy-dress. You're to drive her," Franklin muttered to Luke as the company assembled before dinner. "She'll only say it at the last moment, so that no-one can take it into her head to go with you."

Luke ruefully remembered the last time he had escorted Olivia on an errand for their hostess. Tomorrow, they would have to travel in an open carriage and if they were going into town, he would have to take his groom up behind. Not much opportunity for truly personal conversation, then, although he welcomed the prospect of spending some quiet hours with her.

Tonight she was seated between him and a recently widowed baronet who, to Luke's disgust, was overly attentive. "You and I, my dear Mrs Rembleton, know that life must go on," Luke overheard him say. "My girls need a mother and your children must be in want of a father's guiding hand."

She made a non-committal answer and turned to Luke. "I must apologise for my daughter's importunities. She tells me she begged you for some stories."

"I was happy to oblige her," Luke assured her. "She is a delightful child."

Most of the party were still at breakfast. Luke waited in the corridor for Olivia, who had gone in search of her pelisse and bonnet. As soon as she appeared he took her by the hand saying, "This way" and tugged her through the turret door, closing it firmly behind him.

"Are we taking a short-cut?" she asked

"Later. First I want to talk to you. Come in here."

"How charming," she exclaimed when she saw the turret room. "See how the slanting sunlight strikes jewel tones from the tapestries. And the view!" She went to look out the window. When he did not reply, she turned to seem him standing with his back against the door.

"What's wrong, Luke? I feel almost as if I've been abducted."

"You have," he declared. "I've been trying to speak privately to you for days. And I'm not about to risk a *tête-à-tête* in a curricle, not after the last time."

"But why?" Olivia asked.

"That day in the orchard when I suggested that we marry—"

"You surely don't think you need apologise for that. I understood that it was said in jest."

"Was it?" he asked savagely.

She looked even more puzzled. "Of course it was—just a joke between friends."

Luke felt like banging his head against the door but instead he strode across the room and dragged her into his arms. He kissed her fiercely, his tongue penetrating deep into her mouth. For a moment she stiffened within his grasp, but then her lips softened under his. When her hands rose to his shoulders, he gentled the kiss, leisurely exploring her mouth while he let his hands relearn her luscious curves. At last he raised his head enough to look deeply into her eyes.

"I've been in love with you ever since I saw you going down the dance with the Duke of Gracechurch," he growled. "Remember? That first evening when I asked Miss Rembleton to stand up with me?"

She had flushed delicately but now she paled. She opened her mouth but no sound came and she staggered back out of his hold until she bumped into the chair and sat down hard.

Luke felt an almost savage satisfaction that at last she was truly listening to him. "It was no coincidence that Lady Mary Hope and I sought you out that evening. She was most apologetic later for having misled me about your marital status."

"You—you rarely spoke to me after that and when you did, you were frequently quite odious," she spluttered.

He laughed shortly. "What else was I to do? I knew I couldn't have you, but somehow I couldn't let you go. Then—I was besotted with Thalia after she seduced me so splendidly. And when I found out who she was—and you made it clear there could be not future for us—I had to accept it again. I admired you for it, Olivia. I understood even then how out of character that episode was for you. And later, when you confided in me about your husband, I—I hurt for you."

He knelt beside her and took her hands. "I won't let you turn me into a courtesy brother or cousin, the way you've done with Franklin and Gregg. I've been your lover; your only lover. But I want more. I want a life-long, public commitment. I asked you the wrong way, I know, but you floored me when you spoke of leaving. That is why I wanted to talk to you today."

She still said nothing, but sat stunned, her quickened breathing the only sign of emotion. She drew one hand away, putting it to her breast as if to quieten it.

He recaptured her hand and kissed it. "Olivia," he said seriously, "I know you have many responsibilities and I plan a new life. Will you share it with me; let me share your life? Will you marry me and be my partner in all things? I want to fall asleep in your arms, my head on your breast and I want you to turn to me in the night, for comfort or love."

Luke sat back on his heels. He had stripped himself bare for her, offered his naked breast to her knife. "Olivia?" He gently untied her bonnet and lifted it from her head. She blinked when her eyes lost the shade of the deep brim. Tears trembled on her lashes and he kissed them away, relishing the salty tang. "Sweetheart?"

"It's impossible." Her voice was dull.

"Why?"

"It just is. I can't marry again."

"Why not? Surely Rembleton didn't tie matters up in such a way as to prevent it? Even if he tried, it couldn't possibly be binding."

"No. It's not that." She laid her head against the back of the chair and closed her eyes. Her face was like stone.

"Olivia? Sweetheart? Talk to me!"

She slowly raised her heavy lids. Her eyes were desolate and she shivered suddenly. "Luke, why did you have to do this?"

"Because I'm not happy without you," he said softly. "I have no appetite for life without you."

"What is happiness?" she asked drearily. "It's an illusion."

"Is it? Were we not happy in our orchard?"

"That wasn't real," she protested. "That was—oh, outside time. Like a dream. Real life is work and duty—we must be satisfied with that."

"What of love? Don't you love your children? And your brother?"

"You know I do."

"Do you not think you could love a husband too?" he asked wistfully.

"Once I did. Think so, I mean. I wanted to. But I sold my soul, Luke, when I married Jack. Or my heart, I don't know. But that part of me is gone, bartered for safety. I was a coward. It doesn't matter that he didn't want it. I threw it away. I have nothing left to give." She looked down, wrapping her arms around herself, whether for warmth or protection, he didn't know. He couldn't bear to see his proud Olivia so abject. She was hunched in on herself and wouldn't meet his eye. Frantically he looked around the little room. He needed to take her in his arms, but there was only the one chair and it was too small to take both of them. She was no dainty doll to perch on his knee. He felt a twinge in his ankle and winced theatrically.

"Does your leg hurt?" she cried at once.

"Not really," he said bravely. "I'm not used to kneeling, I suppose." He changed his position so that he sat on the carpet and in a flash she knelt beside him.

"Let me see."

"Got you," he exclaimed with a satisfied grin and pulled her between his legs to hold her close.

"Luke!" She sounded scandalized. "If anyone were to come in!"

"They can't. I barred the door."

"You what?" She struggled to get up but he held her firmly cradled against him.

He sighed, his lips brushing her ear. "I don't know whether to kiss you or shake you or scold you, sweetheart. But let me tell you that I have never been privileged to hear a more nonsensical rigmarole."

Her look of outrage made him chuckle.

"You weren't a coward then, Olivia, if you chose what made you feel safest when your world had suddenly turned upside down. But you will be a coward now, if you insist on hiding behind that decision rather than venture on a new life."

"But supposing I make the wrong choice again?" Her voice was very small, like that of a child.

She didn't trust herself.

"You were ignorant of the world then," he said softly. "You didn't know what to look for. You do now. I'm not asking you to decide this instant, sweetheart. I just want you to open your eyes and see me properly; look at what we could have together."

She rested her head against his shoulder and he smoothed his hand down her back.

"I'm afraid," she whispered. "Whatever I decide will affect the children."

"I swear I would be a good father to all of them," he said earnestly, "yours and ours, just as my mother's second husband is a good father to me and to my brothers and sisters. It would be such a joy to see you carry my child, Olivia, and watch over him or her with you."

"Oh!" Olivia closed her eyes as if dazzled by the visions his words had conjured up. "You would share the burdens with me?"

He stared at her incredulously. "Olivia," he said solemnly, looking deep into her eyes, "I love you. I want to live with you, be a true husband to you and a father to all of your children. I want to be by your side—and have you by mine—for all our joys and sorrows. I want to love you in every way a man can love a woman, and you to love me in every way a woman can love a man."

She smiled tremulously. "That is so beautiful, Luke. Part of me wants to throw myself into your arms and say 'never let me go'."

"If you do, I'll catch you and keep you," he promised tenderly. "But I won't press you for an answer now. Just tell me you'll think about it. Well?" he challenged after a moment.

"I'll think about it, Luke," she said on a rush.

"And kiss me to seal your promise?" he asked hopefully.

She lifted her face expectantly.

"No sweetheart. You are to kiss me."

To his astonishment, this simple request had her all in a fluster. She's not used to kisses, he remembered, recalling Thalia's initial timidity. He waited, ignoring her blushes and reached out to trace the outline of her lips with his fore-finger. "One kiss, a little one," he coaxed and was rewarded when she leaned forward to press her lips to his. He clenched his fists to prevent himself grabbing her, limiting his response to returning the slight, sweet pressure. When she sat back, he followed to return the salute. "*'By just exchange, one for the other given'*," he murmured, smiling at her.

Olivia took a deep breath. "If we are to go to Leicester today, we must be on our way."

She's had enough, Luke realised. Don't rush your fences. He got to his feet and held down a hand to help her.

"Is my pelisse very crumpled?" she asked.

"Turn around," Luke commanded and inspected her. "You'll do, which is just as well, for there is no room for you to act the whirligig here."

She smiled at this reminder but said nothing. He set her bonnet on her head and skilfully tied the ribbons in a flattering bow.

"Take my hand and let me lead you," he said when they were on the stone, spiral staircase. "The steps here are uneven."

Chapter Thirty-One

If Olivia had been asked afterwards what route they had taken or what they had talked about on the way to Leicester, she would have been hard put to reply, but she must have responded more or less rationally to Luke's remarks despite her addled wits. She felt shaky, with a strange trembling in her breast and limbs as if her heart had sent her blood bubbling through her veins.

Perhaps he sensed something of this turmoil, for he said very little. He pulled up his team once so that he could tuck the rug more warmly around her.

"Better?" he asked, and she nodded dumbly.

He closed his hand over hers before taking up the reins again. When they reached their destination, the need to concentrate on her purchases helped clear her head and as soon as she was finished, he took her to the *Three Crowns* where he had reserved a private parlour.

"Have you spoken to Lutterworth about the by-election?" she enquired over fricandos of veal and a dish of mushrooms.

"The writ will probably be moved soon after Parliament is recalled. Two members, Generals Picton and Ponsonby, were killed at Waterloo and their seats must be filled."

"I had forgotten that. Are you going to do it?"

"Stand for Parliament? Yes. Would it affect your decision?"

"Luke!"

"It would mean living in London when Parliament is in session," he pointed out, "but I would buy a bigger house, suitable for a family. You are accustomed to spending some weeks in town each year, so it would not be too great a change."

"I like my home," she said defensively.

"Then I'm sure I will too," he assured her. "We can live there the rest of the time."

"And there are the children. Samuel will start with the rector in a year or so."

"He can have a tutor if necessary."

"And John. His uncle is over seventy. I pray he will live for many years to come, but when he dies, there will be the Rembleton estates to consider as well."

"Might I not help you and John?" Luke asked gravely, secretly delighted that she was prepared to discuss the practicalities of a marriage between them.

"I'm not used to having help, apart from my man of business that is," she admitted rather sheepishly.

"But that is a different relationship, isn't it? I would never try to supplant you, Olivia, only support you. As I hope you would support me in my political endeavours if it comes to that—tease out ideas with me or provide a feminine perspective."

"I wouldn't be alone," she said, almost to herself.

"Or left to your own devices," he agreed. "Who knows, you may finish up wishing me to Jericho."

"Or you us," she retorted. "You are used to a bachelor life."

"Sick of it, more like," he answered gloomily.

As the days passed, Olivia became aware of a change in Luke's behaviour towards her. He concealed neither his interest nor his affection but sought her company, unobtrusively caring for her comfort. He spent considerable time with the children, especially John, who was practising for the medieval fair.

"Mr Fitzmaurice asked if I would like to be his squire," the boy told her proudly. "I shall ride with him in the procession."

"That was kind of you," Olivia said later to Luke.

"The others have fathers and uncles," he explained. "I didn't want him to feel left out."

After all the years of standing alone, it was as if he had wrapped a warm cloak around her. His eyes sought hers when he entered a room; the small smile and nod signalling his pleasure in seeing her and his willingness to serve her. After some time she realised that she, too, looked for him first and that a room was somehow empty until he arrived.

It made her yearn for the sort of contented family life she had experienced over the winter with her brother and Miss Carstairs, but with something more—a little spice, if she were to be honest, the spice a loving husband could provide. The frisson of knowing that the man sitting opposite you would later join you in bed—for comfort, pleasure, lust, love—but not out of a duty to procreate. Although she could imagine the bliss of carrying a child conceived in joy with a man who would be a loving father to it, she had never experienced that complex intimacy. Slowly Olivia dared to hope that it might yet be hers.

Their new closeness did not go unnoticed.

"It's over a year since Mr Rembleton died and he was never much of a husband," one matron remarked to another. "Who could blame her if she sought a little diversion with dear Luke?"

"If you ask me, he is pursuing her, which is most unlike him," her friend opined. "He danced three dances with her last night. One was the opening quadrille."

"She danced every dance. I've rarely seen her dance in town."

"Let her kick up her heels if she wishes. I'm sure I would in her place."

The objects of their curiosity were doing nothing more indecorous than watch Miranda and Samuel trundle their hoops along the drive. Miranda was extremely proficient, but Samuel hadn't quite got the knack. The girl came running back up to them, bowling her hoop before her just as her brother's toppled and fell.

"Stupid thing," he kicked at it angrily.

"It's a poor swordsman who blames his blade," Luke remarked. "I'm sure Miranda had to practise a lot to be so expert."

"Lots and lots," she confirmed. "Papa ran beside me with another stick so that he could help."

"But Papa is dead," Samuel cried despairingly.

"Perhaps I could help," Luke offered, "if Miranda would lend me her stick. What do you think, Miranda?"

She handed it over willingly and watched with her mother as the man and the boy got the hoop rolling. "He's nice, isn't he," she remarked. "I like him."

"Yes," Olivia agreed.

Luke had stopped and crouched beside Samuel, clearly suggesting that the child change his grip of the stick and strike the hoop differently.

"He doesn't have any children of his own, though," Miranda continued.

"No, but he has a younger brother and sister, so I suppose he played with them."

"John doesn't want to play anymore with us," Miranda sighed. "He would rather play with the other older boys."

"I'm told you are a most entertaining reader, Mr Fitzmaurice," Lady Lutterworth said that evening. "Perhaps you would favour us with something. And nothing too sentimental," she added tartly.

"I have just the thing," Sally exclaimed. "Mr Fitzmaurice, I long to hear Mr Collins propose again."

"Your wish is my command, my ladies. But I shall require a Miss Elizabeth Bennet to hear my suit. Mrs Rembleton, I beg you will oblige me by refusing me."

"I should be delighted, sir," Olivia said wickedly.

"Vixen," he murmured in her ear while they conferred over the book. "Shall we take that settee?"

She sat, spreading her skirts so that he was compelled to perch at an awkward angle beside her, his lower limbs disposed in a would-be graceful attitude. He took several snuffling breaths, each one inflating his chest until he was puffed like a frog, tucked in his chin and contrived to look down his nose while simpering in a lover-like manner. He carefully smoothed his hair and nodded to Olivia. She was also to be the narrator, leaving Luke to portray the hapless clergyman in all his glory.

" '*Do not consider me an elegant female intending to plague you, but as a rational creature speaking the truth from her heart*'."

Olivia deposited the volume beside her suitor and retired in obvious dudgeon. He leapt to his feet to gaze after her, protesting all the while that she was " '*Uniformly charming—and I am persuaded that when sanctioned by the express authority of both your excellent parents, my proposals will not fail of being acceptable*'."

A firmly closed door put a period to this prime example of masculine self-delusion and the listeners broke into renewed laughter and applause.

Olivia was still chuckling when Luke came out to the hall to retrieve her.

"You must share in the applause," he said, extending his hand to her. As he prepared to lead her ceremoniously back into the drawing room, he leaned over to whisper, "I trust you will admit that I made my case in a much more convincing fashion than Collins did."

She turned her head so that she could meet his eyes. "Yes," she said simply.

"Olivia!"

"They're waiting for us," she admonished him, ducking her head to hide a secret smile and preceding him into the drawing room where she acknowledged the appreciative compliments with her usual composure.

"I may lay claim to very little of the credit, being merely the foil to Mr Fitzmaurice's genius."

"Ah, but are you not my 'uniformly charming' muse," Luke responded with a smirk that, to his perverse delight, provoked the re-emergence of his severe Mrs Rembleton who looked down her nose at him and said, "You do me too much honour, sir."

"Impossible, my dear lady," he exclaimed, bowing so lavishly in the manner of Mr Collins that she had to laugh.

"A glass of wine," he suggested once the company had turned to other pursuits. A refreshments table had been set up in an anteroom and he led her there, pleased to find it empty apart from the servants.

"Champagne? Or here is a cool cider cup."

"The cup, if you please." Olivia took it from him and walked over to the window where two chairs had been set at a small table. She sat down wearily.

"Tired?" he asked, concerned.

"Tired of people, I think. I'm not used to such large parties where one is surrounded every minute of the day. When I go to Stanton, I have my own sitting-room and may withdraw at any time. Here it is not so easy."

"The countess is an indefatigable hostess," he agreed.

All at once, Olivia was sure of her own heart. She plucked up her courage, feeling her face grow warm as she continued,

"Part of the problem is the castle itself. It's less easy to escape. I wish we could, just the two of us, for a few hours."

He stared at her, utterly confounded and painfully hopeful. "Olivia?"

"I want to talk to you Luke, properly I mean, where we won't be interrupted or overheard."

"Sweetheart!" His hand reached across the table only to be snatched back when another group came into the room.

"Ride with me in the morning," he suggested almost inaudibly. "Before breakfast?"

She flashed a quick smile. "Yes."

"Meet me in the turret room at nine o'clock and leave the rest to me."

Luke stooped, cupping his hands to assist Olivia into the saddle. Once she had settled the folds of her habit and her foot was securely in the stirrup, he mounted his own horse. "We'll talk in comfort later. First we must make our escape."

He set a brisk pace through the park and into the woods. They soon arrived at a neat cottage in a little clearing beside a stream where Phibbs came to meet them.

"I'll take them, sir. Good morning, ma'am. All is prepared, just as the captain ordered."

"Thank you, Phibbs." Luke unbuckled his saddlebags. "This way," he said to Olivia.

The cottage had one large room. It was spick and span, newly white-washed and simply furnished with a settle at right angles to the fireplace, a table and two chairs under one window and a wide daybed piled with cushions. There was a small cupboard in one corner. A fire burned in the hearth where a kettle hung from the crane and a cloth had been spread on the table that was set for breakfast.

Luke shrugged off his riding-coat and lifted Olivia's hat from her head. "Let's see what cook gave us," he said, opening the bags. He looked over and smiled at her astounded face. "Did you think you would get no breakfast, sweetheart?"

"Where are we?"

"Franklin had this cottage refurbished as a retreat for him and Sally. They, too, feel the need to get away from the castle at times." He handed her a small packet of tea. "You'll know better than I how much to use."

She spooned the tea into the teapot. The water had come to the boil and he carefully tilted the kettle to fill the pot. He pushed the crane to one side and stooped to throw a couple of logs on the fire before coming to sit beside her.

She poured the tea. "It's so peaceful," she said, handing him a cup.

"Tranquil," he agreed, nudging a plate of fresh rolls towards her.

It was a simple meal, just butter, honey and a plate of ham to go with the rolls. Olivia found herself remembering that first breakfast with Jack. She felt no such awkwardness now. "How did you manage to arrange this so quickly?"

"I spoke to Franklin last night after the ladies had retired. He sent instructions to Phibbs to come over early and light the fire. Cook provided the breakfast."

"It's very good."

"The fresh air whets the appetite," he agreed, taking another roll.

Olivia finished her tea and smiled tentatively. "I never realised how difficult it must be for a gentleman to raise these matters. Or how much plotting and scheming he must sometimes undertake to have his lady to himself."

Luke felt a huge bubble of anticipation rise within him. "Not everyone is as blatant as Mr Collins," he agreed. "Why did you want to get me to yourself, sweetheart?"

She closed her eyes for a moment, opened them and said simply, "I love you, Luke. I want to marry you and share your life; I want to fall asleep in your arms, your head on my breast and I want to turn to you in the night, for comfort or love."

"Olivia!" The bubble burst, flooding him with joy. Unable to remain seated, he went to kneel beside her.

A tender light filled her golden eyes as she continued, "I want to live with you, be a true wife to you and the mother of your children. I want you to be a good father to all my children. I want to be by your side, and have you by mine for all our joys and sorrows."

He kissed her hands reverently, transported by this repetition of his avowal to her in the turret room.

Blushing deliciously, she continued almost in a whisper, "I want to love you in every way a woman can love a man and you to love me in every way a man can love a woman."

He leaned across their clasped hands to kiss her solemnly, "Olivia, I take you as my wife, and I give myself to you as your husband."

Her lips a scant inch away from his, she answered, "Luke, I take you as my husband and give myself to you as your wife." Their lips met again in joyous commitment. Smiling, he stood and pulled her to her feet so he could take her into his arms. "We shall have to do it officially, but today is the day we shall privately celebrate as our wedding day."

"Yes," she agreed and, unable to resist, reached up to kiss him again, tentatively shaping his lips with her tongue. "Honey has never tasted so sweet," she murmured. "Luke? Will you make me yours now? Before, it was Thalia. Today, I want you to make love to me, to Olivia."

"Are you sure sweetheart? I have nothing with me?"

"Nothing?"

"To prevent getting you with child."

She frowned. "Does it matter? I thought you wanted a child of your own."

"I do. But if we do this now, you must promise to marry me within the month. I don't want to risk any unkind speculation about the reasons for our marriage."

"I see no reason to delay, do you?"

He pulled her hard against him. "Then come." He fingered the high neck of her riding-habit. "How do we get you out of this?"

"It fastens at the back." She turned round. "Make sure you note how it goes, for I rely on you to dress me later."

"Yes, ma'am." He found the fastenings and began to spread the sides of the habit apart, pulling it down over her arms. He loosened the ribbons at her waist and it dropped to the floor in a pool of sea-green merino. "Like Venus emerging from the waves," he murmured appreciatively as she stepped out of it.

Olivia bent to pick it up. "Can you bring a chair over here, please," she asked and shook the habit into its proper folds before placing it on the chair.

Amused and impressed by this practicality, he fetched the other chair for his own use. "Don't, please don't," he begged when she raised her hands to the ruff of her habit shirt. "Let me."

He carefully opened the buttons, pressing his lips to each inch of skin he revealed until she sighed and clutched his head to her. After a last kiss between her breasts, he swiftly unlaced her cuffs and lifted the garment over her head, stepping back to admire the womanly figure displayed for his delight. Plumped by her corset and framed by the narrow shoulder straps of a high-waisted fine lawn petticoat, her breasts swelled above a delicate frill of lace that was threaded with a pale green ribbon. He had never undressed a woman before, he realised. He turned her again to unfasten the petticoat and let it drop.

Olivia shivered when his fingers traced her spine. It felt very decadent to stand before him in her corset and wide-legged pantalettes. She heard him whisper 'Beautiful' and felt his hands smooth over her behind, then slip between her legs.

"Luke!"

He kissed the back of her neck. "Turn around," he commanded huskily.

She obeyed, excited by his eagerness. He took her mouth as demandingly as that day in the turret. She had dreamt of that kiss and now met and answered his passion. He was still fully dressed and she pushed him down onto the bed, standing between his legs to untie his cravat.

"No blindfolds today," he groaned, taking it from her and tossing it onto the chair, before removing his coat and waistcoat. She took them from him and came back to tackle his shirt.

"My boots," he said then.

Her back to him, she straddled each leg in turn to tug the boots off. As she leant forward, her delectable arse was displayed to such perfection that when she was finished, he pulled her back to lie pressed up against him.

"Will we be able to get this back on?" he murmured, running his fingers down the knotted laces of her corset.

"Just loosen them and lift it over my head." With Luke everything was a caress, she thought, bemused by this slow seduction.

Suddenly he sat up and stripped off his remaining garments. When he lifted her chemise over her head and pulled her back down to him, the sensation of skin on skin was shocking in its intensity. He was so warm—like silken fire, she thought, petting his chest and shoulders with her hands. He lay quietly while she relearnt his shapes and textures, impressing them into her very soul so that he would always be part of her.

She could feel his hands at her waist and then her pantalettes were eased down, followed by her stockings. Now they were completely skin to skin, legs entangled, arms enfolding, hands caressing. He slid down the bed and bent to kiss her breasts, nipping and sucking until everything ached with an emptiness that begged for completion. She pulled him closer to her and could feel his erection hard against her belly. Almost instinctively she undulated against him and he caught his breath before gripping her buttocks to clamp her to him.

"Olivia." It was a muttered groan against her lips before he took her mouth again, deeply. He moved a little to one side so that he could trace her feminine folds, first lightly and then more firmly, his fingers dipping teasingly into her so that she opened her legs and pulled him over her.

"Now, Luke."

He gritted his teeth as he began to enter her, nearly undone by the exquisite pleasure of her scalding sheath with no barrier between them. She was tight, so tight, but stretched to accommodate him and when he was deeply seated she opened her eyes and smiled so lovingly that he felt as if he had come home.

"Olivia," he whispered, looking down into her eyes.

"Luke."

I could stay like this forever, he thought, but then she moved, tightening around him and he withdrew and thrust in again and again and again. She responded to his every movement, her hands gripping his arse and her knees raised to cradle him between her thighs. She began to emit little moans at the back of her throat, at first wordless and then "Luke," she was saying, "Luke" until she shattered around him, propelling him to an ecstatic peak that was followed by a fall into oblivion. He collapsed, his head on her breast, his chest heaving. He could feel her heart thrum in counterpoint to his staccato drum.

With an effort, he lifted his weight from her and lay beside her, safe in her arms. He pressed a kiss on her breast. "My love."

Her arms tightened and then like a benediction, she whispered, "my love."

They rode back slowly, after lazily helping each other dress amid kisses and lacings and laughter.

"Only a month," he reminded her firmly. "I can't wait any longer than that and I know we will have to be circumspect in the meantime because of the children."

"You could escort us home," she suggested. "I would like to stop at Stanton and tell Flora and my uncle. They should be the first to know."

"And I must tell my parents."

"We won't say anything here until after the other guests have left. Tomorrow is the tourney and ball. It's Sally's and Vernon's celebration."

"I agree, provided you give me your favour to wear into battle."

"Why not get married here at Stanton?" Flora suggested some days later. "If you have the wedding at the manor, you will have to cope with all the guests. Marry here and you may depart on your wedding journey whenever it suits you, leaving everyone behind. And the children may remain here with Miss Mullins, so you will have some time to yourselves."

"It sounds perfect," Olivia admitted. "I was wondering how we'd manage. What do you think, Luke?"

"I should be most grateful, Duchess," he answered sincerely.

Finale

So this was what a bride looked like. Smiling eyes and curved lips bore witness to Olivia's happiness. Was it the gold thread shot through the pale blue silk of her gown that caused her to glow so? Martin had spread open the collar of blonde lace so that it framed her slender neck and dipped to the valley between her breasts where Luke's gift of an exotic baroque pearl rested, suspended from an intricate gold chain. Her long sleeves were caught at intervals in soft puffs by gold ribbons, the cuffs trimmed with lace and a long golden sash was tied under her breasts so that the ends fluttered seductively. Her unruly hair had been cut and shaped so that soft tendrils framed her brow and temples, while the remainder was caught on the top of her head to create a cascade of curls, now partly concealed by a lace veil.

Smiling, she went to the long mirror. No need to pinch her cheeks or bite her lips for colour today! She picked up her reticule. The children were to come to her sitting-room in ten minutes.

"We're here, Mamma," Miranda said importantly. "Oh, you look beautiful."

"So do you, darling." The sash of the girl's white muslin dress matched Olivia's gown. Samuel stood beside her in a dark blue skeleton suit with a frilled white collar, while behind them John wore a schoolboy's short red jacket with nankeen pantaloons.

"You all look very handsome," Olivia said admiringly. She bent to smooth Samuel's hair and twitch Miranda's skirts to rights. That was how Luke found her, surrounded by her children and laughing at a remark that John had made. His heart turned over in his breast at her loving smile. And she was going to entrust these treasures to him!

"Luke!"

He took her outstretched hands and pulled her to him for a quick kiss. "Are we all ready?"

"Ask him," Miranda hissed at John.

"Ask me what?" Luke enquired. With all the arrangements, he had not seen much of the children in the intervening weeks.

"We were wondering what we should call you once you and Mamma are married," John answered hesitantly.

"You'll be our Papa," Samuel explained helpfully.

"Not our real Papa," Miranda added. "He's dead. But people keep asking us if we are not pleased to have a new Papa."

"And aren't you?" Luke asked carefully. He stole a glance at Olivia. She looked startled, but did not interfere.

"Yes," Samuel answered, while Miranda nodded.

Luke looked at the older boy. "What troubles you, John?"

"We won't have to change our names like Mamma, will we? I must stay Rembleton," John said seriously.

"No. You will all still be Rembletons," Luke assured them. "As to what you should call me, you may continue to say Mr Fitzmaurice if you wish."

"But everyone does that," Miranda objected. "There should be something special for us."

"I should be honoured if you called me Father or Papa, but you must not feel in any way obliged to do so." Luke sat down so that he was more on a level with the children. "But one thing I promise you. When I make my marriage vows to your Mamma in a few minutes, in my heart I shall also be making vows to you three—to love you and care for you as a father should and from that moment you will have the right to appeal to me for assistance of any sort, as my sons and daughter. But this doesn't mean you must forget your own Papa—you must think of him and talk of him the way you always have."

"Mr Adams is your stepfather, isn't he?" asked John.

"Yes."

"What do you call him?"

"First I called him sir, as I would any gentleman, than I called him Father and now I say either—whatever seems appropriate for the occasion. He was content to leave it to me. But I know he regards me as his son."

"He said that he understood we have no grandparents living and would volunteer his services and those of his wife and we should call them Grandpapa and Grandmamma."

"That is very kind of them," Olivia put in, now understanding what had given rise to this conversation.

"Papa would have said that if you are Mamma's husband, that means you are taking his place. Not as our sire, though, that is something separate," John said thoughtfully.

Olivia had to bite the inside of her mouth to stop herself from laughing at Luke's flabbergasted expression. The clock struck the half hour.

Miranda went to stand beside Luke. "You can be my father," she said generously. "I shall say Papa Fitzmaurice so as not to confuse you with Papa."

"Me too." Samuel came to his other side.

Luke did not show his surprise at this novel solution, but put his arms around the children. "Thank you."

John was silent. Luke smiled understandingly. Miranda's suggestion was perhaps too childish for a boy of almost eleven.

"'Sir' does very well between gentlemen, even father and son, John and you may very properly refer to me as your stepfather, so you need not feel obliged to decide anything else today."

John sighed with relief. "Thank you, sir."

Luke held out his hand. "I hope you will let me stand your friend and mentor."

The tension left the boy's shoulders and he clasped Luke's hand. "I should like that."

Olivia blinked, misty-eyed, and smiled at them. "Shall we go and get married?" she asked.

Historical Note

This is a work of fiction, but set in a real place and time. While it would be impossible to list all the sources consulted, I wish to mention the following:

Thomas Creevey's comment quoted by Luke in chapter eight is taken from his letter to Dr Currie of 22 March 1804 (The Creevey Papers, edited by Sir Herbert Maxwell, 1912).

The encounter between Lord Byron and Lady Caroline Lamb at Watier's masquerade on 1 July 1814 described in chapter twelve is based on the Recollections of John Cam Hobhouse and Byron's letter of 2 July 1814 to Lady Melbourne.

René Laennec is recorded as the first person to use a device similar to an ear-trumpet to listen to a patient's heart in 1816 and this is regarded as being the birth of the stethoscope. I have credited my fictional Dr Ferguson with a similar idea one year earlier.

There are innumerable descriptions of the events leading up to the battle of Waterloo and the battle itself. For Luke's experiences with the 1st/52nd, I have drawn extensively but not exclusively on the following accounts.

- William Leeke: The History of Lord Seaton's Regiment, (the 52nd Light Infantry) at the Battle of Waterloo: etc., etc. Hatchard & Co. 1866

- The Life of Sir John Colborne, Field-Marshal Lord Seaton, G.C.B, G.C.H. G.C.M.G., K.T.S., K.Sx.G., K.M.T., &c., Compiled from his Letters, Records of his Conversations, and other sources by G.C. Moore Smith, M.A. John Murray, 1903
- George Hooper: Waterloo or the Downfall of the First Napoleon: History of the Campaign of 1815. Smith, Elder and Co., 1862
- Sergeant-Major Edward Cotton: A Voice from Waterloo: A History of the Battle Fought on the 18th June 1816 with a Selection from the Wellington Despatches, General Orders and letters relating to the Battle. Sixth Edition, Revised and Enlarged, Printed for the Proprietor, Mont-St-Jean, 1862

And finally, Jack and Bart had good reason to be concerned about the danger of being exposed as sodomites. According to the Newgate Calendar, Volume IV of 1826, between 1819 and 1825 fifteen people were executed for sodomy in England and Wales.

About the Author

Catherine Kullmann was born and educated in Dublin. Following a three-year courtship conducted mostly by letter, she moved to Germany where she lived for twenty-five years before returning to Ireland. She has worked in the Irish and New Zealand public services and in the private sector.

She has a keen sense of history and of connection with the past which so often determines the present. She is fascinated by people. She loves a good story, especially when characters come to life in a book. But then come the 'whys' and 'what ifs'. She is particularly interested in what happens after the first happy end—how life goes on around the protagonists and sometimes catches up with them.

Her novels are set in the early nineteenth century—one of the most significant periods of European and American history. The Act of Union between Great Britain and Ireland of 1800, the Anglo-American war of 1812 and more than a decade of war that ended in the final defeat of Napoleon at Waterloo in 1815 are all events that continue to shape our modern world. At the same time, the aristocracy-led society that drove these events was under attack from those who demanded social and political reform, while the industrial revolution saw the beginning of the transfer of wealth and ultimately power to those who knew how to exploit the new technologies.

She has always enjoyed writing. She loves the fall of words, the shaping of an expressive phrase, the satisfaction when a sentence conveys my meaning exactly. She enjoys plotting and revels in the challenge of evoking a historic era for characters who behave authentically in their period while making their actions and decisions plausible and sympathetic to a modern reader. But rewarding as all this craft is, there is nothing to match the moment when a book takes flight, when the characters suddenly determine the route of their journey.

Find out more about Catherine Kullmann and her books at www.catherinekullmann.com or visit Catherine's Facebook page fb.me/catherinekullmannauthor.

Perception & Illusion

And they lived happily ever after.

Or did they? Cast out by her father for refusing the suitor of his choice, Lallie Grey accepts Hugo Tamrisk's proposal, confident that he loves her as she loves him. But what were Hugo's reasons for marriage and what does he really want of his bride?

With chapter headings taken from an early nineteenth century Matrimonial Map, *Perception & Illusion* charts Lallie's and Hugo's voyage through a sea of confusion and misunderstanding. Can they successfully negotiate the Rocks of Jealousy and the Shoals of Perplexity to arrive at the Bay of Delight or will they drift inexorably towards Cat & Dog Harbour or the Dead Lake of Indifference?

Perception & Illusion **is now available.**

Milton Keynes UK
Ingram Content Group UK Ltd.
UKHW040724290823
427678UK00001B/114